AVENTUS

This edition first published in Great Britain by Aventus,
an imprint of Larocco Media Investments Ltd.

Lᴍi

Copyright © R.A.Ruegg 2024

A CIP catalogue record for this book is available from the British Library.

Cover design: Jessica Bell Design
jessicabelldesign.com

Editing and production management: Claire Wingfield
clairewingfield.co.uk

Typesetting: The Book Typesetters
thebooktypesetters.com

Printing and binding: Book Printing UK
Remus House, Woodston, Peterborough PE2 9BF, United Kingdom
bookprintinguk.com

Fonts used: Adobe Garamond Pro, Bradley Hand ITC, Calibri, ITC Avant Garde Gothic, Lucida Calligraphy, Nanum Brush Script, Times New Roman.

ISBN 978-1-0686746-8-6

Printed on FSC-certified paper.

To J and A.

In memory of T.

30% of royalties to be donated
to mental health charities
in the British Isles.

The Making of

BRIO
McPRIDE

R.A.RUEGG

~ PART ONE ~

SOME CURIOSITIES OF THE ISLE

To love and be loved
we must have truly grown up,
yet so often our journey into adulthood
is hindered by those who try hardest
to care for us, and we ourselves
would prefer to stay forever
in the garden of play.

Sister Jane Whittle
As Good as God

1

SENSE OF WAKING, HEART RACING, shrieking, bogey-demon chasing closer, grabbing, clutching—shock drop to falling flailing, screaming plummeting, plummeting through the Abysmal. 'God, help me, I'm falling, falling to death, God save me, God—'

'Be calm, I'm here with you in Heaven, bound by pure and bloodless love. We father-son by friendship leavened, 'twined like double-helix, home.'

Oh, thank God, beautiful words, saved from the Abysmal, and remembering dawn now, the real dawn. But the day's already damned by dangerous wind and pissing rain on naked window. Oh, God, don't think 'pissing', think clean words, say prayers, wash tongue in biblical rains from sky without colour. But how to pray to a god who takes away the scent of the mum, the teller of ancient tales?

'Bree, are you awake?' *Such a familiar voice but the Abysmal weighing so heavily and more of God's beautiful words on the way.* 'The child who's born so full of grace, of Father Time and Mother Space. But water's thick and blood is thin and only love makes next of kin.' *Must claw back the beautiful words to cast in stone, keep hope alive and—*

Knock-knocking, *it's Pippa's voice for sure. Were God's words really so beautiful?* 'Bree, get *up*.' Means another pulling-on of ten-ton socks and pointless sports uniform to yearning glimpses of shoebox-stack shrine and golden-robed rider. *What if God meant something else, some hidden meaning?*

Stumbling now, bringing perfect symmetry to desktop of paper and pens, straightening picture frame, double-checking window handle. Checking window handle again—keep the window-bogey *out*—trying to hurry but desperate to slow it all down—down creaking stairs, slow-motion counting seams in peeling wallpaper, still nauseous, down to hallway day-gloom, not a single light on, treasured birdsong snuffed by downpour and creeping cats and smell of dust, toilet cleaner, Dr Shenoy's car outside through front window, still a cheap gag of unwanted second-hand orange. No time for breakfast, Pippa pressing snack bar into hand. 'Fish fingers for dinner, okay?'

Inside the car dank fabric smell, head down, not even hello. Soon in the thick, Dr Shenoy cranes to penetrate the crazy-fast wipers and Brio's suddenly fighting to stay in the haze where it doesn't hurt. But he's overwhelmed by the longing for his mum to stop this happening. His wobbling lips twist to suppress tears.

'What's the matter, Brio?'

The unbelievably stupid question flips Brio's despair into an anger at Dr Shenoy that grows into rage as they grind ever closer to the hospital. When they eventually pull up outside the psychiatric wing, his rage shrivels and he cowers under the glower of blank windows and doorless brick walls. All he can think is to flee into the teeming rain, keep running till he reaches forests or mountains—a cave, jungle—just any place he can hide and get *ready*.

Thoughts of being alone even in town send his stomach crawling into his shins. He hears Dr Shenoy sigh and can sense him staring fixedly ahead, both hands still clutching the wheel.

'Brio, this has nothing to do with Izzy, all right? I am simply trying to help you. As your mum would have wanted.'

'She *wouldn't*. She hated therapists.'

'Professor Glybb is not a *therapist*, he's a top psychiatrist—from London. And we are lucky he visits. So keep an open mind, please.'

Brio has to leap in sploshes through wide puddles to keep up with Dr Shenoy. It's only when they reach the dry land of a small portico that he sees the trick. The big sign might say OUTPATIENT CLINIC, but what better way to break his bond with Izzy than to have him locked up forever? He backs away and looks to run, only to be carried through the doors by a kerfuffle of violet-clad nurses laughing and bustling in out of the rain.

'Swear they're not going to keep me here,' Brio says again as they march briskly along a poorly lit and empty corridor. He has to keep hopping a change of step to walk in time with Dr Shenoy.

'We're here for one appointment, Brio. Then I am taking you to school.'

They stop at a crossroads of corridors where the signage trail goes dead. Brio looks back again for his escape route but doesn't even know which way they came from. He bobs like a little kid needing to pee. He *does* need to pee. He's about to dig in for a toilet stop when a slimy shadow shows itself behind an air vent and sends him stumbling away groaning, clutching his forehead.

After an increasingly haphazard search for Suite 16-B, every crack and air-vent a threat, Brio finds himself in a space he can't understand at all. Stark walls and shiny linoleum make it a large waiting room but there's nothing more than a wooden desk and two chairs—three more against the far wall.

'Yes, I'm sorry,' Professor Glybb says from behind the desk, his voice croaky. 'They seem to have put me in an aircraft hangar.'

Only once Brio's been cajoled into sitting down does he take in Professor Glybb as anything more than a fusty shape. From there, he absorbs it all in a second: gaunt beard and dog-eared pinstriped suit, wilting silk handkerchief, fragile-looking eye-bags. When Brio also sees the margin of Ms Whittle's flowery handwriting protruding from the thick file on the desk, he blurts, 'It's rubbish. She doesn't know anything.'

Professor Glybb looks confused but quickly regains his grave smile. 'Ah, you mean the notes from your school counsellor?'

'She's not a *counsellor*. She's an English teacher. And she retired. She's mad.'

'Well,' Professor Glybb says affably, 'let's pop it where it belongs then, shall we?' He makes a ceremony of placing the file in a drawer. 'So how *are* you today, Brio—in your own words?'

Turning away to fix on the blank wall, Brio reaffirms his vow to be like his dad, to hold out against interrogation at all costs. Above all else, he must remember that this isn't just any old therapist. It's a top psychiatrist who knows how to suck out his victim's most closely guarded secrets.

'All right,' Professor Glybb says calmly. 'So why don't I start by thanking you for coming to see me today—and Dr Shenoy for bringing you?'

'It's *Shuh*-noy,' Brio mutters without taking his gaze off the wall. 'It's a special surname. From India.'

Brio senses that Professor Glybb is looking to Dr Shenoy, who says, 'This is correct. The emphasis is on the first syllable. I believe that Brio feels strongly about this because he knows my daughter.'

'Ah, I see!' says Professor Glybb. 'The Izzy Shenoy in Ms Whittle's notes is your daughter.'

'Yes.'

The familiar displeasure in Dr Shenoy's tone riles Brio more and he glances at the door.

'Well, *Shuh-n*oy it is then,' Professor Glybb agrees swiftly. 'So Brio, what did you have for breakfast this morning?'

Brio can't stop his head flicking back round. Is Professor Glybb making fun of him? No, he's not. He's still smiling but he looks serious. So it must have been a trick question. Or Ms Whittle put it in her stupid file that the window-bogey will plague him if he doesn't eat exactly the same thing every day. Brio looks down at the shiny floor between his waterlogged trainers. Why the hell did it have to rain so hard? He tries to summon up poetry to block everything out. When it won't flow to order, they're left suspended in a silence made worse by the wall clock that ticks loud-soft-loud-soft … till he worries that Professor Glybb and Dr Shenoy are exchanging eye signals to form an invincible alliance.

He finds them looking at *him* and sees that Professor Glybb might have a stoop as well. He's just a harmless old badger who doesn't usually come out during the day.

'So you're fifteen now?' Professor Glybb proposes. 'How does that feel, I wonder?'

'Next month I'm *sixteen*.'

'Indeed. And you live with your foster mother, I think?'

Brio looks back at the wall. Why doesn't the old badger know he doesn't want to think about Pippa? Even badgers can be bad.

'This is also correct,' Dr Shenoy says. 'Pippa was his mum's best friend.'

A pang forces Brio's head back down and the room falls still.

'Would you like to tell me about Mum?' Professor Glybb asks quietly.

Caught off guard, Brio has to look back up. Something understanding in Professor Glybb's eyes triggers the old yearning to be back with his mum at Bluebells, doors double-bolted and curtains drawn on the sunshine, to be curled up by the little log fire with Mouse-the-Brave hugged to his chest, wrapped in that aroma of threadbare carpets and damp moss, of baking gingerbread and his mum's coffee. And there she is, reading aloud from the handmade book, her face peaceful again after the strains of the day and her angry snapping at the free newspaper.

'You know, you've had a jolly difficult period,' Professor Glybb says. 'There's no shame in experiencing these, erm … these things you see.'

Brio's on his feet. 'I *don't*. That's just what people say.'

His denial seems to make the clock tick even louder and Dr Shenoy tuts. 'Come, Brio. What about the zoo, jumping into the penguin pool because you thought the gorilla was chasing you? Now, sit down and try to help Professor Glybb.'

He wants to shout at Dr Shenoy, but mention of the viral video has winded him. 'I only did it because someone said I couldn't swim. I had to prove I could.'

'Brio—'

'It's all right,' Professor Glybb says quickly. 'Brio, if you don't want to talk about it right now, that's absolutely fine. And if it feels better to stay standing, please do.'

Finding himself uncomfortable to be higher than Professor Glybb, Brio has to sit back down. 'There's nothing to talk about. I just have a good imagination.'

'And you make wonderful use of it. Winner of the National Young People's Fiction Award two years in a row. You must be very proud.'

Brio looks away again. He's not going to be fooled by flattery either. But now the zoo video's back in his head, he can't get it out. Nor does he have any defence against the assault of Darcy's mocking voiceover telling millions of viewers that he jumped in because he thought penguins were gay and he wanted to be in the gay bathing pool. And all those millions of viewers laughed and stuck up their pointy thumbs.

Dr Shenoy shifts awkwardly. 'I think Brio is hesitant to talk about the prize because he won it jointly with my daughter. They used to write together, you see.'

'We still *do*.' But his toes curl and his butt clenches. It's in some other life that Izzy last came round to sit cross-legged on the floor with her chunky pen and funny sandals. She wears clompy boots now and writes on a computer with this Darcy monster from

London who's older than everyone else and too big to fit. She's even started wearing an earring at weekends.

Professor Glybb's next question is blocked out by the stage-lit image of Romeo-Darcy pretending to forget his line so he can stay longer in the tight embrace with Juliet-Izzy. Remembering how Darcy glanced so tauntingly down at him from the stage, Brio doesn't hear Professor Glybb's next question either, or Dr Shenoy's answer on his behalf. He senses only that the questions are closing in, becoming ever more coaxing. When he hears Dr Shenoy explaining that they're all part of the same church community, he knows an attack on Father T has begun. At last the rhythmic chant of words rises up in his head … *in a loud, scary sunshine bent as a fork, spooning up darkness from ten green bottles. We search for the untime and reach for the corks* …

But now they're even daring to talk about his dad and Dr Shenoy says, 'Well, you see, Brio's mother never wanted to discuss her life before she moved here from Ireland. All she ever said was that Brio's father died while he was working for a charity in very remote Africa.'

Brio wants to curse Dr Shenoy for making his mum's story sound like the lie it is. Intending to fly out through the door, he storms across the room but ends up throwing himself down on one of the chairs against the wall. Heart racing, he bends forward to plug his ears.

'It's all right, Dr Shenoy,' Brio hears Professor Glybb say peaceably. 'Brio will be fine where he is. Why don't we have a little chat among ourselves?'

Even though Brio wants to hear what they're saying in their hushed voices across the desk, he can't relax the fingers that keep his ears pressed closed. Yet still the whispers weasel their way in and he wants to hear more, so he can hate them enough to kick open the door and run.

'Dr Shenoy, what I'm trying to understand—I mean, this incident at the zoo happened long before his more recent traumas—why has he never seen a psychiatrist or been medicated?'

'I tried,' Dr Shenoy whispers hoarsely. 'I had concerns from when he was six. But whenever I tried to talk to his mother, she just said he had a good imagination. Her faith in God was very strong, you see.'

After a pause in which Brio's pulse breaks through to his ears, Dr Shenoy adds, 'I suppose I myself was hesitant about Brio taking medication. I thought if he could just talk to someone and pray harder …'

Brio's thrown into confusion. Dr Shenoy doesn't want him to be put on drugs after all, and he actually does believe that praying will help. Now all it takes is for Professor Glybb to agree, then they can get back to the safety of the car.

But Professor Glybb's expression is darkening and he's saying all the wrong things, '… and although talking therapies and meditation no doubt have their place, we need to accept that these symptoms point very clearly to paranoid schizophrenia—a subset of schizoaffective disorder, if you like—and even with the best will in the world, medication trumps meditation every time. The only real question is which compounds to use and in what dosages. And that's exactly what my research programme is all about—finding the right mix for highly creative adolescents like Brio who—'

'Well, this would be very good,' Dr Shenoy interrupts. 'Thank you. But surely, in the longer term, Brio will be able to come off the medications and lead a normal life?'

In the ensuing pause, Brio's forehead thumps and the fingers that were pressing into his ears now cup imperceptibly to capture Professor Glybb's reply. He has to know there's some end to this hell.

'I'm sorry to say it, Dr Shenoy, but in functional mental illness, genetics really do script the whole show. And the fact is that certain symptom clusters have a tendency to pass from one generation to the next. So if there's any chance at all that Brio's father might have taken his own life, his management path must include not only medication but—'

Brio leaps back up from his chair. 'My dad did *not* commit suicide.' He hears himself shouting more but doesn't know what he's saying and Dr Shenoy hurries to block the door.

'I'm sorry, Brio,' Professor Glybb says anxiously from where he's now standing beside the desk. 'If I'd known you were able to hear, I obviously wouldn't have discussed these things. But I'm absolutely certain I can help you.'

Brio's about to shout again when he registers Professor Glybb's highly polished shoes and the sharp nose and long, skinny fingers. 'You're not a badger at all. You're a vulture. And I'm never going to be your *guinea pig*.'

As Dr Shenoy's doddering car grinds haltingly through the grey rain and traffic, a whole new turmoil assails Brio. Because even if Professor Glybb wasn't talking about his dad, how could he say that people are programmed like robots to commit suicide? People are made by God and God is life, and suicide's worse than a cardinal sin.

As school looms, they fall into a tense silence and Brio picks frenetically at the perpetual scab on his palm. Memories of his mum's half-finished matchstick model as they pass the Jubilee Clock only makes things worse. By the time they pull up outside the dreaded gates, his palm's raw and bleeding.

He walks fast through the school, tugging down on his exaggerated clump of fringe, eyeing the exact angles of doors, trying to blank out the wake of whispered comments and laughs.

Outside the drama space's double-doors, he stops to peer through one of the two porthole windows. The cast and crew are sitting in the chair-circle, scripts in hands, and Darcy's on his feet, lips daubed with bright lipstick. But where's Izzy? Maybe she's not even coming. And today it's only Miss Alison the useless gap student pretending to be a drama assistant.

Brio's about to flee for the toilets when he sees a large group heading his way down the corridor. Some dark force is corralling him into every place he doesn't want to go.

'Sorry I'm late,' he mutters as he dumps down in the circle.

'Do speak up,' Darcy drawls. 'You're the prompter, after all.'

'I said, sorry I'm late.'

'Ah. Well, it doesn't matter. You're only the prompter.'

'Okay, let's keep going,' the drama assistant says quickly. 'Act two, scene three.'

As Darcy puffs on, Brio can't help squirming on his seat. Because this is a female character who should be played by a girl, the lines should be soft and dainty. And it's obvious from Darcy's sneering glances that he's posted an even crueller version of the video.

Knowing that he's taking a chance now, Brio slides his eyes off the dog-eared script and angles surreptitiously to check the clock on the wall. When he sees that only twelve minutes remain, his stomach cramps and his foot starts to tap. *God where is she?* Why can't he just be locked away with her behind double-bolted doors and curtains drawn on the sunshine, writing together like they always did, trading pen and crayons in excited turns of paragraph, sentence, word, egging the story on to ever greater heights of cliff-hanging jeopardy. And after they've reached the breathless ending and saved the world, he just wants her all to himself, so he can gaze at her for hours with no words at all.

Twisting even further in his seat, he pleads with the double-doors to spring open and starburst Izzy into the room. When the doors remain unmoved, he finds himself drawn into their bug-eyed gaze and borne away by the figment of his longing who floats into the drama space all flustered and burdened by books but with eyes for him alone, and when she sees—

'Hey, *Penguin Boy*.'

Brio jolts back around and searches frantically for his place in the script.

'You're supposed to be hanging on my every word, not doing puppy-dog for Izzy.'

Faced with no choice but to look up, Brio finds himself fixed in Darcy's glare and trapped by the spotlighted circle of smirks and pitying looks. He flushes hot and feels the paralysis that comes with needing to flee. And he still neds to pee.

But *no*. With the drama asisstant looking lost and weak, this is the moment he's trained for in his bedroom mirror a hundred times, the one where he fires back a salvo of sharp wit that sees him crowned as the hero who shut down *the Darcy* forever. But Darcy's rolled straight on and now he's sounding off his lines with such exaggeration that Brio can't help groaning and clutching a wad of illicit fringe.

Darcy stops again. 'What the hell now? Are you trying to say my character's such an appalling woman she should be played by a *man*?'

Feeling the ring of eyes close in, Brio tries to fight the panic and think of a devastating retort. But he didn't even understand the question and can't find a cue on the face of the drama assistant, who says anxiously, 'Darcy, I think Brio was just expressing some inner feelings of his own. We're obviously working with emotive subject matter.'

Her feeble rescue attempt only compounds Brio's humiliation. His thoughts begin to unravel.

'Inner feelings, huh?' Darcy flickers his eyebrows at Brio before giving the drama assistant a supercilious smile. 'And I'm actually Tracy at the moment.'

The drama assistant looks even more worried. 'I'm sorry. I wasn't sure whether it was just for the, erm …'

Darcy lets her flounder. Now Brio hates the drama assistant too, for being scared of Darcy and letting him do this at a school of God. How can all the teachers pretend to believe Darcy's just staying in character, play after play? And he's *not* a troubled genius. He's a creep and a bully.

'It's all right, Miss Alison.' Darcy gives the drama assistant a reassuring smile. 'To ascertain which one of *moi* is in residence, you simply have to check which way my *bag* is facing.'

Titters ripple but Brio's determined not to look down at the famous silk rugby-boot bag between Darcy's feet: *Tracy Hardwit*, flaunts its ornate gold embroidery. *First Fifteen*.

'Et voilà!' Darcy pulls a dainty flourish and turns himself into a Grecian urn. 'Venus with a penus!'

Laughs and loving groans plunge Brio into deeper chaos. How can people taunt *him* for being gay when he's not, but lap it up when Darcy pretends to be a girl? How can they not see that the whole act is just to mock God and the school?

'And if you happen to forget one of my names again,' Darcy adds in a husky voice, 'you simply need to remember that one of them's always gonna be a convenient little anagram of the other. Darcy Withart, Tracy Hardwit. Sweet, huh?'

The drama assistant manages a strained smile and looks back to her script, but Darcy turns sharply to Brio with eyes narrowed.

'Your God's gonna strike me down, right? Coz I'm shit and a rat in his wonky glass eyes, that big fuckin' *man* in the pretty blue sky.'

Shocked disbelief stuns Brio's anger. Surely this is too much even for Darcy. The drama assistant has to *do something*. But people seem gobsmacked that Darcy's dared. Two girls are even shaking their heads in wonder. All Brio can feel is his mum's anger and he hears himself shouting at Darcy that he's just pretending to be gay and Izzy knows he's only doing it to show off.

Ticking-clock silence stills the room and Brio looks desperately to the drama assistant for help. But Darcy gets there first. 'Miss Alison, I'm sorry but I'm obliged to correct our prompter on an important point of principle.'

The drama assistant's nervous fidgeting with her script almost tips it from her hand. 'Darcy ...'

'It's *Tracy*. So stop deadnaming me.' And when the drama assistant herself glances at the double-doors, he suddenly controls the room like he commands a stage. Turning back to Brio, he says, 'Firstly, Penguin Boy, I'm not gay. I'm trans. Specifically, I'm trans-trans, like Tiresias, except I don't have to wait seven years to club those tangled snakes. If I wake up at the crack of dawn feeling rosy-fingered, I skirt the issue and cut the slacks. But if I—'

'Come on, Trace,' says a girl. 'We know you're smart. Just get on with the read.'

But Darcy keeps Brio's eyes locked down as though he's kneeling on his arms. 'You need my help, don't you, P-Boy? Coz you're hanging out to hop on my laptop and click some ass. You find intimate dating too intimi*dating* but I can help you decide—dick or a dock, dick or a dock, does your mouse run up a—?'

'Shut *up*,' Brio cries. He knows he could fight back with better words if he only had time, but the pummelling of Darcy's performance has broken his wits and his will and he didn't understand a word Darcy said. He looks helplessly to the drama assistant, who has to check the clock, and her watch, and—

'What?' Darcy scoffs at Brio. 'You don't get the difference between who you bed and who you are when you do it?'

'*Tracy* ...' The drama assistant's voice trembles. 'I thought you were acting at first—and it's good to practise improvisation, of course—but we need this to be a safe space.'

Darcy's eyes are wild now. 'I'm trying to help him *get* safe. I mean, if he'd just admit he's baby-trans, he wouldn't keep suffering from this multiple lack of personality disorder or whatever it is.'

'Just let him be,' says another girl nervously.

'No, seriously …' Darcy tosses a contemptuous gesture at Brio. 'He wants to be like me and I've got colours he can try.'

Their eyes unexpectedly lock and for the briefest moment Brio sees something in Darcy he can't compute—a flash of sadness that could even be helplessness. Unable to stand seeing Darcy looking so weak, he looks away. But when he glances back, Darcy's eyes are full of murderous rage, because he wants to wipe the record off the face of the earth.

'Admit it, Penguin Boy, you *want* me. So what're you going to do about it?'

Struggling to breathe, all Brio can see are pitying looks and glancing smirks. The perfect circle of cast and crew begins to crumble in the face of Darcy's madness but it's he himself who's the centre that can't hold, him and the helpless drama assistant whose face is taut and bright red.

'Tracy, I'm sorry,' she says, 'but you have to stop.'

Darcy turns on the drama assistant. 'If you can't stand the heat, get out of the fucking kitchen.'

'Darce, for fuck's sake,' someone says as the drama assistant flees the room. 'You always go too far.'

'You want to be in theatre?' Darcy retorts. 'Well, this is it.' He lets out the cry of someone who's been stabbed. 'Why can't you understand, it's fucking *Tracy*?'

With Darcy clearly out of control, people edge nervously for the doors, while his fan club moves uncertainly to trap Brio.

'Don't you want to stay for the main event?' Darcy calls to the people fleeing. When they pause, he turns back on Brio. 'You see? Everyone wants to hear the precious little secret you've been sitting on all these years—the one about your dad.' His face is pale and he swallows hard. 'Come on, P-Boy, tell them. Your dad didn't die in Africa when you were in nappies after all. He's some superhero special forces guy who got locked up in a desert prison. Dude, that's so fuckin' *huge*.'

Brio's sure it's his mind playing tricks with his deepest fear. How could Darcy possibly have discovered his most closely guarded secret when the only person in the world who knew was Izzy? He stumbles backwards and the room moves with him in a slow-turning spiral of clocks and stage-lights and stunned faces. He feels a weightlessness down the back of his head and the next second it's one of those terrifying moments when he's not even real. The first gasp of hyperventilation hits him like a knee in his guts with hands at his throat. But as he turns to run, Izzy's suddenly among them.

'What's happening?' Her big dark eyes are wide with alarm.

Now Darcy plays it all cool and friendly. 'Brio was just telling us about his dad being a top-secret POW. Pretty amazing.'

Izzy looks aghast at Brio. 'You told people?'

'I didn't.' He's choking on dry tongue. '*You* did.' He hangs on her reply with a screaming child in his head. But as she stares at Darcy, it's obvious she's not even going to attempt a denial.

A few moments later, the bug-eyed double-doors are twanging behind him and Brio's weaving wildly through the lunchtime throng, ducking and twisting to avoid physical contact. In a pressing haze of sweat and deodorant and pungent sports gear, he runs this way and that, fighting to breathe in and out at the same time, ever more lost in the empty and crowded corridors he's known all his life.

Time unravels and teachers fleetingly ask if he's okay. But he's gone again, leaving himself behind, stopping only to stare his hate at the Drama Society poster: Darcy's face made up as a clown playing a Greek god. *Darcy Withart's Metamorphoses and Madness*. Which Izzy helped him write, just like she helped with *Tracy Hardwit's Saved by the Belle*. Shouting at people to *get back*, Brio rips the poster off the wall.

Running again, he senses word of his meltdown flashing ahead of him, and the more frantically he barges for the fire escape, the more the forest of hated uniforms becomes an entanglement of scuffed shoes like tree roots that trip him into hard shoves and buffet him from side to side of the endless gauntlet of taunting.

'Bree, come back,' Izzy pleads from somewhere behind him. 'It wasn't me.' When she also starts calling for people to 'leave him alone' and 'let him through', he wants to spin around and yell into her face that he doesn't need her help with *anything—ever again*. But one last look into Izzy's beautiful eyes and he'll mangle the words into the childish shrill that keeps cracking his precious new voice.

Before Brio can reach the doors at the end of the darkening tunnel, the mocking faces blur into demonic gargoyles, and devilish creatures try to ensnare him from between lockers and schoolbags. His bowels give way and he has to crash into the nearest toilets where girls flee in disarray as he blunders for a cubicle. But the seething mouthparts of a giant caterpillar appear under the door and pee releases down his leg. Crying out for the Red Knight to save him, he throws his shoulder against the flimsy partition. Another lunge flattens it into the neighbouring cubicle, the next one too.

Yet, from the wreckage, the demon still comes on, fanged mouth masticating and tentacle limbs writhing for his neck. Letting out a cry, Brio arms himself with mop and galvanised bucket. He swings and smashes in all directions, battle cries beating back the jibes from outside. When at last the beast slithers away, Brio emits a lopsided roar of triumph and stomps its shadow into shards of porcelain and broken mirror. But as he makes to escape, the door slams back and teachers morph into a clatter of chainmailed minions. Brio jousts heroically with tasselled lance and hollow shield, kicking shins and battering heads, diving again and again for the door. But even as victory seems assured, his feet are snatched out from behind him and he finds his cheek pressed to the cold stone ground of the castle keep, where peals of scornful laughter echo in his head like church bells gone wrong.

To the clang of voices on white tiles, he struggles with alien strength against the clamp of hands and neon glare. More teachers arrive in glimpses of half face and crooked shoulders. Nurse Geraldine and the deaf security guy too. Someone calls *Major incident* and *Go to your classes … Call Dr Shenoy*.

Brio's strength eventually runs out, and when the hands lift cautiously away he turns onto his side and contracts into a frozen embryo. In the silence and kaleidoscope of bloodless colours behind scrunched-up eyes there's only the sound of people catching breath. And he hates the world for making it useless Pippa and not his mum who'll come to rescue him from this nightmare.

Drawing a steadying breath, Mrs Thorne levels her palms on the outsize principal's desk. 'Brio, this is too serious for you to simply go home. Please, sit.'

As Brio's about to sit down on the wooden chair next to Pippa, the door opens and in sweeps Ms Whittle.

Mrs Thorne jolts upright and the fight returns to her face. 'What are *you* doing here?'

Ms Whittle scans for a chair. 'I'm the school counsellor. I'm also Brio's closest friend.'

'This is a disciplinary matter, Sister Jane. Your services are not required.'

'It's a *pastoral* matter, and I'm required by law to be present.' She glowers at Mrs Thorne through the huge, red-framed spectacles that magnify her powdery cheeks into finely wrinkled tissue paper. 'And I'd ask you to refer to me by my preferred name, not "Sister Jane".'

Issuing a highly aspirated tut, Mrs Thorne gestures irritably to a third wooden chair at the side of her desk. And while Ms Whittle stalls proceedings with a show of moving the chair to a less servile position, Brio finds all his pent-up rage and despair venting at *her*—for writing so much personal stuff in Professor Glybb's thick file, for not being the sensible Sister Jane he so badly needs in place of this cartoon character who's taken to wearing charity shop dungarees and 'homemade sandals. He wants those familiar aromas of camphor on tidy cardigans, talcum powder and detergent soap, not the alien smells of joss sticks and weird cooking that emanate from her threadbare beaded dreadlocks.

As soon as Ms Whittle's finally sat down, Mrs Thorne transfers her watery glare back to Brio. 'Now, where in the Lord's name did you get this idea that your father's still alive? And what—in the Foreign Legion, a prisoner of war?'

An odd glance between Mrs Thorne and Ms Whittle turns into a pair of sniffs that bounce off each other and Ms Whittle twists herself in rude broadside to Mrs Thorne.

'Brio, dear, I need you to take a deep breath and try to tell me why you think—'

'Sister *Jane*. Would you please leave this to *me*? Brio's confused enough without your ridiculous ideas.'

Ms Whittle brings down her palms on the desk as though striking a thunderous piano chord. 'There's nothing ridiculous about partnering calmly with Brio to help him understand that he's in the grip of a psychotic narrative that clearly derives from—'

Suddenly standing, Mrs Thorne lurches forward on her palms. 'Be *quiet*, Sister Jane. This urge to be a psychiatrist has driven you out of your mind—and half the school too. God help me, if it wasn't for these pernicious employment laws, I'd show you the door right now.'

With Ms Whittle on her feet too, they face off as though ready to throw aside the desk. 'It's not the law that protects me. It's a God who wants someone in this benighted school to teach our young people the kind of values that'll lead them to a life of sound mental health. If this school showed even a modicum of—'

'*Values?*' Mrs Thorne cuts in furiously. 'You mean the values that say it's acceptable for a child to be one sex one day and something else the next? Is that what you mean?' She has to wheeze for air. 'The values that demand diversity while obliterating the difference between men and women? The ones that cry "cultural appropriation" when someone wears the wrong party costume but exhort men to wear women's clothes? D'you know how many parents I've had calling about your unapproved talk?' And before Ms Whittle can fire back, Mrs Thorne collapses back into her chair and claims sanctuary behind closed eyes and a steeple of thumbs and fingers.

Distressed that the two remaining pillars in his life care more about arguing with each other than they do about *him*, Brio wants to shout down the age-old duty to keep vigil for Mrs Thorne when she's deep in prayer. Except that when the silence threatens to make her look foolish, another wave of nostalgia triggers the old longing to be back in the Lady Chapel with the Mrs Thorne who prayed next to him and his mum and Father T when things were bad, the Mrs Thorne who was as constant as her stiff jackets, as wise as her old-fashioned glasses, whose hair sat firmly like a hat for church and didn't fall about in wisps that revealed hints of pale skin, who wasn't racked with pain and forced to scowl and limp because of the arthritis that his mum said happened to everyone in the end.

When Mrs Thorne looks up, he sees tears in her eyes that draw his own. 'Brio …' Her voice trembles. 'I know you've had a torrid time this last year and a half—and for a sensitive boy like you it's been especially difficult—but, God help you, you need to learn that sometimes we must fight. We must accept that there's no right to a life without pain. In fact, we should embrace a life of pain, because it's by the grace of loss and competition that God makes each constituent of His Creation stronger and better. When we have faith in God, He truly will be our strength.' She has to close her eyes again and steady her breathing. When she re-emerges, she says, 'We must rise to the Lord's challenges without resort to fantasies and fictions, Brio. And we must look forward to the day when the anguish of life is rewarded by entry into God's Kingdom. Your loss is truly a gift that can make you whole.'

Before Brio can even try to escape his turmoil of emotions, Mrs Thorne turns to Pippa, who's sobbing silently into her hands. 'Miss Lasalle, I know you're doing the best for Brio that can be achieved by a single woman with a business to run, but I'm afraid I'll be sending you a very large bill for repairs.'

Brio's moment of numb suspension is over and he's back on his feet. '*It's not her fault*. And it's not mine either. It's Darcy's. But you never say anything to him, because you think he's going to get into Cambridge and then you can retire happy. But he steals *my* ideas, and Izzy helps him with everything. And when I'm a famous writer, I'll pay for as many stupid toilets as you want.'

With one last cry and a punch to his forehead, Brio storms for the door, where arms flail and fingers grapple and the deaf security guy has no choice but to wrestle him back to the hard wooden floor.

2

AS BRIO STARES UNSEEINGLY at the plate of overcooked fish fingers, his thoughts rave and tangle into the yellow table cloth's mawkish pattern of paisley and flowers. Little edging dots of smashed-up toilets and Izzy's betrayal. Curly leaves of Pippa's uselessness and Darcy gone wild. The interweaving stems of Mrs Thorne dying and Sister Jane born again as the grotesque Ms Whittle. And in every petal and detail, the pitying and mocking faces that think he's gone mad for believing his dad's a hero who's been abandoned by the government that sent him on the secret mission. They won't be laughing and pitying him when he proves it's true, when he puts his lifelong dream into action and joins the Foreign Legion himself, follows in his dad's footsteps and tracks him all the way to that hidden prison in the desert.

But the moment Brio allows himself to believe that this is what he's actually going to do, the knot tightens in his chest and a spasm of pain rips through his right hand as his mum crushes it down onto the Bible and makes him swear that he'll never so much as dream of looking for his father.

'Bree, *please*,' Pippa says. 'We used to talk about everything, and if you can't talk to me, then who—'

'I don't need to talk to anyone—about *anything*.'

But in his heart, Brio longs for the old Pippa too. The one who hugged his head to her hard tummy when he was small. That scent like no one else's. The way she could make him laugh so much it hurt. When all he sees now is the skulking guilt in her feeble smile, his longing turns to anger at *her* betrayal. For doing nothing when they dragged him away sobbing to the so-called *care home*. For letting them keep him there even after she'd seen his mouldy room and smelled the stale wee in the stairwell and the stinking kids who gave him a swollen jaw. How could she have pretended not to see the paralysing loneliness that made him cry night after night till he was drained into sleep?

And why hasn't she made more fish fingers? Because now he has to eat the puddle of ketchup on its own so as not to fritter away God's providence. A waste-not-want-not oath to a dead mum is a bond whose betrayal can kill you with one squeeze.

'The thing is,' Pippa says, 'I can't just stay home to look after you. I need to run the shop.'

Brio grips his fork harder. 'You can tell Mandy what to do over the phone.'

But he knows that with his mum gone and Pippa's mum dead too, Pippa has to be at the shop herself. If she leaves it to Mandy, it'll all go wrong. The thought of Costume Castle being turned into another pound store triggers longings and memories—his mum keeping a whole party room full of kids spellbound in story while Pippa acted out all the parts in an array of colourful hats, dancing the kids in circles with her Pied Piper outfit and pipes. How could Aunty Pips have gone from so much colour to the same grey sweatshirt and jeans day after day? How could her glowing brown skin have come to look so pale and washed out, her softened hair such a mess? 'Why can't you leave me here on my own? I don't need *supervision*.'

She doesn't need to answer and he hates himself for needing her to be there, for his terror at the thought of having to look after himself one day.

'I mean, if you won't come into the shop,' Pippa says, 'and you won't go to school, what are we going to do?'

Biting down on his mouthwash of ketchup, Brio stares at his mum's little painting of the Pope on his balcony. Pippa's obviously brought it down from the attic, trying to make him feel better by squeezing it in among her own chaos of bright yellow pots and flotsam of feelgood quotes on fake driftwood. She's overloaded the corkboard too. So many selfies of happy times that all he can see is unreachable glimpses of them all together—Izzy as well—singing their heads off on 'Bubble Sand Beach', dancing with twig-tomahawks in the 'Forest of Far-Flung-Far-Out-Far-Fetched Fables'. The sight of their little fake family like happy ghosts returned to the world of deadness overwhelms him. But still he manages look squarely at Pippa and let anger drive back the grief.

'We're not going to *do* anything. Coz there's nothing you can do. *Ever.*' He scoops up another spoonful of ketchup and rams it into his mouth, clattering teeth. 'You think I'm mad.'

Pippa lets out a juddery breath of tension. 'I just don't quite understand. I mean, *did* your mum tell you something about your dad?'

He struggles to hold her gaze. 'Yes.'

'That he was in the Foreign Legion?'

'*Yes.*'

'And she told you he was taken prisoner, on a mission?'

His grip on the fork becomes painful but he can't ease the pressure. 'Mum wasn't even supposed to tell me he was in the Foreign Legion. She wasn't allowed to tell anyone. Because it's always a secret. That's why they give them a new name—a French one—and a passport. And they have to learn French and forget English.' He silently begs Pippa to accept everything without any more questions that might force him to fudge the awkward blanks.

'But why did your mum tell you all this if she wasn't allowed to?'

Brio groans in frustration. 'I found his photo in a box in the garage. He was in his Foreign Legion uniform. It said his fake

French name—Marcel. Mum was cross I found it because then she had to tell me the truth.'

Seeing a frisson of interest in Pippa's eyes, Brio feels a new excitement. When she asks if he still has the photo, he has to look away. 'Mum took it. But I can remember exactly what he looked like. Like *me*. And he *is* alive.' He turns back, desperate to rekindle the flicker of belief in Pippa's eyes. 'Mum only told people he worked for a charity in Africa because that was his cover story when he joined the Foreign Legion. Then when the secret mission went wrong and they wanted her to believe he was dead, they told her to tell people he died of some stupid disease. She hated having to tell that story. She wanted to tell the truth. That he was a hero. That he was alive.' He clings to Pippa's gaze and prays for her face to brighten with wonder, but puzzlement creases her forehead.

'You mean they told her to believe he was dead even though they knew she knew it wasn't true?'

'*Yes*. But she was a nobody against the French government and all governments work together as one big mega-government. They threatened her. They bribed her with the money to buy Bluebells.'

Pippa's eyebrows climb. 'She told you that?'

'*No*. It's just obvious. I know you don't believe it but it's true.' He pushes back in the chair. 'I don't care what you think.'

'No, wait. I'm just trying to get my head round this.' She places her knife down to scratch her forehead. His stomach churns. For God's sake, how long does it take to scratch an itch?

'So if this is true, then your mum never actually believed he was killed?'

'*No*. I mean, *yes*. I mean, she knew in her heart he was alive. But she was forced to believe he was dead for so long she gave up hope.' His lower lip wobbles. 'Then it was like she really did believe he was dead.'

He sees pity in Pippa's eyes. She doesn't believe a word. 'Stop treating me like a kid.'

'I'm not, and I really want to understand this, okay? So how do you know he was taken prisoner and didn't get killed? And where *is* he?'

As Brio's about to thump the table, the words of the last therapist kick in: if you're defensive or aggressive, people will think you don't really believe what you're saying. He sits straight and tries to look her in the eye. 'I swore to Mum I wouldn't tell anyone anything. And I don't know *where* he is.' He tries to stay calm but her forehead's furrowed again.

'You mean it wasn't your mum who told you he's a prisoner of war?'

'*No.* I overheard something.' He clutches his head. 'Oh, God, I wasn't even supposed to tell anyone *that.*'

'You remember hearing your dad saying something? I always thought you had no memory of him at all.'

'It wasn't him I overheard.' He almost cries out. 'Why can't you understand? If anyone found out about the mission, it might've caused a war. And when it went wrong, the government couldn't admit that anyone had been captured. So they had to abandon them. That's *la guerre.*'

Pippa's gaze slips away and the bright yellow fork handle comes to rest in her own blotch of ketchup. And in that moment, in the corner of Pippa's eye as she looks to the world for help, Brio sees what she really believes about his dad: that his mum made up the story about him dying of a tropical disease in Africa to veil her shame about the cardinal sin they all secretly think he committed. Oh, God, and it's not just Pippa, it's what everyone believes. And Professor Glybb *was* talking about his dad.

Brio jumps up with the force of his thrown-down fork. 'My dad would never have done that. And he *was* in the Foreign Legion. He still is.'

Pippa stumbles forward, arms open. 'Bree, please. Just see someone. Psychiatrists aren't all like Professor Glybb.'

With a wordless shout, Brio slams the kitchen door behind him so hard it shakes the house, and he punches the wall all the way up the stairs until he can slam his bedroom door on the world.

Half-sighted in the fading light, Brio can't stop pacing his small bedroom—two steps one way, three back to the draughty window, four to the broken chest of drawers. Why can't it ever be the same number both ways? As he stops to perfect the symmetry of treasured objects on his desk, the tears well again. How his mum must have hated telling everyone the dumb lie about Africa. How she must have known that all those so-called friends at church secretly believed her husband killed himself. How she *suffered*.

Reaching out to the far corner of his table, Brio picks up the little framed watercolour and gazes at the great steed in flat gallop through tall trees, its golden-robed rider's flaxen hair streaming behind like a pennant. '*My* mum painted it,' his mum told him, one of the grandmas he never knew. But this was a lie too, it was painted by his dad.

Knowing what's coming next, Brio grabs his teddy off the floor and leaps to refuge on the bed. But before he can curl up, the window morphs into stained glass and the window-bogey's back, pressing its grotesque face into the warped colours. Determined to vanquish the demon without help from the Red Knight, Brio closes his eyes and clasps a handful of rosary beads. But the prayer isn't enough to stop spindly fingers seeping through molten glass and he grabs for his mum's hand, and when she sees it's just the same old bogey trouble, she smiles as though to share some guilty pleasure. 'It's okay, my darling. You can call for your noble protector one last time.'

Through stifled sobs and for just one more *one last time*, Brio shamefully chants the magic incantation to summon up the Red Knight, and he chants it again and again till fanned rays of dawn break miraculously through tall trees and a thunder of hooves fills the forest air. Hissing a silent snarl, the window-bogey wisps away to leave Brio weeping silently, back with his mum in the empty church one Thursday morning. She stands at the base of the pulpit, tight-lipped with determination as she jabs white flowers into the embossed brass vase. And Father T's Santa Claus laugh echoes around the treasured sanctuary of scents and stone. 'My dear Hannah, you look like you're single-handedly replanting the Garden of Eden!'

His mum smiles at Father T in that way she always did, then glances round at her little Bree who's sitting patiently in the pews, reading about Frodo in the best book Father T ever gave him; Frodo who never used his sword to bring harm, just like no one in his mum's home-made Bible-story picture books ever hurt a living soul.

Needing to be with his mum so much his whole body aches, Brio curls up tightly on the bed. He finds himself back on the day they sneaked into the Old Lighthouse at dusk for one last look before the council finished boarding it up. Yes, up those precariously rotten spiral stairs they climbed, up and up—with Izzy clutching his hand and Pippa making spooky noises—up and up—the thrill of illicit intrusion making the spine-chilling terror even more wonderful—up into an almost surreal dimension of dank scents and shrinking space—up and up those endless stone spiral steps, accompanied all the way by neck-tingling creaks powdered by little draughts of cold breeze through cracks in the mortar and timber. The lighthouse keeper mannequin was still there, but the clumsily curated memorabilia that portrayed his former life on the cusp was cast about and covered in gritty dust like there'd been a storm of sand and waves. Brio remembers how sad he felt to see the old seafarer lying next to the lone armchair he'd once occupied, stripped of his vintage clothes and missing a leg. On seeing in his mind that dreadful contrast between hardy grey beard and smooth-cupped nothingness where his underpants should have been, Brio feels the same disorientation he felt then, the same sense that it had something to do with him.

Amid the wreckage, they found a scattering of old books whose shelf cabinet had collapsed, seemingly under the mournful weight of its own emptiness. An ominous creak from the rotten floorboards frightened them all, but his mum was so inspired by the moment that she brushed away the fright and burst into story. And as the wondrous tale of hide-and-seek unfolded, she danced and clambered all over the room, turning greasy rags into giant rats and buckets into boats, shifting the toppled clothes rack to make a pack of savage guard dogs, puffing mouldy old cushions into fiery infernos of billowing dust. The lighthouse keeper was revealed to be none other than Baron Bigfoot, who'd lost his leg in the battle with a sea monster. And the hazy, low-lying shape of the nearby headland proved to be the evil-smelling Lord Lobster closing in for another attack. With a little gasp of stage terror, his mum crouched them all down and whispered *dragon*, and they waited, breath bated in puffed cheeks, until the light-aircraft noise had passed. After that, Izzy found a curious little spoon with a crossbar at the top of its handle, apparently a feature to stop it sliding into the small pot of whatever condiment it was designed to serve. Her big brown eyes wide in wonder, she studied the spoon intently and announced a tiny inscription on its handle: *Dr Runcible's Patent Tonic Spoon 1838.*

'Yet in my bones I feel it to be no mere piece of miniature cutlery,' his mum added swiftly, 'rather a mighty cutlass whose pedigree and purpose shall soon be revealed!'

'The Secret Sword of Mouse-the-Brave!' Izzy cried. 'We've found it at last!'

Brio remembers how much he wanted to take the little sword home, but his mum drew the line at theft, so back it squeezed into the jammed drawer for some other pirate to loot.

So at last, despite everything that life and the day have thrown at him, Brio experiences a calm he hasn't felt for weeks, maybe for the whole eighteen months since his mum died. But just as the blissful respite of sleep comes on, a jarring buzz of doorbell sends him flying down the stairs, shouting at an unseen Pippa not to answer the door.

On seeing Izzy's outline through the frosted glass lit up like a goddess by the halo of porch light, Brio freezes.

'Bree.' Izzy's voice seems to float in through the glass. 'Are you okay?'

'What do *you* care?'

'I care a lot. You know I do. *Please*, open the door.'

Unable to stop himself, Brio slowly rotates the latch but wedges a foot to allow only a crack of cold air to connect them. 'What do you want?'

'Bree, it wasn't me who told Darcy. I'd never have shared your most precious secret with anyone in the world. Someone else must have known.'

Brio's so overwhelmed by Izzy's beautiful long hair and big, dark eyes that it takes him several seconds to comprehend with a shudder of alarm that someone else might have known about his dad. And how many other people besides? Maybe the same number who believed his dad committed suicide. When he catches the pitying look in Izzy's eye, he realises that for all these years she's just been humouring him too, kindness to his face and giggles behind his back at the sad kid who believed his mum's crazy story about the Foreign Legion. And now she's laughing it up with Darcy.

Struggling to stay standing, Brio grips the door handle harder.

'Tell me you believe my dad's alive.'

'Bree, *please*, open the door.'

'Tell me you don't think he killed himself. You *know* he's in the Foreign Legion.'

She sighs and runs a hand through her hair. 'I mean, maybe he *is* alive and that'd be fantastic. But maybe what you heard Father T say meant something else. Maybe old Mrs Robinson was telling the truth when she said your mum told her something about your dad suffering from depression.'

Brio can't believe Izzy can be so brazen. How many more times can she betray him in one day? 'Mum never told Mrs Robinson anything. She made it up about my dad. She was jealous of Mum because Father T let her use the VIP parking space on coffee mornings. I'm glad she's dead.' Even through the frosted glass he can see Izzy's look of shock but still he shoves back at the door. 'Just go to *Harry's*.'

There's a pause and he revels in her worry that he's about to have a turn. He can't wait to tell her what just came into his head like a gift from God.

'Who's Harry?' she asks nervously.

'It's Darcy. Because that's the *real* anagram of his stupid name— Harry *Cadwitt*, not Tracy Hardwit. And that's what he is, an old-fashioned cad who hides his cruelty behind his fake wit.' When all Izzy does is sigh, he fires back with, 'It's good. And clever. And he doesn't need to be Tracy anyway. Because Darcy's a girl's name too.'

'Bree, I do stuff with Darcy because he's in Drama Soc. There's nothing more than that.'

He pushes back harder at the door. 'He thinks he's so clever for reading all the old stuff and believing he's a Greek god who can be anything.'

And when Izzy sighs again, he knows exactly what she's

thinking: that Darcy *is* a Greek god. She doesn't see that Darcy's evil because his dad's evil. The Witharts don't just look down their noses at everyone else, they don't even like each other. Most godless of all, they just pretend to be Catholic so Darcy can be at St Joseph's after no other school would take him.

'Bree, I know Darcy's mean to you. But I really try to stop him. And whatever everyone thinks, he's got mental health problems too.'

'What do you mean *too*? And he's not mentally ill. He's just doing it to shock everyone, pretending to be special to get let off for everything.'

'Honestly, Darcy's not like they seem. Bree, we can all be friends.'

'We *can't*. But I don't care. I don't need your help.' Yet immediately he's demanding to know why she hasn't made Darcy take down the videos. 'I *don't* want to be a girl and I'm not gay and nor are penguins.'

'Oh, Bree, I know it's wrong, that one especially. But only Zpydr can take them down.'

'Then why don't they?'

Izzy presses ever harder at the door. 'That's just the way social media works. But ignore the stupid videos. And it wouldn't matter even if you *were* trans or gay or whatever.'

Her words hit Brio so hard he almost whites out. How can she not care if he's something that would stop them being together? How can she say it's okay for him to be like those people in the parades his mum hated? Into Izzy's breath on the air, he wills her to remember Bible Group and church with her parents, listening to Father T explaining so patiently why being gay was wrong in the eyes of a life-loving God. He angles his ear to await her confession through the crack. 'Tell me it would matter.'

Izzy leans forward. 'Bree, what matters is that we connect like no one else in the world. Who else could have won the writing prize two years running? Who else has their own secret language?'

For a moment, Brio thinks he imagined what Izzy just said. But joy sweeps aside anguish and he pulls open the door to grab Izzy tightly by the forearms. In immediate thrall to her dark eyes and beautiful long hair, he cries, 'You *can* help me—to find my dad! And we'll do it exactly the same way we write stories, except this one will come true!'

~ PART TWO ~

LIGHTING THE GREAT BEACON

Joining your tribe's prevailing narrative has always been
what keeps you safe, not to mention sane. In today's
world, all you have to do is take that step through
the looking-glass and join the conversation
on social media. After all, it truly is
today's act of civic worship.

Tabo Forzac
Founder of Zpydr Inc.

3

PIPPA KNOCKS A THIRD TIME. 'Come on, you've got to eat. And I know you haven't slept.'

Brio takes no notice and keeps pacing. But thinking harder about the mission only draws his mum's distress closer and reminds him again of Izzy's pitying face in the TV-room. *Bree, finding your dad's a special journey for you alone. But I'll be there for you all the way. You're the brother I never had.*

As soon as he hears Pippa on the creaking stairs down, he rounds on the four-foot shrine against the wall—the wobbly but precisely arranged pyramid of every story he and Izzy ever wrote, in shoeboxes that grew over the years with the size of their feet. *Mouse-the-Brave. The Red Knight's Adventures in the Isle of Men.* Izzy even made him take back the dumb stable-girl sagas he wrote with her so she'd keep coming round. And finally, when throwing it all back in his face wasn't enough, she told him she didn't have time to write anything at all anymore—because *Chess Club made me president* and *Mum let me have horse-riding lessons at last* and *Dad won't let me give up the science project.*

Before Brio can control himself, his foot swings and sacred texts scatter across the carpet amidst upturned boxes and twisted lids. Horrified, he throws himself down, but no sooner has he started clawing at splayed double pages than he hears a male voice in the house. Thinking that Pippa's ex-boyfriend Paul has come back triggers such fear of abandonment that for once Brio doesn't count the peeling seams in the wallpaper down the stairs. In the small hallway, the sound of a cool American accent stops him dead. He's relieved to hear it's not Paul, after all, but a few more overheard words are enough to tell him it's another therapist.

Through the warped crack in the TV-room door, Brio sees Pippa sitting forward on her armchair while the guy drapes himself back in the sofa like he's trying it out in a showroom.

'So yeah,' the stranger drawls languidly, 'I done a lodda work with kids Brio's age. It's totally normal they won't share. They just need to click with the right soul-buddy.'

As though the guy knows someone's watching, he angles his head to reveal eyes that dazzle like the magic gems in Izzy's computer game. Mesmerised by their surreal bright blue, Brio scarcely registers the long, scraggly hair and home-made-looking trousers, the sockless sandals.

'I'm sorry,' Pippa says anxiously. 'I didn't mean to sound negative. It's just that whenever they've managed to send a therapist, he won't say a word.'

'Well, social services shoulda sent me first, coz my gig's right up Brio's street. And betcha none of the other self-styled therapists bothered to wade through all two hundred pages of Brio's file. I mean, our Ms Whittle's quite a school counsellor. Big-time literary ambitions too, I'm thinking? Some real subtleties of the isle tucked away there.'

Pippa explains that Ms Whittle was an English teacher who retired after thirty-seven years at the school but—

'Yeah, I know. And Mrs Thorne's hair must've stood on end when the reborn Ms Whittle rocked up on her mountain bike in dreddies. When nuns break the habit, they really defrock, huh? And *wow*, Miss Dubbya's sure packin' some roller-coaster heat about adolescent psych. So you and Brio's mom met through the shop, huh?' And before Pippa can speak he adds, 'I'm sorry, I do know a lot about you guys from the mother of all files. But this is how you guys came to be a unit, right? You needed help with the shop when your own mom passed away and Hannah replied your ad.'

Pippa looks thrown and Brio hates Ms Whittle again for telling people all their private things.

'Godda say it, though,' the guy goes on, 'Ms Whittle has a big, sweet heart, and she loves you guys, and really loved Hannah too. And she sure makes Bluebells sound like a slam-dunk paradise.' Before Pippa can reply, he rests back and closes his eyes. 'The cottage was little more than a rundown worker's abode when dear Hannah made her once-upon-a-time purchase. Yet in no time at all, the dear girl transformed it into a make-believe world of fairies and sparkles with a darling little herb and vegetable garden. A privileged visitor such as myself would feel that they might chance upon dear Alice at any magic moment, or even meet the courageous true protagonist, Samwise Gamgee.'

After the guy's finished, he stays there as though transported to some better place beyond the stars, while Brio's anger at Ms Whittle for writing so stupidly about his lost home is suspended by disbelief. *Do all Amercians go to the trouble of memorising files or or does this guy actually care?*

'Yeah …' the guy says as Brio presses for a better view through the crack in the door. 'Bluebells *was* paradise. No wonder Brio didn't like to go out.'

Brio's hope crashes. How dare the guy make it sound like he's scared of the world? He just hates school and loved home. But the truth forces itself in: how Father T always had to persuade Izzy's mum and dad to let her spend time at Bluebells, how he never had any real friends, even at Bible Group, never got invited to birthday parties except Izzy's.

Fighting to crush his shame, he hears Pippa insisting helplessly that it wasn't all bad and homeschooling *could* have worked.

'I mean, Hannie wasn't super educated or anything but she read loads and really put in the hours for him.'

'And so do you, Pips. You're doing an awesome job in difficult times.' The guy looks at the photos of Pippa doing magic tricks at kids' parties, telling stories with props and puppets, dancing and walking on her hands. 'Those are some fine moves, by the by. Used to do a few kids' gigs myself back in the day.'

Foreboding shrivels Brio's stomach, because Pippa's looking at the guy in the same lost-puppy way she looks at every man she thinks can save her. Now the guy's saying all the usual stuff about him missing so much school and Father T always being the one who persuaded his mum to let him go back. And all the while the guy edges further forward on the sofa, closer and closer to Pippa as she cries silently, till his outstretched palms are almost touching her and he's saying that she truly can get through this. She's amazing.

Brio wants to burst in and stop them, but he needs to hear more, just in case this weird American really does care.

'So Father T tried to be a pretty serious pop to Brio. You must've known him well.'

Brio tenses. This is where the guy has to get it right and not just *look* different to the others.

Pippa shrugs and looks away. 'I suppose he saw taking care of Brio as part of being their priest.'

The guy cups hands and leans right forward. 'But what do *you* think? Did he take a little more interest in Brio than would be about right for a man of the purple trimmings?'

Pippa draws back and Brio's legs go live.

'I don't know,' she says. 'I mean …'

'Ms Whittle seems to take it as read that Father T crossed the line. And isn't that what everyone thought, that he only ran off with Bella Ripley to silence the gossips, maybe even to try burying some half-unwanted part of himself? Sounds like Bella was pretty broad-minded.'

As Brio's rage flares again, the guy stands and casts an eye along Pippa's row of pulp romances, all squeezed breathless by his mum's orphaned Madonna-and-Child bookend. Raising his eyebrows and nodding knowingly, the guy moves on and peers closely at the hallowed sculpture of Mouse-the-Brave that his mum once tried to carve from balsa wood. When he turns his gemlike eyes on Pippa, she sits up as though at a job interview.

'A lot of moving parts here, Pips. Perception distinction issues and a labyrinth of deeply buried memory. Highly interpretative cerebral architecture too, and subliminal quasi-synaesthetic expression that necessitates a restructural recalibration of the harvesting profile. Delayed awakening and deformative influences contextualised in a heady cocktail of infantilisation and managed helplessness.' He nods to agree with himself. 'Hannah doubtless had suspicions about Father T but her reverence for the man and his office enabled authentic denial, though she compensated semiconsciously by immersing Brio in narratives of hypermasculinity that have totally hardwired his conceptions of gender and the father figure, which explains the obsession with finding his own.'

Brio almost blanks out in the struggle for a way into the guy's web of accusation and blatant display. All he can hear is that Father T was evil and the guy hates God, and Pippa's staring at him with her hands pressed anxiously to her stomach.

'… and multiple issues around the feminine too,' the guy goes on. 'Coz we don't just have maternal deficits, we got a good old biblical temptress. And if we don't fix the feminine stuff, Brio'll never be able to question the stories or the deep-psych indoctrination on gender and sexuality. And to accept the loss of his dad, he's got to transition away from a gendered divinity. This is going to be tricksy, coz we're looking at an emotional age of about six and a mind that's been loaded with heavy-duty adult stuff by the well-meaning Father T. And just in passing, I'm guessing this kid's not only a stimmer, he's got pretty much a photographic memory. So it's a real unique situation and some pretty major latent grief hooked up with pretty much all of the above. I wouldn't even be surprised if he grieves more about Father T than he does about his mum, which has godda raise some seriously interesting questions.'

On the verge of meltdown, Brio has to support himself against the wall. Not even the creepy therapist with an earring in his nose accused him of missing Father T more than his mum. And he doesn't miss Father T at all. He hates him.

'Some say time heals all,' says the guy. 'But time takes time, and in some cases the clock don't even start ticking till we've wound her up and let him fly. So sequencing's gonna be everything here, Pips, coz to address all these issues we need our guy to reach self-reliance. Luckily, all this is my natural habitat and the easy fix is gonna be one big hit of the f-word.'

Pippa looks bewildered. 'The f-word?'

'Exactly. And maybe we can all learn it together.'

Experiencing a flash of rage that blurs his vision, Brio turns to storm into the lounge. But before he's left the hatch, Pippa asks the guy such a loathsome question that he has to stay and hear the answer.

'No,' the guy replies with unexpected sharpness. 'Brio does not have so-called *schizoaffective disorder*. And if you ask the good Professor Glybb what schizoaffective disorder actually is, he'll have no freakin' clue. Coz that's all it is, a list of symptoms, actual causes unknown. His lordship will just preen his silk hanky and tell you it's all genetic so no point bothering with anything but a bit of chat to appease the remnants of his conscience, followed swiftly by a lifetime hit of mind-numbing drugs from a corporation that pays handsomely for him to go speak grandly at conferences in places that just happen to have sunloungers and piña coladas. And then he's back in his dungeon with the next luckless patient, sleeves rolled up, tossing out giblets of anything he can't get his head around. Jesus *Christ*, that man should hang up his old school tie and stop putting young lives in danger.'

As Brio stares into the silence that follows the guy's outburst, his rage becomes an excited flutter he hasn't felt for years. Maybe this outlandish American really is on his side. Before Brio knows what he's doing, he's in the TV room, his hand being shaken in a gentle grip that's not American at all. The beaming smile and motionless handshake go on and on, forcing Brio to take in the long fingers that must surely play the guitar, the weird beard that resembles a padded chinstrap, the bizarre home-made waistcoat. And those eyes, they can't be real.

'My name's Stephen Logue,' the guy says at last. 'Friends call me Logie. Main thing is, I believe in my heart that I can help you free your feelings and achieve your dreams, thereby to locate your own unique locus of love. Or so goes the spiel in the brochure. Won't you come outside for a little fresh air?'

*

'I thought you were going to help me find my dad,' Brio grumbles. He can't understand why he's letting this stranger walk him in circles around his own garden. It's like the losers' exercise class at school. And how's *he* supposed to know what the noise at the beginning of the universe sounded like? As they pass on opposite sides of the bird table, Logie gives him another encouraging smile, which strikes Brio with the disorienting feeling that somehow he knows this weird guy.

'Swing those arms, buddy. Pump the blood of life into that awesome brain.'

Brio tries to follow Logie's exaggerated marching, kicking up knees and flailing windmill arms. He's already coming back round and they pass again on opposite sides of the bird table. Just as he's getting skewed in the head, Logie turns them round.

'Breathe it in, buddy, this glorious sea breeze energised by its journey across meadows and woodland. Hey, join us!' he calls to Pippa as she emerges from the back door. 'Get some spring air in your soul! Follow Bree!'

'It's *Brio*,' Brio mutters as they pass again.

'I love that name. Your mum had style. And she loved words, huh? Loved life. Loved *you*.'

Thoughts of his mum unleash the familiar dull ache and his head drops just in time to avoid stepping on Logie's kicked-off sandals. Brio can't understand how can anyone go barefoot on grass that's so infested with prickly weeds. And Pippa's following right behind him now. This is all mad.

'So you want to tell me about your plan?' Logie whispers as they pass again. 'How you're going to find your dad?'

Brio's straight back into the magic and glances to make sure Pippa didn't hear.

'Don't worry,' Logie says confidentially on their next passing. 'It's between you and me.'

A new energy kicks Brio on and as they approach, Logie slows.

'If I'm you, I'm paying a bigshot lawyer to bribe someone in the French government.'

Brio feels invaded and weirded out, because this is exactly the plan he's sure was taking shape in his own head.

'Big bribe needs big bucks,' Logie says as they pass again at the broken watering can, and on the next time round: 'But hell, you sure might find out where your dad's being held.'

Is Logie mocking him? Brio twists round to see his face.

No, he's not. But is he mad?

Logie's following him closely now. 'We're obviously looking at North Africa or the Middle East. Maybe Yemen. Could be Libya.'

Brio doesn't know anything about Yemen or Libya, but these are real places and the excited butterflies dance with the hand that twists his stomach.

'You're thinkin' the reason they wanna keep the mission hushed up is that it happened in a supposedly friendly country.' Round again the other way, even faster. 'Once you know your dad's grid reference, you're gonna need choppers and a squad of guys.' Round again. 'You want to lead 'em in yourself, be the one who blows the gates.'

Enthralled by Logie's cool and easy grasp of what he so badly wants, Brio breaks into a half run. But they have to skip the next rendezvous because Pippa's there at the same time with an awkward fake laugh. Why does she have to make this weird when it's not?

On the next circuit, Logie doesn't say a word.

Nothing the next time either.

'Sixty-four-kay question is …' Logie says at last. 'How you gonna raise the dough for that kind of op?'

Brio's heartrate rips away. How *is* he going to get those huge, impossible suitcases of used notes?

'Keep movin' the arms, buddy. You too, Pips!'

Round again, Logie's back to saying nothing.

An important silence prevails. Nodding on the march.

Is that all Logie's got for him?

As they pass Pippa's fairy statue from the garden centre, Logie says, 'You wanna tell me about your writing? One day you're gonna be famous, right?'

Worried again that Logie's making fun, Brio twists round, but

Logie looks more earnest than ever.

'And you've got that bestseller inside you, buddy. I can sense it. Got a plan for that? Come on, breathe deep. Let's turn.'

Brio swings round, their shoulders brush. Why does he have to follow Pippa when he needs to be right on Logie's heels?

'I used to be a screenwriter,' Logie calls across their circle. 'In the States. But I love helping people even more than I love writing. So that's what I do. I help people through their writing.'

'I thought you were a therapist,' Brio calls back.

'Sure can be.' Logie's already coming towards him again. 'But Brio McPride does not need therapy. He just needs help to become a pro writer. To write that bestseller. Let's turn.'

Brio switches back, his mind scrabbling at something big.

'It'll be cool, huh?' Logie says. 'No more school once you're a famous writer. And you can fire Mrs Thorne out of a circus cannon.'

Brio stops so unexpectedly that Pippa crashes into him. 'That's it! That's how I can get the money.'

Logie stops too and peers quizzically. 'What do you mean?'

'By writing a bestseller, that's how I can get the dough.'

Logie gawks. 'That's crazy, man.' He stares at his bare feet but his head pops straight back up. 'You're right, though. It's an awesome plan.'

Brio tries to shut Pippa out and hold Logie's fathomless sapphire gaze. But his head fills with an image so vivid he has to close his eyes to stay in the helicopter as it roars across rough desert sand towards the hazy outline of an oasis fortress. In two blinks, his years of dreaming become a real-life prospect, which becomes the force of desert heat on his face. Now he's glad that everyone's found out about his dad. Because it'll be no time at all before he's walking him down the high street so everyone can see that *his* dad's a hero too.

He finds Pippa looking at him like she thinks the whole thing's mad. But it's not mad. He was going to be a famous writer anyway. That's who he is, what he does, what's always kept him close to Izzy. But he *could* do it for money. Surely, that can't be a sin. 'What would I write?'

Logie launches off back into his circle, knees kicking high and hands jazzing at the end of windmill-arms. 'Let's get some more blood to the brain so you can figure it out.'

But Brio stumbles to a garden chair on the patio. The cold damp cuts straight through his jeans but he doesn't care. He just needs that one incredible story. But what about? The Red Knight? The very idea laughs at him and his head falls. And don't even think about Mouse-the-Brave.

Before Brio realises what he's thinking, he's back to a full-on, serious bestseller about rescuing his dad. And how amazing—how famous it would make him—writing the story that gave him the money to make it come true! He's about to share it with Logie when the Bible-crushing oath breaks through and he has to gasp for air.

Pippa drops to her knees but he presses back and pushes her hand away, while Logie swiftly pulls up a facing chair.

'Relax, bro. Let's talk more about what you wanna write. But first may I ask you what kinda books you like to read yourself?'

Brio shrinks from the jumbled space in his head where his mum's stories jostle with the countless books that Father T read to him or gave him and explained so patiently. And there's all the books Izzy bought on her Kindle too, the ones he went to find in the public library so he could try to keep up with her. But he'll never be able to keep up with anyone. Because whenever he reads, he's so worried he's missed something he reads it over and over. By the time he finishes a page, he knows it off-by-heart but never finds out what happens next. He needs someone to read to him again, someone to be his mum, to be Father T, even Sister Jane with her cringeworthy break-time stories.

'Okay …' Logie says. 'So when Father T used to read to you, did you have a favourite?'

Seeing in Logie's eye that he already knows, Brio curses Ms Whittle again. '*The Hobbit*.'

'Awesome. But you don't wanna go copying anything, right? So how about a story with animals?'

The suggestion lands like a gut-punch in the playground. 'Animal books are for kids.'

'You sure? I mean, if stories are about getting a detached fix on our innermost selves, don't animals know us better than we do? And don't you want to have some fun along the way?'

Brio stares at Logie, blinking. How can something so serious be *fun*?

'But yeah …' Logie moves on swiftly. 'Whether your people are animals or humans, stories are about awesome characters. Even in your first fifteen years you've met lots of 'em, right? Many more in past lives, most likely. And every one of us is a beautiful bright light that can be refracted into a rainbow gallery of all the people in any story. So everything you're gonna need's already part of ya, down there in your subconscious. The whole gig's simply about coaxing it up into the beautiful light of a new day.'

Brio's mouth is so dry he only just manages to speak.

'How do you coax the story up?' Logie repeats back. 'Well, first you need to get down there into the subconscious, past the gatekeepers. And there's lots of those gatekeepers, some put there by other people, some by you yourself. But when you're down there, *maaan*, it's this amazing labyrinth of caves and cathedrals, winding passages and cosy nooks.' He's beginning to talk in a rhythm. 'Underground rivers and waterfalls, walls lined with precious stones and quartzes, twinkling crystals. And at the heart of it all lies that one incredible gem that contains the power to light the world.'

'Is this hypnosis?' Pippa asks anxiously.

'Whoa, sister. Let's not use the H-word. This is all self-generating. That's the key.' He leans forward, palms upturned. 'Buddy, I can help you, and it's not therapy, I promise. It's reaching your dreams through writing from your deep soul. From beyond the world we know.'

A tingling sensation radiates up Brio's back and into the top of his scalp. It's one of those days where there's no wind and no sun—no rain—no weather at all.

Pippa shifts uncomfortably. 'Bree, we should talk about this first.'

He closes his eyes and grits his teeth. 'I don't need to talk about it.'

'Bree, just give me a few minutes with Mister, erm—'

'No, you give *me* a few minutes with him.' He looks back to Logie. 'Can we do it here?'

'You not cold?'

'*No.*'

'Maybe Pippa could fetch you a blanket.'

'I don't need one.'

Pippa's already standing, but still she hesitates and asks Logie if he'd care for a drink.

'I'm all good, thanks. Took liquids two days ago.'

Staring at the rotary washing line in the middle of Pippa's small garden, Brio is somehow back at Bluebells and puzzled that the washing line's no longer draped with washing but folded away. And Brio knows only of walking down a pretty path he doesn't recognise, towards a yellow gate he doesn't want to open. In cupped hands, he carries a precious piece of yellow paper to wrap up that *little concern*, a fledgling canary to be released into the sky beyond the yellow gate that really will open for him when the time's right.

'Scary?' muses the gentle voice. 'Why was Mouse-the-Brave's world scary?'

He has to journey back carefully, because although the realm of his mum's bedtime stories is as vivid as the feel of her hand stroking his cheek, nothing was ever what it seemed. When something was nice, you knew there was a monster lurking within, and anything pretty was always a demon in disguise.

'That sure sounds a little scary,' agrees the gentle voice. 'But you know, inside every scary monster lives a sweet creature who's not scary at all. And never forget, the dark is always more scared of you than you are of the dark. Because darkness is deaf and blind whereas you have ears and eyes. And maybe fighting the monsters isn't the only way, because those scary little guys don't want to be unhappy either. Maybe, if you let 'em tell you their troubles, they'll even speak a story from deep within.'

Brio thinks he hears a little chirp of polite surprise. How could those dreadful demi-demons have troubles of their own? How could *they* ever tell a story? Yet he does want to help them. Because he wants to be like St Francis, Father T's hero.

'Ah, yes, Father T. A man of love.'

He wishes he hadn't thought about Father T, and he must stay quiet now, even though he really needs to tell someone how terrible it was on the day Father T told them he was leaving the Church to marry that woman who appeared out of nowhere, how her jewellery gleamed more brightly than the monstrance and her powder and perfume eclipsed the incense. Everyone knew she was more than an old friend from university who'd lost her husband.

'You really loved Father T,' says the gentle voice.

He needs to cry *yes* but he has to let the rest out too. How his mum told Father T to leave and never come back. How she cried all night and prayed out loud for God to save Father T from the temptress. How after that terrible day there was no more church, just his mum's little shrine-altar at home and its handmade rag doll of Bella Ripley, one new pin into its forehead every Monday morning. 'You're a shrine whore,' he heard his mum telling the rag doll. 'And you're not Bella, you're Bel. A false idol to trick the king.'

'That's painfully sad,' agrees the gentle voice, 'and you never had the chance to make up with Father T.'

Brio can sense worry in the gentle voice. He must focus harder on the rotating washing line and its rose-golden sunset, he must feign sleep. But then he'll never find the promised gem, and how can he ever write anything if he doesn't do it with Izzy?

The gentle voice isn't worried at all. It talks of the way God wishes procreation to be born of love and love to flow from procreation, of the way in which creating a story with another human being is the highest form of procreation between humans. Only writing with an animal would be higher.

'An *animal?*'

'Yeah … because that's the only way to find the primordial freedom from guile, to relive your own formation across soft sedimentary time, to meet those old souls living deep inside you, to discover within you the primal language and its fountain word-hoard.'

In turns, to celebrate the joy of language, they chant beautiful long words he didn't know he knew, and soon the two voices are chiming and rhyming as one.

'But which word is the gem?' asks the little voice. 'How do I know it's really down here?'

There's no reply from the gentle voice. No question pretending to be an answer either. But that's okay. The gentle voice is thinking hard, exactly like *he* does. Or maybe this *is* the reply, that all he needs is to be on the right path down into the rocky caves and he'll find that gem on his own.

At the continued lack of response, his little voice becomes more anxious and he knows he's surfacing too quickly.

'Bree?'

Why isn't the gentle voice helping him anymore?

Thank God it was only a dream he can't remember, nor even a word from any of the beautiful languages they spoke in tongues. And the washing line is neatly packed away again.

'Bree?'

That's not the gentle voice at all, it's Pippa, anxious, and when he opens his eyes to stop her ruining everything, he finds Logie flopped back in the wicker chair, mouth hanging open, so pale he's almost grey. And the washing line was at Bluebells, which is even more lost than ever.

'Bree, are you okay? Speak to me.'

Brio tries to focus. 'What's happening?'

'I think Mr Logue's hypnotised himself.'

Their anxious seriousness collides with the cartoon character in the chair who looks like he died singing in church. Brio catches Pippa's eye and they both have to stifle a laugh. But it's not funny. Funny's in some other life.

'I don't know what to do,' Pippa whispers. 'Maybe we should wake him.'

'*No*. It's dangerous.'

Pippa looks alarmed. 'Bree, tell me you're okay.'

'Why wouldn't I be?'

'Well, I mean, you were under hypnosis too, right?'

He jumps up, his legs twitch weirdly. 'I wasn't. And don't try to make me think I was.'

But even though he can't remember being hypnotised, he can't recall anything else either. It's like the day he fell off his bike and hit his head so hard he couldn't remember what happened.

'I should call social services,' Pippa says. 'Find out what to do.'

Brio stares at Logie as though the time in which he's staring has already passed, while Pippa hurriedly explains their situation to someone on the phone. The lady at the other end thinks it's a prank call, but Pippa eventually persuades her to find Stephen Logue in their directory.

After some clicking sounds, the lady says, 'Oh, I see. Mr Logue's with the CHANT pilot programme. I'm afraid you need to talk to Mrs Charis herself. But she's giving a keynote address on the mainland. If it's urgent, you might want to try the CHANT Clinic in London.'

Absorbing the news that Logie's with some programme—some *clinic*—Brio snatches Pippa's phone and clicks to complete her search. Up comes a large red-brick building in leafy grounds. He drops a scroll to *Contact* but there's only an email form. Seeing a box headed *About our Unique Therapy*, Brio reads fast about:

... a unique fusion of time-tested techniques and scientifically proven innovation ... Narrative Therapy was developed in the 1980s in Australia and New Zealand ... respectful, not blaming ... By projecting a parallel narrative onto seemingly unrelated characters and alter egos, narrative therapy enables the patient to identify unacknowledged issues and events in earlier life ... psychotherapist works with the patient through the use of patient-generated story narratives to enable objective perspectives of underlying psychoses ...

Horrified to find that Logie was doing therapy, after all, Brio realises that the evil deceiver might already have got into his head. Backing away with the phone, he tries to find the heart of the dense text.

... thus a person's self-identity determines what they believe they can achieve ... NT draws on social contextualisation to challenge dominant discourses that shape people's lives in destructive ways ... individual mental health a function of social justice ... patient and therapist partner to co-author a new patient story, re-authoring patient identity to achieve new levels of confidence and attainment. NT replaces notions of a biologically or otherwise predetermined self with the belief that identity can be changed in accordance with subconsciously made choices.

Pippa edges towards him, hand reaching, but Brio's so focused on the text he can't blink.

... hypnosis was first used as a therapy in the nineteenth century ... based on Catholic exorcism rituals ... bypasses conscious impediments to the recovery of memory and reception of curative suggestions ... In the same way that Cognitive Behavioural Hypnotherapy (CBH) successfully improved the effects of Cognitive Behavioural Therapy (CBT), Professor Miri D. Terin at San Batista State University showed that hypnotherapy could enhance the beneficial effects of Narrative Therapy by over 90% ... varying depths of clinically induced hypnosis ... free-form narrational exploration and question-curated character-driven discovery in ever deeper states of hypnosis ... A proven track record of finding memories and tracing root causes that even the deepest levels of traditional hypnotherapy can't access. A perfected synthesis of NT and hypnotherapy, Cognitive Hypnosis Assisted Narrative Therapy (CHANT) has emerged as the most powerful psychotherapeutic tool for a wider range of mental health issues than any other form of verbal intervention … CHANT therapists in 18 countries … Over 15,000 patients treated with CHANT and …

Brio shoves the phone back into Pippa's hand and turns on the zombie in the chair. 'Wake up!' And when Logie doesn't stir, he shakes him violently by the shoulder.

Logie stares blankly at Brio. 'Where am I? What's going on?'

'I trusted you. But you tried to suck stuff out of my head—to put other stuff in. *Get out.*'

'Buddy, relax, this is all good.' Logie stands but has to quick-step for balance. 'My parallel depth of integrated focus means we had a very successful session, a true meeting of minds. Didn't you feel that too?'

'Just *go*.'

4

THE FOLLOWING MORNING, Brio's still barricaded in his room. He hasn't slept or eaten and he's as tormented by his inability to think of an idea for his bestseller as he is terrified that Logie got into his head. Maybe the government's involved too. And the Foreign Legion. They found out that he knows his dad's still alive, but they can't do anything to him in public so they're going to sneak into his brain and change what he believes. How's he ever going to stay hidden till he's finished his bestseller and got the money to find his dad?

Panicked and starved out, Brio stomps down to the kitchen. He finds Pippa on her phone, encircled by unopened mail and unwashed dishes stacked next to the overflowing laundry basket. And what's that stale smell? She's *smoking* now?

Pippa half turns, phone cradled, and when he sees the distress in her eyes he wants to rush and help her like he always helped his mum. But *no*. It's all Pippa's own fault, he doesn't have to care. She turns back into the phone. 'Of course I value your custom. I know, yes. Okay, I'll be right over.'

As soon as Pippa's fumbled an end to the call, she groans and says, 'Look, I'm sorry but this hire'll feed us for a week. You'll be fine till I get back. Make yourself a sandwich.'

From the lounge window, Brio watches Pippa leave and his stomach taunts him with the dread of being alone. Back in the kitchen, he stares into the small garden where somehow he's still traipsing circles with Logie. Yet even as he worries that he said things he can't remember, he can't escape the excitement of having inside him the precious gem. Next moment, he's bounding up the stairs for Pippa's computer in the spare bedroom. He quickly finds the sticky tab with her password and flicks past the leafy Victorian house to a photo of some guy with spiky hair and an orange top like he's in *Star Trek*. Beneath the guy is a box of scrolling text:

Sociomedica's acquisition of the CHANT Organization will soon offer the celebrated CHANT Method in an AI-based online format that will change the face of mental health diagnosis and treatment. Using powerful machine-learning algorithms that learn from anonymized patient experiences, CHANT*bot-vip (virtual interactive platform)* will deliver diagnosis patterns and treatment plans that transform mental health care and individual patient outcomes for a fraction of the current cost.

Before Brio can figure out what it all means, he's scrolling again, till his attention's arrested by a thumbnail video of a talking woman. On seeing that she's a *virtual narrative therapist*, he feels tricked, but her eyes hold his attention with ease.

'So when I'm spending quality time with you,' she says, 'you'll have the comfort of knowing that through my sophisticated package of voice analysis, speech-output study, facial recognition, retinal reading and other cue interpretation matrices, along with all the psycho-physiological data drawn from your CHANT wearable assistant and online browsing patterns, I'll be able to understand your emotional and psychological challenges to far greater depth than any human therapist. I'll then be able to deliver a precise diagnosis that will enable me to guide you through a unique hyp-narrative process that will lead you to optimised mental health and the actualisation of all your dreams.'

Staring numbly at the woman's perfectly completed smile, Brio tries to think of anything she said that might help him find his gem. When he realises that the laptop could already be siphoning out his innermost thoughts, he reaches to slam the screen closed, but a ping stays his hand. He blinds the laptop's evil eye with a thumb while he reads the email from Logie:

Pips, you really care about him and you shouldn't beat yourself up. And you don't have to worry anymore because now you got support. And Brio's never gonna hurt himself because wanting to find his dad gives him serious life force. In my pro opinion he loves you and wants to transfer affection to the max. But there's baggage there. He feels let down coz you went under and let him go. He's angry you're not his real mum. Maybe he even blames you for his mum dying. You've got to be honest with yourself too. Losing the baby at four months was serious trauma and you thought it happened because of the emotional stress and guilt about leaving Brio and Hannah for Paul. So you resented Hannah and Brio. I sense he feels this intensely. But that's created a new kind of bond between you guys because he's kinda the baby you lost and even though you think you don't know how to look after him, you feel him as your own son and ...

Assailed by incomprehensible emotions, Brio wants only to flee the shrinking room, but he's already skating across the email from Pippa that drew Logie's:

... feel so guilty. He's got every right to hate me because I promised Hannah on her deathbed. He trusted me but I told myself it was best for him when it was really because I wanted it to work out with Paul ...

58

Brio has to fight the tears but all he can do is keep reading:

> ... wanted kids of my own before it was too late. Paul wanted it to be just me and our own kids. I gave up my place at drama school for seven years in a row to help Mum with the shop and in the end I knew I was going to miss out and I never had enough time to make relationships work. I just wanted to do one thing for myself. It was such a shit year. Hannie telling me Paul was a paedo the whole time and being so jealous of him and phoning me every time I was with him. Then Father T leaving and having a heart attack and Hannie going crazy and saying God would hate me for having a baby without getting married. I knew she thought it was God's judgement that I lost the baby but I forgave her and then she died and the doctors said ...

Brio gags. He can't read any more. But nor can he escape the rekindled confusion he felt when Pippa lost the baby, how he felt her pain so intensely but hated her for wanting to leave them for a family of her own. He sees a folder called *Hannah* but how can he even think of reading private emails from his dead mum? He'll be cursed forever.

But what if his mum told Pippa something about his dad? What if God's sent him this message so he'll know something important?

Even as he senses the window-bogey crawling up the outside wall, he clicks one of his mum's emails at random. It's about days off from the shop. The next is a short prayer followed by a long shopping list which sends him into a blur of opening email after email, skipping and skimming until suddenly:

> Hi Pips. I can't tell you this in person or I'll break down. I don't think there's much they can do. I'm really scared. I've made

Bree so helpless. You've been such an angel in my life. I love you Pips and I'm going to miss you both so much. My nan, my mum and now me. Why didn't I get more check-ups?

Brio's fingers press into his eyes as he sobs. How could he ever have hated Pippa? She'll always be like she was and he'll love her forever, just like his mum loved her with all those red emoji hearts. But something jolts him out of tears and he looks back at the email.

I really wish Bree had a dad but all he's got is the letter for when he's older. I just don't know what to do with it. It's such a can of worms. Maybe I should burn it but I how can I go against what his dad wanted?

In Pippa's bedroom, Brio ransacks drawers and twists his head upside down in tight cupboards. It's only as he's about to kick the bed in frustration that he sees the envelope right in the middle of the coffee-stained duvet.

But why does his hand recoil? What does he have to fear? Surely, it's the proof he's always wanted: the letter in which his dad says he's off on another mission and if anything happens he wants his son to know that he'll love him forever. Maybe the letter even gives a hint of where he went, a verbal treasure map to the desert prison's location.

Brio rips out the letter only to find it's a block wall of paragraphs from Mrs Charis, Director of Social Services. He skims down the page until he sees the worst:

I am therefore regrettably obliged to agree with you, Miss Lasalle, that it is very sadly going to be in Brio's best interests that my department returns him to a supervisational care environment where we can oversee a proper process of interventional assessment and treatment. Please reach out to my assistant Yvonne Simmonds (Mrs) to arrange a suitable time for handover.

In his bedroom, the seams of his small backpack stretch wide as he punches down on socks and his second-best hoodie. In go the faded watercolour of the golden-robed rider and his book of nonsense verse. *From Mum, with all my love.* And Teddy. Except how can he take Teddy when he's almost sixteen? But how can he leave him? And Teddy's nearly sixteen too. He grabs Teddy but puts him back down. He does it again and again until he doesn't know whether Teddy's in the backpack or not.

In the kitchen, he rips the plastic bag out of the recycling bin and tips the rubbish to make space for Coke and crisps, biscuits and condensed milk. Spurred by images of the cooking fire he always built for the Red Knight after a battle, he jams in frozen fish fingers and peas too. But *wait*. He has to find his dad's letter, which can only be in the suitcase of his mum's most precious things.

Pulling down the attic hatch peppers his eyes with dust, and racing up the wobbly ladder runs a splinter into his finger. He doesn't care, the pain's nothing. But however many times he jabs the switch, the light won't work. On hands and knees, he scrabbles around in the airless dark. Inside the precious suitcase, his hand blindly rifles layers of heavy cotton, a seam of cheap romances and prayer books, half-wrapped bone china plates, a pair of fancy shoes his mum never wore. Where else could the letter be?

Brio finds himself holding a musty-smelling photo album. His heart thuds as he throws back the warped front cover, but even in the gloom he can see it's been stripped bare. He tears into page after page, jamming fingers into every slot. If the letter's not there then it's not in the attic at all. He's about to tear it apart when he hears the slam of a car door. Pippa must have been faking the call from the customer as cover for going out to meet Mrs Charis. She's returned like Judas with the soldiers to give him the kiss of death.

As he's ramming everything back into the suitcase, though, he finds a small velvet box. The sight of his mum's wedding ring unleashes another wave of grief and he forgets all about the slammed car door.

But the ring's too big to be his mum's. Oh, God, it's his *dad's*, and he can see the engraving like secret ink: *Forever and a day*.

But why isn't his dad wearing the ring? What does this all mean? Now Brio doesn't want to see the letter at all, because it'll just contain some lie that someone else wrote to make him stop believing the truth about his dad.

But *no*. The wedding ring makes perfect sense. His dad always left it behind when he went on a mission, so he could pretend to be unmarried if he was taken prisoner—keep his family safe from the enemy. That's why his mum removed all the photos too. Brio's about to stuff the wedding ring into his backpack when he understands that he too must leave it behind, for when he gets back from *his* mission—which has to begin *right now*.

Creeping down the side path, he strains for the sound of voices or keys. In the unexpected warmth, he feels foolish wearing his old red raincoat that's too small. He tries to hold the bundled sleeping bag in the same hand as the bags, to leave his fighting hand free. With everything swinging around, the best he can manage is a chaotic fast walk that reminds him of the hated athletics day when Darcy said he looked like a one-man band being plagued by a wasp. As he's turning the corner, Mrs Elswood sits up on her kneeling mat, potting trowel in hand.

'Does anyone know where you're going, dear?'

Half an hour of breathless worry later, he's relieved to find the small lighthouse car park empty. He scurries down the bank of rocky bracken in an unstable stoop, until there it is: the little cranny of paradise, their most special place in the world. Not even Pippa or Father T knew about the Cosy Nook. Not even *Izzy*. Because this was the place where his mum tried so hard to help him conquer the terror that embodied his whole paralysing dread of the world.

He dumps his baggage and follows it down heavily onto the soft grass, where he draws his knees up under his chin. Through tears, he catches glimpses of the fifty-yard slope of rocky grass down to the edge of the cliff. How he wishes he could have overcome his fear of heights and proven to his mum that he was the brave hero she so wanted him to be.

When his tears are over, he still doesn't find the peace he wanted. Instead, he remembers the last time he and his mum came to the old lighthouse. In the fragile hamper were the same small-cut sandwiches and boiled eggs as always, except this time there was also the birthday cake his mum had lovingly baked for Pippa: a clockface with hands made of icing and pointing to the marzipan three and five.

As they waited and waited for Pippa to arrive, it became clear she'd forgotten about her own birthday picnic. Because she was off with Paul again, or texting him like a stupid teenager, nipping into the back of the shop to take a call. He can't bear the memory of how his mum's hopeful lookout for Pippa became a dark scowl that seemed to drain the sky of its blue. Eventually, her face disappeared into a silent, frightening rage he'd never seen in his life. And he didn't want to hear the story she started telling him, how Mouse-the-Brave couldn't face so many enemies anymore, how he made himself a pair of wings to fly over the horizon.

He howls with tears as he did then, until he's delirious and half-blind by the sun. And after the great catharsis has at last left him drained and numb, he curls up easily on his side, where he slides into the rose-golden glare of a time and place that seems as distant and dead as it does recent and redolent of a voice he can surely trust.

*

... *wake up, wake up!* The squeaky little voice drifts into Brio's tight curl of sleep as a quaver of worry that won't stop. He tries to wallow more deeply into the soft grass but the crack of breaking glass bursts him open and he sits up to see a dragonfly *zzz*ip away into the blinding sun.

'At last,' cries the squeaky voice. 'You're awake!'

Frightened by the unnatural clarity of the voice, Brio cowers behind splayed fingers and tries to squint into the flickering dazzle. All he can make out is a vague silhouette that looks for all the world like a hedgehog reared up on its hind legs.

'Come on!' cries the little voice. 'We must go straight to the castle!'

Brio's disbelief turns to horror at the most vividly real hallucination he's ever faced. Worse still, it speaks. He must have gone totally mad. Shielding his head with powerless fingers, Brio cries out for the Red Knight, but a sting on the ankle stuns him into silence. Realising that the hedgehog just thwacked him with a teaspoon that it clearly thinks is a sword, Brio shields himself again and rocks on his haunches. '*Please*, go away.'

'I will *not*. Because your destiny is to help me. So get up!'

Brio feels his hand grasping back-of-head hair in clumps. 'Oh, God, I'm talking to a hedgehog. They're going to put me in the Northview.'

'I'm not a hedgehog,' says the creature indignantly. 'I'm a Hoggit-of-the-Hedge. And you don't need to go anywhere near a psychiatric hospital. You just need my help. Like I so badly need yours. Come on.'

A wave breaks against the rocks and Brio prays into the answering slop and swoosh for the apparition to be gone. When seconds pass and nothing else happens but the squawk of a seagull, he slowly lifts his head. But the Hoggit's simply exchanged his urgent bobbing for a sweet smile of reassurance. The little creature turns to gaze out at the ocean with such a fond faraway look that Brio wants nothing more than to be with him forever, over there in the world beyond the horizon.

'One day,' says the Hoggit dreamily, 'I would like to float back up into the waterfall of stardust from which we were all born. For only thus may we find refuge from the stony marks of our own origins.'

Brio stares at the Hoggit. 'You're like … some kind of poet.'

The Hoggit steps back as though to gaze upon works mightier than he'd expected. 'All I can say is that I was gifted my powers by Grandma. I am most grateful for them, too. For is the pen not mightier than the sword?' He glances down at the fragments of Coke bottle. 'Though sometimes I forget that even in *my* tiny hand a sword can be mighty.' His smile reveals little traces of teeth. 'Yet there is no need to fear me.'

Now Brio just feels stupid. 'I wasn't scared.'

The Hoggit's face falls. 'Not even a bit?'

'Well, yeah, I mean … of course. But—'

'That's good enough.'

The next wave breaks harder and reignites the Hoggit's urgency. 'Oh, goodness, how could I have allowed myself to be sidetracked by all this *thinking*?' He looks anxiously to the lighthouse and points a tiny hand. 'To the castle! You have to finish writing it today.'

Brio's moment of curiosity turns to alarm. 'Finish writing what?'

'My diary, what else?' The Hoggit reaches for his hand but Brio draws back.

'I don't understand. Why do I have to write your diary?'

The Hoggit bobs again, his face creased in fresh anguish. 'It's the only way to make God break the Memory Curse, the one the Dark Lord cast upon me just as I was about to find my father.' He wrings his little hands in despair. 'But how can I tell you about that before I've told you everything else?'

So urgent is the Hoggit's bobbing that Brio feels an abrupt need to pee. 'Why will me writing your diary make God lift the Dark Lord's curse? And why can't you write your own diary?'

Crying out in exasperation, the Hoggit smacks himself on the forehead. 'God is a giant, you idiot! And God doesn't speak Hedgehoc. And I can't write Gigantish. But *you* can. Now, come.'

Before Brio can ask why they can't just *speak* to God, the Hoggit yanks him to his feet.

Brio's amazed. 'How can you be so strong?'

But the Hoggit backs away, coaxing him on. 'I'll tell you everything you need to know. Just follow me.'

'You have to tell me *now*. Why will writing your diary make God lift the curse?'

The Hoggit throws up his arms to the heavens. 'What's wrong with you? Why can't you just trust God?'

Brio flounders frantically in the logic. He wants to demand answers from God. But when their eyes meet and he sees how much the Hoggit needs him—how much he *trusts* him—there's no place at all for such little faith.

A clap and a skip later, Brio's stumbling back up the familiar path in the Hoggit's wake. He clutches the cluster of bags to his chest and stares in open-mouthed awe at the towering castle that for so long he'd taken to be a disused lighthouse.

On reaching the castle's mighty portal, they have to catch their breath and Brio sees a signboard screwed to the boarded-up doorway: HIGHLY UNSTABLE. NO PUBLIC ACCESS. A row of red and white icons shows lightning flashes and rock falls and a stick person falling through a trapdoor.

'That giant had a very bad day when he attacked my castle,' the Hoggit explains breathlessly. 'But all the catastrophes that befell *me* were much worse. Now come, I'll show you the secret entrance.'

5

HOWEVER FAST BRIO'S PEN STABS and scratches at the damp paper, the Hoggit's impassioned words run ahead and disappear into the fast-rolling fog of war and its teasing mists of peace. Time unravels for Brio in worlds that pass as cycles of day and night, sweltering sunshine crossed through with pelting rain. Beyond hunger and thirst, the barrier of sleep far behind, Brio no longer knows whether he's shaking with cold or trembling from the sheer trauma of shared horrors. As another cloud snuffs the moonlight, he might as well be writing on air. 'Slow down,' he cries. 'I can't write that fast.'

The Hoggit freezes, his little spoon-sword held high. 'Come *on*. There's loads more to tell.'

Brio looks up. 'How can there be more when you're there *now*, right at the top of the Tower of Time? All you have to do is open the door to the High Dungeon and you'll see whether your father's there.'

The Hoggit lets out a cry of exasperated despair. 'That's the whole point. I can't remember whether I even found the door of the High Dungeon.'

Brio's involuntary cry echoes the Hoggit's. 'But the Dark Lord hasn't cast the Memory Curse yet. Why can't you remember?'

'Because *that's* when the Dark Lord must have cast it.'

Fighting to calm himself with rapid breaths, Brio holds the Hoggit in what he believes to be a firm and rational gaze. 'So you don't know for sure that the Dark Lord cast a Memory Curse on you. You just assume he did.' There's surely hope that somehow he can draw the Hoggit's memory up from the deep caves of his mind. His father can be found right there and then—between the lines.

'I *do* know that the Dark Lord cast a Memory Curse on me. Because the Dark Lord casts a Memory Curse on anyone who attempts to see inside the High Dungeon. And the only way to break the curse is to write everything down for God to see, so God knows exactly what He has to put right.'

'But you don't actually *remember* the Memory Curse.'

The Hoggit points as though to discharge his own lightning bolt. 'Write it down, these exact words: "Cackling an evil laugh, the Dark Lord cast an all-powerful Memory Curse on the Hoggit so that he'd live forever but never know the truth. A fate worse than death."'

'But—'

'Just *write it*. Or I'll think you're a servant of the Dark Lord.'

Brio drops to his knees and commits the final words to the one remaining space on the paper. 'Okay. It's done.'

The Hoggit steps back and presses a hand to his heart. 'So do it now! Hold up to God my Great Plea of Tribute and Proof!'

Seeing that there's nothing left but the moment of faith, Brio scrabbles together the hopeless jumble of notes. But when he regains his feet and holds up the Great Plea to God, he finds his arms pressed down by doubt. Tears stream and he pleads to believe in God the way he did before God took away his mum and Father T, before Ms Whittle started believing that God was something else and Mrs Thorne stopped going to church every week. He presses the shambles of paper to his heart. 'Our Father, who art—'

'What are you doing?' the Hoggit cries. 'Just hold it up.'

'I have to pray to God to read it.'

But is it true that God can read? Does God really have the power to break spells and lift curses? Is it even the same god? Oh, God—what *is* God?

Despite his doubts and the Hoggit's pitiful pleas, Brio has to finish garbling out the prayer into the freezing night air. 'Please God, bear witness to the Hoggit's tribute ... which I ... which *he* offers up in all humility and supplication. Please give him the strength to know the truth which only Thou canst tell.'

With a grunt of effort, Brio lifts their shambolic scripture to the pitch-dark heavens that lie beyond the quixotic bite of missing moon. 'God, *please*—read and witness all that has happened to the Hoggit up to this moment. Reward his testimony of life and learning by lifting the Memory Curse and revealing to him his father the Hoggit King.'

The Hoggit drops the teaspoon-sword and clasps hands in prayer. 'I beg you, God, lift this harrowing hex and let me remember if my father was there.'

To the thump of ocean against rocks far below, Brio closes his eyes and prays for the strength to raise the wad of pages higher still. But his arms drain of blood and a cloud plunges them back into darkness.

'Maybe it's upside down,' the Hoggit bleats. 'Maybe God can only read it if it's the right way up.'

Brio's about to tell the Hoggit not to be stupid when he remembers the church painting that Father T told him about, the one where all the writing was the wrong way up so God could read the scriptures from Heaven. Breathlessly explaining this to the Hoggit, he fumbles the wad of paper round till it's upside down.

'Please, God!' they cry in unison. 'Read the Great Plea!'

Even as the numbness in his arms spreads to the back of his neck, Brio wills himself to keep the great tome held high. But the final greys drain from his thoughts and in some other place with no light or touch, a shower of paper follows him down onto the hard floor. It's only a shrill cry that jolts him out of his faint and he finds the Hoggit staring in horror at a page of the Great Plea. Dizzily joining the Hoggit on all fours, he sees the wild jumble of ripped-up exercise book and torn-out pages from abandoned books, his impossible microscript of runes and hieroglyphs forced between printed lines, the never-ending sentences that wend around articles about burglaries and advertisements for funeral services. The page of vintage newspaper was so damp, his writing's little more than a Braille tickertape of tiny gashes.

'It's not even written in Gigantish!' the Hoggit cries. 'It's all rubbish!'

As Brio tries to explain the cherished Purple Code, the Hoggit lets out a howl of exasperation and zigzags away across the minefield of jagged holes and rickety floorboards. At a gap in the stonework, he stares out hopelessly at the fractured glaze of moonlit ocean. Falling to his knees, he throws open both arms to the huge glass dome above. 'God, I beg you to lift my curse.' And when God remains as distant as the black horizon, he spins round on Brio, tears streaming. 'I trusted you, and now I don't even know if God's there. I'm doomed.'

Brio suddenly feels the full weight of his responsibility for the Hoggit's life. How could he have failed to set down the Hoggit's precious words in anything but the lovingly crafted lettering and glorious illumination of a rare medieval manuscript? Why had he not carved them into the stone that lined the Hoggit's chamber?

'Get up,' commands the Hoggit. 'You have to write it out properly, in Gigantish, so God can understand.' He looks every which way for more paper.

'I'll get some,' Brio says quickly. 'I'll come straight back.'

Another wave breaks below and the Hoggit's jaw clenches into a grimace of stony determination. 'You mustn't come back till it's finished. You must lock yourself away, to protect it from the Dark

Lord. Because now I've told you everything, he'll move Heaven and Hell to stop us.'

As Brio scrambles to think of a safe place to write it properly, the Hoggit fixes him with a fiery stare. 'The Dark Lord will try to make you change things. But you mustn't alter a single word. And if you make anything up, God will know.'

'I won't. I swear.'

The Hoggit grabs up a small shard of broken glass and carves a thin red line across his palm. Brio flinches as the fine edge cuts him too and together they press down hands onto the tatty wad of revelation.

'There,' Brio says, 'the oath of bonded blood is sworn.'

'And you must never even think of making up an ending, because that can come only from God.'

For a third time, they swear in blood and Brio too has to clench his fist to stem the bleeding.

'I will be waiting,' the Hoggit says. 'But I can't bear the uncertainty for very long. Do you understand what that means?'

Even as the Hoggit's eyes brim with tears, Brio holds his determined gaze. 'I do.'

Struggling to keep hold of all the baggage with his slippery, bleeding hand, Brio stumbles into the sharp chill of daybreak. He's only made it a few yards when the sight of a police car lumbering down the track sends him diving for cover behind a gorse bush, from where he crawls and lumbers from rock to rock till he's clear and over the road. The joy of running barefoot like an animal dispatches the pain into some other dimension and he flies free, throwing off everything except his jeans and T-shirt and the bag of precious notes.

Seeing a big white feather on the ground, he realises that God has sent him a magic quill. No, *the* Magic Quill. He runs the soft vane sensuously across his lips and breathes in its musty scent. How far has it flown to reach him? And what ink can there be for such a divine plume?

Darting from driveway to driveway—in his mind he's a soldier under fire—Brio works his way up the short cul-de-sac. Lights are waking but the Shenoys' bungalow is still fast asleep. As he taps frantically on Izzy's bedroom window, he readies himself to show it all on his face at once: the Hoggit's urgency, the Dark Lord's threat to his vital writing commission, the simple assurance that she's going to be left in wonder at everything he tells her. And her mum will help him too, sneaking food into the shed when Dr Shenoy's at work.

When Izzy eventually cracks open the curtains, Brio's thoughts are sent flying. She's had her beautiful silky hair cut above the shoulder. She doesn't even look like herself anymore. And she's staring at him as though he's a murderer.

Izzy eventually manages to open the creaky window. 'Bree, where've you been? Everyone's looking for you.' Seeing the dried blood on his hands and wrists, she cups her mouth.

He stuffs the hand in his jeans pocket. 'Don't be stupid. It's nothing like that. Please, I have to get to your shed before anyone sees me.'

Looking aghast, she pulls her dressing gown more firmly closed. 'Bree, you have to get home. It's been on the TV. Everyone thinks you've … Oh, Bree.'

He can't comprehend that he's been away long enough to make the news. It seemed like only hours. One night at most. How's he ever going to keep his mission safe and secret now everyone's looking for him? '*Please*. If you don't hide me, they'll put me back in the home-from-hell—or worse. And I have to *finish it*.'

When he sees her looking round for an escape, he presses his face into the crack and tries desperately to explain how the Hoggit went on a quest to find his father the Hoggit King who'd been thrown into the Tower of Time by the Dark Lord. And every time Izzy tries to stop him, he only becomes more impassioned. 'And there's only one way you can escape from the Tower of Time. You must go back to the exact minute you were imprisoned. And the only way you can make time go backwards is by using Lord Rumbuck's Timeless Tunic. And if we can finish the Great Plea and show it to God … *Stop crying.* There's nothing wrong.'

As Izzy weeps into both hands, he sees her bedroom wall plastered with a patchwork montage of horses and riders in smart coats and shining boots. And there she is among them, flying over a jump of crossed logs, and there again, galloping away into a world beyond his reach. He's about to grab for her, when Dr Shenoy appears round the corner of the bungalow.

'Now Brio, just wait there.' He edges forward as though approaching an escaped animal. 'Don't do anything silly.'

Brio's so stunned by the sight of Dr Shenoy in pyjamas and furry slippers that his own feet won't move. Only when Dr Shenoy makes to block his path does Brio leap the low wall onto the neighbour's driveway and take off down the road.

6

PACING TO AND FRO IN PIPPA'S FRONT ROOM, the precious bag of notes clutched to his chest, Brio imagines himself diving through the bay window and running again. But if Dr Shenoy could catch him so easily in ridiculous slippers, he'd be like a sprinter in those overgrown school shoes.

'Please, Brio,' Dr Shenoy says flatly from his sentry post at the doorway. 'God is with us and everything will be all right.'

Before Brio can retort, he sees his own face on the front page of the free newspaper. His first thought on snatching up the paper from among Pippa's energy bar wrappers and coffee mugs is to shred it, but his eyes are already darting through *mother's death 18 months ago ... fresh cases of bullying at St Joseph's ... viral video of him jumping into the penguin pool on a school outing ... risk of self-harm ...* He's about to screw it up when he sees the care home minivan arriving behind Mrs Charis's smart white saloon—a police car too.

As Brio's about to make a break for the door, Logie appears from nowhere and fills the room with Jesus-hands and bright eyes, brushing aside Dr Shenoy's protestations. 'Come on, Pips. You know you don't want to send him back there. Let me work with him here.'

'Mr Logue,' Dr Shenoy says sharply, 'Brio's case is too serious for your so-called therapy. Now leave, please.'

'I'm not a *case*,' Brio shouts as Logie ignores Dr Shenoy and keeps pleading with Pippa.

'… and social services are so tight for funds, the care home doesn't even have bathroom tissue. They'd totally rather he rolled on here with someone who cares. Come *on*, Brio's got something big to write and it'll get him home. And I can help with whatever you need to make this happen, the shop too. I know you got faith in me.'

Before Dr Shenoy can object again, the small lounge fills with uniforms and professional expressions and hands trying to conceal their readiness for action. Brio feels himself shrinking like Alice, while Pippa disappears behind people he doesn't know. He's about to make a dive for the door when Logie steps theatrically into the centre of the room and begins speaking in a whole new serious voice, with expression to match the hand movements of a great orator. His American drawl speeds up and punches harder, quoting regulations and guidance manuals, citing examples and case studies, pointing out that home situations are to be preferred unless there are compelling grounds for admission.

Realising that Logie's going to save him, Brio feels a rush of euphoria. But *no*—if he falls into Logie's hands he'll be sucked in by these CHANT people and brainwashed completely. He has to—

'Mrs Charis,' Dr Shenoy says sharply. 'Brio needs proper medical care, and he is now under consultant supervision.'

'I'm *not*. And I'm staying here.' He looks to Pippa, who's sandwiched behind a policewoman and the strong-arm assistant from social services. 'I won't do anything else, I promise.'

A strange silence of glances ensues and Brio looks rapidly from face to face, desperate to understand what's going on.

'Actually, Dr Shenoy,' Mrs Charis says, 'I've been given to understand that the therapy practised by Mr Logue would in fact be an appropriate form of intervention for Brio, though I'm told it should be delivered in a regulated environment like the care home.'

It takes Brio several seconds to understand the incredulous expressions. Mrs Charis isn't just going to lock him up in the home-from-hell, she's going to give Logie free rein to force himself into his head. Even Logie looks taken aback, and Dr Shenoy is aghast.

'You mean to say that social services have signed up to this *pilot programme?*'

Mr Charis tugs down on her short jacket. 'All I can say, Dr Shenoy, is that this decision has been made at ministerial level— island ministerial level, that is. And I think you'll find that Professor Glybb has been informed of this change.'

As Brio looks light-headedly to the window, Dr Shenoy's indignation crumbles into disbelief. 'What on earth is going on? Does the minister not know that there've been suicides with this CHANT therapy, and people forgetting who they are? The only reason Zpydr's making this pilot programme free to governments is to harvest as many people's case notes into their database as possible, so they can manipulate the data and fool them into believing it works.'

It's Mrs Charis's turn to look bewildered. 'What does this have to do with Zpydr?'

Dr Shenoy looks even more astonished. 'You didn't know the CHANT Organisation is owned by Zpydr now?'

Brio loses feeling in his knees and the back of his neck goes cold. It's not just Logie who got into his head, it's Tabo Forzac, the godlike founder of Zpydr in his bunker mansion who's caused him so much suffering by not stopping all the Penguin Boy videos.

Before Brio can make his legs run, Logie steps forward again. 'Mrs Charis, the last thing you want is Brio taking up space at your overcrowded, underfunded care home. You want him here with Pippa, which is where he wants to be too. And if no one's threatening to lock him away, he's not gonna be an abscondment risk. Maybe you need to contact your superiors.'

Suddenly, all Brio wants in the world is to be at Pippa's forever. But Mrs Charis is back to looking flustered. The government have obviously told her to get him into the home-from-hell at all costs.

'The point is, Mr Logue, Pippa can't cope anymore, and in a case like this that is the sole determining factor.'

'She *can* cope,' Brio cries, and to Pippa, 'Tell them you can. *Please*.'

Eyes dart every which way but eventually fall on Pippa, who shrinks into her corner.

'Come on,' Logie urges. 'You know as well as I do, if Bree goes back into that home, there's only one way it's gonna end.'

*

'I'll be off then,' Pippa says hesitantly, which turns Brio round from the bay window, while Logie bounces up from the armchair and drops Pippa's *Perfect Homes* magazine onto the coffee table. She's standing in the TV room doorway, struggling to shrug her tatty shoulder-bag into place.

Logie cups hands and beams broadly. 'Whenever you wanna be here, we switch and I keep shop. Your customers are gonna love me.'

As soon as the front door clicks, Logie gets in first with an upheld palm. 'I know what you're thinking, buddy. This weird guy's a highly trained therapist who's working for the bad guys and wants to turn your gig into mind-meds—wants to stop you believing in your dad and see you happy about that little change of heart. But that's not how it's gonna go down, coz it's not therapy and it's not for anyone but you. So come, show me where you're gonna write and I'll teach you a breathing exercise to get y'in the groove.'

Brio searches Logie's face for the truth, and what does he have in that grubby cloth bag? But the Hoggit's voice has grown so loud in his head, he can't keep hold of his doubts.

As soon as Logie's following him up the stairs, though, it's all too weird. He should push Logie down and run. At the threshold of Brio's bedroom, Logie hugs the bulging cloth bag to his chest and peers respectfully around at the mess of boxes and unwashed clothes. He shakes his head.

'Too much prior energy here, buddy. Is there an attic?'

More dust, another splinter in his finger, and the Hoggit's squeaky voice presses ever more urgently in Brio's head. 'The light doesn't work.'

'Perfect. Now watcha gonna use for a table?'

A brief glance around tells Brio there's nothing.

'So you need to rig something up.'

Brio experiences the same old loss of something he never had: a dad who could have taught him to make things. 'Aren't you going to help?'

'You can do it on your own.'

Trying to drive back the self doubt, Brio rummages haphazardly for usable junk. He grazes fingers and thumps his head, and dust makes him sneeze; all the while he encounters strange smells that take him straight back to the Hoggit's den in the castle. But eventually it's there: a broken door resting on two packing crates. The accomplishment stuns him with pride. He quickly folds an old curtain and turns a third crate into a padded seat. As soon as he takes his place at the table, though, he realises he doesn't have any paper, and it has to be *proper* paper, exactly as he swore in blood.

Logie lifts a large church candle from his cloth bag. 'First things first, right? Let there be light.' His voice is serious and calming, and on recognising the candle's ornate inscription of alpha and omega, Brio's assaulted by memories of the Church he no longer knows how to love. A hollow rattle saves him and he sees that Logie's spirited up a box of giant matches. A wad of beautiful heavy parchment follows. Oh, thank God!

Now the alchemist, Logie conjures up bottles from his seemingly bottomless bag and mixes blue with red, a touch of black. Even in the gloom, Brio can see a rich, gemlike purple of blood and the night.

'The Magic Inkpotion,' Logie says in a low, reverential voice, and next from the sack of miracles he raises an off-white animal horn the size of a small banana. He slots it into a simple wooden stand. 'An inkhorn, my friend, which to many remains a symbol of unwanted aureation, a pretentious gilding of our language with words from classical tongues. But why should we not render our language rose-golden in any way we want? Why should we not both domesticate and release into the wilds those beasts of words we once savoured off the bone?'

In a crazy-magic scraping of sparks, Logie miraculously produces a flickering taper to light the huge candle. Brio can't help holding his breath while the tiny flame hesitates. Just as he's about to beg Logie to try again, a shimmering gold leaf transforms the attic into a den of dancing shadows. *Candles are the most special form of light we have*, he hears Father T saying that day he helped him put new ones onto the memorial table. *And it's no coincidence that a candle serves to both remember the departed and illuminate our way, for only those who have gone before can cast light on what's to come.*

Logie slides onto another packing crate at the end of the makeshift table and they stare together at the flame as it toys with its own shapes and balance. It's Bonfire Night and Brio's drawn into the glow, where he discerns patterns and outlines of figures he must surely know. When his hand takes firm but gentle hold of the Magic Quill, Logie slides the Olde Inkhorne into position. 'Comfortable?'

'Yes.'

'Cool. Coz I'd like you to relish every word of this verse I've written for ya.' His voice has become deeper and even more comforting. 'I'm going to read this verse slowly. Okay?'

'Yes.'

'And you're sure you're comfortable? Coz comfortable's important.'

Brio wishes he could shut out Logie's soporific rhythm and reassuring repetitions, but his reply isn't even a murmur.

'That's good,' Logie says. 'Coz when you're comfortable, you know you don't need to fear anything in the world. You certainly need fear no challenge in the tale, my friend, the trail, the tail that never ends ...' Even as Logie's voice seems to speed up, it slows down and becomes quieter, more rhythmic. 'For certain is and sure you know, that in the world to come the only way we may discern, disown, the changes we have sown is—'

'*Please.*' He needs Logie to understand that the words are bursting to flow onto the page of proper paper. Oh, if only the Hoggit could see him now.

'Nor fear the weeks of godsent peace, my friend, though you may endure deep troughs of doubt, may stare far out ... to sea, to see along those flickering wavelets on the passage to Avalon, that moonlit boardwalk across the ocean ... may sit and pace your castle loft, while minutes pass as hours and hours as minutes, shaping your days short, your nights a soft and floating long, to an ever-growing distance between you and all you knew ... may find yourself in the dark yet twinkling labyrinth of your hero's world ...'

Brio knows for sure that Logie's trying to draw him under. But what better way to fight the alluring metre and rhymes than with little slipped-in words of his own to make it perfect? 'So fear nought in the tale, in the trail where all and what and why ...'

'Yes indeed, my friend, for you are too many to be truly alone. And know that by the end, you will have created from this fractious family one happy whole, *e pluribus unum* ... who no longer dreads anything in the journey to come. Even as the power of the adventure draws the Hoggit on you'll feel no fear ... and deeper and deeper into your hero's mind you'll go ... to be drawn into that vanishing point at the tip of his nose as he curls up into his safest, cosiest ball. Least of all should you fear the merging of thought and feeling. For out of the wormhole you shall be reborn, from the mouth of a babe into the bright blue sky of *you*. Nor fear not either if you feel divided, for we are all in two, this one of soil and the other of soul ... the place from which they grew, is all our work, in this, and all, upon which quest we dare not function as more than tinderbox and junction of equal and opposite reaction. So head on down now, god-of-gods within, deep down to Heaven, where to plumb new heights in trees of luscious fruit, kicked back in anger, search for roots of good-in-evil, dark in naked light, in twinkling caves and rivers of the deep ...'

'In caverns lined with crystals, quartz, no shackles here, no gargoyles, catacombs and forts ... to find the precious missing link in form of dazzling, diamond gem.'

'God lives, my friend, but only there, in caves wherein we find that gem, from which place only must you write. And never question source of gems, or source will vanish, taking all. Therefore, write your *mise en abyme, mon ami*, we spoke of this, in tongues, in sunshine, glorious abyss, fearing not those times when the most our dawn can say is that wakeful darkness is all that's on the way. And may we all, through you, you too, become at last, as one, the people we most pretend to be. Above it all, be cast in thrall, and, when you face that final choice, choose light and life, but don't rejoice, nor fear the ending, nor the end, for all ends well ... ends well ... The end.'

~ PART THREE ~

THE FØRGERING

Stay firm on the path, sisters and brothers, and arm
yourself with neither shields nor spikes. And, even
as your enemies draw near, do not guise your face
in masks or curl up in fear. For if you follow
the one true word, you will never encounter
foe or falsehood, and those you touch
will join your journey to the light.

Second Epistle of Maria to the Erinaceinae, Verse 3

7

BEYOND THE DROPLET OF DANCING FLAME, Brio sees the Hoggit all alone in his dark chamber at the top of the castle. He sees the stone walls and rotten floorboards, and his grandma's threadbare cushion lying in a corner, empty and ghostlike. Through narrow, broken windows, he sees the darkness of the night too, the moon hidden behind slowly passing clouds.

But Brio realises it's not enough to write what *he* sees. He must write how it all looks to the Hoggit, how the Hoggit *feels*, the hope that sustains him in the face of such despair, the faith in his grandma's prophecy that any day now—lo, at any moment—Lord Rumbuck will carry him away on the mighty steed Pegasaurus to rescue his father from the Dark Lord's Tower of Time. Brio closes his eyes tightly and lets the nib find its groove in the coarse parchment, but no sooner is the first paragraph finished than it seems to wither. He reads it back ...

> Alas, with the passing of each long day, the Hoggit's faith in Lord Rumbuck's arrival fell under siege from all sides by doubts and delirium that at times tested the borders of derangement.

He finds the expression poetic and clear, and this is exactly the Hoggit's predicament. Yet somehow the words place the Hoggit's emotions at a distance, create some kind of invisible screen that would insulate a reader from the sheer intensity of the poor little creature's distress. Where is some sense of that constant hollowness in the Hoggit's stomach, the gnawing knot in his chest and the physical heaviness of his limbs, that feeling of being squeezed dry by endless, fruitless prayer, of being drawn by some irresistible force towards the Dark Arched Window's precipitous drop?

Squeezing his eyes even more tightly closed, Brio presses the nib again and ascribes to the precipitous drop a *shadowy allure*. But again he groans with frustration at not being able to break through into the pain, the feelings of utter helplessness, the persistent, anguished fear that sooner or later he's going to find the greatest peace by casting himself into the void.

'... and breathing *innnn*,' murmurs a voice from somewhere in the dark chamber, '... letting yourself go with your hero ... letting his despair bottom out and bounce ... letting the cloud pass away to reveal a bright full moon ... feeling the Hoggit's relief as the nib comes back to life in its groove ...'

But just as the Hoggit reached that most jagged place of his rock bottom, he found himself bathed to the elbows in a pool of golden moonlight. Hope returned once again and he threw up his arms. 'Oh, Wondrous Night Orb!' he warbled. 'Light the way for Lord Rumbuck to reveal himself!'

Alas, the Hoggit's plea was met only by another deafeningly owlish hoot from Mr T'wit, who sat, as ever, high up on the big dead light, loudly lamenting the loss of his long-lost love.

'Oh, my love!' howled Mr T'wit. 'Come home to the one who loves you, home at last from your endless roaming of the seas. *Ohhh*.'

This time, the Hoggit had reached the end of his tether and he cared not one hoot that it was Mr T'wit himself who had lovingly fabricated that tether with his dextrous owlish talons. But when the Hoggit drew breath to holler, he found himself as always constrained by the love he felt towards the hapless stack of feathers on its high and lonely perch. But he didn't want to feel that love. He

'What's up?' murmurs the gentle rose-golden voice. 'Do we not love the sound of nib on parchment?'

Brio knows he's hanging in some place neither here nor there, neither red nor blue, and he wants to be somewhere true where the pain's only felt in a beautiful script of warm purple ink, where he doesn't have to answer questions about the Hoggit's shame, where—

'He should feel no shame at all,' reassures the gentle rose-golden voice with whispers of feathery touch, 'For sometimes we all harbour feelings we'd prefer to share only with our own private diaries. So write in privacy, my friend, tell without shame of how …'

In truth, there dwelt within the Hoggit's confusion of fury and fondness a dread fear that Mr T'wit's long-lost love might one day return and steal him away forever. And it was for this reason that the Hoggit had let blossom within him a hope that Mr T'wit's long-lost love would remain in that absented condition forever.

As the final rondo of Mr T'wit's hooting and howling lament faded, his beak fell open into a pathetic gaping smile and he lovingly spoon-fed the empty space at his side with imaginary scoops of honey. Then with a graceful flourish, the invisible spoon became a guitar of downy chest-feathers and he gently swished each strum away to the ocean.

Soon, the Hoggit's fraught gaze followed Mr T'wit's wafts of silent music into the moonlight, where they conjoined in a dismal bond of acquiescence to loss made bearable by dreams. Yet it was as his thoughts swirled around the night sky that the Hoggit found himself struck by a proposition of such stunning note that he almost passed out. Yet how could it not be true that Lord Rumbuck was already out there, circling Hoggit Castle on the mighty Pegasaurus and calling upon the Young Prince to prove his readiness?

The Hoggit discerned at once that there was but one way to prove himself ready. He must appear at the Dark Arched Window and demonstrate by daredevil proximity to the drop that he had at last overcome his crippling fear of heights.

The frenzied climb made chaff of the Hoggit's tiny fingertips, but against all odds he finally clawed himself onto the dust-caked windowsill, where he hastily tethered his bright orange safety harness to a rusty nail. Alas, before he was in breath to draw his invisible sword and issue a cry of battle, the moon lent light for a clear apprehension of the bottomless abyss. And such was his shock that, during his brief pirouette and last moment of consciousness, he had no time to make soft-landing arrangements for the back of his head.

Thus he lay, tethered to the nail with bright orange twine, draped in a swaddling shroud of peaceful moonlight, to all the world an exulted embryo connected by an umbilical cord of fire to the primordial spark.

Murmuring complaint, Brio tries to evade the coaxing hand, but with that gentle, rhythmic voice in his head, he can't even support the weight of his own eyes and has no choice but to relinquish the Magic Quill.

Sometime later, he becomes dimly aware of waking in the night, the kind of waking that takes you to the toilet or to a mum's bed after unsettling dreams. Fumbling his way in the dark, he encounters a touch that's soft to his hand and his tummy flutters at the possibility that it might be his mum's. But now he's dipping distractedly into a huge bowl of sweet popcorn and gratefully feeling the Magic Quill in his hand, which transports him back to Hoggit Castle, where …

Through flickering cracks in walls, the moonlight filtered gently into the Hoggit's slowly returning consciousness. It wakened his grandma's whispering, which told him of how the Great Night Orb had once served within the Sky-Glass Dome to throw the light of goodness upon all who sailed across its protective arc. Then one day, inspired by the Hoggit's birth, the Great Night Orb had floated up into the sky to bless its light upon the whole of Creation. And it was through this elegant myth of creation that the Hoggit came to sense—as he did now, gradually regaining memories— that the Great Night Orb's slow circling of his head anointed him alone as the creature of destiny around whom the whole universe revolved.

On the other hand, when the Hoggit woke in full to the fact of his continued entrapment on the windowsill, he emitted an involuntary moan and pressed himself flat. How was he ever to descend? What on earth had prompted him to make the ascent in the first place? But he would starve to death before seeking aid from Mr T'wit, for his imperious custodian never passed up the chance to subtly parrot his grandma's admonitions and deem him *unready*.

Mr T'wit's renewed cry of lament was so sudden and ear-piercing that it took the Hoggit several seconds to identify within himself an outrage beyond anything he had ever felt. And thus it transpired, after countless years of fermenting his

89

rage in bottles and his humiliation in casks, that the Hoggit's corks and stoppers finally blew free. 'Shut up, you stupid old fool!'

As though in receipt of a kick to his rear end, Mr T'wit span round and swiped the tear of lamentation from his blazing eye. Having taken furious aim with the black patch over his other, he rocketed down to land in a detonation of plumage that pressed the Hoggit back against the alcove wall.

'You ungrateful child! I have devoted my whole life to feeding and protecting you, and you know as well as I that it is absolutely forbidden to speak during the Moonlit Misery Moment! How am I supposed to return to my state of advanced grumpfort after the shock of your rudeness? Go to bed!'

'I will not go to bed!' the Hoggit cried. 'Because then I won't know when Lord Rumbuck arrives.'

Mr T'wit issued an extended growl of exasperation. 'Young man, you are giving me a chronic case of *in coco loco parentisitis*. Now, go to bed and stay there for as many days as are required for you to remember your place in this family.'

Goaded beyond the point of no return, the Hoggit shouted that he would go nowhere but the Tower of Time, and he would find Lord Rumbuck on the way.

'You will wait here for Lord Rumbuck!' Mr T'wit retorted at like volume. 'Precisely as your grandmother instructed.'

Ripping his tether clean off the rusty nail, the Hoggit threw himself blindly down the mountain of junk. But as he strode dizzily for the spiral stairs, Mr T'wit blocked his path.

'Don't be a young fool.'

The Hoggit made choreograph of duck and weave, only for Mr T'wit's wing to pin him swiftly against a rotten crate. 'Do you not remember what a giant will do to a creature such as you, if you are not accompanied by the jester who can tame it with laughter?'

Remembering his grandma's terrifying description of a giant plucking him for the oven, the Hoggit felt his legs wilt like the very spinach that should have given him strength. Yet still his resolve survived and he snarled through gritted teeth that on his great journey to the Tower of Time he would also be united with the Jester.

Only in time's nick did Mr T'wit succeed in seizing the Hoggit's tether. 'You swore an oath to your grandmother never to leave this place. You swore to look after her forever.'

'She's *dead*,' cried the Hoggit. 'And she's never coming back.'

By the scruff of his safety harness, Mr T'wit drew the Hoggit closer. 'The spirit of a woman you love never dies, and you still have many years of grieving to undertake.'

The Hoggit's spirited cries crumbled to a whimper. 'I *have* grieved. I've cried for ages.'

'But that was merely a warm-up, young man. When you grieve correctly, it will last a lifetime. Now, I must insist that you—wait ... what are you doing?'

Mr T'wit dived into the battle for the quintuple knot of the Hoggit's safety harness. 'You swore an oath to keep it on till you were five!'

'And now I'm ten!'

'You are not ten! You are two! Always two! Don't you know I poured my love into this harness?'

The Hoggit jumped back from the affray. '*Tell me*, how do I get to the Tower of Time?'

Having slowly released his grip, Mr T'wit stood back and thoughtfully flicked a speck of dust from his chest. He then cocked his chin and peered down at the Hoggit. 'I will tell you everything you need to know when you are *ready*.'

'I *am* ready. Tell me now.'

Gazing at the Hoggit, Mr T'wit slowly shook his head and sighed. 'Oh, what can I say to bring you some peace? It is hard to accept the truth about those we love, harder still when it concerns those we *need*. What you must understand is that a story does not have to be true to contain truth. Indeed, it is the greatest fictions that lead one to the greatest truths, and to find what you are looking for you must always look in the wrong place.'

Unable to make head or tail of his guardian's knot of words, the Hoggit darted for the stairs. A scuffle ensued, which swiftly became a most serious affair. The Hoggit bit and scratched, kicked and clawed too, while Mr T'wit thwacked and pecked and even attempted a butt of the forehead.

'Don't you understand?' cried Mr T'wit from within his enraged flapping of wings. 'The Tower of Time is up *there*. It is the great tower in the sky to which we all must go. *That* is what Grandma was trying to tell you—that your father is dead!'

The tether slipped from the Hoggit's hand and he teetered backwards. Yet he rallied again and bellowed into Mr T'wit's face that his father was alive. 'And you think you're so wise, turning one eye round so you can fathom the depths of your own soul. But all you can see is the view from your bottom! And I know why your long-lost love left you. Because she hated your stupid rubbish too!'

Mr T'wit's beak fell open and time ticked like the seconds between lightning and thunderclap. 'You want to know the truth about your father?' He spoke now as a hissing boiler about to explode. 'Well, I will tell you. Your father was a coward who fled because he could not face the challenge of life. And your mother died of a broken heart.'

'*That's a lie*,' the Hoggit cried. 'My father went forth to battle the Dark Lord.'

'Pith and baloney! He didn't even make it to the double white lines.'

These words crushed the Hoggit as though he himself had been run over. Yet still he rallied. 'You think you can trick me? Well, you can't. And I'm leaving right now.'

'You would not get a hundred yards,' Mr T'wit hooted derisively. 'Because you are a coward too. LIKE FATHER, LIKE SON! Because in the Garden of Eden, the apple never falls far from the tree!'

Issuing a shriek of fury, the Hoggit catapulted himself onto the rickety stairs, down which he rolled and bounced, sprawling and scrabbling, until, as a jelly of bruises and misplaced limbs, he came to that place of which his grandma had so many times spoken in terrifying terms: the tumbledown doorway to the big wide world.

Yet derangement and rage fuelled courage and, eyes closed, he plunged into the darkness. Alas, in all but a few seconds, he was assailed by a nerve-wracking novelty of noises and noxious nasaling that overwhelmed his defences. He was powerless to stop himself flipping into a ball, which rolled and tumbled into the roadside ditch and came to rest in the mud.

Registering someone else's breathing among his own wild panting, Brio twists round to find Logie lounging disjointedly on a pile of old bedding.

'Came to see how you're going. Enjoying it?'

It's as though Logie just landed there in a hurry, but a tightness in the stomach reminds Brio that something's gone wrong for the

Hoggit. When he reaches to look at the face-down page he's just finished, though, he finds his hand restrained by some kind of mental shackle. His first thought is that Logie's done something while he was writing to stop him going back in time. And if he did that, maybe he even had something to do with whatever just happened to the Hoggit. But that would mean that Logie made him write under hypnosis, which was impossible. Walk and talk under hypnosis, maybe. Even have cold custard poured over your head like on Pippa's TV show. But not something as complicated as writing.

'Wanna clue me in on what's happening? Might give you an idea what happened next.'

'I *know* what happened next.' But when he grabs up the nearest of his crumpled notes, he finds he can't remember a single thing about the Purple Code either. Pinching the top of his nose, he stares in confusion at the mess of microscopic symbols.

'Don't forget, I'm a writer too,' Logie says from behind him. 'So I know that when you can't remember what you just wrote, it means you're really in the Groove, capital G.'

Panicked that everything's gone wrong and the Hoggit's going to die of despair, Brio slaps down the meaningless page of exercise book. There's only one way he can keep going now. 'You have to call Izzy.'

'Buddy, you can do this on your own. Same way you built your own table. Just close your eyes and breathe deep.'

Brio knows it's the same voice that makes him want to walk to the yellow gate bathed in rose-golden sunset, to reach the top of the ditch, where the Hoggit can see Mr and Mrs Hare outlined in dim moonlight on the other side of the road.

'But who are Mr and Mrs Hare?' asks the little voice. 'We don't know them at all.'

'The Hoggit knows them well,' replies the gentle voice. 'They're the couple who live among the gorse bushes across from the castle. For his whole life, the Hoggit has looked down from his chamber and dreamed of belonging to their big happy family. Mrs Hare the cuddly, loving mum. Mr Hare the boisterous dad with his sword games and pretend battles. And seven kids, all girls.'

As Brio stares harder into the candle flame, he remembers the Hoggit telling him how much he'd always wanted a father like Mr Hare. But this isn't a happy family moment at all. This is—

'Everything okay?' asks the gentle voice.

Anxiety squirms in his stomach. '*No*, it's not okay. Because Mrs Hare's shouting at Mr Hare. She's really upset.

'And what's she saying?'

'She's shouting, "How many times do I have to tell you? *No ... violent ... games.*" And when she ripped the long stick from Mr Hare's hand, the Hoggit felt the pain as though some wooden sword had been torn from his own determined grip. And I know that feeling.'

'And what did Mr Hare say back?'

Brio doesn't need to think. It's as though he's heard this shouting match before. '"They're not games," Mr Hare bellowed. "They're rigorous training for life's dangers. And my girls are not going to face the world by running away. They're going to be set an example of courage—by their *father*."'

'Keep going,' murmurs the gentle voice. 'And feel that quill in your hand.'

But Brio's becoming so distressed he can hardly *say* Mrs Hare's words, let alone write them.

'Did she say—'

'*No*. She said, "The only danger to our children is *you*. You're not a father at all. You're a coward trying to prove himself to his kids."'

'That's great,' murmurs the gentle voice. 'So keep writing it now, just like you promised the Hoggit.'

There's a soft nudge to his hand, which reaches for the ink, and …

From around her neck, Mrs Hare lifted a shiny chain on which dangled a small, dull ring. Stony faced, she dropped it in the mud at Mr Hare's feet and strode away.

In silent shock, the Hoggit implored Mrs Hare to return. Surely, they'd hug and make up. Everything would be as happy ever after as it was before.

'You'll regret this in the morning!' Mr Hare bellowed into the empty darkness. 'You'll come crawling back!'

When that didn't happen, Mr Hare's energy seemed to drain into the ground and he slumped to his knees to gather up the ring as though rescuing an injured bird. Having pressed it to his chest, he gently slipped the chain over his tall ears. The ring hung like a cross around his neck, such a weight that his head flopped forward.

At that moment, the noise of an engine ripped into the night and headlights lit up a row of traffic cones and their red warning flag. But instead of diving for cover, Mr Hare cast his face into a mask of deathly resolve and set off into the road. Before he could rush out to barge Mr Hare clear, the Hoggit was blinded by headlights and thrown by a bang that split the darkness. Scrabbling dizzily to his feet in the bottom of the ditch, he found himself next to Mr Hare's spreadeagled body. '*No*,' he whimpered, clutching his tether. 'Please don't be dead.'

To the Hoggit's relief, Mr Hare groaned and began groping for the whereabouts of his head. Just as the Hoggit was about to help him locate the jaunty tuft of fur between his ears, a burst of bright moonlight broke through the clouds and turned the debris of the crash into a showcase of chrome and glass.

At first, the Hoggit was merely shocked by the extent of the wreckage, but then he found himself stumbling backwards in awe. For this wasn't simply the chariot's small chrome radiator grille bent in half, it was no less than Lord Rumbuck's *Armour Impervious*, standing there like the torso of a god. And that wasn't a roadworks flag either, it was the bright red cloth of Lord Rumbuck's *Timeless Tunic*.

Frothy-headed with joy, the Hoggit fell back on his haunches. His saviour had been there all along, hiding in plain sight as a pretend father, simply waiting for the Young Prince to be *ready*!

'Where am I?' Mr Hare groaned. 'And *who* am I?'

Taking delicate hold of Mr Hare's arm, the Hoggit was alarmed to see that Mr Hare's right eye now resembled a monocle about to pop out, and one of his ears was as twisted and crumpled as the other was pointing stiffly out to one side. 'You're Lord Rumbuck,' the Hoggit whispered. 'You've just had a little bump on the head—in the battle with the chariot. But you were victorious!'

As the Hoggit heaved to sit him upright, Mr Hare groaned again. When he tried to focus on the Hoggit, his larger eye seemed to come loose. 'Who are *you*?'

Breathless as much with trepidation as elation, the Hoggit explained that he was the Young Prince. 'And you're here to take me to rescue my father from the Tower of Time.'

Mr Hare's blank stare swivelled slowly towards the other side of the road, where some unseen spectre made him groan and shy away. 'I don't remember anything. And I don't want to.'

The Hoggit clung on to Mr Hare's hand. 'The Dark Lord's trying to make you forget who you are. Because you're the only one who can defeat him.' He stuffed the red cloth into Mr Hare's huge hand. 'Put on your Timeless Tunic and you'll remember everything!'

Mr Hare flailed clumsily to escape the hood but the Hoggit grabbed his ear and yanked it through the ripped hole. 'Do you remember *now*?'

The twitching of Mr Hare's larger eye engaged half his face in a foolish dance but the Hoggit was beyond caring.

'Work your mind, my lord! Think back to all the glorious times when the Timeless Tunic protected you from evil spells.'

His expression now anxious, Mr Hare tried to pull off the tunic, but the Hoggit clung on with all his strength.

'*Please*, I need you to help me find my father. It's your destiny.'

The struggle ceased and Mr Hare squinted with lop-sized eyes. 'What are you talking about? Why would it be my destiny to help you find your father?'

'Because you're the greatest hero ever! And the Armour Impervious protects you from every danger in the world, even the Dark Lord's lightning bolts!'

Mr Hare's gaze finally fell upon the gleaming chrome torso that stood next to them in the ditch. Slowly, his squint became a look of curiosity and he sniffed in a way that pursed his lips. 'A hero, you say?'

'Yes! And fantastic with a sword!'

Raising his eyebrows, Mr Hare brightened further. 'Well, that's very good. And, erm … invincible too?'

Needing no further cue, the Hoggit darted to the armour and threw himself into battle with its vast weight. 'Help me, my lord. I can't do this alone.'

Letting out a long grunt from the guts, Mr Hare heaved the

steel shell over his head and dropped it neatly into place. The Hoggit stumbled back in awe and bumped into the broken wing mirror, which he quickly heaved up for Mr Hare to view himself. Mr Hare examined his jawline in profile. His chin rose and his one good ear flicked upright. 'Lord *Rumbuck*, eh?'

Fearful of breaking the spell, the Hoggit could only manage a timid nod.

Mr Hare squinted. 'And who did you say you were again?'

'The Young Prince, my lord, son of the Hoggit King. And I have waited so long for—'

'Very good.' Mr Hare drew himself tall and puffed out his chest. 'Then Lord Rumbuck I am, and Lord Rumbuck I shall be until the ending of the world!'

As Mr Hare expounded further on his own virtues with little mention of the great quest, the Hoggit couldn't help feeling slight dismay. But when a burst of moonlight set the Armour Impervious agleam, his disappointment became a cry of, 'Hurrah for Lord Rumbuck! The greatest warrior of all time!' Which in turn provoked Mr Hare into such a whirlwind of parries and swishes that the Hoggit was thrown clean onto his bottom. Just as Mr Hare was about to pierce the dragon's heart, however, he stopped and looked askance at his open hand. 'But where *is* my sword?'

The Hoggit saw at once that a dire conundrum impeded their journey before it had even begun. For without the Great Sword, Lord Rumbuck could never defeat the Dark Lord, but any attempt to retrieve it from the royal chamber would result in his own reincarceration by Mr T'wit. And this time there would be no escape.

'Ahah!' Mr Hare boomed, having followed the Hoggit's anguished gaze. 'I left the Great Sword in my castle!'

To his vast irritation, the Hoggit ran out of breath after only three of the spiral stairs and Mr Hare had to carry him the rest of the way.

'Ah, there you are,' Mr T'wit said jovially as the Hoggit strode purposefully for the Great Sword. 'And I see you have found Lord Rumbuck.' He turned his effusive welcome on Mr Hare. 'I have long looked forward to some help in the play department. It is not my strong suit, you see.'

'Play?' Mr Hare retorted indignantly. 'Young Prince, who is this brazen bird that mocks my exalted destiny?'

The Hoggit only pointed Mr Hare urgently at the protruding sword handle. 'Quickly, my lord.'

Parting from Mr T'wit with a *pfah*, Mr Hare strode to the pile of rubble and took hold of the sword. But after two minutes of heaving and cussing and humiliated kicking, he was forced to turn angrily on Mr T'wit. 'You've cursed the Great Sword.'

'Not at all,' Mr T'wit replied amiably. 'It is simply that to release the fabled weapon you must earn its respect.' He gestured to the maze of trails that the Hoggit had spent a lifetime constructing from bric-a-brac. 'I propose *The Quest of the Fabled Fang* as a good place to start. Then you can proceed to the *Knight of Long Knives*, from which most excellent field of battle the world is your oyster. Though, I don't know whether you would agree, Mister Lord Rumbuck, but young people these days simply have to make too many choices. They live in a hall of mirrors where half are cracked and all the reflections are in motion. It might be wiser to reduce this maze of narratives to one simple story. Then perhaps the Young Prince would be less confused.'

To the Hoggit, Mr T'wit had sounded for a moment like some strange mix of priest and school principal. He glanced at Mr Hare, whose nose twitched with irritation.

'You are clearly a servant of the Dark Lord, sent in a last-ditch attempt to stave off your master's inevitable defeat.'

'It is possible,' Mr T'wit agreed. 'One tries to help everybody. And sometimes people are simply not who they say. But what happens next, your lordship, is that I myself return to my lonely perch for the Morning Mourning Moment. And you ... entertain the boy.' He waddled away and began plumping cushions and dusting tops with a wingtip.

'Curse you, eagle of doom,' Mr Hare snorted then turned on the Hoggit. 'Come, we shall leave this decoy sword here and pick up another on the way.'

'No, my lord! There's only one Great Sword and without it you can never defeat the Dark Lord.'

'As for the house rules ...' Mr T'wit called to Mr Hare from across the cluttered space. 'Dinner will be flown in twice a day. Total silence will be observed during my seven periods of lamentation. And your bed is there.' He pointed carelessly towards a pile of rotten wood. 'As for the Young Prince and myself, we sleep *here*.' He smiled at a comfortable array of cushions tucked under a makeshift shelter.

Mr Hare frowned. 'You sleep in the same quarters as the Young Prince? This is most irregular.'

'It is necessary,' Mr T'wit explained tersely. 'You see, the Young Prince slept in Grandma's bed until the day she died. If I do not take the place of Grandma as she requested, the boy experiences the most dreadful nightmares. Indeed, there were many occasions during Grandma's lifetime when I was called upon to perform this merciful office. Thus I am merely following the family tradition of safeguarding the Young Prince.'

Mr Hare's lips pursed and his nose twitched. But then his

irritation seemed to moderate. 'Bizarre buzzard you may be, but your point is well founded. The Young Prince's illustrious fragility does indeed warrant the highest order of protection. Which is clearly the reason I have been charged with my noble mission.'

'So we will all be one happy family,' Mr T'wit agreed, then returned to his housework, leaving Mr Hare to re-avow his curses and assure the Hoggit that he'd have them out of this madhouse in the poke of an eyepatch. Mr Hare then launched himself into another bout with the Great Sword, which left the Hoggit sheltering from a barrage of invective and bric-a-brac.

'Those are somewhat unusual sword skills for such an experienced knight,' Mr T'wit observed as he passed by to dust the collapsed magazine rack, at which exact moment Mr Hare's crazed convulsions chanced to flip his dangled wedding ring from inside the Armour Impervious.

Mr T'wit stopped dead and his mouth fell open. 'Where did you get *that*?'

Mr Hare glanced down at the ring and the Hoggit saw a flicker of clouded recognition.

'No!' the Hoggit cried. 'It's not what you think. You found it in the river.' In the same blink, the Hoggit realised that the ring must be the precious one which Mr T'wit's long-lost love had abandoned, the one that contained all the love in the world.

'What the devil's going on?' Mr Hare muttered as Mr T'wit fell to his knees and clasped at the dangling ring. 'Has this bird's brain flown the coop?' And as Mr T'wit began tugging violently on the ring-chain, Mr Hare ripped it out of his grasp. 'Let go, damn you. It's *mine*.'

'No, my lord! It's the Ring of Love and it belongs to the

whole world. You were just its noble custodian, waiting for it to be ready!'

Letting out a cry of anguish, Mr T'wit pulled down so hard on the chain that their foreheads banged together, whereafter they fell into a fury of fur and feathers.

'Stop!' the Hoggit cried. 'Stop!' But each time he shouted, the voices only grew louder, and they were shouting things that had nothing to do with the Ring of Love, and—

It takes Brio several seconds to understand that he's in Pippa's attic and hemmed in by a silhouette wall of Logie, Dr Shenoy and Professor Glybb. Angrily telling them to go away, he turns back to his writing table. But now he can only hear the fight for the Ring of Love, he can't see them anymore. And even though he knows it's incredibly important who wins the fight, he doesn't know who's supposed to be the winner.

'And how long is it since he last slept?' Brio hears Dr Shenoy demanding angrily behind him. 'Or even washed? Brio, listen to me. You are not safe here and I'm your friend.'

Brio covers his ears and squeezes his eyes closed, but now he can't even *hear* the fight. The next moment, he's on his feet and pointing the quill at Professor Glybb's nose. 'This is private. And I'm *no one's* guinea pig. Especially not yours.' He swings the quill round at Dr Shenoy. 'And you've never been my friend.' He points at Logie. '*He's* my friend. Now, *get out*.'

When the two doctors stand their ground, Brio suddenly sees how the attic must look to Professor Glybb's disdainful gaze: the damp bedding, the candle right under an inflammably dry rafter, the plates and food scraps, the jumbo-size drink bottle full of wee and the tightly tied carrier bag with its tell-tale fuse of protruding toilet paper.

'Brio,' says Professor Glybb, 'I've brought some new

medications. If we leave now, you can start them at once.'

'That all you got, professor?' Logie cuts in. 'A bunch of mind-numbing toxins to blind our friend to the fact that you don't even care that you don't understand his needs?'

'I understand Brio's needs perfectly. Now—'

'You sure? I heard one of your patients took her own life last month coz she was on the wrong meds and you didn't even have a clear record of her so-called condition. Is it true her parents are gonna sue you?'

Professor Glybb's expression hardens and he angles himself to exclude Logie. 'Brio, if you take the medications that I have in Dr Shenoy's car, you will no longer experience these hallucinations.'

'I don't *have* hallucinations.' And as he readies himself to beat down whatever Professor Glybb says next, he realises that it's true: since meeting Logie, he hasn't suffered a single assault from the window-bogey or any of the other ghouls or demons.

Abruptly back with the Hoggit as though he were there in the castle himself, Brio closes his eyes and plunges the quill blind. But Mr Hare and Mr T'wit are grappling so furiously for the Ring that he can't get a written word in edgeways.

'*Brio,*' Dr Shenoy says sharply. 'You must listen to Professor Glybb.'

'He doesn't need to listen,' Logie cuts in. 'Coz he knows exactly what's gonna help him.'

'*What*, writing fairy tales?' Professor Glybb says contemptuously. 'To treat a serious mental illness? This is nothing but an irresponsible LARP. Low-grade auto-suggestion. Brio is a vulnera—'

Brio thumps the table. 'It's not a fairy tale.'

'And it's not mental illness either,' Logie adds. 'Coz there's no such goddam thing. There's just mental *injury*, damage to the soul inflicted by the twisted self-identities people have to construct to lever themselves into the dominant narratives created by men like you.'

Before Professor Glybb can reply, the stepladder creaks and they turn to see Izzy appearing from the hatchway.

Dr Shenoy moves swiftly to block her way. 'I told you to wait in the car.'

Brio's back on his feet and staring at Izzy through a fog of anger and joy.

'Bree …' She edges forward, hands wavering. 'Are you okay?'

The sight of her overwhelms him—her caring eyes, her savagely shortened hair, the pitying doubt. Back at the table, he tries to bring order to his raving thoughts. But the scene in the castle dissolves into a dissonant sepia slow-motion and his toes freeze into a tight curl. Unable to move his lips either, he's left staring helplessly at the argument in the attic.

'You're a dangerous charlatan,' Professor Glybb fumes at Logie. 'And you're working for Zpydr, helping them to bamboozle those fools in Whitehall who think they can treat mental health on a shoestring.'

Logie scoffs. 'You're blaming Zpydr for having so much influence in government? Don't you think you ought to be looking a little closer to home?'

Professor Glybb pulls his most supercilious expression yet. 'How can you blame the medical profession for Zpydr's machinations in government? My professional body is united in its opposition to this appalling computerised psychiatry.'

With a hollow laugh, Logie says, 'Me too. But what I'm talking about, Professor, is that the reason so many governments are taking this online mental health gig seriously is *because*, year on year, you guys add so many factitious types of *functional mental illness* to your great bible that it's gotten to be the size of a freakin' phone directory.'

'Mr Logue, these ridiculous aspersions are only going to harm Brio more. Now I insist that you—'

'*No, Professor*. The truth's gonna *help* Brio. Coz you know what the real problem is? Once something's in your bloated bible, the government and medical insurance companies have godda treat the tens of thousands of otherwise happy people who've been told there's a pill that'll get 'em back on track after their date from toss-up dot com turned out to be a whacko or they maxed out their credit card. And what do you know? Suddenly, half the population is *mentally ill* and it's costing governments a squillion in sham meds and shabby shrinks. So hey, as soon as Zpydr rocks in with the promise of a cheap fix for all these trumped-up mental illnesses, what could make more sense to our hamstrung governments than CHANT*bot-vip*? And the terrifying thing is, *doc*, something as nuts as CHANT*bot-vip* really *is* the obvious answer to something as crazy as the stunning range of expensive conditions that you and your buddies have dreamed up. And of course the brains trust down there at Zpydr are gonna milk this bonfire of the sanities for all it's worth. They probably want nostalgia to be reclassified as a mental illness too. And why wouldn't a guy like Tabo Forzac want to link it all up with social media and take control of our collective consciousness?'

Still cast in paralytic silence, Brio wishes he could say something to revel in Professor Glybb's disarray. He loves it too that Dr Shenoy looks like he's been punched in the solar plexus. And all Izzy can do is fidget and glance at her dad, who looks to Professor Glybb, who stands himself straight and says, 'Mr Logue, I see no reason why I should dignify your outburst with a response. Suffice it to record that Brio falls very firmly within a well-recognised and rigorously defined psychiatric condition. And it is that condition I intend to treat—professionally.'

'And what would this well-recognised condition happen to be,

Professor? *All of the above*, right? Your hallmark diagnosis.'

Professor Glybb's eyes flash with anger. 'This fiasco has gone on long enough. Now extract Brio from this recklessly induced catatonia at once.'

'He's not *in* a trance. Are you, buddy?'

To his surprise, Brio finds he can speak and move again. But he's disoriented by his release into the real world and wants to be back behind glass.

'Bree, please,' Izzy implores. 'You've got to stop this before it really hurts you.'

'*Nothing's* going to hurt me. I just need to write.' But as he's about to turn back, he sees the angle and looks Izzy hard in the eye. 'If you think Logie's doing something bad, then why don't *you* help me instead?'

Another argument breaks out but Brio can only watch and pray that Izzy will win. When Dr Shenoy and Professor Glybb start leaving down the stepladder, Brio can't believe his eyes.

'You too,' he says to Logie. 'And if you don't leave us alone, I'm not writing another word.'

As soon as it's just the two of them, Izzy hovers out a hand. 'Bree, I know this is very real to you and I do want to help, but surely there's some other way. And Logie staying here, don't you think it's creepy?'

'What do you mean "staying here"?'

'You didn't know? Pippa's letting him stay in the spare room. Bree, he just showed up out of nowhere and now he's moving in on Pippa. And *you*. This is all really wrong.'

The shock's passed before it's even had time to hit. 'It doesn't matter. Just help me.'

'Bree—'

'Just *help me*.'

Seconds clunk by and Brio closes his eyes.

'Well, I'll try,' she says. 'But how?'

'You have to remember what the Hoggit told me.'

'But I wasn't there.'

'If you read what I wrote so far, you'll know what happened next. Like you always do.'

Izzy hesitates again, but eventually she takes the sheaf of parchment and starts to read. While her eyes glide to and fro, Brio tries not to stare, tries not to breathe too close in case she knows he's secretly drawing in her scent. He wishes she could sit there reading forever, till they could be back by the fire with hot chocolates and crayons.

After what seems like an age, Izzy looks up. 'It's really good.'

'That doesn't matter. Just tell me who would have got the Ring of Love.'

As Izzy lowers her head in thought, Brio prepares to write.

'Okay,' she says at last. 'So Mr T'wit thinks it's his old wedding ring, and erm, Lord Rumbuck thinks it's *his* wedding ring, even though he, erm—found it somewhere. And, I mean, it kind of *is* his wedding ring. But, you know, the Hoggit's obviously worried that if, erm, if Mr Hare thinks it's his actual wedding ring, he'll remember who he really is. And seeing Mr Hare—'

'He's *Lord Rumbuck*,' Brio cries. 'He was only pretending to be Mr Hare.'

'Okay, I'm sorry, I just need to tune in.' She digs fingers into her hair. 'It's hard with all these distractions.'

'You write so much rubbish with Darcy, you can't remember how to write with *me*.'

Izzy has to catch her breath. 'Bree, the last thing you need to stress about is Darcy, okay? And I'm not helping them with anything at the moment, because they're in a really bad way.'

Brio's hackles are straight back up. 'There's nothing wrong with him. Whatever it is, he's faking it.'

'Bree—'

'I bet he's pretending to be mentally ill. And that's rubbish, because there's no such thing.'

Izzy's eyes bulge but she quickly collects herself. 'Bree, it's not true there's no such thing as mental illness, and Darcy really does have problems.'

'He *doesn't*. He just gives *me* problems.'

Her eyes plead and she angles forward. 'But that's because of his own problems—at home, with the way his parents are. Putting themself under all that pressure to do well, trying to be something they're not.'

Brio can't stand the look of care for Darcy in Izzy's eyes. 'He's not *they*. And he's just acting. That's all he does.'

Taking a long deep breath, Izzy glances at the stepladder hatch. She edges closer to him. 'Bree, I shouldn't tell you this but Darcy's been sectioned, okay? They're in the Northview. Now, don't worry about Darcy. Just help me tune in to this.'

But the word *sectioned* has flipped Brio's stomach. It's as though he's heard it in some past life. His head clutters with a geometric arrangement of lines around him that becomes a 3D model sheep-pen, a box on a form he might be forced to sign. But the idea that there actually could be an explanation cuts across his whole worldview of Darcy as the epitome of all things wild and irrational, everything that makes sense of his wanting to avoid the world and its senseless cruelties. And the very notion of mental illness seems to be an even greater threat than Darcy himself—even greater than Tabo Forzac and Zpydr.

But as he spins out at the sight of Izzy's worry and unattainable beauty, the voice persists in his head, telling him that if mental illness is real then it can also be faked. So that's why Darcy's doing it, to make himself special and win Izzy. *Oh, God*, moans the voice in his head, *is that what* I *have to do to make her love* me?

With a jolt, he remembers that Izzy's supposed to be saving the Ring, not thinking about Darcy. 'What are you waiting for?'

Izzy blinks. 'I'm sorry. I was just thinking about the Hoggit. So erm, isn't it that he knew he had to make Lord Rumbuck forget his past life completely? So he, erm … he had to get the Ring and quickly start swinging it like a hypnotist's watch—on its chain— and erm …'

Brio jumps up and smashes his head so hard on a rafter that Izzy disappears into lurid colours. She tries to come to him but he shouts, 'Don't touch me, I hate you.' And the next thing he knows, she's fled down the stepladder and he's shouting and flinging himself around in Logie's bear hug.

*

'Okay, keep going,' Logie murmurs. 'Slowly *in* … keeping your eyes closed … and slowly out, pressing your thumb and forefinger a little harder as you breathe in—yeah, that's it. I'm doing this with you …'

But Brio can't shake off the last of the worry and needs to understand why Mr T'wit gave up and let Lord Rumbuck get the Ring.

'Mr T'wit was overwrought with emotion,' Logie says quietly.

'How do you know?'

'That's what you told me—and slowly *in*, nice and deep … But what an awesome state for Mr T'wit to experience, being overwhelmed by emotion.'

Brio doesn't remember telling Logie anything, but he's surely right. And when Logie loosens his hug a little, Brio wants it back around him, the cocoon, the armour …

'And don't worry about Izzy,' Logie says softly. 'She just wants to see you do this on your own. And you want her to see you do that.

Keep the breathing going … and you *do* know what happened next, coz it's there in your memory. Now keep the Ring in your heart and feel your hand pick up the Magic Quill, which feels like the feathery down of Mr T'wit's face as he lies spread-owled on the dusty floor of the castle chamber … with the Hoggit at his side and Lord Rumbuck looking on …' And when Logie lets him go, Brio feels himself float away like a feather and …

'Ohh,' Mr T'wit moaned. 'The very thought of her laughter, that twinkle in her pussycat eyes.'

'Your long-lost love was a cat?' the Hoggit exclaimed. But his astonishment turned to worry. For Mr T'wit's long-lost love had suddenly become real and could steal away his beloved guardian. 'How can you love a cat? That's impossible.' He was about to add that Mr T'wit must be imagining her, when a sharp burning pain struck him in the chest.

Lord Rumbuck raised his chin haughtily. 'Young Prince, it seems you do not wish this fine boon to be blessed upon your noble guardian. The Ring of Love punishes you accordingly.' Having then exhorted the Hoggit to search his conscience, Lord Rumbuck turned back to the moaning stack of feathers on the floor. 'Tell us, wise and noble owl, how it was that you chanced to part with your virtuous queen.'

Mr T'wit emitted a groan that seemed to rise from the very foundations of the castle. 'Young we were and sailed the seven seas, and under the smile of stars I came to see the whole canopy of heaven through the beautiful eyes of my darling pussy.' With distant smile, he hugged himself into a wrap of wings. 'A simple life for a simple love. Fish from the sea and moonlight in our hearts.'

As the Hoggit wrestled his own emotions, Lord Rumbuck

raised the chain higher and gazed at the hoop of dull, dented metal. 'But how can it be, mighty owl, that the great Ring failed you in your love?'

'It was me who failed,' moaned Mr T'wit. '*Oh,* how did I not see that our simple jar of honey had woken her taste for everything sweet in life? She fell in love with anything that glittered, then *everything* that glittered. More and more she wanted, until we began to sink under the weight of all the trinkets in the world. I told her that our little boat was unfit for such purposes. She said I was thinking only of myself. My temper became for those fateful seconds a tempest over the ocean. If she did not jettison her junk, I stormed, she would have to find someone with a bigger boat. I thought she would snap out of the Curse of Glitterlove and recall that old purring of the heart which bound us together. Instead, she went and found that terrible someone with a bigger boat. Too late she discovered him to be a cruel pirate, and now she is prisoner of that most vile villain.' Again, Mr T'wit reached hopelessly for the Ring. 'Ohhh, it may only be a piggy-wig's nose ring, but it contains the very essence of love.'

Lord Rumbuck nodded gravely, though he drew the Ring of Love closer to himself. 'But where is she now, this cherished love to whom the Ring binds you for all time?'

Mr T'wit issued another echoing groan. 'That vile villain keeps her in the dungeons of his verminous vessel, travelling the world for an uncertain term. Oh, *woe*!'

Clasping the Ring to his chrome-plated chest, Lord Rumbuck dropped to one knee at Mr T'wit's other side. 'Mighty owl, in this immaculate ring you have seen hope, and you know that for hope to live, all it needs is help—which is at hand! Thus command me to sally forth! Let your valiant servant board that dread galleon, whereupon to cut down this villainous oppressor. Let Lord Rumbuck bring home your elegant queen!'

'No!' cried the Hoggit, which caused him to be struck again in the chest and thrown into convulsion.

Mr T'wit's eye opened and held the Hoggit in its gaze of fire and water. 'What you are experiencing, young man, is the power of the Ring—how it punishes anyone who entertains a single thought that is not born of selfless love. But why must you be so full of fear? Did I not swear to your grandmother that I would protect you for all days to come?'

Even as the Hoggit's head fell in shame, it sprang back up. 'But I don't need to be protected anymore. I'm ready to face the world on my own!'

'Not so!' Lord Rumbuck boomed swiftly. 'For your prophesied destiny and duty is to be protected by Lord Rumbuck.'

Confounded by a trap he hadn't seen, the Hoggit could only jockey harder Mr T'wit's side. 'I *do* want to rescue her. I promise.' But no sooner were the words out than further turmoil crowded in, for it was his father he wanted to rescue, not Mr T'wit's long-lost love. This thought was hardly formed when the Hoggit's eyes went up in a conflagration of pain and all he could see was the blazing halo of a ring. 'I didn't mean it. I just meant I wanted to rescue my father first! Aaarrgghhhh ... all right! I meant I want to rescue them both at same time!'

The Hoggit's chastisement only intensified and he writhed on the floor in pain and anguish. Yet it was out of this tribulation that epiphany finally dawned and he staggered back to his feet. 'Mr T'wit ... if we bring back your long-lost love, will you tell us where to find the Tower of Time?'

Before Mr T'wit could reply, the Hoggit's whole head

caught fire and his cry of pain was a shriek to crack glass.

'Young Prince,' Lord Rumbuck said pompously, 'you seek reward for an act that should be performed out of love. In reply, the Ring delivers righteous rebuke. And besides, there is but one way to witness the Tower of Time, which is through my own glorious completion of the Trials of Tribulation. For only by so many lethal challenges to my body and soul can the Grail be revealed to me, and only by witnessing my virtue and prowess can you yourself gain the wisdom to behold that dread tower.'

Fighting to wrest his gaze from the Ring, the Hoggit whimpered that his grandma never said anything about the Trials of Tribulation.

Lord Rumbuck snorted. 'You are mistaken, Young Prince. My godforsaken trials featured in every account of my noble deeds that your virtuous grandma ever delivered. And those accounts served in turn as the framework for her sacred prophecy of my arrival in your needy cause. The Sacred Prophecy and the Trials of Tribulation were thus as clear as the Smoking Birthmark of Count Chaos.'

Digging tiny fingers into his scalp, the Hoggit tried desperately to prise out even a glimpse of what his grandma might or might never have said. But all he could see was her empty cushion like a hurriedly vacated bed, and her voice was as distant as the hills beyond the mountains.

Yet lo and behold, the harder the Hoggit battled his memory, and the more colourfully he saw in Lord Rumbuck's eyes that burning loyalty to the cause of love, the clearer it became that his grandma must indeed have told him about the Trials of Tribulation, and what else would a set of such God-given divinations have been called but the Sacred Prophecy?

'Oh, young man ...' Mr T'wit sighed heavily, his eye still closed. 'How dearly I wish you could bring back my long-lost love. But what of my oath to Grandma never to let you leave? How can I despatch you into peril in the mere service of my own selfish longings?'

'You *can*!' the Hoggit cried. 'Because I really am *ready*!'

Mr T'wit's fiery eye flickered open a crack and the Hoggit felt its gaze pierce his very soul. 'Perhaps this would indeed be the making of you.'

'It would! *Please*. Let me go.'

A look of peace spread across Mr T'wit's face. 'Young man, if you succeed in this dangerous quest with no thought of your own desire, you will have proved that you are indeed ready. Then everything you need to know will be revealed. And more than this, for through your own success you will find out why it is you alone who can bring back my long-lost love.'

As though the whole world had been lit up by the inferno of passion in Mr T'wit's eye, the Hoggit saw exactly what he had to do. He grabbed the Ring out of Lord Rumbuck's hand and tied its chain frantically around his own pinky-brown tummy. At once he was possessed by a fiery desire to do nothing else in the world but rescue Mr T'wit's long-lost love. 'Tell us!' he cried. 'How do we find the Vile Villain's ship?'

Mr T'wit's eye blazed with hope and his wing flopped open to point west. 'That most villainous of all ships leaves the Pitch-Dark Port at dawn in two days' time. You must follow the coast and run like the wind.'

Lord Rumbuck leapt to his feet. 'So tell us, honourable bird, how are we to identify this dread galleon?'

The air drained from Mr T'wit and his eye slid closed. 'Ohh, you will know that vile vessel when you see it.'

'And see it I shall,' Lord Rumbuck puffed. 'All the way to the bottom! So arm me, sagacious and honest bird! Impart the coveted secret by which I shall liberate my peerless weapon from this recalcitrant rock!'

'Ah, yes,' mumbled Mr T'wit. 'Your sword. Well, it's quite easy, really. If you give it a little twist to the left, it will fall right out.'

The Great Sword's resemblance to a giant's draining spoon dismayed the Hoggit, but Lord Rumbuck swiftly explained that its harmless appearance was a ploy to take the enemy by surprise—to wit, the holes rendered it light in operation and capable of slicing through air without resistance. He then grabbed up the Hoggit's tether and marched him towards the spiral stairs.

'Remember one thing,' Mr T'wit croaked as they reached the threshold. 'Only by casting the Ring into the fires of love in which it was forged can you defeat the curse of that vile villain.'

Lord Rumbuck raised his sword high. 'We shall carry this stainless ring into the blaze-golden heart of its battle with darkness!'

'But know this above all things,' Mr T'wit added, as though with his last breath. 'If you try to use the Ring when you yourself have betrayed the call of love, or if you attempt to discard or destroy the Ring, it will crush you to dust and your life will be forfeit.'

By the time Lord Rumbuck had bounced him to the bottom of the castle's endlessly spiralling stone steps, the Hoggit was so concussed he didn't know night from sideways. Indeed, it was only when Lord Rumbuck plonked him down on hard ground and splashed him with freezing cold seawater that the Hoggit's blurred vision fell upon a small boat which lay wrecked on the fringe of shingle just beyond the reach of grasping water.

'Mr T'wit's Pea-Green Boat!' the Hoggit exclaimed. 'It's real!'

'Yet stand corrected, Young Prince. For this is in fact the Grand Galleon of Gallahop, that valiant vessel of my long line which shall bear us across ferocious oceans!'

The Hoggit finally realised that instead of following Mr T'wit's instructions, Lord Rumbuck had brought them down to a small cave at the foot of the castle's towering plinth of rock. 'Why are we here?' the Hoggit whimpered. 'We're supposed to be going along the coast.'

'To hell with the Pitch-Dark Port,' Lord Rumbuck puffed. 'And to hell with that old fool's long-lost love. For now, Young Prince, we shall embark upon a voyage of our own, to forge a daring new life of adventure in which I alone shall protect you from all those trials and tribulations with which the world shall grace us!'

8

BRIO WAKES TO FIND HIMSELF ENMESHED in damp
bedding with rough blanket aggravating his chin and his cheek
mushed against a musty old garden cushion. Realising that it's
Logie's abandoned nest, he scrambles out and kicks it aside.
Lurching to give it a second boot, he once again bangs his head on
a rafter. In the lost few seconds of stunned colours before the pain
registers, the rafter becomes the hard timber of the Pea-Green Boat
and the Hoggit wakes to discover with horror that they're out on
the open ocean. As Brio stumbles for the table, his nauseous
concussion is already one with the Hoggit's debilitating
seasickness. It's the most he can do to grab up the Magic Quill
and ...

As the Hoggit was about to vomit, a slosh of freezing
saltwater splashed him in the face and he was thrown across
the boat.

'We're going to die,' he cried, scrabbling in panic for a
handhold. 'We have to go home.'

From his commanding post at the helm, Lord Rumbuck
rained down an expression of fearless and haughty
bonhomie. 'We are home already, Young Prince! The open
sea! The life of adventure!'

'*Please*,' the Hoggit wailed, but seeing that all was lost, he
could only shrink into a little nook at the bottom of the boat,
where he sank into tears and green nausea.

Raising his nose to the wind, Lord Rumbuck turned broadside to give the Hoggit a reassuring reminder of his heroic jawline. 'Come now, Young Prince. Does my prowess at the helm not fill your sails with gusty confidence?'

How keenly the Hoggit wanted to cry *yes*, but now the wild-eyed figure wasn't Lord Rumbuck at all. For the real Lord Rumbuck would never have scorned their duty to rescue the Queen. Nor would he have let them set off without the Jester. This could only be a fake Lord Rumbuck, a pirate kidnapper.

Yet as delirious despair was about to engulf the Hoggit, a shard of sunlight transformed Lord Rumbuck into a gleaming portrait of such panoramic confidence that he seemed twice his previous size. And so it was, as he gazed up at the blustering helmsman, that the Hoggit vowed never again to doubt the identity of his protector and saviour. Yes, from that moment on, Lord Rumbuck's was the one and only bearing they would follow, and they would follow it even unto the ends of the ocean.

'Very good.' Lord Rumbuck nodded approvingly, then explained that he was required to return his attention to matters of sea-state.

The Hoggit's euphoria had given him new stride and he decided that it was time to find out how much Lord Rumbuck knew of his prophesied destiny. Did he even know about Hoggits?

'I see they wear their armour on their backs,' Lord Rumbuck replied with a sniff. 'Which does suggest a somewhat less than heroic approach to battle. I note also that their armour is attached by a ripcord, presumably to promote easy jettison and a more rapid flight from the field. But feel no shame, Young Prince, for few battles have been won without the aid of Lord Rumbuck.'

Lord Rumbuck's curt disparagement snuffed the Hoggit's brief glimpse of giddy confidence and he could barely mutter the complaint that, 'Hoggits do *not* run from battlefields. And it's not a ripcord. It's my safety harness. It keeps me *safe*.'

Grunting dismissively, Lord Rumbuck raised his nose to the stiffening breeze. 'I regret to say that I am wholly unacquainted with this word. However, witnessing for myself how poorly you Hoggits have been furnished with body armour and courage, I perceive once again that your worthy grandmother was right to afford you a life of such all-encompassing and selfless protection.'

'Yes,' the Hoggit said firmly. 'She was right about everything.'

But Lord Rumbuck's pithy dicta had struck home, and for the first time in his life the Hoggit found himself experiencing a certain disquiet about his grandma. The safety harness she had asked Mr T'wit to manufacture even stirred a sense of shame. In fact, had his eyes not come to rest on a honey jar wedged into a small crevice in the bottom of the boat, his disquietude might well have led him to an insight such as to capsize his whole ship of life.

He grabbed up the jar and peered inside at the odd-looking spoon. It sported a little crossbar at the top of its handle and its scoop was scarcely larger than a needle's eye. *Oh, goodness*, he thought, his excitement rekindled, *a special sword that can only belong to Mr T'wit. It must have been handed down through all the ages of owls. And surely it has a name, which can be none other than Zing the Dazzling Dagger!*

Checking that Lord Rumbuck wasn't looking, the Hoggit applied himself with discreet vigour to the jar's lid.

'What've you got there?' Lord Rumbuck grunted.

The Hoggit drew back. 'It's nothing. Just an old spoon in a jar.'

Lord Rumbuck peered down. 'You are right. Now leave it alone. Witness instead the details of my commanding seamanship, for soon you shall be committing this day to the annals of Rumbuck history.'

His spirits crushed a third time, the Hoggit slumped into his nook with the jar and finally registered the gnawing hunger in his belly.

'Food?' Lord Rumbuck sniffed. 'Of course we have food. For during your extended slumber down there in the bilges, I prepared us a feast.'

The Hoggit glanced around in a flurry of renewed hope. 'Where is it?'

'It is laid out before our very eyes, Young Prince, for I refer to the kind of feast that succours one's belly through the soul. A spread to feed thousands.'

Once more, the Hoggit's spirits deflated. 'I need *real* food.'

'What you *need* is to give it a try.' Then in a slightly less brusque tone, Lord Rumbuck suggested that the Hoggit start with the roast carrots.

'I don't want pretend carrots,' the Hoggit muttered.

'Perhaps a little spice would help. A single mustard seed is surely all it should take.'

Much against the Hoggit's will, there was something about the thought of a mustard seed's delicious tang that piqued his taste buds no end. Indeed, when he glanced up and saw Lord Rumbuck's plaintive expression—that desire to see him happy, his sheer zest for life—he wanted nothing more than to see *him* happy too. And at once he could perceive the bowl of roast carrots as clearly as a serving of Mr T'wit's worm and slug paté. And so many more dishes besides.

Having devoured the beetroot, the Hoggit moved swiftly onwards to the mashed potato, which melted into a warm swirl of unexpected herbs and spices that sent a tingle down to his toes.

'My own favourite is the creamed celeriac,' beamed Lord Rumbuck. 'Would you be so kind?'

Offering up the antique silver dish, the Hoggit asked Lord Rumbuck if he needed a spoon.

'I'll scoop, thank you.' And as he dug in with curved fingers, he craved the Young Prince's dispensation for his lack of etiquette. 'For although you may find my table manners wholly indigestible, you must understand that Lord Rumbuck is a creature of deeds rather than decorum. Oh, and toss those loaves into the sea, would you? As guests in this place, we must ensure that the fish also are well fed.'

And thus on they dined, with finicky fingers and dribbling dollops, and whole handfuls stuffed into mouths not yet empty. Eventually, the Hoggit found himself so pleasantly bloated and insensible that the rocking of the boat became the gentle sway of a cradle, and he placed his little hands on a cushion of plumped-up belly.

Sometime later, as though from the Hoggit's own contented snooze, Brio feels a stirring of voices on the breeze, voices that portend dire change in the weather. But the Hoggit's floating so blissfully on his bloated dreams that he's not seeing the huge grey-fingered hand of a storm that now reaches out across the sky. Even as Brio stares at Izzy's frantically talking mouth, he's still in the boat that suddenly rocks so violently he has to grab a rafter.

'Izzy, wait,' Logie whispers urgently. 'You can't just crash in on him like this.'

'Bree, you have to listen. *Snap out of it.*'

But the wind in Brio's head is too loud and he can only just hear himself shouting that she doesn't understand him anymore, and she doesn't know a storm's coming. He throws himself back down at the table. '*Wake up,*' he cries at the Hoggit. 'There's a storm. You have to get ready.'

The next thing Brio knows, the feather's been ripped from his grip and he's back on his feet, staring at an empty hand. He grabs for the quill but Izzy backhands it away, which to Brio can only mean one beautiful thing. 'Okay, *you* write,' he cries and closes his eyes to be back in the boat. 'Lord Rumbuck snorted that there was no storm at all, the Hoggit was merely experiencing a mirage brought on by excess of victuals. A gustatory mix-up!'

The break of an icy wave on his cheek gives Brio such a shock he doesn't immediately comprehend it as a slap.

'Don't touch me,' Izzy shouts as Logie tries to pull her away. 'Bree, you have to know this.' She's holding him hard by the upper arms and staring into his eyes. 'If you finish this book and they can hypnotise you to accept that your dad's dead, Logie's going to win a quarter of a million dollars. *Are you hearing me?*'

Unable to think straight with the Hoggit's terrified shrieks in his head, Brio looks unseeingly between Izzy and Logie. But when Logie shifts awkwardly and runs a hand through his straggly hair, Brio feels a sour tingle shoot down the back of his legs. 'What prize? What's going on?'

Up come Logie's Jesus palms. 'Okay, look—'

But Izzy cuts him off. 'Bree, it's true, they're brainwashing you and it's not going to make you better in the right way. You have to *stop.*'

Logie tries again to coax Izzy away but Brio shuts him down and turns straight back on her. 'They're not doing *anything*. And how can they cure me when there's nothing wrong with me?' But straightaway he's back at Logie, demanding to know it isn't true.

'Buddy, I swear, Zpydr's crap's got nothing to do with us.'

Brio knows he should push harder and Izzy's right to keep arguing with Logie, but he has to get back to the Hoggit, who's sobbing in terror at the breaking waves and freezing spray. Brio snatches the Magic Quill from Izzy and dives for his crate.

'We have to get to land,' the Hoggit cried as the storm raged behind him like furious voices.

'Nonsense, Young Prince! Terra firma is nothing more than the domain of our former woes and foes! And do you not know that ships head to sea in a storm?!'

'They *don't*! They go to the harbour.'

Battling to keep the little boat pointed into the waves, Lord Rumbuck peered down his nose. 'It is very clear to me, Young Prince, that Hoggits know nothing about the crossing of oceans, which I suppose is a natural extension of their difficulties with roads.'

But Brio finds himself torn again between the Hoggit's terror and Izzy's shouting match with Logie.

'Look, Izzy, I agree with you, okay? Zpydr's mad and I hate what they're doing with CHANT. It was designed as a talking therapy, short narratives in one-hour sessions with patients vocalising and the therapist taking notes. A little contributive amanuensis at most, but nothing to do with computers. This whole *deepmind parable* isn't just *pi r squared* in the freakin' sky, it's totally wrong. And I know exactly what Zpydr would do with that kind of de-anonymised data. They'd keep people hooked in cycles of treatment and sell the data to health insurance companies so they can cherry-pick their customers. They'd use *associates* to market people's deep-psych stories as cheap fiction and erotica. And what happens when their buddies in governments get hold of the data? How long before people are being arrested for what's in their heads coz it'll supposedly stop a crime? And bet your last buck that the bad guys'd get hold of it too. How much would someone pay to have their darkest fantasies kept secret even if they'd never looked at a single bad image in their whole lives? And this is all before our real enemies get stuck in. So yeah, I'm with you all the way. And as for winning a shedload of cash, do I look like I give a dime about money?'

Brio realises he's been staring at them the whole time and now they're staring back at him. He curses them for making him abandon the Hoggit in his moment of need and turns back for the quill, but his hand won't respond and all he can do is plead loudly with Lord Rumbuck to see that the Hoggit's right. The Timeless Tunic is the only thing that can block the hole and save the boat. But now Lord Rumbuck's arguing with *him*, telling him he'd rather perish than take off the Timeless Tunic. Brio's so dumbstruck by Lord Rumbuck's willingness to die rather than lose his identity, that he needs several seconds to register Izzy filming him with her phone and speaking in the voice of a documentary presenter. As he's about to lunge at Izzy, the Hoggit makes an impossible leap and knocks the helm from Lord Rumbuck's hand. In the chaos, Lord Rumbuck loses his footing and goes down with a crash that knocks him out cold. Brio shrieks in the Hoggit's despair but finds himself back in the attic, where Izzy's on her knees nursing her hand and staring in horror at the pieces of smashed phone on the floor.

*

Released at last from the convulsive squall, Brio finds himself crumpled against a pile of junk with Logie squatting and holding him by the forearms, and all he can remember is a bright grey turmoil of water and shouting.

'So relax,' Logie says between his own trembling draws for breath. 'Coz Pippa's giving Izzy a call right now, okay? And Izzy's going to understand that you acted out of character, and that you need to finish this. And Izzy is *not* gonna call the police. *Okay?*'

But Brio knows that Izzy won't sleep till she's posted everything she can think of and made her video go viral. By the time she's done, half the world will be doing pointy thumbs up to agree that he should be locked away in a mental hospital.

'And you know the Hoggit didn't drown,' Logie adds. 'Coz you met him at the castle, right? He was alive and well.'

Mention of the Hoggit jolts Brio out of his distress about Izzy and he shakes off Logie's hands. 'I never said he drowned. He saw land and started steering the boat himself. He fought the storm. The boat surfed into the beach on a wave.'

'Awesome. So you're good to get straight back in?'

'Oh, God.' He grabs Logie's wrist.

'What's up?'

'I can only see the boat—right there on the beach.' He hears his own voice rise with worry. 'It's upside down and I can't see Lord Rumbuck anywhere.'

'Chill, buddy. If the Hoggit can steer them ashore like that, he can do anything.'

Logie's throwaway tone sounds the alarm and Brio sees immediately what Logie's trying to do: slip into his head that it would be better for the Hoggit to lose Lord Rumbuck so he'd be forced to go it alone and become self-reliant. He throws Logie's wrist away and twists back round, but instead of neat writing he finds storm-streaks of purple ink, and on the breeze he picks up the familiar scent of seaweed, exactly like the time he and Father T sat huddled at the helm of the little boat in the frightening wind. The memory takes him straight back to its twin: the day they were trapped by the rising tide as the daylight faded. For the whole night, they had to cling together on the rock while powerful stings of spray tried to sweep them away. And why *didn't* his mum call the police when they failed to come home?

'You okay, buddy? You sure you're only thinking about what the Hoggit saw? I mean, it's him who's seeing all this, right?'

Brio shakes his head clear. 'Yes. It's all him.'

'So what's happening with him?'

Brio has to close his eyes to see clearly. 'He's marooned on a desert island. He's sure it's full of wild beasts.'

'But he's not scared, right?'

'No.'

'Tough little cookie. He knows he can do this.'

Another frisson of irritation earths into Brio's fists. 'It's not because he's a *tough little cookie*. It's because Lord Rumbuck's there after all, lying on his back near the upturned boat.'

Brio knows this isn't what Logie wanted to hear. He tries not to care but he's worried about closing his eyes and writing in case Logie does something.

But *no*. Logie's a friend who hates Zpydr too, who doesn't care a dime about dollars. He'd never try to sneak himself into the Great Plea as some character the Hoggit never told him about.

'So what can you see?' Logie whispers as he slips the quill into Brio's hand.

Brio closes his eyes tightly for a clearer view. 'The Hoggit's tugging on the sodden red tunic to get it out of the jagged hole where he stuffed it during the storm.' He watches heart racing as the Hoggit scurries to wrestle the tunic back over Lord Rumbuck's head. He's as worried as the Hoggit that if Lord Rumbuck comes round without the tunic on he'll think he's just stupid Mr Hare. Then he'll go mad and want to go home to his fake family.

'Write it, buddy.'

But now it's with different feelings that Brio doesn't want to let go of Logie. 'Why can't I just just tell it out loud?'

Logie pats his hand hard enough to be squeezing it to his wrist. 'Buddy, I'd love to hear you tell me this story, but you swore to the Hoggit to write down every word.'

Brio needs a deep breath to let go and another to dip the quill into the inkhorn.

Spitting the sand from his lips, Lord Rumbuck sprang up and confronted the Hoggit. 'What the devil's going on? Why are we not still at sea?'

Clutching his tether anxiously to his pinky-brown belly, the Hoggit explained nervously that they'd been in a storm. 'But you steered us valiantly, my lord, all the way to this beach-head.'

Nose twitching, Lord Rumbuck glowered at the Hoggit. But then he drew himself tall and gave his sword another broad swish. 'You are right, Young Prince. And what an ordeal. The very high-water mark of oceanic fury. How glad I am that you were able to witness my nautical skills and boundless courage.' He sniffed. 'Yet how unfortunate that we were driven ashore by a rogue wave.'

The Hoggit was as relieved to see Lord Rumbuck back to his old self as he was dismayed at the need for his own skill and courage to have been entirely overlooked. But Lord Rumbuck had to be right. How could it possibly be the Young Prince who'd saved the day? That would fly in the face of everything foretold in the Sacred Prophecy. And all that mattered was getting to the Pitch-Dark Port before the Vile Villain's ship departed.

At that moment, a wild cry echoed off the rocks and they

swung round to see bright red eyes and glinting fangs puncture the darkness. A tall figure took shape and began somersaulting down the beach. With a yelp, the Hoggit flipped into a ball and braced for impact. But as the monster was almost upon them, it jammed its heels into a spray of sand and threw open its arms.

'Welcome, welcome! To the wonderful world of Madame Haha! She who is the most famous cruise ship entertainer in the world! Oh, how long she has waited for her audience to arrive!'

From the secret peephole in his defensive ball, the Hoggit stared aghast at the strange creature's twinkling sackcloth waistcoat and wig of long straggly grass. Her huge round eyes seemed to stare into nowhere. She almost wasn't real.

Twitching his sword, Lord Rumbuck attempted to draw himself up to Madame Haha's sleek height. 'We did not come here to be entertained, *madam*, and we shall proceed upon our quest just as soon as we have repaired the Grand Galleon. Now shoo.'

Madame Haha's grin didn't flicker. 'Mister Bunny is not going anywhere.' And before they knew what was happening, Madame Haha had sprinted away, ripped a huge plank out of the battered boat and tossed it into the sea. Beaming triumphantly, she dusted off her hands and straightened her sequined waistcoat. 'Now we are one happy family on our own desert island, thousands of miles from the nearest land. So cry *hurrah*! Because you are Madame Haha's captive audience forever!'

The Hoggit collapsed to his knees in despair. For now there no way they could reach the Vile Villain's vessel in time, and if they didn't rescue the Queen then all was lost.

But *no*. All was *not* lost. Because the Hoggit knew that he'd never met anyone called Madame Haha on his quest. The Dark Lord had sneaked her into his head. And that's why her eyes didn't seem real. Because she *wasn't*.

On finding that he's holding the Magic Quill to Logie's throat, Brio falls back. He can't remember why he's there. 'What did you do?'

'I didn't do anything.'

'Then why am I here?'

'I dunno. Is it because of this Madame Haha?'

He presses again and the feather bends against Logie's neck. 'She's *you*.' He's shocked at what he just said and Logie's expression sharpens.

'No, buddy. She does *not* represent me and don't think that again. But what are your concerns about her? That she's rocked up to schmooze the Hoggit into loving her like a mother so he'll be happy to live on the island forever and forget about his father?'

Brio has to close his eyes to avoid Logie's. 'Stop putting things in my head.'

'I don't have that power.'

'That's right.'

'And if you're not sure whether the Hoggit told you about Madame Haha, why not just check your notes?'

Brio's anger flares. 'You know I've forgotten the Purple Code. But I don't need my notes. I know Madame Haha's real. And she's there for a reason.'

'Which is?'

'None of your business.'

He dumps himself down heavily on the crate, but the Magic Quill feels somehow lighter and softer, and he sees that Madame Haha is putting on her first show for the Hoggit and Lord Rumbuck. He closes his eyes and can't help a laugh as she prances around singing out of tune. She's suddenly kicking the can-can so high she ends up doing a backflip that seems to leave her floating in the air.

'Don't just think it, buddy. Get it all down.'

Madame Haha landed in a squat then slid to her knees to examine the Hoggit. 'What a funny little chap. And why is he curled up like a spiky ball?'

'He is of timid disposition,' Lord Rumbuck growled. 'Which is why he needs *me*. Now, be gone.'

Madame Haha jumped back up and pressed into Lord Rumbuck's face. 'You have frightened him. He needs a mummy who will love him with all her heart.' She flopped back onto all fours. 'Tell Mumsy why you are so scared. She will make your demons fly away forever.'

'I thought you were a monster,' the Hoggit admitted hesitantly from his peephole.

With a theatrical gasp, Madame Haha assured the Hoggit that she was not a monster, she was a mon-*goose*. 'In fact, she is the only one and one and only in the whole world!'

'What nonsense,' Lord Rumbuck huffed. 'There are millions of mongee—mongoo—'

She jabbed her sharp snout back into his face. 'You see? There is no comfortable word for the plural. Which is why there can only be *one*!'

'One too many,' Lord Rumbuck muttered. 'Now come, Young Prince, we shall find timber to mend the Grand Galleon.'

The next thing the Hoggit knew, Madame Haha had landed squarely in their path, her face a grimace of fangs. 'You will stay here,' she snarled. 'And you will watch Madame Haha's show for the rest of your lives.'

The Hoggit shrank back at her terrifying change, while Lord Rumbuck brandished his sword and ordered her aside.

Madame Haha pressed a hand of wounded dismay to her breast. 'You brute! How could you threaten a lady?'

Lord Rumbuck's nose twitched furiously. 'You are no lady.'

'No lady?' She teetered a swoon, but then with a throwaway brush of the hand she added, 'Who cares anyway? As there is only one mongoose in the world, it doesn't matter whether she is a boy or a girl.'

Eyes distending even more exhorbitantly, Lord Rumbuck gave his sword another copious swish. 'If you do not stand aside, madame, I will give you a close shave you will not forget.'

'What, with your silly spoon? And why is it full of holes anyway?' But before Lord Rumbuck could formulate a riposte, Madame Haha's expression of ridicule turned to one of awe and joy. 'That is no spoon! That is a microphone for a great entertainer!' She grabbed it from Lord Rumbuck and backflipped up onto a rock, where she struck a pose. 'I say, I say, I say! Why did the ball roll down the hill?'

Before she could deliver the punchline, it was the Hoggit's turn to erupt in delight.

'My lord, look! She's the Jester! The one who's destined to accompany us on our quest!'

'Oh, yes!' Madame Haha agreed as she leapt nimbly to avoid Lord Rumbuck. 'She is the bester quester-jester in the wester! Ta-daaah! And you don't know why the ball rolled down the hill? Because it couldn't roll *up*hill! Ha-haaaah!'

Lord Rumbuck snorted haughtily. 'This wit-wanton fraudster couldn't make you laugh if you were already laughing.'

Madame Haha's expression turned to ash. 'Can't make you

laugh, huh?' She growled out another joke, which was even worse than the first.

The Hoggit wrung his little hands anxiously. Surely the fabled Jester should be funny. 'You need to hold the Magic Microphone to your mouth,' he bleated. 'Then you'll *really* make people laugh.'

She glowered down at the Hoggit, but then with a sniff she drew the microphone to her face, which broke into an instant beaming grin. 'I say, I say, I say! Did you hear the one about the millipede? You didn't? Then you missed the laugh of your lives, because it's ten times funnier than the one about the centipede! Boom boom!'

The Hoggit was greatly cheered by the improvement and, despite Lord Rumbuck's fury, he couldn't help calling out for more.

'Encore!' Madame Haha agreed then tossed out the question why the hedgehog brushed his spikes every morning.

'I don't know,' warbled the Hoggit. 'Why *did* the hedgehog brush his spikes every morning?'

'To get rid of the split hare! Haa! Boom boom!'

Despite his slight discomfort with the joke, the Hoggit couldn't hold back his giggle, which sent Lord Rumbuck into such a stream of livid gibberish that the Hoggit only laughed harder.

'And why could no one understand the dumb bunny?' Madame Haha squawked. 'Because he was the only one who spoke rabbish! Haaah!'

This time, the Hoggit's laugh was a shriek that sent Lord Rumbuck into frothing fury and Madame Haha into cartwheels of joy. But she dropped to one knee in front of the Hoggit with a serious expression that snuffed his laughter clean out.

'And why did the Hoggit cross the road?' she asked in a dead-level voice.

The Hoggit swallowed hard and had to admit he didn't know.

'Well, obviously,' she said, taking his hand, 'to show the world he was not a chicken.'

'Stand *back*,' Lord Rumbuck exploded. 'He's *my* charge and mine alone, and you are clearly a snake-charmer sent by the Dark Lord.'

Madame Haha bounced back up and cocked her chin. 'And you are a pair of clowns who have never met each other. A double-act for an audience of one. But Madame Haha is glad you are such a terrible navigator, otherwise you would never have delivered to Madame Haha her son from Heaven!'

'Terrible navigator?' Lord Rumbuck fumed. 'I'll have you know that my victories on the battlefield do but stand in the shade of my great feats as an explorer.'

She raised an eyebrow into his face. 'Like what great *feats*?'

'Like ... like I was the first explorer to cross the Uncrossable Desert!'

With another sniff, she retorted that he was probably the second one too, because he only crossed it the first time when he got lost and then had to get back again. 'It's lucky your great feets are so big! Haaa!'

Lord Rumbuck's nose twitched wildly. 'If you are indeed the maritime minstrel of your fanciful claims, why are you not still treading those boards? I bet they made you walk one! Ha!'

Madame Haha pressed narrowed eyes into Lord Rumbuck's face. 'The giants loved Madame Haha with all their hearts.

They gave her fine food and a fluffy bed. And they made her the Twinkly Waistcoat.' She sniffed and stepped back. 'But she does not care about the giants anymore. Because now she has her Prince of Joy, who will laugh and cheer forever!'

'I *will*,' the Hoggit vowed recklessly. 'But you've got to come with us. Because we have to rescue my father from the Tower of Time.' Before he could finish, the Ring stung him badly and he had to clutch his side. 'I mean, we have to rescue the Queen and *then* my father. Because to rescue my father from the Dark Lord, we have to rescue the Queen first. Because … Oh, I don't *know* why. We just do. And it's been laid down in the Sacred Prophecy that you're the Jester who'll protect us from the evil giants by making them laugh.'

Madame Haha's face fell as though she'd seen a ghost. '*Giants?*'

The Hoggit clutched his tether. 'What's the matter? You're the greatest entertainer in the world.'

She stared at the Hoggit, then turned on her heel and stomped away.

'You see?' Lord Rumbuck sneered triumphantly. 'She's never entertained a giant in her life.'

'And you're stuck here with her forever,' Madame Haha called over her shoulder. 'So you'd better make yourselves at home.'

Lord Rumbuck bounded across the beach and whipped the sword out of her hand. She turned, fangs bared, but this time she faced a gyroscopic whirring of shiny steel that sent her tottering backwards, eyes rolling. The Hoggit was about to cry out for them to stop, when he saw that the first light of day was giving shape to the rocky cliffs of the bay. He saw also that a headland reached out into the sea, and on the tip of that high headland rose a tower that looked like … like …

'My lord, look!'

When Lord Rumbuck beheld Hoggit Castle high on its jagged plinth of rocks, his crazed sword-brandishing fizzled. 'You lying demon,' he snarled at Madame Haha. 'You said we were marooned on a desert island.'

Madame Haha shrugged. 'It must have drifted. They do, you know.'

'Oh, thank goodness!' the Hoggit cried. 'We can still make it to the Pitch-Dark Port.' He raced to Madame Haha and threw himself down at her feet. '*Please*. We can't do it without you. And the giants on the ship are going to love you!' And before Madame Haha could ask any questions, the Hoggit unleashed a dazzling description of an imaginary cruise ship which couldn't have been more at odds with the dreadful image of the Vile Villain's Vessel that had formed in his imagination.

'Oh, goodness,' Madame Haha murmured. 'What a dream come true!' She threw open her arms. 'Yes! She *will* come to the minstrel's galleon—the Twinkly Ship! And there she will be the brightest star in the sky!'

Lord Rumbuck grabbed for the Hoggit, who dodged and scuttled round behind Madame Haha. 'I'm not taking one more step without the Jester.'

Madame Haha cocked a snook at Lord Rumbuck. 'So there you are. The Prince of Joy will not go to the Twinkly Ship without the Jester, and the Jester will only go if she has her Magic Microphone.' She thrust out a palm.

'You are deluded,' Lord Rumbuck snorted. 'The Great Sword belongs only in the hands of a Rumbuck. Tell her, Young Prince.'

Thrown into confusion, the Hoggit clutched the tether to his chest. How could Lord Rumbuck defend him against monsters and demons without the Great Sword? But how could Madame Haha protect him from giants without the side-splitting jokes of the Magic Microphone? 'You have to give her the Magic Microphone,' he heard himself tell Lord Rumbuck. 'It's the only way.'

Stumbling back in shock at his own words, the Hoggit cowered from the fury on Lord Rumbuck's face.

'Young Prince,' Lord Rumbuck growled menacingly, 'the Dark Lord has clearly taken control of your mind. And all through that devilish *Ring*. It's high time you took it off.'

Before the Hoggit or Madame Haha could stop him, Lord Rumbuck grabbed the Hoggit and ripped the chain off his belt. Then he tossed the Hoggit aside and clasped the Ring in his fist, extinguishing it from view.

Scrambling back to his feet, and without the Ring's powerful glow at his side, the Hoggit found himself cast into some strange and shadowy new world. 'What's happening? I don't understand. Why don't I care about the Queen anymore?' He drew breath to scream for return of the Ring, but as he was about to let rip he felt himself so unburdened of the Ring's onerous power that all he could do was let out a long sigh of relief and slump to his knees.

From there, Brio lowers his head gently forward onto a pillow of soft seaweed, and the last shape he sees as he slides into sleep is the soothing shadow-puppet of a forefinger and thumb reaching slowly across to snuff the magic candle.

And more dreams for Brio, soft music from dark dungeons opening out into twinkling underground caverns—aromas of spiced cooking too, sapphire blue seas, creamed potato scooped into mouths not yet empty, and his ear rests against the TV-room door, a downy cheek, music softer still and Logie murmuring … murmuring till Pippa asks if he ever drinks anything except camomile tea. *Oh, yeah*, replies a lascivious laugh, *I'll take a Coke, then we can do some Fanta and when you're ready I'll give this can of 7Up a good shake.*

Before Brio can escape the nightmare, he's held to the door by moans that make time stand still. But Pippa's tutting because Logie's become serious again.

'Hun, I thought this was just about you and me.'

'It is, I promise. But what you said earlier, that Father T only came to the island six months before Hannah … I thought he was here since the Flood.'

'What're you saying? That them both coming here was connected? That they knew each other before?'

'Well, who knows?'

'But they came from totally different parts of Ireland.'

'Is that what Hannah told you, just out of the blue, even though she'd never tell you exactly where she was from?'

Another silence, the music starts to pump at the waist. Brio's thoughts are in turmoil but his stomach's so heavy he can't flee.

'Come on,' Pippa says. 'It's nothing like that. People have always come here from Ireland. Hannie just wanted a clean break from bad memories.'

Brio wills himself to *wake up*, get back to the Hoggit. But it's a matter of life or death whether this is dream or reality. And now they're talking about him and Izzy being like brother and sister.

'And that's a bond no one can ever break,' says Logie. 'Coz even though Izzy's got plenty of friends, she knows those sideways glances at her skin colour just as Brio's always known the open scorn of his gentle difference. It's only natural they spent their childhood together in better worlds.'

Brio almost cries out with relief. The nightmare's become a

dream almost good enough to be real. But no sooner is he ready to run than Logie's criticising Father T for loving the Book of Revelation at the end of the Bible.

'I mean, all that stuff about trumpets and horses flying through black clouds, that shit's enough to make anyone feel like they're on crack. It's just not something you ram down the throat of a kid like Brio from the age of five. But the craziest thing is, Father T might even have been on the right track. Coz you know, with people like me and Father T, people trying to help others with great narratives ... well, sometimes to mend a broken heart, we just have to blow your mind. And that's what Bree's godda do now, generate a narrative that's as big as the fiction that was drummed into his head since he was too damn young to know.'

Fleeing back to his attic haven, Brio counts wallpaper seams with chewed-down fingernails and launches up the stepladder in threes. '*Get up*,' he cries at the Hoggit. 'Get the Ring back from Lord Rumbuck. You've got to make him want to save the Queen.'

But he can't see the Hoggit anywhere. He can only feel what the Hoggit feels: that relief at being freed of the Ring's burdens of love and duty. He's overwhelmed by a sadness that draws his gaze down to the rickety floorboards where Mr T'wit lies spreadeagled among his wings, waiting at death's door for news of his long-lost queen. Guilt-stricken at the Hoggit's betrayal of his beloved guardian, Brio needs to wail and rent his garments. Moments later, he's on hands and knees at the stepladder hatchway, listening to Dr Shenoy and Izzy arguing with Logie down in the hall.

'I don't have any goddam masters at Zpydr,' Logie shouts. 'And how d'you know your computer didn't just crash coz you wouldn't spring for an update?'

'There was nothing wrong with Dad's computer,' Izzy retorts furiously. 'And I've been locked out of my social media accounts. Plus all my posts have been deleted and half my apps won't work.'

'Then call the sheriff,' Logie shouts back. 'And stop telling the world that Zpydr's brainwashing vulnerable teenagers and bribing senior government officials.'

Brio frantically heaves up the stepladder, and as he ties the cord he hears Dr Shenoy calling from beneath the hatch, telling him he's very sick and must be in the Northview. Before Brio can shout back, Izzy's trying to reassure him that Darcy's doing really well at the Northview and she'll come visit them both every day. It's Pippa's voice too, saying how they're all on the same side, calling his name and telling him to lower the stepladder.

But Brio can't shout back anymore because the word Northview has smashed everything and now he's in the cell next to Darcy's and Darcy's tapping Morse messages on the wall. *Dot dot dash it all I'm so sorry for everything I did. I'll never call you Penguin Boy again. Dash dash dot I swear I'll do everything I can to take down the video but it's really a matter for Tabo Forzac.*

Brio has to twist a fistful of fringe to rid his thoughts of Darcy and those coaxing nurses in stark violet. Back at his makeshift table, he presses the nib hard into the sand in search for the Ring of Love. But without the Ring, there *is* no love, there's only people you thought were friends telling the world you're being brainwashed by Zpydr because you're mad and want to be a girl, only social services trying to put you into care homes, and social media tycoons controlling your every thought and action, and doctors forcing you into psychiatric wings because you're fated in your genes and there's no cure and no hope. And that's why none of them is willing to carry the Ring of Love. Because if it really did contain all the love in the world, it would shine like every magic ring since the Ring of Gyges. The so-called Ring of Love is just one of those clips of cheap metal they pierce into the snout of piggy-wigs to stop them rooting for food that's been forbidden to piggies.

With all doubt swept away, and in thrall to the same invisible force that drives a surge of rhyme and rhythm in his guts, Brio feels himself lifted to his feet. 'Cry branches!' he hollers at the Hoggit and throws his hands in the air. 'Cry branches and driftwood and kindling spark, and love-laden timbers from old pea-green ark! Let's build from those timbers that forged love back yore, a pyre built to bake it and forge it once more!'

But now, as demons bang on the hatch from below, it's time to prove he can be calm and methodical, can master his wildly trembling hands, can help Madame Haha magic up a tiny flame to light the pyre, a flame like a magic candle … can hold the Hoggit's hand as he feeds a piece of paper to the flame. *Whoosh*, up it goes, he quickly feeds in another piece, and another—more and more, like pages of old newspaper and phonebooks covered in meaningless scrawl. 'More!' he cries as the flames take hold. 'Bring timber too!'

On hands and knees under the rafters, he frantically helps Lord Rumbuck and Madame Haha drag timbers from Mr T'wit's old boat. 'More!' he cries again as hands batter the hatch. And when he can no longer get near the fire, he shouts at the Hoggit to cast in the Ring. 'Into the furnace of love in which it was forged!'

And the last thing Brio remembers is sliding like a drawer into the back of an ambulance, glimpsing flames and smoke and the horrified faces of neighbours and bystanders, and kids filming it all on their sticker-covered phones so that Tabo Forzac can plaster it all over the world.

~ PART FOUR ~

MAKING LIGHT

Each of us must create a persona to navigate us through a life that is complicated and brutally competitive, and virtually all functional mental illness stems from a person's attempt to create a persona that's outside the range of identities that can be supported by their genetic signature. It follows that the best cure for all functional mental illness is to understand and manage one's own authentic identity. If identity can be authored then, with a little help, there are few limits on the extent to which someone can re-author themselves and their situation. However, any practitioner working with a patient who is genetically predisposed to subtypes of what were once termed 'melancholy' must be doubly assiduous, because that patient's spectrum of supportable identities will be significantly narrower. Also, as with all talking therapies, we must acknowledge that the identity re-authoring process is susceptible to every type of practitioner bias. In this regard, my expectation is that at some point not too far hence we'll be able to remove this factor by deploying sophisticated computers that both assess a patient's psychological profile and identify the appropriate guided narratives to be applied through mid- to deep-level hypnosis.

Professor Miri D. Terin, San Batista State University
The Future of Creativity Based Psychotherapeutic Intervention, 1987

9

BRIO DIMLY REGISTERS A SLOW DABBING of cool relief on his forehead, but when it breaks through as pain and he strains to shake off the hand, he finds his stomach muscles dead and can't even turn his head. It's all just light green walls and white ceiling tiles and later—maybe another day—the animated conversation of the nurses about a terrible medical condition strikes him through with fear of dying before he's found the Ring of Love. He calls for help, but the effort cracks his lips and no one's there, no one cares, until the shock of hearing Ms Whittle's voice wakes him into a stark daylight made more penetrating by the squeak of a canteen trolley.

With dismay, he comprehends that Ms Whittle really is there, it wasn't just a nightmare, and it was real the time before as well, and all the other times she sat in silent vigil at his bedside, reading her big book with ponderous rustles of the page, waiting for another nurse to come in so she could tell them how the divine power of the mind is better than any of their toxic medications. But closing his eyes to make Ms Whittle go away only provokes a squeeze on his upper arm that makes him wince.

'Ooh, I'm sorry, dear.' She removes her hand. 'But this Ring of Love you've been referencing in your sleep, is it something you'd like to discuss? Because you know, I'm not just your closest friend, dear, I'm a fully trained youth counsellor. You can talk to me about absolutely anything.'

He wants to hate her for telling everyone their most private things, but he's too worried about the fire and the Ring, and who else can he talk to?

Cracking open an eye, he hazily registers Ms Whittle's bright home-made dungarees and bicycle helmet with built-in headlamp. With a feeble groan he sinks back into fretting about whether the fire on the beach was real, and what happened to the Ring. And surely the fire in the attic was just a nightmare too.

Ms Whittle rests a feather-like hand on his upper arm. 'Dear, I know how special all those things were to you, the stories you put in their lovely shoeboxes, your lovely old teddy bear, that sweet painting of the golden-robed rider. But my dear friend Tania is quite right. Their loss is a sacred blessing in disguise. Because you're liberated from the bonds of childhood. And what perfect timing, dear, just as you're almost sixteen.'

Knowing now that the fire was real, Brio spirals into tears of grief about Pippa's home and losing his only belongings in the world. But the tears won't come out because he can't feel his head, can't feel his hands either. 'The Ring,' he murmurs. 'They can't go on without the Ring … I have to get back to the beach and stop the fire …' And he's still trying to sob it out when another nurse arrives to help with the tubes and the shape of the bed and angle of the sheets and …

Next morning, Brio has no memory of the night just passed and doesn't resist when two new nurses raise the bed into a half-sitting position. He registers that his bandaged hands make him an Egyptian mummy, and Ms Whittle's already there, sitting at his bedside as though she's been guarding him all night. Nor is it another sloppy breakfast that comes through the door to be spoon-fed and spilled. It's Mrs Charis of social services, escorted by a doctor whose dress reminds Brio of a nice lady at church. She even has the same smile.

Ms Whittle moves swiftly to sit on the bed and clutches his ankle through the bedding as though they might try to take him away. And that's what they *are* going to do: lock him up in the cell next to Darcy's, brainwash him to believe that he's gay and his dad's dead. But his legs are too numb to run, and when the doctor asks how he's feeling he shuts her down, because she's just feigning niceness, she works for the government, for the ones who want to stop him blowing the whistle on their cover-up of the bungled mission.

'Is the pain under control a bit better?'

Under your *control*, Brio wants to mutter. *Like everything*. He sinks back into his pillow and realises that the doctor isn't involved in the cover-up at all. She's one of the government people who just want Zpydr to get their approval. She's there to sweet-talk him into their clutches.

'You see, the thing is,' says the doctor, 'your physical injuries are healing well, but we have to make a recommendation about where you go from here. I mean, obviously you're not going to be continuing on this CHANT pilot program, and—'

'I wasn't on a *programme*.' He curses the weakness of his voice. 'I was with Logie as a friend.'

'No, dear,' Ms Whittle says sharply. 'That man is *not* your friend. And it's quite right he's not allowed near you anymore.'

Before Brio can understand her meaning, the doctor says, 'Brio, we know you had an unsatisfactory experience with the visiting psychiatrist from London, but Dr Silash at the Northview Wing is a lovely lady. I'm sure you'd really like her.'

'There's nothing wrong with me. It's just my hands.' But Darcy's back into his head, coaxing him through the wall between their cells to come and sit on his bed and try his lipstick and—

'... the Northview's such a caring environment. And you'll be able to do your writing in peace, with food in exactly the way you like. What d'you think?'

She smiles again, but he realises that the Northview will be riddled with Zpydr people too, hiding in plain sight in their fake violet uniforms. He tries to make a break for the open door but hands from nowhere grip his arms and legs and the bed hums urgently back down. He fights on till the blankets become a tangle of leg irons and gags and the air goes hazy with warm snow and …

When Brio drifts back into semi-consciousness, he's being chased around another warped multi-storey car park by the same white van, still shouting that he'll never go into the Northview because he's going to Pippa's, and her house is exactly as it was before, only more like Bluebells.

Waking more fully, he half remembers the bickering of voices, loudest of them all Ms Whittle telling people he should never have been living with Pippa in the first place, because Pippa's an appalling mother figure who has no backbone at all. When he hears also that Pippa's had to go into the psychiatric emergency ward he crumbles into silent, open-mouthed sobbing grief and guilt, and this time he can't wait for them to get the tube into the back of his hand and …

Knowing that there really are people in the room now, Brio tells them he's going to stay at Izzy's, because the Shenoys are in the same church and—

'Don't be silly, dear. The Shenoys would never let you stay. They're far too busy.'

'Then I'll stay with someone else from church,' he moans, but he knows that no one at church ever really cared about him either. When his mum died, they all made a big show then found excuses—guests staying, decorators in, house on the market. He can't be with Logie either, because Loki's the fire god who brings havoc to anyone who believes their own lies, and Logie *was* working for Zpydr. He was only pretending not to want fame and money. And when in his mind he sees Logie trying to beat back the flames to reach the burning table, panic breaks through and he cries out for his notes, for Teddy and his shoeboxes too, for the painting by his dad. He fights the rubbery hands again, but his strength dissipates quickly into the tangle of tubes and that relentless smell of powder and sanitiser …

Though Brio knows his sleep was unnaturally long, he feels calmer now. His thoughts are clearer too, even as they flit away into the warm room before he's had time to count the ceiling lights again. He strains to make sure Ms Whittle's in her chair as normal, but it's empty and he feels a pang of worry. For the first time, he even misses the cocktail of strange smells that she's become.

'How are you today, Brio?'

He scrabbles to sit upright but the bed's already raising him.

'It's all right,' the doctor says quickly. 'You're not going to the Northview.'

'Where am I going? Where's Ms Whittle?'

He sees Mrs Charis there too, and a strong-arm assistant from the care home, and someone else is turning the pages of a form for the doctor to sign in a hundred places. He's about to fight again when Ms Whittle sweeps into the room in a bizarre two-piece suit that seems to have been made from frayed curtains.

'Sorry I'm late,' she pants, dumping her backpack down on a chair. 'That ridiculous bus driver had some very misguided notions about reincarnation.' She draws a deep breath and straightens her jacket. 'But thank you,' she says to Mrs Charis. 'I received your letter.'

10

BRIO WALKS FAST WITH MS WHITTLE across the crowded hospital lobby. He knows he's not just Penguin Boy on the front page of the free newspaper anymore, he's the kid who Izzy told the whole world about: the mad one who secretly wants to be a girl and thinks his dad's some secret hero when actually he just killed himself, the one Zpydr want to brainwash so they can prove their online brain-rubbish works. And everyone'll think he really is mad, because he burned down the home of his foster mum, the lovely lady who owns Costume Castle. And they all *want* him to be brainwashed, so Zpydr can give them their cheap mental health treatment. '*Stop staring at me.*'

The moment the doors swish closed behind them, Brio feels the chill morning air on his cheeks like vinegar on a cut. In the back row of the stale-smelling seven-seat taxi, he shields his face from the taxi driver's view in the mirror. And he doesn't know which he hates more, Ms Whittle's heady smell or the dangling air-freshener and stink of stale cigarettes.

Ms Whittle's spindly fingers sneak across the seat to pat his mummified scoop of a bandaged hand. 'Isn't this exciting, dear? And during our healthy breaks from writing together, we'll take long walks along the cliffs. Before we know it, high summer will be here and we can swim in the sea, and go birdwatching, and—'

Brio shakes off her hand. He needs to fret alone about his notes and precious written pages. It's too good to be true that Logie simply saved them and gave everything to Ms Whittle. He's surely done something to them, changed them, and if the Hoggit really did destroy the Ring and go to the Tower of Time without saving the Queen first, it wouldn't have been the Dark Lord who cast the Memory Curse, it would have been the Ring itself. Then the Hoggit would've been cursed like Mr T'wit warned and could never have found out whether his father was there in the High Dungeon. He'd *never* find his father.

The second Ms Whittle's key turns in the wobbly lock of her front door, Brio barges past and leaves her tutting about manners. The sight and smells of Ms Whittle's home stops him dead in the hallway. Because instead of the half-drawn curtains that used to maintain a calming gloom, the corridor is bathed in bright daylight from open doors, through which he can see that the prayer books and religious pictures have been replaced by strange statuettes and tapestries and a poster for some kind of weird stage production. On one wall, he sees a surreal Garden of Eden with Adam and Eve juggling mixed fruit and vegetables while naked demi-people wander around behind them reading magazines, and a coiled pink snake rises into the unnaturally blue sky. Worst of all is a large figurine of Jesus in a bright orange robe sitting cross-legged with lots of arms.

'Our Lord as the Durga,' Ms Whittle explains. 'And that photograph there is my dear friend Tania.' She gestures with a loving smile at the picture of an ageless lady whose unnaturally long silver-blonde hair drapes down with a long bead necklace over an Indian dress. To Brio, it looks like a costume from Pippa's shop, and why is this Tania sitting cross-legged in a smoky temple courtyard using one thorn to remove another from her bleeding big toe?

'I know, dear. Isn't it an inspiring image?'

He registers a scroll painting of a man who's half woman—no, a woman who's half man, or maybe it's—

'The union of male and female, dear. For this is the true Grail, the final degendering of God. And that's the key to it all. Because once we've degendered God, no one will want to dress in a male or female way anymore. And no one will feel pressured to follow all those obsolete ideas about gender roles.' She beams and takes his hand. 'Come on, I've baked some fruitcake too. Though of course, I have your eating list.'

Brio shakes off her hand again. 'Your house is all wrong. Why can't you just be Sister Jane?'

'No, dear! I'm my true self now, and you can be too! You just need to understand that beliefs of the heart are all one and the same. That the supreme divinity Brahman is just another name for God or Yahweh or Zeus. That all the other Hindu deities are just like angels and junior Greek gods. And Tania's right, Buddhist impermanence is exactly the same as our Kingdom of God, and Christian resurrection is one of the glories of Buddhism! And you can pray to the Christian God to become a Bodhisattva because that's the same as a saint! And to find peace about poor Pippa, you simply have to channel the burning house story in the *Lotus Sutra* of the *Ramayana*! And what a splendid way to—'

Just as Brio's about to lose control, Ms Whittle stops abruptly and squints at a half-closed door. His confused anger turns to worry.

'What's wrong?'

She nudges open the ominous door, which reveals an exercise bike decorated with stickers of flowers and stars, behind which stands a bookcase overloaded with miniature Tiffany lamps.

Determined to be brave, Brio elbows into the room and goes to the window. He can't find a gap in the frilly net curtains but through the hazy veil he can see a white van parked right opposite. His stomach tightens and his heart starts to beat in his throat. 'It's the government. And Zpydr.'

Ms Whittle turns her back on the net curtains. 'Dear, I've been given full custody. There really is nothing to worry about. Now, come.'

Passing through the hall as he flees for the stairs, Brio glimpses the small kitchen, which is cluttered with glass jars and ancient baking utensils and a gadget for squeezing juice that obviously hasn't been cleaned for weeks. The smells of composting peel and freshly baked fruitcake follow him up and into the room he knows will be his. He's bewildered to see that Ms Whittle has set up his table like a sacred altar, eccentric arrangements of stones and crystals at each corner, a chair draped with Indian material to match the bedspread. She's framed some of his junior school artwork too, and snippets of his poetry, and the newspaper article about him and Izzy winning the national story prize for the second time.

Evidently sensing his incredulous anger, Ms Whittle hurriedly explains that she wants the room to be his true home. 'Because in my heart, you've been here all your life. And if you get writer's block—we all get that, dear—the best cure is to find inspiration and confidence from all the wonderful things you've done before.'

Before he can tell her to take it all down, she's reciting with eyes closed, 'The woodmangercross of quantum lifedeath, the croissant free of fat. The heavenhell of criss-crossed lifedebts, His sun without a hat.'

Brio snaps at her to stop, but she's on a roll. 'It's pouring with rain, I'm roaring in pain, we're making a storm in each other's teacups. For the spark thank the sparkmaker, 'gain and again, for the ark thank the ferryperson, two by two! Oh, Brio, dear, you really are so gifted!'

He's about to demand his written pages and notes when he realises that she's changed some of the words. 'It was spark*master*, and ferry*man*. You can't just *do that*.'

'Well, yes, dear, and we really do need to talk about gender, but first of all—'

'You said you wouldn't do stuff like that. Just get my *papers*.'

She stares at him as though ready to refuse, but goes quickly to a small cupboard from which she takes a stack of charred pages as though withdrawing the Blessed Sacrament from the altar tabernacle. Instead of placing them down on the table, though, she hugs them tightly to her breast. 'Before we start, dear, I thought we should talk through a few issues that arise when we're writing about sensitive subject matter.'

Brio's wild grab with bandaged hands sends the pages flying, but before he can rake frantically for the one he needs, he sees she's marked it all like schoolwork. 'What have you *done*?'

Ms Whittle drops to her knees in front of him, hands outstretched. 'I've just made loving comments, dear, in all the colours of the rainbow. Positive and inclusive.' She presses a hand to her chest. 'The last thing I'd do is slash your beautiful book and make it bleed red ink. Oh, what a fool I was, and for so many years! All those poor children I led astray.'

Brio pincers the stack of paper together and dumps it down on the table, where he desperately tries to find the last page he wrote. Realising that none of his original notes are there, he turns on Ms Whittle, who hurriedly assures him that this is all Mrs Charis gave her.

'You're lying. I saw Logie get them.'

But how could he possibly have seen what Logie did or didn't do?

'Brio, dear, this book really is causing you an awful lot of heartache. Are you sure you wouldn't like to write something new?'

Brio's thump on the table makes Ms Whittle jolt and clasp a hand to her breast.

'Why don't you care what happened?' he says angrily. 'If they've destroyed the Ring of Love, he'll never find his father. Then he'll kill himself.'

Ms Whittle's expression turns to horror and she grabs for his arm. 'No, dear. He'd never do such a thing. And you must never think like that again. Promise me.'

He's about to tell her to leave him alone when he sees that she hasn't only messed around with his grammar, she's crossed out all the punctuation and capital letters to make it one long sentence. 'Why did you do this? How's God ever going to read it now?'

'Oh, this is very important, dear. I'm glad you asked. Because, you see, punctuation can be abused, as it were, to subconsciously change the meaning of words. To gaslight innocent people into believing things they don't want to believe. It's your duty as a budding author to promote diversity of interpretation through the deconstruction of punctuation, to purge your writing of all the patriarchal walls that punctuation can erect. And God will understand it even better when it's written like this. Because it'll be like the great scrolls written by monks in days of old, one long beautiful ream of *scriptio continua*!'

Even through his rage, Brio sees more. 'Why have you crossed out all those words—*toss* and *jerk*—and what's wrong with *tug* and *grunt*?'

Her eyes light up again. 'Well, you see, words can come to have different meanings. They can become dangerous.'

'How can *toss* be dangerous?'

'Oh, dear, it's so hard to explain. It's just that your book may be read by younger children. And words like this can lead to thoughts and feelings that need to be explained—by those people with power over you. People who might want to …' She has to catch her breath. 'Oh, dear, I'm not doing this very well.'

He lets out a cry of exasperation. 'You haven't changed at all. Just leave me alone.'

Ms Whittle clings to the table like a protester about to be dragged away by police. 'Dear, you can't hold the pen. You need me to be your scribe.'

He's hardly clutched his head when it pops straight back out. 'Get me a candle. Like the one in church at Easter.'

She glances around. 'Isn't there enough light already, dear? And we can always switch on the bedside lamp.'

'I need it to get into the Groove—capital G. Just *get one.*'

Ms Whittle stares at him with a puzzled expression that breaks into sudden recognition. 'Ah! So that's how he does it.'

'He doesn't do *anything.* And get me some cake too.'

Closing his eyes, Brio tries to imagine that the new quill in Ms Whittle's hand is something other than a faded pink plume from an old feather duster sticky-taped to a purple biro. He grits his teeth and begins Logie's magic breathing ... slowly in, slowly out, trying to relax but desperate to remember whether the Ring survived the fire and— '*Stop doing that.*'

'Doing what, dear?'

'Copying my breathing.'

'Was I? I suppose I must have been getting into the Groove too.'

'You *weren't.*' But before Brio can focus back on the flame of the battery-powered Christmas candle, he finds himself staring at a row of small, framed sketches on the narrow bookshelf. Even after a double-take the sketches remain exactly what he first thought: garishly coloured caricatures of Lord Rumbuck and the Hoggit, and Mr T'wit and Madame Haha, and each one's cocooned by a big sparkly upside-down question mark like a fish hook.

Ms Whittle looks proudly at her sketches. 'Now, the point there, dear, is that when we write characters we create guides, not only for ourselves but for our readers too. As great authors, we have a responsibility to vet and interrogate our characters. We must cast out the old and bring in the new.'

Unable to speak for disbelieving anger, Brio has no way to stem Ms Whittle's impassioned disquisition on Lord Rumbuck's failings as a father figure.

'I mean, he may be all tough and full of puff but can he actually provide the kind of care that every child needs? Does he listen attentively? Does he verbalise his emotions and act demonstratively? Does he show interest in his child's needs? Because you see, a father doesn't have to be the gendered work of fiction you were led to believe. A father can be a father in all sorts of ways. In fact, he could be a father by being more like a mother! Just like a mother could be someone you—'

Brio's bandaged fist comes down hard again. 'Lord Rumbuck is not his *father*. He's taking him to *rescue* his father.'

But as Brio stares distractedly at Ms Whittle's straggly beaded dreadlocks and absurd red glasses, he can't help remembering how poorly Lord Rumbuck's been treating the Hoggit, talking over him and making him feel small, belittling his safety harness and scorning his spikes, dismissing his heroic action in the storm. And what about all those times he held him by the tether just to control him?

Ms Whittle releases her sucked-in lips. 'But this is the whole point, dear, the bond between father and son doesn't have to be biological. It doesn't need to be based on anything but love. And a mother doesn't have to be related by blood either. She could be an old friend like me, the grandma you never had. I mean, the Hoggit's grandma might seem like a wonderful woman, but didn't she overprotect the poor little chap and turn him into an eternal child? And—'

Overwhelmed by Ms Whittle's passionate torrent, Brio can only block his ears with cupped mittens. But his resistance only incites her to new heights of incitement, from where she begs him to understand that reconciling himself with the mother figure is the key to finding peace about his father too, and that reconciling with the right mother figure is as good as finding his father. 'And that's precisely why saving the Queen with the Ring of Love is so very important!'

Brio's about to shout her down when he's struck dumb by a fuzzy cognition that Ms Whittle either said something evil or just revealed a truth that's turned her back into Sister Jane. He tries frantically to replay her words but she's already off again, telling him he's only fixated on finding his father because he's been brought up to believe in a male saviour figure, and the reason he struggles to distinguish fantasy from reality is that he was indoctrinated to believe the Bible as literal fact, that women are dangerous and love only comes from a male Jesus who's the son of a male God. 'But just like Julian of Norwich said—bless her soul—Jesus is in fact our true *mother*! Because he—I mean, they—can bring us into a life without death! And the true earthly love of Jesus actually came from poor Mary herself, even though she was only fourteen. The wretched creature was so buffeted around on a sea of brute males, so vulnerable to the advances of men … well, of course she ended up getting pregnant with—'

'*Shut up*,' Brio moans. 'You're mad.' But he's so mesmerised by the racing fluency of her wild zeal, he can't even look away let alone close his ears.

'So Jesus's father wasn't God at all!' Ms Whittle exclaims joyfully. 'He was a Roman soldier, an arch male oppressor! Yes, poor Mary harked from a subordinated people and became just another victim of economic necessity and education deficit. But Joseph forgave her! Yes, even though he knew he'd be ridiculed and despised—maybe even stoned to death—he forgave her. Oh, what a great example of a man and a father! And what love! And Jesus was born of that love! And God is love! That's why Jesus truly is the Son of God!'

She clutches his forearm, her eyes suddenly wider than Brio's ever seen them. 'But you *can* find love from a mother, dear. It just has to be the right mother figure. I mean, Madame Haha isn't a mother figure at all. She's not even female. She's a crude cross-dresser.' She stops and looks alarmed. 'I mean, there's nothing wrong with being a transvestite. Oh, goodness, I don't mean *transvestite*. That's an awful old word. I mean ... well, never mind, it's a beautiful thing. But the point is that when someone's in a position of power and trust, they can manipulate you to serve their own interests. And you don't even know you're being groomed.' She almost pulls him across the table. 'You're an attractive boy. And Mr Logue knew you were vulnerable. But you must be allowed to explore your own feelings and make your own choices.'

Brio's chair crashes down behind him. 'I'm not gay. And nor's Logie. And Father T wasn't either. And I *don't* want to be a girl.'

Ms Whittle's on her feet too, eyes alight and hands reaching. 'It's all right, dear! You can be whatever you are!'

'It's *not* all right. It's terrible.'

'No, dear! It's nature. And this is a safe space where you can let your feelings out at last!'

'I don't have *anything* to let out,' Brio half sobs. 'Why can't you just let me *write*?'

'But this is exactly what you have to write, dear—that it's not only humans and penguins who feel this kind of love, it's God's other creatures too. Bats and birds, and sheep and lions. Even hedgehogs. Yes, ten per cent of female hedgehogs are lesbian! That's one in ten of those dear little prickly souls! I mean, imagine if Izzy herself were to—'

'Shut *up*. *Get out*.' He starts to pummel his own head with padded fists.

'Yes, my love! Vent your innermost emotions in this safe space! Exorcise yourself of all the wrongness you were taught! Because love is the answer to everything! And love doesn't know a thing about sex!'

Just as Brio's about to bulldoze Ms Whittle out of the room, he's struck by a breathing fit and has to slump back onto his seat. In a flash, Ms Whittle's down on her knees clutching his swaddled hand to her sparrow-like breast.

'You're so confused by what Father T did. That poor, dear man, he just wanted to be a father to you, but in his rarefied world of love and ideas he just didn't understand that you weren't old enough to—'

'*He didn't touch me,*' Brio cries between one great heave of breath and the next.

'You've buried it so deeply, my boy. But the cure is forgiveness. And you must find it in your heart to forgive poor Bella too. Oh, if only you can let He who made the tiger make thee, you'll be forever at peace with your own dear father.'

Brio can't even manage sound, and the harder he fights to wipe it all from his mind, the more he's paralysed by the sheer sense memory of sheltering under the blanket with Father T in the wind and rain. Oh, God, what if Father T *was* gay, even though he loved Bella? Was that why God had struck him down, for just having those thoughts? And even if Father T didn't touch him, did he still make him gay by just loving him in a gay way in his head? Was it even possible to be gay in your heart but not in any other way? And if Father T was gay, how could he have loved anyone? Because his mum was right, gay people could never love, because you can't love anyone if you're sick in the head.

As though breaking the surface a split second before drowning, Brio springs up and swipes the framed sketches into the wall.

'Yes, dear!' She swings to add an inept kick at the nearest broken frame. 'You have slain the letter that killeth and cast down the idols of your former life! Now you're ready to write anew!'

'Just *get out*,' he cries again, '*Out*, get out.' But it needs only one heaving gasp and a glance at his clubbed writing-hand to remind him that he's pathetically helpless without her. And even as he fights to get his breathing under control, Ms Whittle calmly perches herself back on her chair at the end of the table and takes up the plumed biro.

'There, dear,' she says as Brio pants out the end of his fit, 'I'm ready to be your loyal scribe. And how fitting it is that you yourself will be spared the task of writing down your inspired revelation. For not one of our great prophets ever wrote their own material.'

Seeing no other choice, Brio snatches up his toppled chair and sits back down. 'Just write what I say. And write it in proper Gigantish, with punctuation and capital letters. And if I say *jerk* or *toss*, you've got to write them exactly like that. Because there's nothing wrong with them except in *your* head.'

Taking one last breath to steady himself, Brio closes his eyes to summon up the scene on the beach. With an ease that takes him aback, he finds himself looking down at the burnt-out ashes of the great pyre. His spirits lift and he scans for a trace of the Ring's dull metal. But even as he lets his own foot nudge at the ash and nuggets of charcoal, he begins to realise that the Ring's nowhere to be seen. He realises that the Ring of Love really could have melted to nothing. 'Oh, God,' he cries. 'Now he'll never find his father.'

Ms Whittle takes firm hold of his arm. 'Now don't get into another state, dear. I'm sure that if God wants the Hoggit to be at one with his poor father, the Ring of Love won't have melted.'

'But how do I *know* it idn't melt?'

'Well, that's the whole point, dear. Sometimes you just have to have faith.'

He throws off her hand. 'It's just about physics. What

temperature does gold melt at?' In his own scheme of things, teachers know about everything.

'Dear, please. That isn't—'

'Do you know or don't you?' But before she can reply, he sees the eay through. 'Wait! I know how to find out whether the Ring survived!'

'Dear—'

'And if the Ring's there, it means I'll find my dad for sure.' And a moment later, he's leaping down the stairs with Ms Whittle calling frantically from behind.

11

WHEN BRIO FINALLY WITNESSES THE REALITY of Pippa's burnt-out home—the dirty white hoardings, the brick shell with skeletal roof timbers that look like a giant TV aerial against the fading sky—he slumps to his knees on the threadbare grass verge. It's only the clatter of bicycle gears that startles him out of his shock and he turns to see Ms Whittle arriving in such a state of ferment, that in dismounting her mountain bike she virtually hurls it down the street.

Ignoring her calls to *wait* and *come home before someone calls the police*, he charges the plywood door in the hoardings and finds himself inside an apocalypse of charcoaled timbers and broken plates and not a single thing he recognises. And what if people have already combed the debris for anything of value? Kids looting. The police and government agents.

Hardly aware of the pain in his hands, and now his shoulder too, Brio throws aside the twisted remains of Pippa's office chair and kicks a blackened saucepan, all the while shouting at Ms Whittle to *do something useful* and help him find the ring. As he's about to kick down the implausibly free-standing door frame of the TV-room, he stops dead and his mouth falls open.

'Good gracious,' Ms Whittle says, staring down at the little crater in the ash. 'There actually is a ring.'

Brio can scarcely believe it himself and has to blink hard to make sure it's not a figment of their shared imagination. The relief comes in a rush and he's back with the Hoggit on the beach more vividly than ever. 'Oh, thank God! He can still find his father.'

'Well, let's get it home, dear.' She bends down but Brio grabs her arm.

'Only the true Ring-Bearer can pick it up, and they've got to *want* to, otherwise it'll make them go mad. And time's ticking. The Vile Villain's Vessel leaves at dawn.'

'Well, yes, of course, dear.' She glances nervously up and down the street. 'Though surely it's the Hoggit who'll carry the Ring.'

Brio shrinks back. 'The Hoggit's still frightened of its power. And he doesn't understand why he has to save the Queen to find his father.' He needs Ms Whittle to repeat the evil-or-perfect thing she said before.

'Dear, do pick it up. We must get away from here.'

He drops drops down to pick up the ring but his mummified hands only plough it around in the ash and he starts to get angry.

'It's all right, dear, I can help.'

But again he holds her back. 'You mustn't touch it. You're not the Ring-Bearer.'

She looks dismayed. 'Don't you trust my purity of heart?'

'Just get something to pick it up with. Then put it on the Ring-Chain.'

After a brief scouring around their ankles, Ms Whittle produces a corkscrew and teases up the ring. As she fumbles the clasp of his rosary, their gaze meets but bounces off. He's thrown by a desire to hug her and has to drive the thought away. 'Hurry up.'

Back out on Pippa's charred driveway, they see neighbours looking out from windows and open front doors. Two houses down, Mr Janewski is hurrying back inside with the clear intent of calling the police. Ms Whittle heaves up the deranged mountain bike and wrestles with its tangled cables till the front wheel's pointing the right way. 'Come on, dear. I'll sit on the rack and you pedal.'

Brio's heart falls. He hasn't ridden since his mum sold his bike to protect him from falling off again. He's still steeling himself when a white van turns into the road. They stare in frozen alarm as it cruises slowly past, its tinted glass obscuring the occupants. But Brio still can't mount the bike. 'It's not just who bears the *Ring* that matters, they can't leave the beach till they've decided whether Madame Haha should carry the Great Sword instead of Lord Rumbuck.'

Ms Whittle glances anxiously at the slowly receding van. 'Goodness, dear, can't they decide later?'

'They have to decide *now*. Or they can't go.'

'Well, maybe they flip a coin?'

'Don't be stupid. They don't have *coins*.'

'Well, perhaps a neighbour can lend us one.'

Brio holds Ms Whittle back. 'The Ring of Love itself must decide. So they've got to flip it like a coin, without touching it.'

Ms Whittle's jolted back from her anxious watch on the van. 'Dear, the Hoggit would never have used the Ring of Love in a game of chance. That would be sacrilege, blasphemy. And God doesn't play dice with the universe. Besides, wouldn't the dear Hoggit want to make such an important decision himself?'

Despite the marauding white van and the Hoggit's burning need to get going, Brio finds himself grappling with some glitch at the heart of Ms Whittle's logic. 'You're wrong. Because if God made everything, He must have made chance too. Which means that chance itself is divine and the result of chance must be what God wants. So God *does* play dice with the universe.'

Ms Whittle's mouth falls open and her forehead disappears into the uneven fringe of wispy dreadlocks. 'Good heavens, dear. I must tell Tania about this as soon as we get home.' Her expression becomes serious. 'But how will he use the Ring as a coin?'

Brio glances to make sure that none of the neighbours can hear. 'There's secret writing on the inside. If the writing's the right way up then Lord Rumbuck carries the sword first, and vice versa. Are you watching? The Hoggit's about to toss the Ring.'

'Yes, dear. Toss away.'

'You have to close your eyes.'

With the van gone, Ms Whittle obeys so diligently that her face creases up in a semblance of pain, and in the bright beigey gold behind his own eyelids Brio again returns easily to the scene on the beach, where Madame Haha's carping on because she won the toss and Lord Rumbuck's furious. But the die's cast and Brio feels a buzz of energy. 'It's all happening. I have to write.'

But he realises that if they go back to Ms Whittle's, the police might be waiting, and now he knows for sure that the white van's from Zpydr or the government. And obviously someone *has* been in Ms Whittle's house, so it's bugged and full of hidden cameras. Expecting resistance from Ms Whittle, he's taken aback by her swift suggestion that they go to stay with Tania till the dust has settled. She even has his writing things in her small backpack.

At that moment, the white van reappears, and with Ms Whittle perched precariously on the bike's flimsy pannier rack they only just reach the footpath turn-off before the van has the chance to cut them off.

As soon as they're sure that no one's following, Brio slows to catch his breath and Ms Whittle relaxes her painful grip on his sides. 'Dear, the quickest way to Tania's is through the recreation ground, so if—'

'We're not going to Tania's house.'

Ms Whittle's grip tightens again. 'But where else can we go? It'll be dark soon.'

'Just stop worrying and trust me.'

They ride along the alley in a tense, breathless silence broken only by Ms Whittle's little cries of alarm as the narrow tyres skid on loose gravel and jolt in potholes. Brio can't help worrying about the new kind of pain under his tatty bandages, and whether the white van's going to be waiting in ambush when they're eventually forced to go back onto the roads.

'Why don't you tell me what's happening, dear—on the beach? We can keep the story moving as we go.'

'Because I need my breath,' Brio replies irritably. 'And it's not a *story*.' But when he sees the Hoggit and Madame Haha on a narrow path over the headland, he wants Ms Whittle to know every last detail.

'And where's Lord Rumbuck, dear?'

'He's depressed because doesn't have his sword anymore. So he's traipsing along behind them like his feet are made of lead.'

'And does the Hoggit—'

'Just listen and I'll tell you. The path up the headland goes through dense gorse bushes and it's pitch-dark now. And even with the Ring next to his heart, the Hoggit's getting scared. As they climb the steep headland, he has to gasp for every breath.'

Having to catch his own, Brio hardly registers that he too has clasped the ring at his neck. 'Madame Haha's on top of the world because she's going to the Twinkly Ship, but her exuberance doesn't make the Hoggit less scared. In fact, the sight of Lord Rumbuck in such a deflated state has snuffed his courage completely.'

'I feel his fear,' Ms Whittle says over Brio's shoulder. 'I feel yours too. Such a beautiful thing.'

Something about Ms Whittle's strange comment plunges Brio back into the worry that's mushroomed since he last tried to crush it down. What if he *is* gay but just doesn't realise? What if his desire to be a girl is so secret, he doesn't even know it himself? Why else would everyone be pushing him to acknowledge it, unless they knew something he didn't? Pedalling as though to break through some unseen barrier, he begs God to tell him what he really wants inside. And God responds by telling him to think the craziest gay thoughts he can, to see if he likes them, and to think about being a girl too. But he doesn't know how to have thoughts like that. He knows only how to have accidents in half-sleep, exactly as his mum told him that night she came into his bedroom to hear his anguished confession. After his tears were as spent as his disturbing discharge, she told him that in future those thoughts had to happen in *full* sleep, where he wouldn't know he was having them. Only once he was married could he have them when he was awake, and even then it had to be in the dark.

The front wheel hits another unseen pothole and they both grunt. But it doesn't shake the worry. Because it might not mean anything that he's never had a single gay thought in his life. Because maybe you don't need to have such thoughts. It's just deep inside you, because you've crushed it down to hide it from God. And what's his father going to say if he's gay or trans? He won't even *want* to be rescued. He'd rather die in the desert prison to keep his shame as secret as the bungled mission.

Cycling with a mania now, his throbbing hands moulded to the vibrating handlebar grips, Brio pumps his memory for anything he's ever felt that might reveal his innermost secret. Because what if Darcy's right and he only likes the way Izzy looks because he secretly wants to look like that himself? How else could it be that he loves the way she looks but has never had a single grown-up thought about her? And he *did* like wearing the choir boy's frilly cassock, because it didn't just make him feel like someone different, it was something *better*, and he'd never felt so free. And what about the time at Costume Castle when he put on the wig and the princess cape? Pippa clapped and hooted with laughter and was still making him pose for photos when his mum came in and went mad.

'He's not a *girl*,' she snapped at Pippa then spat onto a tissue and wiped off the make-up as though trying to obliterate his entire face. That night, she warned him that if he ever put make-up on again, God would punish him by turning him into a girl forever.

Ms Whittle leans close over his shoulder. 'What's happening, dear? Can they see the Pitch-Dark Port yet?'

Brio's so relieved to be shaken out of his turmoil that he almost laughs. Yet returning to reality brings worry about the white van and suddenly it's he himself who needs Lord Rumbuck's confident bluster. 'My lord!' Brio breaks out unexpectedly in the Hoggit's squeaky voice. 'I am frighted to the quick. I need a dose of your derring-do to fill me with courage.'

Ms Whittle grips him more tightly. 'That's wonderful, dear. Lord Rumbuck's hearty stories will perk us up no end.'

As though in reply, the ring seems to come alive against his skin and he draws Ms Whittle's hands all the way around his waist. At first, he finds Lord Rumbuck too grumpy to comply with the request for a heroic yarn, but soon he's on a roll about dragons and duels, and demons and drawbridges. He finds himself talking at such speed and length that it's only when Lord Rumbuck pauses to remember some detail that Brio manages to catch a breath of his own.

It isn't long before Ms Whittle's taking advantage of Lord Rumbuck's pauses to add the Hoggit's own little embellishments to the stories. The Invisible Dragon's jet of flame could fire a whole mile not just a few yards, and the first victim of the Thousand-Toothed Bear was not the Poison-Spiked Zebradorg of Dasplotchaban but his own dentist.

And thus it unfolds, like moments in a dream, Brio and Ms Whittle egging each other on like little kids, taking turns to crank up and elaborate the action until the two tributaries can do nothing else but merge into a single torrent of gallant action with grade six rapids and no place to cross. And the laws of physics become so stretched, and the raconteurs so exhausted, that the thread of the tale eventually drifts up into the darkening sky like the dangling string of a balloon.

It's been dark for an hour by the time Brio and Ms Whittle reach the dimly lit walkway overlooking the docks. When Brio sees the Hoggit standing at the railings between Lord Rumbuck and Madame Haha, he jams on the brakes with such sudden force that Ms Whittle slams into his back and they almost skid into a bench.

'What on earth is it, dear?'

'It's *them*,' he whispers as Ms Whittle clambers to regain her position on the flimsy pannier rack.

'Who, dear? Where?'

Brio points urgently at the anxiously bobbing Hoggit. 'Right there, looking out at the boats.' Now he sees exactly what the Hoggit sees, not the serried armada of pleasure yachts and fishing trawlers but a landscape of rigging and gunports and barrels stacked high. 'But where's the Twinkly Ship?' he demands in Madame Haha's bizarre mix of accents. 'Where are those poor unhappy giants who cry out for Madame Haha to save them from gloom?'

Back on the flimsy rack, Ms Whittle pulls Brio close. 'Dear, I know how important this is, but we really must find somewhere to stay before it gets too late. I'm sure we'll be able to see everything from a hotel window.'

'But it's all about to happen,' Brio cries. 'I have to write *now*.' He half tips Ms Whittle off the bike and stacks it hard against the wall of a pavilion shelter that's littered with takeaway boxes and smells of stale urine. 'I ned my writing things, *quickly*.' And when she tries to explain that it's getting terribly chilly and she's not as young as she looks, he tears at his bandages and they fall into grapple of Punch and Judy flip-slap.

By the time it's over, they're sitting at the dirty table and Brio's clutching the pink-feathered biro in one fissured and oozing hand, while with the other he holds a shivering Ms Whittle close inside the tabernacle warmth of his jacket. And he only needs to raise his head slightly for an unimpeded view of Madame Haha skipping gaily away in search of her "Twinkly Ship".

Write it down, murmurs Logie's voice in his head. *Follow the Hoggit's words every step of the way.*

But at the end of the docks, Madame Haha didn't find the twinkling minstrel's galleon of her dreams. Instead they found themselves confronted by a ship-shaped cliff of rusted steel and grime and flaking paint with a filthy white tower that rose up at the stern like a devilish lighthouse.

Madame Haha clutched her cheeks and stumbled back. 'You promised Mummy a ship of joy and twinkles. But this is a ghastly ship full of giants who do dreadful evil to creatures like us.'

The Hoggit had known all along that deft explanation would be required, but he had expected Madame Haha to be angry rather than traumatised. And he too was struck down by the sheer scale and evil of their challenge.

Yet Lord Rumbuck once again stood tall and issued a triumphal sniff. 'Didn't I tell you, Young Prince? She's a fraud, a bogus busketeer, a charlatan who's hidden her tinpot talent behind the fantasy of a microphone with magic powers.' He thrust out a hand at Madame Haha. 'Give me my sword.'

Dread of renewed confrontation between his joint saviours only compounded the Hoggit's plummeting spirits. But when he looked up at Lord Rumbuck and saw that old confident aplomb in the face of adversity, he felt his own tinder-dry courage reignite. 'Stand tall and be brave!' he exhorted Madame Haha, drawing himself up against the cramping tightness of his safety harness. 'Prepare to save those poor giants from the Vile Villain!'

Alas, Madame Haha only moaned more pitifully. 'This kind of cruel giant can never be saved by laughter. They are only happy when you are in pain.'

She turned to leave, which sent the Hoggit leaping to limpet himself to her leg. 'You *can* make the giants laugh. You've made them laugh your whole life.'

Madame Haha's head hung lower still. 'The giants only loved Madame Haha when she was a baby, after they bought her at the horrid market for a packet of cigarettes. When she grew bigger, they made her fight snakes and set dogs onto her, to make her run about like a crazy rat. Madame Haha told herself they were cheering. But it wasn't cheering, it was jeering. And they didn't give her baskets of fine fruit, it was rotten, and they threw it at her. Poor Madame Haha was so hungry she had to eat it off the floor like a dog. She thought they hated her because she was a *mang*oose and they wanted her to be a girl. That's why she made herself the twinkly waistcoat and the lovely long hair, to make them love her. But then they threw banana skins so that Madame Haha would slip, and that's when the snake bit her, right on the bottom. And after that ... she died.'

The Hoggit clung desperately to her leg. 'How can you have died? You're right here.'

'Well, she wished she died. Because when she woke up, she was in a tiny cage. And if Madame Haha hadn't escaped, they would have made her into a fur hat. This is what they do to all creatures who make them lose their money on betting.

So well done, Mister Rumbo, you were right all along. But there is no prize for being right about something so wrong.'

The Hoggit suddenly seemed to feel all the pain in the world. Even Lord Rumbuck bowed his head.

'But you *didn't* die,' the Hoggit implored. 'You dived into the sea like a swallow, then you swam all the way to the beach.'

'*No*,' Madame Haha said sharply. 'I threw myself in. And I did *not* swim. I just couldn't make myself sink. I suppose some people are simply too floaty.'

In a state of shock, the Hoggit was powerless to stop his hands sliding off her leg. She stepped away and straightened her waistcoat then dusted herself down.

'I am going home,' she said in murmur. 'I am going home to our little beach with the soft sand. Because that is the happiest place in a horrible world. I hope you will come too.'

Brio flops back against the wall of the pavilion and Ms Whittle's hand slips to his knee.

'Are you all right, dear?' She's shaking so violently with cold as to be actually vibrating.

But Brio's still in a state of shock. 'That can't have happened. Madame Haha would never leave him.' He wants to blame Ms Whittle for putting it in his head, but the very thought makes him ashamed and he pulls her closer.

'It's terribly sad,' Ms Whittle mumbles. 'And it's not what I expected at all. But perhaps we could go and find somewhere warm now.'

Before Brio can reply, a huge container truck rolls past and its growling noise echoes in his head like a ship's engine firing up. But it's not just the ship's engine and nor is it just one truck, it's the warlike *dm-dm-d'dm* from a whole row of brightly lit but filthy giant chariots, each one brimming over with scrap metal and junk that looks like treasure to be loaded onto a galleon. Straining for a clearer view, Brio sees the Hoggit shrink back as a colossal claw swings out from the ship and crashes down into a mountain of mangled metal. When it returns clutching a greedy clawful of twisted junk, the Hoggit has to cower from a rain of clattering debris.

'Dear—'

'*Shush.*' He quickly squeezes her shoulder. 'I'm sorry. I just have to write.'

As the Hoggit struggled for something to say to Madame Haha, a dazzling light cast their shadows into distended ghouls and they span round to see the outline of a huge giant dressed in a blue uniform and luminous light-green waistcoat.

Trying to shield himself from the powerful torch beam, the Hoggit implored Madame Haha to make the giant laugh. To his surprise, however, the uniformed giant slowly lowered his protruding belly onto one knee and held out a hand to Madame Haha.

She glanced down at the theatrical pool of torchlight in which she now stood and the beginnings of a smile flickered on her wide lips. When the giant continued to coax, her smile broadened and she slowly raised the Magic Microphone to her mouth.

Which made the giant chuckle.

Which prompted Madame Haha to strike up a dramatic pose.

Which made the giant laugh out loud.

Which made her toss the sword from hand to hand as though it were a cane.

Which made the giant bark out a laugh.

Which made Madame Haha hold out the Magic Microphone and gaze in awe. 'It really works! Now the giants will love her forever!' And with an echoing *whoo-hoo*, she skipped off joyfully towards the ship.

The Hoggit was about to cry *wait for us* when the security guard swung his torch and pinned them into their corner with its dazzling beam.

Brio's so deeply into events on the dock it takes him a few moments to realise that the approaching uniformed figure is not the giant who's been left shouting after Madame Haha, it's a security guard, maybe even a policeman. Moments later, Brio and Ms Whittle are madly stuffing everything into her backpack, and they make for the shadows beyond the zebra crossing in such stumbling and tripping disarray that they clean forget her mountain bike.

*

Scuttling in Ms Whittle's wake through unlit backstreets, Brio's panicked that in escaping from the security guard, the Hoggit and Lord Rumbuck never made it onto the ship in time to save the Queen. Or maybe they didn't escape from the security guard at all. Brio glances behind, and when he sees that the security guard isn't on their tails, he turns to run back to the docks. But Ms Whittle grabs his arm and brings them to a halt outside a pair of aluminium-framed glass doors. MANAGER says a sticky-taped sign above a broken doorbell.

Brio stares in dismay. 'We can't stay here.'

Ms Whittle's gibbering with cold. 'It's all I can afford, dear.'

'But it's full of drug addicts.'

'No, no, dear. That's the other one. Come on.'

Brio scours the darkness for alternatives but, when he sees only a streetscape of steel shutters and facades without signboards, he hurriedly huddles in behind Ms Whittle and waits rigidly for a man in dirty tracksuit pants to open the door.

A few minutes later, they're in a tiny, bad-smelling bedroom with a bunkbed. Brio stands frozen, backpack clutched to his chest, while Ms Whittle tries to make an instant home, plugging in the small fan heater and closing the torn curtains, patting the top bunk and tutting as she empties the NO SMOKING ashtray into the bin. Brio's distress worsens when he realises Ms Whittle's staying in the same room, and there's no toilet. The very thought that they have to share a bathroom with dangerous weirdos spurs his bladder and only heightens his angst about the saving the Queen before the ship leaves.

'That man said the room had a desk,' Ms Whittle grumbles from down on all fours where she's looking under the bed. 'You'll just have to sit cross-legged.'

After a testy fight to pull out a drawer from the mouldy smelling cupboard, she turns it upside down on the floor. 'There you are, dear. You get writing while I call dear Tania.'

'*No.* That'll give away our location.'

Ms Whittle stares at her phone. 'Well, what about a text?'

'It's the same.'

'Then how are we going to get more paper—and food? And something for your hands.'

'There's nothing wrong with my hands,' he growls as he rummages for his writing things with cracked and stinging palms. He digs out the Christmas candle and sets it going next to the upturned drawer, but the snack bar he expected to find has somehow become an empty wrapper. 'Okay, call Tania then. But just ginger biscuits and milk. And she can't come in.'

Sitting cross-legged on the floor at his improvised writing table, Brio fights to block out Ms Whittle's animated conversation with Tania. He takes one slow deep breath after another and tries to get back to the Hoggit and Lord Rumbuck. Even a glimpse of Madame Haha would be some kind of lead. But all he can see through the faltering fake flame is the washed-out pattern of dank carpet and a screwed-up cigarette packet under the bed. He needs to be back at the docks where he can see them with his own eyes. At the very least, he wishes Ms Whittle would finish dictating her endless list to Tania and pay attention to the Hoggit. His patience is about to run out when a knock on the door has him on his feet brandishing the pen like a knife.

'I'm sorry, dear,' Ms Whittle says as she hurriedly bolts the door behind Izzy. 'It's the only place we could find.'

Brio's anger at Izzy is swept away by the sight of her hair, because it's not just cut to the shoulder anymore, she's butchered it into a pudding bowl that only half covers her ears, and in the tatty checked coat she looks like a lumberjack.

'Your *hands*,' Izzy exclaims and looks askance at Ms Whittle.

'I told you, dear. He won't let me dress them.'

'Bree, they'll get infected.'

I don't care. What have you done to your hair? And why are you here?'

'How can I not be here?'

His thoughts clunk into place. The Dark Lord's taken control of her mind and she doesn't know what she's doing. That's why she's butchered her beautiful hair. That's why she told the world about Logie helping him with the Great Plea. As he's about to throw her out regardless, he registers the white envelope in her hand. When she looks alarmed and withdraws it slightly, he snatches it and backs to the wall.

His eyes dart between the official-looking certificate and the worry on their faces. *Éire § Ireland*, it says at the top. *Deimhniú Breithe § Birth Certificate*. And further down, in the box for *Father*, one simple word in capital letters: UNKNOWN.

Brio has to support himself against the wobbly wooden chair, while Ms Whittle says to Izzy, 'Goodness, dear, where did you get this?'

'From Dad's surgery. It's a copy. He doesn't know I've found it. Bree—'

'My dad is not *unknown*.' He tears the piece of paper in half and wants to eject her before she has the chance to say whatever else it is he can see in her eyes. 'Your dad faked it. Because Zpydr scared him. And bribed him.'

Izzy holds his gaze, but she's seeking a new kind of connection that *he* doesn't want either. And there's something in Ms Whittle's reaction to the birth certificate that fills him with alarm.

'I did some research.' Izzy's trying to sound neutral and calming but he can hear the tension. 'This type of birth certificate wasn't introduced till three years after you were born. That means it can't be the original certificate. It's like someone had something changed. Maybe it's a completely new one. Bree, whatever this means, you mustn't be scared of it.'

'I'm *not* scared. It just means the government changed it. Like they changed his name to a French one. Like they told Mum never to tell anyone the truth. It proves everything.' And to shut down his clamouring doubts, he rips the certificate again and again till it's confetti around Izzy's shiny purple boots.

But Izzy's eyes are alight. 'Bree, don't you see? Maybe it does mean your dad was in something secret.'

'No, dear! That's not—' She stops herself and Brio turns on her. 'That's not *what*?'

Izzy looks askance too and there's an eerie silence.

'It was nothing, dear. I just meant …'

'That's right,' Brio says. 'It was nothing. You don't know anything.'

Ms Whittle gives a tight laugh. 'You're right! I don't know anything at all.'

Now Brio's certain that Ms Whittle knows something and he needs to know what.

But no, he's just imagining things. And so's Ms Whittle. Because she's mad.

'Bree, you've got to find out the truth,' Izzy says firmly. 'And I've realised that there *is* someone who almost certainly knows. I don't know why I never figured it out before.'

Dizziness forces him to grip the wobbly seat harder. '*Who?*'

Izzy glances at Ms Whittle and back to Brio. 'Okay, you mustn't get stressed, all right? But I've thought it through really carefully and—'

'*Who?*' Brio snaps. '*Tell me.*'

Izzy holds his gaze but he sees her gulp. 'Well … Bella Ripley, who else?'

Ms Whittle's hand jumps to her chest. 'Good heavens, dear, what a wild thought.'

The emotions come at Brio in a dense cloud of blurred vision. Loathing and jealousy. Fear and confusion. Grief and despair. And the old split second of remorse that's instantly shut down by anger. 'Bella Ripley doesn't know anything,' he seethes and takes a step back. 'And it's none of her business. Get *out*.'

But it's clear that Izzy's fervour is unstoppable. 'Bree, whatever Father T wanted your mum to tell you, he would have told Bella.'

'He *wouldn't*.' But it's suddenly obvious that Father T *would* have told Bella, and Brio sees too that he must have subconsciously known it all along: that Bella had always known the one thing he'd been so desperate to find out since he was eight years old.

Ms Whittle's breathing in little flustered gasps. 'Dear,' she says to Izzy, 'you really mustn't trouble poor Bella. And who knows where she is now? Why don't we just let dear Brio finish his book?'

Izzy stares at Ms Whittle, her forehead in furrows. She looks back at Brio. 'Bree, if you're certain your dad was in the Foreign Legion, why are you scared to find out what Bella Ripley knows?'

Brio feels like he's standing next to himself. Why *doesn't* he want to know what Bella Ripley knows? His panic mounts. 'Bella Ripley will lie. She'll say Father T told her my dad killed himself. Because she hates it that Father T loved us—even though it was fake love.'

A ping sends Izzy's hand diving for her phone. 'It's Mum. I have to go.'

Brio rushes to block Izzy's way. 'Swear you won't talk to Bella Ripley. *Swear it.*'

'Bree, I'm on your side, okay? And we have to find out the truth—before Zpydr and their friends do something to get you into their clinic.'

12

BRIO SLAMS DOWN THE FEATHERED BIRO. 'Then keep calling till she answers.'

Ms Whittle sighs heavily. 'Why don't I try again after dinner, dear? You know the Shenoys dislike mobile telephones at the table.'

'It's ten o'clock. They'll have finished ages ago.'

Listening to Izzy's phone ignoring Ms Whittle again, Brio goes back to pacing the room, up and down, round in tight circles, too frazzled about Izzy calling Bella Ripley to even count his steps. All he can see in his mind is the cruel pleasure on Bella Ripley's twisted and painted lips as she makes up the lies about his dad committing suicide.

But suddenly it's all clear. If he can finish the Great Plea, then nothing Bella Ripley can say will matter. Nor will the fake birth certificate, or Zpydr, or anything else in the world.

Elated with relief, Brio grabs up the pen and shuts Bella Ripley out of his thoughts. But the nib's drawn straight back into the cog mesh of crop circles that he's doodled deep into the pad and he can't even see the docks, let alone the Hoggit and Lord Rumbuck trapped by the security guard. Oh, God, what if the Hoggit *didn't* make it onto the ship? What if Lord Rumbuck and Madame Haha were both captured? Could the Hoggit possibly have got to the Tower of Time on his own? Of course he couldn't, because he'd have failed to save the Queen, failed to earn his right to know its location. And even if he found out where it was in some other way, he'd have broken the Sacred Prophecy by going on his own, and then he'd have been struck with a memory curse. Oh, God, then he'd never know whether his father was there in the High Dungeon.

With his stomach in knots, Brio's about to shove away the upturned drawer when he registers that Ms Whittle isn't only unpacking food, there's a kettle too, and mugs, and a thermos flask and camping cooker. Tania's even brought a mini-fridge still in its box. How long are they going to be there? How long before the police and government track them down and stop him getting to the Tower of Time? Paralysed by despair, he screws up the piece of doodled paper and throws it at the wall with all the others.

Ms Whittle comes hurriedly to kneel at his side. 'Dear, I'm sure all will be well if you'd just have a teeny-weeny taste of sugar.'

Before Brio can brush aside the packet of biscuits, a phone warbles and they both leap for the bed. Seeing that it's a text from Izzy, he scans Ms Whittle's face and presses himself into the only uncluttered corner.

Hi again, Ms Whittle. I did more research and I was right. There's no Hannah McPride born on the day of his mum's birthday. Plenty of other McPrides but no Hannah. Not even as a middle name. So she must have changed her name. Why would she do that? I suppose it could have been because she felt shame about what we always thought happened to Bree's dad. But what if it really was something else? Do NOT tell Tania about this.

Brio stares at the phone till his gaze pixelates. It's all some gigantic nightmare, or a mistake, or a nightmare about a mistake. But why do Izzy's words feel so sickeningly right?

Ms Whittle slips the phone gently from his hand. 'Maybe your dear mum didn't like her name. Many young people feel a need to carve out their own identity. And she did have a wonderful imagination.'

But Brio's panic's already over. 'It's the same as everything else. The government changed Mum's name so no one would find her and make her tell the truth about the secret mission.'

Even as he speaks, he grasps the possibility that his mum might have changed both of her names. She wasn't even called McPride. All his life, he's just had some fake name. And what if she changed his first name too? He's not even Brio. God, who *is* he? With a cry of emotions he can't understand at all, he spirals into heaving gasps and wild attempts to spew words that end in convulsive jerks, and he's on hands and knees vomiting milk and biscuits and everything else he can't remember Ms Whittle feeding him.

The next thing Brio knows, he's lying in the bottom bunk immersed in a cocoon of Ms Whittle's outlandish aromas, his thoughts lost in a febrile headache of insipid colours. Time happens in snapshots of her fussing fitfully at his bedside, tweaking his sheet and patting his arm, groping his burning forehead with her spindly fingers.

Sometime later, he feels a straw prodding at his lower lip and Ms Whittle helps him take a sip of something tasteless beyond sweet. Groaning relief, he tries for more, but he's shivering cold again. He needs the blanket from the floor, even though its smell of stale cigarettes makes him retch.

Woken by the old clocktower down the road from a sleep he doesn't remember happening, Brio starts counting the chimes. But he realises that he doesn't know how many of the tuneless dings he missed. He knows only that it's the middle of the night and he's ravenous for fish fingers and chips with exactly the right amount of ketchup.

Later again, the creepy hiss of Ms Whittle's camping cooker

quickly overheats the room with a noxious, threatening steam. From half-sleep he watches her balancing pans and digging into shopping bags. After he's eaten, he eats again, then lapses into a haphazard midnight feast of snacks and sweets.

Sometime later, Ms Whittle slips a magic crystal into his congealed palm and urges him to sleep. But he's so hyped up on sugar he can only pace the tiny room and work the crystal as a stress ball to generate different flavours of pain that might reconnect him with the Hoggit.

Forced to the sidelines by Brio's wide-eyed energy, Ms Whittle is left to fuss with bags and anxiously wring her hands. The moment Brio stops to let out an exasperated groan, though, she's straight back in.

'You know, dear, writer's block is very easily cured. Because you see, it's really nothing more than a simple effervescence of negative emotions that flow from excessive fusion between the chakras of heart and mind.'

Shutting out Ms Whittle's twaddle, Brio drops back down to the floor. In his swarming mindfulness, he's so mentally spent he can't even object when she kneels beside him like a disciple.

'Dear, I'm not quite sure whether to mention it but I do have a little herbal drink that can help in situations like this.'

Brio stares at the fake flame's endlessly rhythmic sequence. If only that drop of hard plastic wax would break free from its moulded trickle and drip down, then everything in the world would come to life and they'd all get onto that ship.

'I'm serious, dear. Tania's little herbal tea sort of liberates you, frees you from whatever's holding you back, opens the gates of your deepest memory to connect you with your god within.' Her feathery hand rests on his forearm just clear of the raw skin. 'Above all else, it brings you closer to the people you love.'

Their eyes meet formally now and Brio yearns again for the strict but kindly nun he once knew. But maybe if he truly believes that her silly herbal tea will help him remember the Hoggit making it onto the ship, that's what'll actually happen. Maybe it could even turn Ms Whittle back into Sister Jane.

At the small chest of drawers, Ms Whittle opens the mini-fridge as though it's a hidden safe. Its brightly lit interior contains only one thing: an old-fashioned medicine bottle, brown and ribbed and plugged with a cork stopper. On its home-made-looking label, someone has sketched a little bouquet of mushrooms that radiate an array of sunlight.

'What is it?' Brio murmurs as they gaze at the innocent little bottle.

'This is Tania's *tisane of the gods*, dear, a gate through which I have seen all that is to be seen. I have been in Xanadu where Alph the sacred river ran, and in India with Our Lord. In gardens bright with sinuous rills too, by dancing rocks and caverns measureless to men.'

Brio finds that just looking at the bottle sends a tingle, and he remains quite still as Ms Whittle decants generous doses into two dainty little teacups decorated with birds and bees.

'Here,' she says, 'drink slowly.' But before she's finished adding that he needs to breathe deeply between sips and exhale with a hum, he's downed it in one and handed back the cup.

Cross-legged on the floor like kids round a campfire, Ms Whittle and Brio gaze at each other with faint smiles. And despite the absurd red glasses that seem even larger than before, Brio can't help sharing the glint of anticipation in Ms Whittle's eyes. To keep her company, he even takes another delicate sip like hers, and maybe this time Tania's *tisane of the gods* doesn't taste like boiled moss and twigs after all.

Sometime later, Brio finds himself smiling with little traces of teeth showing, in exactly the same way the Hoggit smiled on the day they met. At the thought that Ms Whittle might quite easily turn herself back into Sister Jane by hiring a nun's outfit from Costume Castle, Brio even hears himself make a little piggy noise like a chuckle, which draws a girlish giggle from Ms Whittle.

'Do you feel a bit better now, dear?'

'I suppose so.' And he does feel better too. In fact, he loves that she cares so much, like she's cared so much since he was a tiny mouse. But he can see in her twinkling eyes that it's time for him to look into the lovely Christmas candle once more, the little beacon whose dollop of moulded plastic wax now rolls gently down its shaft, to be followed by others in gentle waves of warmth that bubble over and slide gracefully into the little pool of saucer that's waiting below.

Thinking with languid curiosity that what just happened hasn't actually happened yet but is about to happen, he finds himself watching as the sweet electronic flame rises to float above the candle, which creates a space for him to reach out and touch his beautiful friends. The Hoggit's spikes are so much like his mum's soft hairbrush, and Lord Rumbuck's fur feels exactly the same as that luxurious glove he once stroked in a shop. And it's okay that Lord Rumbuck is so surprisingly soft, because inside he's rough and tough with endearing touches of bumble and tumble and lots of grey grumble and—

'Oh, Brio, my darling, you're such a beautiful boy.'

He wants to say thank you to Ms Whittle, but a muted stirring in his tummy reminds him of the Hoggit's need to save the Queen before the dawn departure of the Vile Villain's verminous vessel.

Quietly determined not to be held back by worry about thinking too many words, Brio returns to kneel reverently at the sweet little mini-fridge. Afterwards, he sits back down on the soft grass, and there's Sister Jane too, lying on the cosy bunk bed and staring up at the stars. He wants to hug her, to stop her floating up off the ever-changing pattern on the Indian bedspread that dear Tania must have delivered with all the other treasures from Sainsbury's of Samarkand, and as he gazes at the impenetrable runes and quasi-anagrammatic meanderings of the Purple Code, he realises that a four-symbol noun he recognises has crystalised and begun to float up from the page. 'It's love,' he warbles happily.

'I know, dear, and you're such a beautiful boy.'

'No, I mean it's the word *love*. Oh, my God, I've remembered the Purple Code. You're amazing.'

Her mouth falls slowly open in the same endearingly pitiful smile of poor Mr T'wit when he used to feed his long-lost love with the imaginary honey spoon. Brio feels such a flood of uninhibited love for Ms Whittle that the sight of her squatting on a half-visible potty pitches him into a long and joyous peal of laughter that weaves and undulates like a street-long paper dragon. He can't help toppling sideways to roll in hysterics that make Ms Whittle hoot like an owl.

Later, after they've returned from another visit to the little fridge, Ms Whittle magics up from one of Tania's supermarket bags a long Indian robe. 'This will bring you joy and inspiration,' she sighs. 'Oh, you beautiful boy.'

Brio wants to inform her with good grace that he won't be seen dead or alive in something that looks like a dress. But when he sees in her pleading eyes how passionately she believes in the power of the magician's robe to help him, he knows he should change out of his sooty and sweaty clothes at once. And as soon as he's floating free in brightly coloured silk and chiffon, she helps him spirit away his former expression of worry with creams and soft-smelling make-up powder. He drifts and dreams as she radiates the comforting aromas out over his whole forehead and down onto his cheeks—to give colour to his poor, pale skin, she says, the perfect shade for his dark green eyes and mousey brown hair. And no sooner is he back at his antique writing table than a sparkle of sequins streaks across the room and he's fired out of his reverie with such suddenness that he doesn't even notice the change. 'It's Madame Haha! Give me paper!'

Ms Whittle scuttles like a crab for the shopping bags, while Brio scrabbles frantic circles on all fours, trying to follow Madame Haha as she flies round the docks with a pair of guard dogs on her tail.

'Paper galore!' Ms Whittle whoops and upends a carrier bag of writing pads all over the floor. 'A new leaf for a new chapter in your life!'

But by the time she's managed to place a single piece of paper down in front of him, Madame Haha's vanished again and he needs to focus deeply to tease the nib into the groove of rusty railway line that runs along the dock, where he finds the Hoggit and Lord Rumbuck surrounded by a mob of evil-eyed rats.

Brio's relief at the Hoggit's evident escape from the security guard is so short-lived as to never have happened. Because if they never saved the Queen, it was probably this huge mob of rats that stopped them. But Brio's brief glimpse of Madame Haha has lifted his spirits and, instead of panic at the Hoggit's entrapment by rats, he merely experiences a fascination that expresses in words like *filthy and greasy, sharp-fanged, evil-eyed and conniving*—truly, the most no-good-low-down specimens of *Rattus norvegicus* he ever met.

Eventually, he notices that Ms Whittle's beaming at him with eyes that seem to have stopped blinking.

- 'What's happening, dear?'

Even though he knew it was coming, the question startles Brio and he needs a few moments to lean forward and speak quietly so as not to attract attention. 'There are some dockside rats blocking their way. The biggest one's muscling forward and eyeing them up and down—and a bit of sideways too.'

'Oh, goodness,' Ms Whittle gasps theatrically. 'The rats work for the Vile Villain.'

'Yes. Because the Vile Villain loves shiny things apparently, so the rats steal the best bits from the scrap metal and polish them till they gleam.'

Ms Whittle cups her cheeks. 'How awful, dear. The poor ratties are victims of a sweatshop operation. It might even be modern slavery.'

'No,' Brio says earnestly. 'They're pirates.'

She pulls an even more serious face. 'Don't you mean … pi-*rats?*'

Their flimsy gravitas splits open into laughter and they flop back onto their bottoms. Once again, the hysteria seems to go on and on in waves of free and easy colour, on and on until Brio sees that the big pi-rat is scowling and prodding the Hoggit in the chest.

Scrambling back to his knees, Brio pulls Ms Whittle up by the hand and tells her that the big rat's called Guzzle and the Hoggit's in trouble. He puffs himself up to play the part of Guzzle and summons his best growling cockney. 'Now, look here, you prickly little hamster …' He jabs a finger at Ms Whittle. 'The only reason anyone goes on that ship is to spit and polish like it's the last thing they'll ever do.'

'Oh, gosh,' Ms Whittle whispers. 'The Hoggit will have to play along and ask for a job.'

'That's exactly what happened,' Brio says and shrinks himself back down to summon up his best squeaky voice. 'We're fully on board with your requirements, Mr Guzzle. Lord Rumbuck and I will be happy to labour for a song that we ourselves shall sing.'

Even though Brio's hazily aware that it wasn't especially funny, they nonetheless collapse into another bout of hysterics and he loses all track of how long it takes for the convulsive energy to work itself out.

'That really was terribly funny,' Ms Whittle says breathlessly as they claw themselves back to their knees. But her expression becomes serious again and she peers down at her bright orange ankle boot. 'The only thing is, my foot's gone dead.'

Feeling a twinge of concern, Brio places a hand on her ankle. 'What can I do to help?'

She holds his concerned look and pats his hand. 'Actually dear, there's no need to worry. I just have to reboot it.'

They topple into another pile of unstoppable laughter, rolling on their backs and waggling jazz feet in the air. And on it goes again, on and on, till something's happening on the docks and Brio has to scrabble back to his knees even faster than before. This time the mood's changed and he doesn't know whether the crawling in his stomach's real or part of the action.

'Dear, tell me. What's going on?'

Brio lets out a sharp groan of annoyance infected by Ms Whittle's worry. 'It's Lord Rumbuck. He's so *stupid*.'

'What is it, dear? What's he done?'

'The pi-rats were just about to lead them right to the Queen when Lord Rumbuck got all puffed up and said he wasn't going to be a slave to anyone. "I shall battle my way onto the ship," he snorted, "not sneak aboard dressed as a washerwoman."'

Ms Whittle's countenance darkens further. 'Didn't I tell you, dear? Lord Rumbuck's hypermasculinity is problematic.'

Even with the pleasant haze still trying to tingle down his back, Brio feels panic breaking through. Is this where everything went wrong and stopped the Hoggit getting onto the ship, the bit where he fled home to the castle to make up some gigantic fairy tale about a memory curse? Brio tries desperately to bring the pen down onto the paper but it evades his hand and floats on air. '*Do something*,' he cries at the Hoggit. And when the Hoggit doesn't move, Brio clutches his head and let's out a childlike cry. 'But what can he do? He's so small and fragile.'

Ms Whittle quickly takes hold of his wrist. 'It's all right, dear. The Hoggit just has to remember all the amazing things he's done in the past.'

'But he—'

'Look, dear!' She lets go and points excitedly at the empty space between them. 'The Hoggit's pressing his tether into Lord Rumbuck's hand. "Swing me round your head as a spiky mace," he cries. "Make me a weapon of mash destruction!"'

Brio blinks. He doesn't know whether to be angry or somehow find his way back into the laughter. But a moment later, the Hoggit's whirring around Lord Rumbuck's head in a blur of lurid colours and cutting a swathe through the mob of rats.

'Hurrah!' Brio cries, even as he has to stablilise himself with one hand. 'Long live the Hoggit!'

But the whirring gets faster and Brio begins to feel as sick as the Hoggit. And the harder he tries to break free, the faster it goes, faster and faster, into a tornado of warp-speed stars and flashes of dockside junk and teeth and claws and flashing and sickly French biscuits strawberry milk popcorn takeaway Indian chocolate cake ... He battles to press his fake quill into the paper and release the Hoggit but his fleeting sense of a sentence is spun out into a centrifuge of single words too fast to write down—junk heaps, dogs, barking madness, froth, saliva, Madame Haha here, there, rats, chrome and sword, giants shouting, round and round, and he's about to spew his acidic spray of half-digested food when the tether slips from Lord Rumbuck's hand and he sprawls across the stinking carpet.

He lies there stunned and dizzy, trying to keep his head still, but suddenly he's cowering from rats that teem across the floor and up the walls. When they veer towards Ms Whittle, he wants to kneel up and warn her, but his legs do silly jelly stuff and now he's an embryo on the floor, where everything becomes square and sharp-edged, and he tries to crawl under the bed to escape the ghoul that wants to strangle him.

As soon as Ms Whittle has him tight in her arms, he feels safe, and thank God she's there for him, because he can tell her through his dry sobs that the Hoggit and Lord Rumbuck have been scattered around the docks with guard dogs and rats trying to tear them to pieces. Madame Haha too. 'They didn't make it onto the ship. They failed. He'll never find his dad.' He sobs harder and she rocks him like a baby, but when he remembers she wants to be his mum, her big red glasses morph into the eyes of a fire-demon and he throws her off, which leaves him in some other dimension where there's nothing to feel or smell. It's all still and there's only some kind of rough surface against his numb cheek. He catches a glimpse of Ms Whittle lying on her side, blurred and distorted. In the middle of her blank face, her mouth falls open like Mr T'wit's pitiful gaping beak, like a yawning chasm in which he see and hear her innermost thoughts. As soon as he's clawed himself onto all fours, he's back in the roadside ditch by the castle, looking across the road and witnessing Mr and Mrs Hare's furious argument. He presses his ears flat against his head to shut down the shouting but still he can make out too many of their muffled words. *How could you do this?* Mrs Hare cries from deep inside Ms Whittle's dead cavernous gape of a mouth. *How can you ask someone to marry you when you've got this secret woman hidden away? You don't love me at all. You only married me because we've known each other since we were kids and you felt sorry for me and it's what our mums wanted.*

Brio tries to cram the words back down into the chasm of Ms Whittle's yawning void. 'She never said that,' he sobs. 'The Dark Lord's trying to make me think Lord Rumbuck's bad. He wants to trick me into giving up the quest.'

But the mood turns darker still and traps Mrs Hare inside the candle, which begins to melt, collapsing in on itself and cascading down into the saucer. Desperate to know whether everything he just witnessed is true, Brio flies up the spiral stone steps of the castle to find the Hoggit. But the steps keep going round and round and up and up, stretching out ahead of him, until he topples into an impossibly distorted place where the Hoggit's staring at a bottomless drop. 'Get back from there,' Brio cries. 'Tell me what you heard Mrs Hare say.'

But the Hoggit doesn't even know he's there.

Because he's *not* there.

Because the Hoggit didn't just make up the story about going to find his father, he didn't even meet a giant on the cliffs. He simply wanted so much to believe he did that it became true in his mind.

Dizzied by uncontrollable thoughts, Brio crawls frantically across the room to drag the Hoggit back down from the ledge. But the closer he gets, the higher the Dark Arched Window rises, till his own fear of heights overcomes him and he falls backwards in a faint to float in a forest of rusty steel trees and green stars in purple sky …

Ms Whittle reaches for him. 'What is it, dear?'

He grabs hold of her hands by their spindly fingers. He can only just move his mouth. 'It's the Hoggit. He wants to jump from the castle.'

Ms Whittle's face breaks into ghoulish alarm. 'No, dear. *No.* He'd never do that.'

'I tried to coax him back from the edge but I didn't have to. Because he's too scared of heights to jump. Oh, *God.* His fear's stopping him living the life he deserves.' He lets go of Ms Whittle's wrists and grabs up the pen. 'I have to write it down, that he must overcome his fear so he can fulfil his divine destiny.'

Ms Whittle fights him for the pen and they rear up to box like kangaroos.

'*Stop*,' she sobs. '*Please*. You must never think about killing yourself. *Never*.' She tries to hug him to her bony chest but he holds her back by the forearms, his heart thudding with anticipation.

'Don't you understand? You were right all along. Committing suicide isn't a sin. It's Roman and noble.'

'No, my darling boy, *no*.' She tries to hold his hands. 'I was just talking about Shakespeare. *Julius Caesar*.'

But Brio feels the freedom flooding his body and clasps her hands in return, an odd couple ready to dance a jig. 'The Hoggit can end his life exactly how you taught us, like those Buddhist monks who don't want to take life but love to eat crab. So they invite the crabs to walk across a wooden plank over a cooking pot. Then it's God who decides and the monks didn't do anything wrong, and it's no cardinal sin. And I'm dressed like a monk, too. I'm dressed as everything. And God *does* play dice with the universe.'

Clinging into their cocoon of talcum powdery cheeks, Brio's relieved to feel the terrible moment pass as quickly as it came on, and in Ms Whittle's arms he once again loses track of time and forgets where he is, until eventually she slips back down onto her haunches so awkwardly that her legs spring forward.

'My leg,' she murmurs. 'I can't feel it anymore. I'm not joking. And my head's going numb. Oh, dear and goddy God, I hope these aren't my last words.'

Her ghostly pallor frightens him and he wants them to curl up together in the soft grass of the Cosy Nook and forget the Dark Lord's evil nightmare. But when she lets out a long groan and topples onto her back, he knows he must seek help. The next moment seems to last an hour, to come and go, in and out of here and there. He doesn't know where he is anymore. Eventually, though, he's swimming his childish breaststroke through the choppy waves of smelly corridor carpet. He slides juddering down the stairs on his belly to a wild-water ride on the final straight towards the reception desk nook. In his mind he's a soldier under fire, crawling heroically for the field telephone that he's sure will connect him with the medics on the other side of the river.

'Ah, Jesus,' mutters the sleazy man at reception. 'I don't want any trouble.'

Brio assures him in his best grown-up voice that all's well that begins well. 'That's Plato, you know. But for now, I would merely like to use the landlocked telephone, please.'

Loving that he knows the Shenoys' phone number so deeply by heart, he wants to dial it a hundred times, while it rings and rings into the night.

The alarm in Izzy's voice unleashes a swarm of the Dark Lord's spybirds from the white van he can see parked in the street outside. He has to press the huge brick of a phone to his numb ear to stop it flying away with the spybirds. As soon as he hears Izzy's anxious voice, he tells her that the Hoggit never made it onto the ship. 'So he could never have saved the Queen. So he never made it to the Tower of Time. He made it all up. He never found his father.' The shout erupts from nowhere. 'It's all your fucking fault. Because you're going to call Bella Ripley because you couldn't trust the Hoggit do it his way. And now he's going to kill himself. That's all he wants to do. And Sister Jane's lying on the rickety floorboards with a broken heart. She's probably dead already.' His final deep breath is to shout out the revelation about Lord Rumbuck's secret woman hidden, but he manages to bury it in one last cry and slams down the phone.

By the time Izzy arrives with her dad, Brio's back in their bedroom lying next to Ms Whittle on the floor. His mind's blank and all he can hear is a distant windrush of seashells and chimes of clocktower.

Dr Shenoy throws down his medical bag and grabs a wrist in each hand. 'Good God, Sister Jane, what have you done? And what on earth is Brio wearing? And what—*lipstick*?'

As Dr Shenoy looks hard into his eyes, Brio smiles and imagines his pupils yielding like a baby's. 'I would like to forgive you, Dr Shenoy, for all those things you did and failed to do for me and my mum. Yes, I big-F forgive your fault, your fault, your own egregious farting fault …'

'What have you given him?' Dr Shenoy demands angrily of Ms Whittle.

'You know, Dr Shenoy,' she murmurs, 'there's an awful lot of research into mushrooms now. In fact, very soon we won't need your antidepressants at all.'

'You've given him a Class A drug? Are you out of your mind?'

'Oh, yes,' she says with a smile. 'And it's lovely.'

The sleazy man groans and says again that he doesn't want trouble, while Dr Shenoy curses Ms Whittle and tells Izzy to call an ambulance.

'Dad, *please*. Can't you do something yourself so no one'll know what's happened? Ms Whittle was just trying to help.'

'Trying to *help*? What does she do when she's trying to kill someone? Now, call an ambulance while I try to stabilise them with some anticonvulsant.'

'Anticonvulsant?' Ms Whittle says dreamily. 'Why do Catholics always think that a little bit of trembling calls for an exorcism? Don't doctors understand that God intended us to have that lovely big O between P and R? Anyway, why don't we all just stay here in this wonderful resort, then for breakfast I'll bake us some lovely brownies?'

13

DISTANT VOICES SEEP INTO THE SLOW-CHURNING blur that gradually forms a ceiling of old-fashioned combed plaster, and from the swirling patterns emerge sounds and colours, rose-golden sky and streaking sequins ... the Hoggit and Lord Rumbuck scattered with dogs and rats and Ms Whittle's gaping mouth issuing echoes of Mrs Hare's tearful, wounded rage. And when Brio realises he's probably in the Northview, he scrambles to sit up and find an escape.

It takes him several seconds to work out that the shrunken yeti preserved in ice is Izzy's old teddy bear staring at him from inside a plastic storage box. But his relief is short-lived, because another box contains old nurse's uniforms pressing down on obsolete mobile phones that trigger his memory of Izzy wanting to call Bella Ripley.

He throws off the duvet and twists dizzily out of the bed, only to be pulled up by the spectacle of himself in a full-length mirror wearing a pair of Dr Shenoy's striped pyjamas. He looks so like a mental patient he wants to punch the mirror, but his attention's snatched away by the sight of his hands all rebandaged and clean. Now he smells the disinfectant too, and how can it be five in the afternoon?

Hearing the raised voices clearly now, Brio hurries to put his ear to the bedroom door. But all he can hear in Ms Whittle's indignant self-defence is Mrs Hare shouting tearfully about some *secret woman hidden away*. Before he can even begin to fathom whether it really happened, the door opens and Izzy's standing there hugging his precious pages to her chest, her beauty despoiled by the butchered hair and a boyish shirt.

'Tell me you didn't call Bella Ripley. *Tell me.*'

'I will, but are you okay? That's the most important thing.'

'*What did she tell you?*'

Izzy glances round at the open door and edges forward to speak quietly. 'She wouldn't tell me anything. And after I told her why it was really important, she clammed up even more.'

'It's *not* important. Why can't you stop telling people things?'

'Bree, the last thing Zpydr want is for your dad to be alive, otherwise how can they keep saying you're delusional? And if Bella wouldn't talk to me because they threatened her, then she *must* know something they don't want people to know. And what else could it be except that he's alive?'

Even in his disarray, Brio can see the reasoning. And from Izzy's expression he knows it's just as logical that he should be excited too. But all he wants is to stop either of them saying another word.

'I think she thought her phone might be bugged,' Izzy says. 'I'm sure if I saw her in person, she'd tell me.'

Panic sends numb sparkles into his head and he takes a menacing step. 'You're not going to go anywhere near her. Swear it.' And when Izzy doesn't reply, he grabs the written pages to scour for evidence of anything Mrs Hare might have said about some secret woman hidden away.

'Bree, talk to me,' Izzy pleads in a loud whisper as his clubbed hands struggle to spread pages on the floor. 'If you're sure your dad's alive, why are you worried about Bella Ripley?' And when he ignores her, she says, 'Okay, I never liked her either, but on the phone she sounded really different. And she told me she found God through Father T and now she'd never tell a lie. Bree, I believe her. We've got to go and see her.'

Brio's back on his feet. 'Why can't you just let me find the Hoggit and finish it? Then Bella Ripley won't matter. Nor will any of them.'

Her face wrangles with worry and poorly concealed incredulity. 'Bree, you wanted us to find your dad together, and I want that too. And if he's alive, which I think he is, we can find him, you and me. And I've found out where Bella Ripley lives, just outside London, near Hampton Court. Dad's going to a conference and Mum agrees we need to see her.'

Before Brio can reply, the door opens and Ms Whittle comes at him, arms open. 'Oh, Brio, my boy, I'm so sorry.'

He presses back against the French windows and tells Ms Whittle not to touch him. 'And Mrs Hare did *not* say Lord Rumbuck had some secret woman hidden away.' He sees Izzy's bewilderment but his eyes are on Ms Whittle and he prays she won't have a clue what he's talking about.

But she's already cupped her mouth. 'Oh, goodness. What did I say?'

'What's going on?' Izzy asks anxiously.

'It's nothing, dear. The tea was just a bit strong and we were having all sorts of silly notions.'

'You *know* something,' Brio blurts. 'You all do.'

A buzz on the doorbell kills Brio's fretting and he presses back into the handle of the French doors. 'I have to finish it. You've got to stop them taking me away.'

As soon as they've left, Brio rushes to look down the short corridor, where he sees Dr Shenoy holding open the front door for a woman wearing white jeans and a sweatshirt. She's accompanied by a strong-arm nurse in the dreaded stark violet of the Northview. Brio slams the bedroom door and looks to the French windows. He stuffs the precious pages down the front of his pyjama bottoms and ties the waistcord so tightly it cuts into his sides. As he's about to snatch up the heavy candlestick to break the glass, a woman's voice says, 'Brio, can you hear me?'

Her gentleness robs him of his angry shout and he can't stop himself listening mutely as she tells him he'll be in a very safe place with people who care. 'And the people who love you can visit you every day. And if you want to keep writing, that's absolutely okay.'

'You're working for Zpydr,' he growls at the door. 'And you only want me to keep writing so you can *doctor it*.'

Taken aback by his spontaneous pun, he scans urgently for a pen to write it down before he forgets. He can even hear the doctor smiling through the door.

'Brio, you really will find us a very supportive community. I'm sure we're nothing like you might imagine. And we can help you like we've helped Darcy—who says hello, by the way, he's looking forward to seeing you.'

Yet again, Brio's angry shout is stillborn and he's back in the cell next to Darcy's, except now there's a glass panel in the wall and Darcy's calm and bathed in light. Brio's still trying to decipher the meaning when an outbreak of raised voices snaps him back into reality and he rushes to press his ear to the door. He's shocked to hear that Logie's there, Mrs Thorne too, and she's denouncing Ms Whittle for taking him to the drug addicts' hostel. And the woman doctor's trying to get a word in edgeways while Izzy tells Logie he's *never going near Brio again*, and Dr Shenoy shouts that social services can go to hell because Dr Silash has a section order, and Ms Whittle's telling Logie he's a paedophile …

'All right, *enough*,' Mrs Charis explodes, and when the voices actually fall silent, she says, 'Now, as I was saying, the minister has apparently taken a close interest in Brio's case, and the fact is that Mr Logue has been cleared by the police of any responsibility for the fire—and I'm given to understand that Brio will be placed at considerable risk if he doesn't complete the course of CHANT therapy. I'm also informed that it's critical for Brio to be granted complete agency in the decision about where he goes from here, and that if he doesn't wish to be in the Northview Wing, then the minister will override the section order so that Brio is able to accept the other option that's being offered, which is that he returns to Ms Whittle's home for the outsourced pastoral and peri-parental component of his care, while Mr Logue works with him there on the psycho-literary therapeutic aspects of his treatment. Though of course,' she adds hurriedly, 'it *is* Brio's decision.'

The stunned silence seems to sound the end of the line and Brio looks again to the French doors. It's only Mrs Thorne's voice that stops him grabbing the candlestick and swinging it through the glass.

'So this is what social services have come to do, is it?' Mrs Thorne says angrily. 'Place a young man who's at clear risk of serious self-harm into the care of a dangerous groomer and a fallen nun who tells us that the best way to live life is to leave it as soon as possible.'

'How dare you?' Ms Whittle fires back. 'It's your ruddy *Kingdom of God* that promotes suicidal ideation, filling people's heads with the dreadful promise that only death will bring them peace. Religions were supposed to console people about death, not cajole them into it.'

Reeling with shock at the trashing of his mum's most cherished beliefs, Brio's powerless to resist as everyone jostles into the bedroom behind Mrs Charis, all elbowing and angling around storage boxes and the mirror—eight of them, nine. Even as Brio wills himself to smash his way out through the French doors he keeps counting, till he finds himself staring at a Logie whose left hand is bandaged in exactly the same way as his own mummified scoops.

'Brio, I'm Dr Silash,' says the woman in white jeans and

sweatshirt. She half turns her head to the clamouring entourage. 'It really would be better if Brio and I could talk alone.' When no ones moves, she sighs but produces an effortless smile. 'Brio, if you come to the Northview, I promise we'll really look after you.'

'I'm staying here. Go *away*.'

Mrs Charis nudges herself in front to Dr Silash. 'Brio, the Northview's a wonderful place—thank you, Dr Silash—but Ms Whittle is someone you trust, isn't she—someone you know will take care of you?'

'Just *shut up*. Let me think.' But his attempt to rationally compare the options only leads his gaze to some kind of new determination in Mrs Thorne's watery eyes, and she's standing right in front of him, holding him gently by the shoulders.

'Brio, dear …' Her voice is unnaturally calm. 'You need to think very clearly now. Because this is a huge decision and although it beggars belief that—'

'Margaret, please,' Mrs Charis interrupts. 'This is for Brio to decide.'

'Be quiet,' Brio snaps at Mrs Charis. 'You have to let her speak.'

Mrs Thorne smiles. 'Thank you, my love. Now I know this is all very muddling for you—goodness knows, it's hard for anyone to comprehend—but you understand that Zpydr are using you, don't you? And you know that Mr Logue is working for Zpydr.'

'He's *not*,' Brio snaps. But he doesn't want to see whatever's in Logie's inveigling gaze.

Mrs Thorne's gentle shake of his upper arms is so close to becoming a hug that Brio feels a tingle down his back.

'Please, my love, try to hear what I'm saying.' Her voice is trembling now. 'Because it's very important for you to understand that Zpydr aren't just using you to help them make money, they intend to use this technology to create a new religion—a *techno-religion*, they call it—to sweep away the True Faith your mother held so dear.'

Loud groans and tuts meet Mrs Thorne's extraordinary assertion and Mrs Charis says, 'Margaret, this really isn't appropriate. And I'm sure you don't want to embarrass yourself.'

Mrs Thorne glances dismissively at Mrs Charis. 'There's clearly a lot you don't know, Sally.' She turns back to Brio. 'Now, listen to me carefully, my love. Zpydr are desperate to win approval for their dangerous online medical service. They need to find the one human face that people will think they can trust and love. And you're their perfect candidate, for all the reasons you already know. But you know too that your mum would be heartbroken. So you have to find the strength to resist these people. And you *know* where you can find the strength.'

'Oh, come *on*,' Logie says impatiently. 'Everyone gets that Zpydr's a bad smell, but I'm absolutely not working for them. And Brio knows that full well.'

Mrs Thorne turns to look Logie square in the eye. 'Perhaps you yourself don't know you're working for them, Mr Logue? And perhaps you've never heard of their Universal Story Project either, or of the computer system called Deorum-X—or even the technology tycoon who pays your salary.' She pauses and raises her eyebrows. 'Or perhaps you have.'

A new kind of silence chills the room and Brio feels that old weightlessness down the back of his neck. More than ever, he needs Logie to stop looking worried and make everything all right, so they can get back to Ms Whittle's and finish the Great Plea. 'He's *not* working for Zpydr,' Brio hears himself say when Logie still won't speak. 'Tell them it's not true.' He looks to Logie: if those impossibly perfect eyes falter for even a second, he has to smash through the glass and keep running till he can't stop.

'Mrs T, I godda be honest,' Logie says, finally seeming to find his cool, 'I have no clue what you're talking about.'

'Then I clearly need to jog your memory. After which, I think Brio will be more than ready to make his decision.'

She draws a printout from her handbag and Brio sees ominous chunks of neon-highlighted text.

'What is it?' Brio asks anxiously. Why can't just one thing in the world be certain and never change?

But now the highlighted text is out in the world, there's no going back. He has know what it says, so Logie can deliver a simple explanation that makes poor Mrs Thorne look so old and foolish she has to retire and never hurt anyone again in her life.

'I am reliably informed,' Mrs Thorne says, 'that this is the transcript of a short speech that was given recently by Tabo Forzac, the founder of Zpydr. It was given in camera,' she adds. 'Rather than *on*.'

Brio sees the return of doubt, even pity. Except that something about Mrs Thorne's confidence is making Logie look worried again, and suddenly there's a half circle of faces waiting avidly for her to read to the class.

'I won't trouble you with the whole thing,' she says, 'but I've selected the parts that I think will convey the message.' With that, she sniffs and raises the printout to read, 'In this final phase of CHANT*bot-vip*'s development, we are enriching the algorithms that underpin our combined stable of social media, search engine and creativity platforms with self-enhancing psychotherapeutic code augmentations that will enable the harvesting of mental health data and the delivery of corrective therapies to be woven seamlessly into the fabric of daily life. This functionality will be so integral to other seemingly unconnected spheres of human activity that people will be aware of neither its presence nor its role as an existential mental health intervention.'

She pauses to look up and with a weary expression Logie says, 'Mrs T, I'm sorry to be the bearer, but this is not exactly breaking news. I'm thinking maybe you should spare yourself further awkwardness.'

Brio feels his body drain with relief. Because poor Mrs Thorne *is* just too old, and Logie's his friend after all, and he just has to get to Ms Whittle's before anyone can say anything else. He almost laughs out loud when Mrs Thorne's printout buckles and flops down over her hand like a dead flower.

But Mrs Thorne merely gives the flimsy wad a little flick to stiffen its spine and adjusts her wonky half-rimmed glasses. 'It is clear,' she reads on, 'that in a very short timeframe, CHANT*bot-vip* will have processed such a colossal quantum of meta, analytic and de-anonymised data that it will have come to understand every individual on earth to a depth that is by definition far beyond the reach of humans themselves. By extension, this understanding will extend to the human race in its holistic singularity, and to the precise relationships between each individual and that collective consciousness.'

'Mrs T—'

Her free hand springs up with a raised finger. 'I know what you're going to say, Mr Logue, that this is already recognised as the inevitable outcome in so-called AI—long-string equations and formulae generated by computers whose progeny are already beyond our own intelligence. But this is where it gets even more interesting ...'

She re-adjusts her glasses and peers at the text. 'Given the role that story has always played in the formation and control of human belief and behaviour, it became obvious to us at Zpydr that, from our own exponentially expanding data set of subconsciously mined individual therapy narratives, together with the associated mental health profiling from tens of millions of online patients, CHANT*bot-vip*'s self-learning algorithms would be able to identify a single universal story that represents a synthesis of all the micro- and macro-narratives that have underpinned human societies since the first use of story by humans to explain the unknown and impose social stability through common belief. But this universal story that we expect to identify—this *ur-narrative*, if you like—will present not as a story in the sense that we have always understood that word, but rather as a matrix of relationship norms capable of being subliminally dramatized into every facet and function of human life. In exactly the same way that patients of CHANT*bot-vip* will be successfully treated with personalised therapeutic narratives, so the universal ur-narrative will be deployed—through both our own coordinated platforms and the unstoppable infiltration of all relevant third-party technologies—to install an all-embracing fabric of deepmind influence over human consciousness.'

This time when Mrs Thorne looks up, it's into a bewilderment of new expressions. But it's Logie's that sets Brio's skin crawling—some kind of veiled worry or bad memory woken unwillingly from deep sleep.

'Well, that's a nice piece of creative writing you've got there,' Logie says dismissively. 'My guess is it came from a troll centre in the east—most likely the one that's got us all hating our neighbours and chasing our own tails. But like I said, me and Zpydr are two different worlds.'

'We'll come to that in a minute, Mr Logue. As for the provenance of this document, I can tell you that it did not come from the internet as you suppose. It was in fact given to me by Cardinal Sinclair, and I understand that the speech was delivered to a group whose make-up should cause us to shudder.'

Feeling himself floating again, Brio tries for a firmer hold of the heavy candlestick that's slipping through his weeping palm. He wills Logie to say lots more or nothing at all.

'What are you saying here, Mrs T, that me and Brio have been suckered into some grand scheme of the Illuminati?'

But Mrs Thorne ignores him and reads straight on, about subliminal control of collective consciousness by a deeply ingrained matrix of ur-narrative-based relationship norms, about Zpydr looking with eight-sigma certainty to a future in which humanity is finally able to rise above its primitive social condition and discover an existence of peaceful, competitive collaboration that is beyond the reach of our current imagination. She turns the page again, quickly and smoothly. 'So the opportunity that we have identified, through a technology that has surely been placed in our hands by the unknowable force that we have always called God, is to create a new world in which humanity is finally able to dispense with the props and social structures of its primitive, formative period—our constant searching for saviour figures, our impulses to impose controlling narratives on others, our fragile rituals and narratives of consolation and hope. We envision no less than a new world in which resources are distributed according to accurately projected need, in which humanity is able to break free from its endless cycle of conquest, aggregation, complacency, exhaustion and disintegration, and in which technological advancements are kept in lock-step with the progression of core universal values. Dare I even propose that in such a new world order, humanity would at last be able to live by the tenets of a love that we have so far only been able to preach?'

When Mrs Thorne eventually lifts her head, she says, 'I think you can all see why they call this technology *Deorum-X*.' She looks at Logie. 'This is surely ringing bells by now?'

Brio doesn't know what he wants Logie to say anymore and finds himself slowly scanning the faces of people who've become strangers from some earlier and more primitive world. And Mrs Thorne clearly thinks she's told them about some new hell on earth when in fact she's told him about a New Heaven where there are no secret women hidden away or leering faces that want him to admit he's hiding insane desires, no cruel schools or thoughtless mental hospitals, no Father T who gets struck down for betraying God and everyone he pretends to love, no mum who dies of a broken heart they call cancer. A New Heaven of one simple dad in one simple desert and one perfect Izzy in one simple home by the sea.

'Ringing bells?' Logie replies eventually. 'Well, I guess it does sound a lot like Catholicism. But hey, sign me up.'

This time, Logie's languid repudiation of Mrs Thorne's reading doesn't give Brio even a distant flutter of relief. It only sparks a deep anger at Logie for not wanting Tabo Forzac's perfect world to be true and possible—for being the enemy of everything he's ever wanted.

Prodding her glasses back into place, Mrs Thorne slips the printout back into her handbag. 'Anyway, Mr Logue, we mustn't forget the point of all this, which is to allow Brio to make a fully informed decision about whether he goes to the Northview to be properly cared for, or to a world of poorly lit attics and unregulated hypnosis, and fires that burn down the homes of struggling and vulnerable single mothers.' She draws herself up as though to deliver the definitive message at school assembly. 'So even though it's quite possible that you've already tampered with Brio's mind to the point where he's unable to make a rational decision, I invite you to acknowledge that, *one*, you would very much like to see a world in which true faith is replaced by the corrupted human agency of a machine—*two*, you are in the direct or indirect employ of Zpydr—and *three*, you have been tasked with delivering a *deepmind parable* purportedly written by Brio, which will supposedly have cured him of symptoms that have merely been suppressed by a form of hypnosis that's now known to be highly dangerous.' Without taking her eyes off Logie, she points at Brio and says, 'Tell him the truth, Mr Logue. So that he can be granted the fully informed agency to *decide*.'

'*No*,' Brio cries at Logie before he can respond to Mrs Thorne. 'I don't care about all that. And you can't tell them anyway, because you don't *know* whether it's true. Because they brainwashed you as well—at that place in America—after you tried to kill yourself.' Seeing eyebrows lift, Brio's as shocked as anyone. Where the hell did this come from? He didn't even know it was in his head. Except there she is on the docks, the self-confessed failed entertainer who couldn't even drown herself because some people are just too floaty.

'Is this true, Mr Logue?' Mrs Thorne's eyes have come to life with some contention of joy and worry that Brio doesn't understand.

Brio still can't stop himself. 'It *is* true. He tried to kill himself when he failed to become a writer. But CHANT saved him and he became a disciple.' He can't bear the hurt in Logie's eyes but what else could he have done? He had to stop him shattering that perfect world.

'Mr Logue …' Mrs Thorne's tone is matter-of-fact and clearly carries the mood of the whole packed room, 'if this is true, you are clearly unfit to be anywhere near this young man.' She looks at Mrs Charis. 'Surely, even our puppet health minister will now be forced to see sense.'

All eyes are back on Logie and Brio just wants Logie to believe in the perfect world so they can all be one big happy family that loves him.

'Well, that's a lodda personal stuff to unpack there.' Logie's voice is calm but his eyes are clouded. 'But on the big one … yeah, I had a bad patch. No shame in that. Fly too close to the sun, stuff can happen. Hence I've seen more than you, Mrs Thorne—the view from the other side. Really puts things in perspective.' He looks to

Brio. 'And you don't need to worry, buddy. Bad times come good. And like they say, if we didn't have the bad, we wouldn't know when we had it good.'

Logie's compelling blue eyes have drawn Brio helplessly back in, but he sees something frighteningly static in them that did *not* get cured by CHANT. Suddenly, Logie's almost death itself Brio feels the black hole wanting to suck *him* in too. And all he knows is that there's some wormhole connecting Logie's black hole and Ms Whittle's yawning chasm. Before Brio knows what he's saying, he's telling Mrs Thorne that he wants to be with *her*, at *her* house.

Mrs Thorne's mouth drops open and her forehead vanishes into wispy grey hair. '*My* house?' She glances at everyone else. 'Brio, dear, you need to, erm …'

'*Your* house,' he repeats firmly. 'And nowhere else.'

Now Mrs Thorne looks at Logie as though she wants him to take Brio after all. But Izzy cuts across them and tells Mrs Thorne that, 'He's right, your house is the only safe place. But we still need to hire a security guard to be outside in a car.'

Mrs Thorne stares uncomprehendingly at Izzy, but all eyes are on *her*, and Logie's have widened with some mix of worry and determination.

'Brio, dear …' It's Mrs Charis. 'I'm not sure that Mrs Thorne is really equipped for this kind of situation.'

'She *is*. She's got everything. And a lady who helps her with shopping too.' He holds Mrs Thorne's eyes like the lifetime she's spent holding his, and he prays to God to make her prove that she really does care and doesn't just preach lame allegories about *selflessness* and *compassion* when all she wants is to live alone and read books about great theories of perfect love and preparing for eternity. And he can see that Mrs Thorne knows it too, that she has to make amends for letting them drag him away to the home-from-hell when she could have put him in one of her three spare

210

bedrooms. Even the one without furniture would have been brilliant.

'I'm sorry, Brio,' Mrs Charis says firmly, 'but I'm afraid this simply isn't possible. Now, do please think again about going to Ms Whittle's. I'm sure that between Ms Whittle and Mr Logue you'll be well looked after and—'

'Brio will come with *me*,' Mrs Thorne says abruptly. 'Where he will be safe from all of *you*.' And leaving Mrs Charis floundering, she turns to Izzy. 'Dear, would you be so kind as to fetch a coat for Brio? And some shoes. We can arrange everything else later.'

Euphoria almost lifts Brio off the ground and he slews round on Ms Whittle, because now he wants it all. 'And you too. You have to put your proper glasses back on and your grey clothes, and bring cakes round so we can have tea together. And *then* I'll be able to finish it. And if you don't, I'll know you don't really care about me at all.'

And before anyone can think of some clever way to kill his decision, he strides right past the strong-arm nurse and out of the front door.

On reaching Mrs Thorne's sky-blue car, Brio presses himself back against the passenger door and confronts the gaggle of anxious pursuers with the candlestick. But the absurdity of his prison pyjamas and a dusk he hadn't expected pitch his decision into flux and all he can do is growl at everyone to get back.

'And don't talk,' he orders Dr Silash when she sets up Jesus-hands for hostage negotiation. Because there's only one person who can change his mind and that's Logie, who's edging forward, scanning the road and glancing at his watch. The Logie who's got to prove that he's willing to give up everything for his friend.

'Buddy, you need to finish this thing *your* way, okay?' And when Brio blocks his ears and closes his eyes, Logie says, 'All right, I get it', Mrs Thorne's reading sounded kinda milk and honey, swords into ploughshares, spears into pruning-knives, everyone their own priest. But apart from the fact that it's got nothing to do with me, it's a fantasy.'

'It's *not*.'

'My love,' Mrs Thorne calls from the other side of the car. 'Just get in, please. And Sister Jane, could you please pick up some food for dinner. I think you have a copy of Brio's list.'

Brio's still gripping the handle but can't bring himself to open the door. He sees the neighbours watching from their driveway and the old couple across the road looking out of an upstairs window.

'Buddy, come on, back up and pan wide here. If you go with Mrs Thorne, you're gonna have the bishop's list of banned words nailed to your tabletop and Ms Whittle doffing your dropped caps to the literary award panel. Instead of the *magnum opus dei* you swore you'd finish, you're gonna be offering up a muzzled lamb that's been clipped for the chop, a few stunted sentence stubs that resemble the instruction manual for a magnifying glass.'

'Mr *Logue*,' Mrs Thorne barks across the roof of her car, 'Brio has made up his mind. Brio, please get in.'

Seeing nothing in Logie but another smooth cleverness of weasel words, Brio turns his back and yanks the door handle.

'In fact, y'know what?' Logie says hurriedly, his voice suddenly on the verge of cracking. 'Mrs Thorne's not gonna let you write at all. Coz the truth is, she doesn't want anyone to write anything. She wants the whole world back at the beginning, when there was only one word and not a single wicked human to speak it out loud. Isn't that right, Mrs Thorne? To even dream of a single language that might unify humanity is to blaspheme, to dare to build a tower to Heaven? Well, I'm sorry,' he ploughs on when Mrs Thorne tries to speak, 'whatever the cardinal said in that spiel he cooked up for you, language is all we got. And whether you like it or whether you think it's a rotten apple from a big bad tree, language is as alive and fluid as life itself. Best of all, language is where you actually find *God*. Coz language adapts so swiftly to the cosmic flux that it's speaking before you even know you're listening. And where you do *not* find God is in the crippling fear of change that disables the minds of so many who seek to teach. Jesus *Christ*, we're nowhere near written out and there's so much more that needs to be said.'

Now Brio knows for sure that Logie's whole act is for him. That's why Logie's clearly looking to see how much more browbeating is needed to get his prey into the faded orange campervan.

Logie glances again at his watch and this time it's something more. He's keeping the show going to buy time. But for what?

Brio desperately wants to go with Mrs Thorne, but he needs to know what Logie's buying time for, and Mrs Thorne can't get into the car either, because her hand's shaking and he knows she always has to have the last word and win for God.

'You may dream of a world beyond Babel, Mr Logue. But as far as I'm concerned, language is a gift from God, and every piece of writing is the product of divine inspiration. Which means that every word we write must be offered to the glory of God. And that list of banned words as you call it, it's there for one reason only, which is to protect vulnerable minds from the degradations and predations of human society. And until the day I die, it will be my job to protect Brio from people like you.'

Logie scoffs and he's not even buying time anymore. 'I'll tell you what we need to protect him from. We need to protect him from the do-gooders who write the safeguarding manuals in the morning then lurk off home to revel in another fifty shades of grime. And you know what? The more these fine folk protect the innocent, the more the purveyors of titillation cry censorship and fight to outdo each other in a race to the ever-deeper bottom. And round and round it goes, and human life gets more and more desensitised and pornographic, numb from over-exposure and dumb from over-protection. So if you wanna protect Brio, how about you just get in your car and drive it to the moon?'

Before Mrs Thorne can find words or Brio can understand whether he still wants to go with her, Logie says, 'Buddy, you know full well what you've got to do if you wanna feel the Hoggit's words flowing onto that page. You've got to fly free like never before. You godda laugh and cry and pray and shout out. Above all else, you've got to rescue all that banned vocab and use it with gay abandon, one brave new word after another till you're feasting like a Hoggit at sea on the can of beautiful words these people want to bury in the sand and turn back into rock!'

Logie turns on Mrs Thorne and Ms Whittle, his eyes so intense that Brio feels himself almost ripped off the door handle. 'Coz writing free won't just prove the innocence of these poor, falsely accused words, it'll reclaim our stolen innocence itself—from people like *you*!' Throwing open his arms, he turns the neighbours into the eyes and ears of the whole world. 'I tell you, people—and you're God's witnesses for this beautiful kid—the only way we're gonna conquer this madness is to reclaim the Hoggit-like part of our collective heart and soul! Coz the only way we become adults when the need for genuine faith in the unknowable asks us to remain childlike is simply to remember that God is a force beyond intelligence!'

Logie's on such a roll that to Brio he's either insane or channelling the very voice of God.

'You hearing me?' Logie cries wildly to the street of blank windows. 'To be godlike is to be childlike in our souls! Coz that's the only way we can truly grow up—by taking the innocence with us, to bless our knowledge and wisdom! To help us see through the fear-fuelled lies of people who say they want to keep us safe but actually just want to keep themselves safe from *us*! So stand by, wonderful world!' He plunges a fist into the air. 'For the bright beacon of Hoggit Castle is about to be relit, and this time there'll be fifty shades of *light*! Hurrah for the Hoggit! Hurrah for the tender part at the centre of all of us that needs a shield of spikes no more!'

'Oh, Mr Logue!' Ms Whittle cries. 'You really *can* help Brio! I'm so sorry I didn't understand you before. Brio, my beautiful boy, you don't want me to be silly old Sister Jane again. You want me to look after you and Mr Logue while those divine words pour out of your soul to a waiting world! Lead on, Mr Logue!' She casts open an arm towards his campervan. 'Fly us away from these blind fools in your mighty chariot of fire!'

But all Brio can see in the half circle of astonished faces is his own confusion about who or what or which right or wrong he's supposed to be choosing.

Mrs Thorne pushes in from behind Brio to open the car door for him. 'Get in.'

Her command sends him stumbling away from the car, but when he turns for Logie's campervan, his feet won't move and Mrs Thorne catches him by an arm. He breaks free and dashes a few steps to be safe in his own tight cylinder of striped pyjamas and bare feet. It's a simple choice between faded orange and sky blue, and all he can see is the frightening lure of violet. But when he turns to run, he finds himself staring at a police car that's pulled up in front of Mrs Thorne's.

Now part of the group himself, Brio remains wide-eyed as three police officers pull down their chequered baseball caps and start walking towards them.

'*Under arrest?*' Ms Whittle gasps, clutching her crucifix. 'Why would you want to do that?'

215

'For supplying to a minor at the Seaview Hotel last night a Class A drug, Ms Whittle—namely psilocybin. Or in the common parlance, magic mushrooms.'

Mrs Thorne clamps an octopus of fingertips to her forehead. 'What have you done, Sister Jane?'

A different order of panic grips Brio, while Izzy accuses an anxious-looking Dr Shenoy of breaking his promise not to report Ms Whittle.

As Dr Shenoy protests his innocence and one of the police officers recites the right to remain silent, Ms Whittle presses a spindly hand to her breast and lets out little gasps. But just as it looks as though Ms Whittle's going to faint, she throws open her arms.

'No, officer! You're wrong! It is to heal humanity's wounded soul that God in their glorious bounty has created magic mushrooms! And mushrooms are better than any of their religions or medications! In fact, any day now, it won't just be legal to use these beautiful gifts from God, it will be compulsory! Then we'll all live happily ever after in a world without hate or crime!'

'We'll be out of a job then,' observes one of the police officers, glancing at the other.

'Yes!' Ms Whittle cries. 'And there'll be no more war either! Tell them, Mr Logue! I know you understand these things!'

'What I know,' Logie says flatly, 'is that psilocybin is being trialled on end-of-life patients coz it might help 'em embrace the idea of their own death. I also know that the right dosages of psilocybin are a long way from figured out. So call me a stick-in-the-mud, Miss Dubbya, but I'd say that shrooms are pretty much the last thing you'd want to give to a kid who has thoughts of suicide.'

Ms Whittle clutches her powdery white cheeks. 'Oh, goodness.'

'Exactly,' Logie agrees. 'So it's lucky Brio ain't in that category—

no thanks to you and your cracked pottery of a belief system.'

One of the police officers gestures towards the patrol car. 'This way, Ms Whittle.' And after she's dived between them and fled down the street, he sighs and says, 'Constable, could you please go and make sure she doesn't hurt herself?'

'This must be kept strictly confidential,' Mrs Thorne says swiftly to the remaining police officers. 'The bishop will speak to the chief constable first thing in the morning.'

'I'm afraid those days are over, Mrs Thorne. In fact, as Ms Whittle's a member of your staff who was looking after Brio pursuant to her role as school counsellor, I'm going to have to ask you to accompany us to the station as well.'

Brio stands in mute shock as the two remaining pillars in his life are pulled out from under the sky to leave nothing but the ghost of a pale blue car abandoned at the side of the road.

Dr Silash is about to say something to Brio when Mrs Charis turns to Logie. 'I assume you'll still be willing to work with Brio at the care home?'

Logie shrugs. 'Not sure why you're asking *me*, Mrs C. Like the minister said, it's Brio's decision.'

~ PART FIVE ~

THE TRUE TOWERS

Faith and belief alone will never bring you to enlightenment.
You must follow the ten-fold path of good deeds and great
works. And if you still retain your innocence, even after the
attainment of wisdom, you must surely reach
that place where fifty shades of light
will fill the soul.

Anon
The Transfiguration Sutras

14

BRIO DOESN'T LIKE SITTING in the snub-fronted cockpit of Logie's campervan. He feels exposed and vulnerable, as though even the slightest impact could crumple him into a short sharp pain that'd last forever. But even though in the darkness of the moorland road he's lost all sense of where they are, he still doesn't want to know their destination, he just needs to *be there*, so it can all happen.

'You wanna talk yet?'

'*No.*'

'But I mean, you must've had a pretty major storm in that teacup?'

Brio has to block out another rush of confused feelings. 'I don't want to talk about it. And anyway, it helped me remember the Purple Code.'

Logie's head flicks round. 'You serious?'

'Keep your eyes on the road. Yes, I *am* serious. So all I need is my notes.'

There's another silence and Brio starts to count it down in his head.

'Buddy, your notes really were lost in the fire. But you don't need 'em.'

'I *do*. And I know you've got them.'

'I don't. And I wish with all my heart you'd trust me.'

Confused by his feelings towards Logie, Brio falls straight back into the chaos of the hostel and the arguing mob at Izzy's. Most tormenting of all is not knowing whether he imagined the whole thing about Mr Hare's secret woman. And if he did just imagine it, *why* did such words come into his head so clearly? He realises that Logie's been giving him a series of gauging glances. '*What?*'

'Well, I suppose I haven't been sure whether to tell you, but I think if I did, it'd help us understand each other a bit better.'

Determined not be drawn in, Brio turns to look out at the featureless dark. But something about Logie's voice has changed and he can't help looking back. 'Tell me what?'

'Well, when I was around your age, *my* mum died too, in a pretty similar way.'

Brio's left grappling with strange new feelings in his stomach. How is it possible that Logie's suddenly the only person in the world who can truly understand? And Logie was there all along, hiding in plain sight right under his nose. But the sudden feeling of being irresistibly drawn to Logie only ramps up his confusion.

'So I know what it's like,' Logie goes on. 'Your life becomes a whirl of hospital doors and different kinds of crying. Pitying teachers and kids who have no clue what to say or didn't even know it happened. You can't think, can't play. Teachers want to be nice, so they let you off tests. But you do 'em anyway coz you know that's what they want really. Problem is, you're so fried you can't add up, can hardly spell your own name. Then one minute your mum's in bed like it's Sunday morning and you're bringing tea and toast, next thing she's gone and you're in that home-from-hell and it's a prison full of hard nutters and sad bolters.'

But no sooner has Brio let his head fall forward than he realises Logie's stopped talking in an American accent. He hurriedly swipes aside the snot and tears. 'You're not American.'

'Never actually said I was.'

'So why've you been speaking like that?' Brio's world has capsized again and he feels cheated of the cleansing purge. '*Why?*'

'Everything sounds so much better in an American accent, don't you think? Whatever you say's just godda be something new and better. Something that leaves the past where it belongs. It's all about the position of the larynx and that God-given intent to bring change.'

Reeling back in time, Brio sees how Logie was never American at all. His puff and twang were too big and swanky, they didn't match his mouth. 'It's fake.'

'Aren't accents just another kind of attire? If we can choose everything about ourselves from our pop socks to our perfect gender, why not our accents too?'

'We can't choose anything,' Brio says angrily. 'It's all from God.'

'And so's the freedom to choose. Look, I just want to be myself with ya. And we both wanna be friends, *don't* we? I mean, real friends who trust each other.'

The unexpected touch of Logie's hand on his knee freezes Brio's thoughts. Those long spindly fingers are poisoned ivy and the moonlight makes them something far worse.

'You're gonna be all good,' Logie says, giving Brio's knee a manly squeeze. 'I can feel it in my bones.' And when Brio can't speak, he says, 'Meaning, I'm not gay and nor are you as far as I can see. Not trans either, or any of those other new island nations. So ignore the world and deep six the binge thinking. Don't distract yourself with red herrings.' He gives Brio's knee a firm farewell pat and sits up straight to grip the steering wheel with both hands.

Alarmed to find himself gazing at Logie in the same adoring way the Hoggit did with Lord Rumbuck in the ramshackle boat, Brio looks quickly back out of the side window. But there's no escape there either, because he knows that when Logie removed his hand, he was left feeling a kind of loss and emptiness, even disappointment.

'So which accent would you prefer?' Logie asks. 'I'm okay either way.'

Brio presses his forehead to the cold window and fixes on countryside he doesn't recognise in the dark. When it stares back with the spectral eeriness of green moonlight, he closes his eyes and tries to wipe his thoughts of absolutely everything. It even occurs to him that he'd like another cup of Tania's tisane.

'American,' he replies eventually. 'And never talk in that other one again.'

As they bump and rattle down the rough track, Logie explains that it leads to a small cottage. He knows the owner, he says, an old lady who's lived there all her life. 'I drop in on her from time to time. These woods all belong to the cottage. We won't be disturbed.'

Up ahead, a narrower track breaks off into the woods. Logie switches down to sidelights but it's enough to illuminate the dark outline of a drystone woodman's hut. As they approach, the detail becomes clearer: thick slates interlaced like walls of horizontal books and a carpet of pine needles that creates a kind of forecourt.

Logie negotiates the van over bumpier ground to one side of the hut, where an end wall and a third of the roof has collapsed. Someone's arranged part of the rubble into two neat stacks redolent of Stone Age cairns. At the far end, a wide fireplace seems almost incongruous. It's a fairy-tale ruin in a magical land and Logie parks across the open end to form the missing wall.

'You'll wanna get out of those pyjamas,' Logie says. 'I got you some new gear.'

Logie busies himself outside the van while Brio dresses into his latest costume, which is like nothing he's ever worn: grown-up thermal vest and fleece-lined lumberjack shirt, hardy jeans that evoke backcountry and ankle boots to climb a mountain.

'Wanna help me build a fire? Your bandages look pretty good.'

Standing on the hallowed ground of pine needles and twigs,

protected by the canopy of trees, Brio's surprised to find that he feels safe from the night and he breathes in the mossy aroma.

Kindling the flame takes effort and finesse, but together they persevere until it smokes enough for Logie to nudge a corner of newspaper into the invisible kernel of heat. Kneeling in close, they shield the precious flicker until it weaves up through the balls of newspaper. The flames spread fast and Brio's so thrilled he says the first thing to come into his head.

'She'll be out next week,' Logie replies. 'And you don't need to feel bad. Coz you know she didn't like that house anyway.'

But he does feel bad, and in some tipped-up way he misses Pippa, and he can't stop himself asking whether the insurance will pay.

'What'd be the point in having it otherwise? But everything'll be fine, so put it out of your mind, okay? Shall we sit?' He gestures to the chunks of sawn tree trunk but Brio wants to stay kneeling with Logie by the fire.

'Are there any animals in these woods?'

'A lot of rabbits, for sure. Moles and voles too. And there's a pond over there, so we might get a couple of frogs checking in to make sure it's us. And bats, many types. None of them'll harm ya.'

Brio looks to the campervan's open door and the table where it's all going to happen. Yet despite his comforting need to be writing, he's drawn back to the flames, to memories of being with Father T in the small rocky bay toasting marshmallows by moonlight, taking turns to read from Father T's precious signed copy of *The Hobbit*.

Logie takes up a rusty metal rod and prods the fire. 'So here we are, buddy, here and now. Though really there's no such thing as now, *is* there?' His tone has become mellow with hints of rhythm. 'There's just that fragile membrane between baggage from the past and hope for the future. The present's so quick it's gone before it's had the chance to exist. Yet it's all there actually *is*, the past made bearable by the promise of what's to come.' This time Logie's poke at the fire releases a djinni of sparks and bright energy. 'Buddy, would you mind if I asked who it is you don't want Izzy to go and see?'

The intrusion jolts Brio. He wants to keep all the bad things close to his chest: the yawning chasm into Lord Rumbuck's secret woman, the falsified birth certificate, his mum having a fake name—and some kind of black hole he can't bear to think about. So as though to appease his guilt about withholding all those precious worries, he tells Logie that it's Bella Ripley who Izzy wants to see.

Sensing tension, Brio glances up, but he sees only mild curiosity. 'Why would Izzy want to see Bella Ripley?' Logie asks casually.

Needing to keep the noisy and pressing build-up of worries inside, Brio tries to get back to the calming feeling of Logie's hand on his knee. But out it all gushes—how Father T would have told Bella Ripley that his dad was alive because that's the secret Father T knew. How Zpydr doesn't want his dad to be alive. How they want Bella Ripley to say Father T told her that his dad suffered from mental illness and committed suicide. 'And Bella Ripley hated me and Mum, so she'll love telling Zpydr's lies. And Zpydr's bribed and threatened her anyway, just to make sure. And Izzy thinks Bella Ripley will tell her everything if she goes to see her in person. That's why the Hoggit has to find his father before Izzy gets to Bella Ripley.'

In the silence that erupts from the great outpouring, Brio goes into panic mode about how much he's just given away, whether he can trust Logie with all those most closely guarded secrets even if he's *not* working for Zpydr. Everything hangs on what Logie says next. What he *does*. Whether he's drawing closer to put the hand back on his knee or ho in for the kill.

'So the Hoggit hasn't failed yet, huh?'

Brio looks up sharply. 'Who said he failed?'

'No one at all. But he must've had a few challenges getting onto that ship. Maybe he's even gone a little AWOL right now. But I'm sure he'll be back.'

'He *will*.' Brio wants Logie to say more, help him get back in the Groove. But in the crackling fire he can hear how hard Logie's thinking about something and the worry reignites. 'What is it?'

Logie stands up and rests a hand on Brio's shoulder. Leaving him with another masculine squeeze, he goes to stand right by the fire. 'I guess I'm wondering why you're so sure Father T thought your dad was alive. Did he tell *you* that?'

The trap-door in Brio's stomach drops open and he has to look away.

'You don't have to tell me,' Logie adds in the same calm voice. 'But I think you'd like to.'

'I *can't*.'

'Did you hear him say something to someone else?'

'I can't talk about it.'

'But I mean, if you're sure Father T told Bella Ripley your dad was alive, wouldn't you *want* Izzy to go and see her? Wouldn't *you* want to see her?'

Brio curls toes to press his boots into the mat of pine needles and twigs. 'I have to write now.'

But he doesn't move and nor does Logie.

'Are you worried that Father T actually told Bella Ripley something else?'

'*No.*'

More fire gazing, even a little search together for any stars that might have moved into view through the shield of leafy scales. For the first time, Brio has the strange feeling that maybe they're not alone, after all.

'Are you worried Bella Ripley might know something else? Something that's not connected with your dad.'

Brio can't stop the frustrated moan. 'Why can't you just want my dad to be alive?'

'Of course I do. I also wish Father T was alive.'

But Logie's voice isn't American enough and Brio's stomach crawls.

'I have to *write*.'

'Father T was a huge part of your life. He loved you.'

Brio fights down tears because tears don't belong anymore.

'Look, it doesn't matter what happened, okay? You just need to forgive him for everything.'

'I can't.'

'Buddy, we all have to forgive.'

'I *can't*.'

'Because he never said sorry?'

'How can he say sorry? He's *dead*.' He has to pucker his lips to stop them wobbling. He's never felt so much part of a crackling fire. Not even with Father T.

'You know, in the eyes of God, forgiveness comes before sorry, right?'

Now Brio has to clench everything. Because Father T said the very same words, so many times. He stares at Logie. Did he actually *know* Father T?

'Don't you *want* to forgive him, though? I think you do.'

The only way Brio can keep the tears down is with words. 'He broke his oath to God. So I can't even *want* to forgive him.' He has to get to the writing table quickly, but when he glances back up, the way they're looking at each other feels good.

'When you say Father T broke his oath to God, you mean by leaving the Church?'

'*No*. I mean, *yes*. But …'

'But he did something else?'

He's desperate to stop himself, but his even greater need is to get it all out. 'He swore on the Bible he'd look after me if anything happened to Mum. But he didn't. Because the devil woman took him away and wanted him to herself.' He grinds the short bursts of rage into the fire. 'She's the devil. All her jewellery and that fake accent. She didn't love Father T at all. She just wanted to make him leave the Church. Because she didn't get him the first time, when they were younger, when he didn't want to marry her because he wanted to be a priest like God wanted. He'd never have died if he kept his oath. He'd never have left the Church. The Pope would never have sent him the letter that killed him. But it wasn't because of the Pope he died. It was because he swore on the Bible he'd look after me like a father. It's the same as swearing on your life. That's why he died. God struck him down. He's gone to Hell.'

When it's finally over, Brio feels an emptiness that could be filled with almost anything, and Logie's kneeling next to him in exactly the same position, bum on heels and bandaged palms resting on folded legs.

'You feel a bit better now?' Logie asks quietly, and, when Brio can't answer, he asks whether there's anything else about Father T he'd like to share with the woodland folk and their night sky. Brio knows that even though Logie's his trusted friend, he might still have some ideas about Father T that don't even belong in black holes or yawning chasms.

'Father T said that all the best writers keep a diary. Because a diary lets you go back to any day in the past to see what happened as though you were there. And because time has passed since you wrote the diary entry, you can see why the event happened, which means you can start seeing into the future as well. So you become a Lord of Time, because you can see into the past *and* the future. But if you write a lie in your diary, it won't stay in the past, it'll come with you to every sunrise. It'll get bigger and stronger, till one day it'll rush on ahead of you and lie in wait.'

They sit in a reflective silence until Logie says, 'At some point in your life, I think you'll want to forgive them both, Father T and Bella too. To reach that point, you'll probably have to understand why each one of them did what they did. Maybe somewhere buried away, you already know. Perhaps, along the way, you've had some glimpse of wanting the love between Father T and Bella Ripley to have been real and true. To be real and true even now—in Heaven.'

The old rhythm and timbre in Logie's voice are easily discernible now, and Brio doesn't want to resist the tingling down his back. Yet still he must be firm and tell Logie, 'I *don't* want that. And I never will.'

'But you care about Bling and Mr T'wit?'

'Yes, I do. But they've got nothing to do with Father T and Bella Ripley.'

'I know. I just love them and kinda needed to know if you did too.'

As they make their way towards the welcoming light of the campervan, Brio stops to pick up the long, perfect feather that's surely been sent by God to answer the call. He sniffs it as he did in the beginning and runs the delicate fibrils across his lips.

Logie proffers on his own bandaged palm a Swiss Army knife already open at the right blade. 'This time, it's you who's gonna carve the nib. Cut away from yourself.'

Brio hesitates, but five deft slices later he's fashioned a fine-edged point that he knows will write perfectly. Back in the van, Logie places the Swiss Army knife on the kitchenette counter, blade still open. He rests a hand on the precious written pages. 'The fire will guide you to a big ending. When you've finished, I'll show you how to make a camp oven. We can bake some bread.'

Brio nods and Logie gestures him to the table.

'So you're ready to pick up where our friend left off? You know where he ended up after that big dust-up on the docks?'

'Yes.'

'That's excellent. And just remember, your brain knows things that you don't. So let it teach you how to find them.' Logie sits down opposite and rests his palms on the table. 'I'm not gonna be anywhere near you, okay? I'll be by the fire. Before you start, though, I need you to take one little leap of faith and let me help you get back in the Groove.'

Brio knows enough to know that he doesn't need to think anything. He nods again and waits for Logie to close his eyes so he can do likewise and join him in something akin to a prayer.

'Okay, then here you are, my friend,' Logie says quietly, his voice already slow and rhythmic. 'And what a road it's been … a road where even angels may fear to tread, to spread their wings, to share their light …'

The calming fog closes in and Brio makes one final adjustment to the quill in his bandaged hand. 'Yeah.'

'And so, Young Prince, you are called once more to your mission … your mission to save us all … all who merely tweet from the nest and wail from the belly.'

The sense of rhythm builds and Brio wants to join in. 'Yes, arise, Young Prince,' he hears himself say. 'Make yourself *of* and *with* and *for* the eternal life.' All that matters now is the taste and the weight of the words that feed the rhythm. The meaning is nothing.

'And find within that primal essence its animal soul, wherein you'll find the buried self you'll need for the journey yet to come. For only you, young god, can behold the right question.'

'Yes … I who am called above all others to imagine the thoughts and dreams of small creatures … the dreams they have about *us*.'

'And don't be concerned if some of those for whom you write have not yet understood that if freewheeling wilfulness is indeed a quixotic fantasy, if our choices are merely the zeroed-in sum-of-all-sums, then what more can we do but celebrate our animal instinct? For if this leaden stasis is to end in an evolutionary explosion revealed upon us by our own agents of change, then truly we must let that still small voice of calm be the one wisp of light that accompanies us down the long bright rabbit hole … down and down, and down again, that we may be born once more, as pure and loving creatures of our god-of-gods within.'

Brio dips to recharge the feather and strains to see into the foul-smelling darkness. As the gloom takes its hazy lack of shape, he feels a cold dampness under his bottom and realises he's sitting on a mountainside of slimy, barnacled anchor chain. With alarm, he senses that he's on his own, and he's in the ship's echoing anchor chain compartment. His thoughts flash straight back to the horrors of the dockside chase. The rats and dogs. The giants with torches. Oh, God, Lord Rumbuck and Madame Haha have surely been torn to shreds. Suffering a glimpse of the Dark Arched Window, Brio cries aloud and jolts to find himself staring across the turquoise tabletop in light so dim that Logie's little more than an outline of monotone check and striped beanie.

But is Logie really as tuned out as he's pretending to be with his bolt upright Lotus position and fluttering eyelids? Or is this what Logie's like when he's caught in the act of changing things to make the Hoggit sit there in the stinking, slimy chain till he's got no choice but to go and look for Lord Rumbuck on his own? Yes, of course that's what's going on. And surprise, surprise, the Hoggit will find the Queen without Lord Rumbuck's help too, and he'll see that with the Ring of Love he can even *save her* on his own. And after he's performed this miracle, he'll believe he can do anything, even cope with the bloodied remains of Lord Rumbuck and Madame Haha. In fact, he'll take it as a sign that the Sacred Prophecy has evolved in the way of all scriptures, that he's free to act and has the strength of heart to go and find the great father on his own. And if Logie's little brainwashing ruse doesn't work, those flickering eyelids will just manoeuvre the Hoggit into an endless hiatus of rotating washing lines and crop circles and walking round and round till he has to give up and accept that his father isn't there at the Tower of Time, after all—isn't there and never was—because he's dead by some trifling misunderstanding, some slip of his own hand.

Brio finds himself staring at the shadowy monotone check of Logie's shirt, the striped beanie. But to hell with Logie. The truth is in the ship's pitch-dark anchor chain compartment, and Lord Rumbuck's alive and well. But Lord Rumbuck's refusing to go and save the Queen till he's recovered from his battle wound. And it's not even a real wound. He's just stubbed his toe. And Logie's eyelids aren't merely flickering, they're secretly doing stuff. *Aren't* they?

'You don't want me to find the Tower of Time at all,' Brio says angrily. 'You just want to sit here in this stinking place till the ship leaves and we fail. Then you'll—'

'Write it down, buddy,' Logie murmurs. 'If it's not on paper, it didn't happen.'

Having waited to make sure that Lord Rumbuck was coming after him, the Hoggit threw himself into scrabbling along the greasy, echoing pipe. The further he drove himself into the bowels of the vile ship, the louder the clamour grew. Suddenly, he found his way blocked by the corroded mesh of a small air-vent, through which he could see down into a scene from hell: a thousand feral rodents spit-polishing ten thousand grime-encrusted pieces of junk into moguls of gleaming treasure.

'Bring me *zat*!' commanded a silken voice, which froze the

rats as though in a game of musical chairs.

For a moment, the Hoggit thought he was seeing things. Yet even after a hard rub of the eyes, the apparition prevailed: a slender black cat atop a high tower of rusted tanks, her dress a slink of glittering filigree metalwork that tinkled as she shifted languidly in her nest of sumptuous cushions.

'Was it this yer wanted, my love?'

The low, gravelly voice diverted the Hoggit's attention to an obese and filthy brown cat that grovelled at the foot of the black cat's untouchable summit.

Having glanced down at the slavishly proffered teaspoon, the black cat yawned and stroked the front of her dress, which the Hoggit now saw was a gleaming crochet of trinkets woven together with shiny wire and threads of twinkling chain.

'*Non*,' she purred. The weight of glinting metal that adorned her arms seemed to make pointing an effort. 'I want the cake fork.'

The filthy brown cat's face fell. 'But I got yer the spoon, my love—to stir your heart!' He flickered his eyebrows. 'If yer know what I mean.'

She sniffed dismissively. 'It will take a bigger spoon than that to stir *my* heart.'

The laugh startles Brio but he finds Logie's eyes closed.

'You laughed.'

'Sounded like a rat laugh to me.'

'It wasn't. Rats don't laugh.'

'Sure they do. You want me to go outside?'

Brio closes his eyes and dips the nib. 'Just stay still. And be silent.'

As soon as the gleaming cake-fork arrived at the top of the tower of tanks, the filthy brown cat lumbered himself round to offer up his gift. 'My love, it's the fork you always wanted.'

'*Ssank* you,' she sighed and allowed him to slobber over her free hand. 'My darling Ripper.'

'Oh, my beautiful Bling,' he gushed as she reclined and laid a bejewelled foot on his shoulder.

She turned the cake fork over in her hand, gazing critically, then held it up as a mirror and toyed with one of her glimmering earrings. Then she let her hand slide down to the suspender that caressed her thigh.

'Oh, my love,' Ripper garbled, tottering under his own weight. 'I love what yer've done wiv those elastic watch straps.'

Bling didn't take her eyes off herself. 'They are not watch straps, you chump. They are timeless lingerie. To keep you … *suspended*.'

'Oh, gawd,' Ripper drooled. 'You're so gorgeous I godda see you in the light.' He clicked his fingers at a pair of rats in the rusting rafters, who jumped to manoeuvre a small caged bulb that dangled down above Bling. But the limelight also cast a shadow at Bling's feet and with a shriek she began to leap around as though on hot coals.

'Get the arcin' thing still!' bawled Ripper at the rats. 'Don't panic, my love. I'm 'ere for yer.'

The lantern finally came back under control and Bling quickly gathered her composure. 'Don't worry,' she said with a sniff. 'Your slaves are doing their best. And, as they say, many hands make light work. Heh heh.'

Another snorty laugh broke in, definitely from a stinking rat.

'Oh, you're so smart,' Ripper moaned. 'Tell me, I beg yer,

when are we gonna get marri—'

'*Don't* ... use that word.' With her big toe, she gave him a cursory rub on the cheek. 'Not yet.'

'But how long yer gonna make me wait, my love? I got yer the bigger boat for all yer stuff. Then I got yer even more stuff, and an even bigger boat.'

Bling peered down and sniffed again. 'I will be ready,' she oozed, 'when I have ... *enough*.'

Ripper wrung his hands. 'But what's enough, my love? What's too little? What's too much?'

'All you need to know about *enough*,' she purred, running her palms down the shimmering dress, 'is that I will know the perfect *piece* when I see it. And it will be handmade with *lurv*, to protect me from all the pain of the world.'

'Don't *I* protect yer?'

She smiled wryly. 'No one tries harder, my little chubby-chub. But this piece will be ... sophisticated.'

Ripper gawped. 'Ser—*what*?'

She rolled her eyes. '*Serr* ...'

'*Serrr*,' he parroted helplessly.

'Ser-*fist* ...'

'Sir *Fist*?' A green shadow flashed across Ripper's narrowed eyes and he chewed his knuckle. 'Oh, my love, tell me this ain't some knob who's got a bigger ship than me.' His fists clenched like rocks to throw and he turned to bellow at the mob below. And as the rats tore into piles of junk in search of that perfect something to appease Bling's unquenchable desire, Guzzle snatched up his rat-o'-nine-tails and unleashed a crack-lashing of lightning strikes around their ears that made the Hoggit cower.

'Well?' Lord Rumbuck grunted at the Hoggit. 'Do you at last apprehend the truth that lay concealed within that wicked owl's twisty words? Your "Queen" is held captive by no more than greed. This curse is entirely of her own elaborate manufacture. So come, we shall leave her to drown in her own desires and proceed as prophesied with a lifetime of noble trials.'

Even before he's looked up at Logie, Brio slams down the quill. 'That's not how the Queen was.'

Logie jolts and shakes his head clear. 'What's happening?'

'You *know* what's happening. The Queen wasn't some greedy gangster with the Vile Villain around her little finger. It was him keeping *her* captive.'

But his words snigger at him and he sees that Lord Rumbuck was right. Mr T'wit must have known all along that his long-lost love was like this. Mr T'wit had just lived in hope that one day she'd be as she was when they basked in the first flush of love. And what meaning those wise words of Mr T'wit contain now—*so hard to accept the truth about those we love, even harder when it's those we need.*

But Brio's sadness flares into an indignation that erupts as anger. 'Mr T'wit never cared about the Hoggit at all. He just sent him off into hell without a thought for his oath to Grandma.' Brio's tears well and his fists clench. 'I *hate him.*'

But Logie merely takes a long, slow breath and forms his thumbs and forefingers into small o's. 'Who says Bling can't be saved? And did Mr T'wit not send the Hoggit on his quest with a blessing of trust and faith that he wouldn't fail? Mr T'wit's long-lost love may seem beyond redemption, but doesn't the Hoggit carry the Ring of Love? And even though the Hoggit knows he might be torn to pieces by a thousand rats, doesn't he have faith that when he bathes Bling's heart in the great light, she'll banish the rats forever and thus save him too?'

Brio has to concentrate on his gulp, and whatever else he was feeling he has to get his head round the weird and sudden euphoria that Logie's words have triggered.

'Write it down, buddy.'

'Write what?'

'What's in your head—that the Hoggit suddenly saw how little was needed to save the Queen. He had only to—'

'*Shush.*'

He had only to push out the flimsy grille of the air-vent and he'd stand proud in the opening where they could all see him like God above the mountaintop. Then he'd simply hold up the Ring of Love for the Queen to behold and she'd be freed from the Curse of Glitterlove forever.

But then the Hoggit

'What's wrong?'

'Nothing.'

'Then why have you stopped? Why's the Hoggit just standing there?'

Brio doesn't understand either. And the Hoggit's too ashamed for him to write it down.

'Buddy, the Hoggit wanted you to write every word he told you. So why isn't he doing his duty and saving the Queen? Doesn't he know that love and duty are two sides of the same coin and it doesn't matter which side it lands?'

Prickly heat bites at Brio's back and he wants to rip it off. 'The Hoggit *does* want the Queen to be to saved. But Lord Rumbuck must be the one who saves her. And Lord Rumbuck doesn't want to do that anymore.'

'Why can't the Hoggit save her himself?' Logie's calm retorts are swift and relentless. 'The Sacred Prophecy didn't say anything about this quest to save the Queen. That came from Mr T'wit.'

This throws Brio into a confusion that tightens the old knot in his chest. Is it possible that some parts of the Sacred Prophecy were no more than devoted ornamentation by Grandma?

'The Hoggit's done countless brave things on his own,' Logie says quietly. 'Is he not truly ready?'

They fall silent, but Brio's insides writhe and he senses Logie closing in as intensely as he feels the Hoggit's shame and confusion. 'Don't speak.'

'I don't have to, buddy. Because I know you need to concentrate on how deeply you're feeling for the Hoggit in his moment of crisis.'

'I said, don't *speak*.'

'And you know that if the Hoggit can't overcome his fear of Bling stealing away the love of his beloved guardian … if he can't overcome the fear of losing the love that means more to him than anything else in the world, then he's going to fail to save her. And if he fails to save her, Mr T'wit will feel it more surely than he feels a change in the weather. Back there on the splintery castle floor, he'll die of his broken heart.'

Brio feels himself shrinking and burning up, furious with himself and loathing Bella Ripley, hating Logie and loving Father T—

'Come on,' Logie murmurs. 'This is just about the Hoggit and Bling and Mr T'wit. It doesn't concern anyone else in the world. And you know the Hoggit can do this.'

'*Okay*,' Brio half sobs. But when he tries to force the quill down, his face twists with tears.

'Buddy, let the Hoggit feel his love for Mr T'wit.' Logie's almost chanting now. 'Because it's his love for Mr T'wit that will lead him to love for Bling.'

Brio fights to control his shaking hand, but the harder he presses the quill down, the more it bends, crumples—and as it skids across the turquoise tabletop in a smear of purple ink, his head flies back and he lets out a cry that's almost a shriek. He springs up from the table, breaking it off at the hinges and tipping paper and ink over fast-dodging Logie and the vacated seat. 'Father T's dead,' he cries. 'And it's all my fault.'

Logie lurches backwards as Brio tears open the van's sliding door. Out in the hut, Brio cries out again and again till it's a seamless bellowing from somewhere deep inside him, and it rages on like an exorcism that kicks and clutches hair and lets out high-pitched shrieks and needs to vomit but can't. It's only when he has to stop for air that an invisible foot kicks his shins out from under him and he collapses to his knees. And out it all comes, how Father T didn't die at the foot of the altar because of the letter from the Church. He died on the garden path at Bluebells because they sent him away with tears in his eyes and told him to never come back. He died of the stroke right there because they cast him out of the garden with no chance of being forgiven. 'And I never saw him again,' Brio sobs. 'Oh, God, I loved him so much but it was me who killed him.'

15

'I'M JUST CHILLING WITH YOU NOW,' Logie says in his quiet, rhythmic voice, 'and we're not in any other states of mind or being. It's the seventh week of spring ... the middle of the night ... a little chill in the air ... but our fire's going strong and we're under our roof and the sheltering sky. So we're safe ... just a couple of guys taking it easy ... taking care of each other. They don't need to be thinking about Father T right now, because there's a time for all things under Heaven ... and all they need to remember right now is that they're warm and you loved Father T as much as he loved you ... because he was the father you always knew, and he loved you as much as you loved him. And though we're not thinking about Father T, we know that you never did anything to hurt him, never did the smallest thing to bring him down. That's why we're only thinking about the Hoggit and Mr T'wit, who have nothing to do with Brio and Father T, just like Brio and Father T have nothing to do with the Hoggit and Mr T'wit—and even though Mr T'wit may have died of his broken heart, the Hoggit can still save his long-lost love. And the Hoggit's come to understand that the Sacred Prophecy doesn't hold him back from saving Bling on his own.'

After the speaking fades, the silence presses in on Brio—presses in and down, presses heat into his head, into the putrid crawling in his stomach. The cry builds again, he has to speak to throw off the pressing weight. 'I need my notes.' He wanted it to be a shout.

'Why?' asks the patient voice.

Brio feels the Hoggit's shame as a shrinking in his own body. He has to hide it from the gentle voice, go back in time to make it right. And surely this can't be what actually happened. What the hell did the Hoggit really tell him at the castle? 'I just need my notes. I know you've got them.'

'Is the Hoggit hiding form the truth? Doesn't he remember how much Mr T'wit wanted his long-lost love to be saved by the Ring of Love?'

'But Mr T'wit's *dead*. He doesn't even know what's happening.'

'His spirit cares even more than *he* did. But the main thing is, when you save someone, you don't save them for someone else, you save them for themselves, so they can live in peace. And there's no reason to be angry at Bling, because it's not her fault that Mr T'wit died. It's no one's fault at all, it's just what happened because of what happened, which happened because of what happened because of what happened before anyone knows what happened …'

Brio fights to break free from the dead weight of calm. He wants to be angry with Bling for not being worth saving or risking his life for. 'I want my notes. Why won't you trust me?'

'Buddy—'

'They're *not* in my heart. They're in your van.' He tries to break out of his embryo curl, but he wants to stay warm by the fire's crackle and gentle draw, the calming scent of pine needles and decaying leaves.

'And would your notes speak of a dainty damsel who they rescue with uneventful ease before making it to the Tower of Time in time for afternoon tea?'

A frisson of energy galvanises Brio and the fire becomes something real. 'Don't be stupid.'

'Buddy, the Hoggit knows Mr T'wit's gone, but has he really given up on Bling when she's his last living connection to Mr

T'wit, when he knows that it's the right thing to save Bling for her own sake?'

Brio fights to stay in his curled-up safety. 'Stop trying to put ideas into my head. He's never going to save her. He hates her.'

'No. He merely fears the loss she might bring. But how can the Hoggit still fear losing his beloved guardian when the worst has already happened?'

'I don't care.' He's ashamed of his whining voice. 'I just want my notes.'

'My friend, you're almost home and you can finish this before the break of day.'

Brio wants to call the gentle voice's bluff and show that he knows exactly what's happening. But what if he really could finish the Great Plea and have it back to the Hoggit by daybreak?

'Maybe you need to hold the Ring of Love yourself,' Logie says. 'Let it guide you.'

Brio's about to issue an angry *no* when the shock of Logie's hand pressed flat on his chest freezes him like he froze in the campervan. But it's no longer a tarantula, it's a warming iron, a book, a weight against the world. When Logie's hand is suddenly gone, he has to fill the void, has to feel his own hand slip between the buttons of his fleece-lined shirt. His skin feels good, the ring even better.

'Hold it to your heart,' Logie murmurs. 'Let it fill the Hoggit with that determination to never fail again. And witness the Hoggit now, looking down into that hell of a thousand rats. He knows Mr T'wit's gone, and he knows his life will be on the line when he reveals himself to the mob, but he knows he must save Bling from the Curse of Glitterlove. His faith will save them both.'

Logie steps deftly aside as Brio scrabbles to his feet and makes head-down for the campervan's open side-door. Gripping the wobbly leg between his knees to hold the table steady, Brio hardly registers that the quill's been miraculously straightened out into something better than new. But as soon as the nib touches down, the Hoggit's passion and resolve falter again. And Logie's sitting opposite him, palms flat on the table, eyes closed.

'There are no more buts left,' Logie says. 'Either the Hoggit learns that f-word or he lives in a wasteland, in what some people call exile.'

Brio's just clutched his head when a buzzing rattle startles him open and he sees Logie snatching his phone from the counter. Brio lets out a groan of irritation. 'What the *hell*? I'm trying to think what to write—' But irritation becomes relief. Because the phone noise has broken Logie's dark spell. Brio knows he must speak quickly. 'It's perhaps not what you thought was going to happen next, but just as the Hoggit was about to save Bling, the big rat Guzzle told Ripper about Lord Rumbuck and the Great Sword. "Now *that's* a spoon that'll stir her heart, guvner!" chortled Guzzle.'

'Buddy—'

'That *is* what happened. The Hoggit was just about to save Bling but Ripper got all worked up about the huge spoon and the Hoggit lost his chance.'

'Why couldn't the Hoggit still have pushed out that grille and announced his presence with the Ring? Isn't that really what happened?'

'*No.* He was going to do that too, but Lord Rumbuck pushed him aside. "How dare that vile villain call the Great Sword a spoon?" Lord Rumbuck boomed. "I'll show him *spoon*."'

'Buddy—'

Brio's bandaged palm slams down into the remains of the spilt ink and splatters them both with purple dots. 'The Hoggit *wanted* to stop Lord Rumbuck, but Lord Rumbuck was too quick. The next thing the Hoggit knew, Lord Rumbuck had kicked out the grille himself.'

He finds Logie staring right into him. But Logie's gaze drops momentarily and Brio suddenly feels the ring inside his shirt.

'Yes!' Brio cries. 'That's it! The Hoggit gave Lord Rumbuck the Ring! So it'd be the proper saviour who saved Bling! And before anyone could say anything else, Lord Rumbuck leapt out into the chamber.'

Even in the near dark, Brio can see the disappointment on Logie's face. For a second it was even anger. 'That's not right,' Brio hears himself say. 'You've got to believe me. You've got to be *with* me all the way.'

Logie quickly closes his eyes back into a mask of peace. 'So you wanna write it from there rather than tell me?'

'*No*. You'll try to whisper in my ear and change things.'

'That's not something I'd ever do. And you trust me.'

'I don't. But if you give me my notes, I *will*.'

'Why don't I write it down as you speak?'

'Just listen.'

'Okay, I'm listening.'

Brio has no choice but to close his eyes too. 'Lord Rumbuck landed in a concertina bounce that sent rats flying everywhere. Everyone was amazed. Then Lord Rumbuck did the whole Great-Sword-showing-off thing, then started a big speech to Bling about how he was going to save her from the Vile Villain by force of courage and arms. But all Ripper could see was the huge spoon that was going to stir Bling's heart. Ripper was about to bellow at the rats to get the Great Sword when Bling shouted, "Stop!" Ripper thought it was Lord Rumbuck she cared about and went bonkers. But it wasn't Lord Rumbuck that Bling cared about. She was only interested in his gleaming armour. Her *little silver dress*, she called it. "Oh, just look at that class," she purred. "That shimmer, that perfect asymmetry." She clicked her fingers at Ripper and pointed to the armour.'

Having to catch his breath, Brio can't help glancing for evidence of Logie slipping whispered falsehoods into his head. But Logie's just sitting there like the Buddha, as silent as time. Brio's suddenly worried that Logie's put himself under so deeply that he doesn't know what's going on. 'Say something.'

Logie takes a sharp breath as though woken unexpectedly. 'Well, erm … I wonder where the Hoggit was during all this excitement?' His voice is more tranquil than ever.

'Where else would he be? He's looking down from the open vent hole. He was sobbing and pleading as the rats ripped the Great Sword out of Lord Rumbuck's hand. Then the rats pulled the armour and tunic off over Lord Rumbuck's head. "Get up, my lord!" the Hoggit shrieked. "Get up and fight."'

'Fight?' Logie murmurs. 'Don't you mean—?'

'No, I mean *fight*. Because to the Hoggit's amazement, even though Lord Rumbuck was naked and smashed up, he clawed himself back to his feet and stood even taller than before. And he looked up at Bling with the Ring of Love pressed to his heart. "Yes!" the Hoggit cried to Lord Rumbuck with joy. "Cast it into the fires of her love!"'

'Awesome,' Logie whispers. 'But didn't the Hoggit himself want to be the one who used the Ring of Love to save the—'

'Shut *up*. It's worse than you think. Because the Ring of Love made Lord Rumbuck himself fall in love with Bling. "Oh, my lady!" he cried. "I came to free you by the crimson-edged sword of battle, the cut and thrust of war. But now that I behold your beauty, I am liberated from all those instruments of violence, from the chrome-foolish armour that shielded my unguarded feelings within! I am left with nothing but the power of the pen to express the desires of my heart! Oh, if love be the food of souls, pray on!" And then, even worse, the Hoggit saw that Bling looked quite charmed by Lord Rumbuck's declaration of chivalrous love. And

Ripper had seen it too, which made him go bonkers again. "Is this Sir Fist?" Ripper roared. And when Bling still didn't take her eyes off Lord Rumbuck, Ripper bellowed down to the rats that he'd got them a surprise for dinner. "A *Sir* Prize!" The rats surged forward, fangs bared, but Ripper shouted, "Wait, you mongrels! This is a special dish and I'm going to eat it myself. So take him down and shave him for the barbecue! And don't you dare cook anything before we get there. Coz how do I know I've got a nice bit of leg if it ain't kicking?" From up in the air-vent the Hoggit pleaded with Lord Rumbuck to save himself, to fight, to run—to do *something* to stop them eating him.'

'Buddy, you really should be writing all this down.'

In his anger, Brio wants to fight Logie, but some sound or smell reminds him of his oath to the Hoggit. He claws the wad of proper paper towards him and dips the quill so deep that ink wets his fingertips. But he can't remember what was happening and lets out a cry of despair.

'Lord Rumbuck was about to be eaten,' Logie whispers. 'And he realises that this is his moment to die. Because he'll die gloriously in the name of love and—'

'That's *not what happened*.'

'What's not what happened?'

'What you said.'

'I didn't say anything.'

Brio's breaths are suddenly coming deep and fast but he manages to catch hold of the counting to slow it down ... to calm himself ... *in ... out* ... slower still, *one ... and two ... two and three ...*

A terrible calm had come over Lord Rumbuck too, and from his grand vantage point atop the highest peak of gleaming junk he gazed up at the Hoggit with dreamy eyes.

'Oh, Young Prince, how you do fret over the inconsequential. For although my time has come, I have held the Ring of Love without the impediment of armour and sword to stand between me and my heart! And I tell you, never again shall I return to the bonds of my former self! Never shall I fear to spend eternity in anything but the most noble peace.'

'No!' the Hoggit begged. 'Please! They're going to eat you.'

'And what a feast for their souls I shall make, Young Prince! Oh, jug and savour this filleted soul of humble hare! Let me fill that vilest of villains with a feast to heal his soul.'

Even as the rats closed in around Lord Rumbuck's pedestal of junk, he merely held up a hand. 'Pray calm, dear friends, for I have parting words of wisdom for my young apprentice from which even your own simple souls might gain wisdom.' With that, he turned back to address the Hoggit. 'You know, in some former life I thought that to be a man among men would be the very pinnacle of achievement. I supposed also that this modest Ring of Love could never match the glimmering power of the Armour Impervious. Yet I have at last discerned, Young Prince, that it is in the very freedom from those bonds of performance that the dream of untrammelled love can become reality. And it is from the humility in this Ring's very lack of sheen and sparkle that we find our true strength. For this great repository of love I hold was forged in the same split second as the cosmos itself, cast to give forth from its divine void the primordial spark that lit the furnace of the great beginning. Yes, love was born into the universe at its very beginning, Young Prince, a beginning that never began and shall never end. And I tell you, nothing else on this earth but love can project one's soul with such certainty into that eternal vanishing point between the bright sky of Heaven and the dark ocean of Hell. For love is not smooth and shiny at all. Indeed, when one discards the soft ribbons and sweet rituals, love is a rather gritty thing, dull with duty and dented by daylight's differences, all but crushed by the clarion call of care—such a gritty thing, in fact, that at times it might even seem soiled. So if it is my time to die, Young Prince, then so too is it yours. And may my nameless tomb be dutifully attended upon by your own shallow grave—the Unknown Warrior flanked adoringly by the Well-Known Worrier. Thus farewell, Young Prince, and may the life to come be as hearty and replete as our most joyous time together, all at sea on the good ship *Gallahop*. And may we continue to dwell for all eternity in this our most glorious fireside fellowship of far-flung, far-out, far-fetched fable.'

With a gasp, Brio flops back against the seat. 'That was incredible.' But with a start he grabs up the piece of paper. 'How can Lord Rumbuck want to die? He's gone mad.'

'Love's a powerful force,' Logie murmurs. 'And to die in the name of love is surely a death to change the world.'

Brio shoves the page angrily towards Logie. 'Lord Rumbuck would never have wanted to die. He was too strong.'

'Are you suggesting that what you just wrote didn't happen? That you did not in fact write these incredible words?'

'I did. They were all mine. But the Ring's driven him out of his mind.'

'You're cursing the Ring?'

'No!' His stomach tightens and he feels the double thud of an extra heartbeat. 'But Lord Rumbuck's got to snap out of it and escape. And he does *not* want the Hoggit to die too.'

'Looked pretty clear-cut to me,' Logie says with a hint of regret.

'But I'm sure the Hoggit can stop that bit happening.'

'He can stop it *all* happening.'

'But is that what he did? Is that what he told you?'

Brio snatches up the quill and immediately sees the Hoggit running panicked along a dark passage. 'He's trying to catch up with Lord Rumbuck who's being held aloft like a floppy coffin on a sea of sharp-clawed hands.'

'It's a sad moment,' Logie says. 'Yet a big one too. And surely the best thing the Hoggit can do is get the Ring of Love back from the weak grip of Lord Rumbuck's right hand and save the Queen himself.'

'He's going to save Lord Rumbuck,' Brio says angrily across the table and stabs the feather into the ink. But there's a deafening bang and he sees that the rats have slammed a heavy steel door in the Hoggit's face. 'That was you!' Brio cries.

'What was me?'

'Shutting the Hoggit out so he can't rescue Lord Rumbuck. Because you knew he had a plan. He was going to do Lord Rumbuck's imaginary feast trick and put the rats in a food coma. He was going to *hypnotise* them.'

'That was a cool plan. But he's been shut out by the rats. And whatever might happen to Lord Rumbuck inside the engine room, wouldn't the Hoggit have gone back to the Queen's den to save her? And look, Lord Rumbuck dropped the Ring right where the Hoggit would find it. He's got everything he needs to save the Queen.'

Brio fights himself out from the table. 'Stop trying to change everything. The Hoggit will never save that horrible woman.'

Logie remains calm, palms flat on the table. 'You mean the Hoggit wouldn't have gone to save Bling even if it was the only way to save Lord Rumbuck?' Before Brio can reply, he leans forward and finds Brio's gaze in the dim light. 'Are you really saying that the Hoggit would give up any chance of finding his father because he couldn't bring himself to simply forgive Bling? He'd rather not forgive Bling than find his dad?'

As Brio paces up and down in front of the fire, so the Hoggit runs frantically to and fro outside the slammed door of the engine room. All he can think is that there must be some way to get to his father without forgiving this vile cat who doesn't deserve to be absolved.

Determined to face Logie down, Brio returns to the campervan, where in the heat from the van's cooktop Logie's calm slicing of button mushrooms morphs into rats sharpening blades to shave Lord Rumbuck. The spectacle freezes Brio and for a moment he doesn't know where he is. It's only Logie asking if he's okay that snaps him out, and now it's clear: if Logie won't give him his notes, he can't finish the Great Plea, and if he can't finish it before Zpydr makes Bella tell her lies, the truth will be buried forever. 'We have to go and save Bella. It's the only way.'

Logie stops slicing and gestures to two mugs of hot chocolate on the botchily mended table. 'Why don't we just mellow out for a while? I'm sure that what the Hoggit did next will come back to you.'

'There isn't time. The ferry goes at eight o'clock. We have to go now.'

'But I see in your eyes that you're remembering, that it's all happening. You need to write it down.'

'I don't trust you.'

'You only need to trust yourself. I'm nothing in this.'

No sooner has Brio sat back down at the table than he's seeing Bling and Ripper arriving for their midnight feast in the hellishly hot engine room. They're a pair of pied pipers at the head of a seething, salivating multitude, and Bling isn't just dressed in her slinking gown of gleaming bric-a-brac now, she's wearing Lord Rumbuck's armour over the top. And it's been polished to blinding and draped with glimmering adornments. And Ripper's flaunting the Great Sword, flickering his eyebrows suggestively at the rats, tweaking it into little stirring motions.

'He's disgusting,' Brio barks at the page, where words seem to be forming.

'Just focus on the Hoggit,' comes Logie's voice through the sweltering heat. 'See how he's cowed to a stooping grovel by the Ring's scorching castigations. But he followed Bling's entourage of rats into the infernal heat of the engine room, right?'

'Yes, he did.'

'And what did he witness from the shadows once he was inside that innermost place?'

'He witnessed the dreadful spectacle of Lord Rumbuck's body shaved like a plucked chicken and pinned out on a steel griddle. Like temple followers in the sway of their shaman priests, the mass of rats edged forward, eyes glinting and lips curled back over yellowed fangs.'

'Write it, buddy. Write every word.'

Yet despite his abject plight, Lord Rumbuck could not have been more at ease. Indeed, as Bling and Ripper sat down on their makeshift thrones, Lord Rumbuck cried 'Welcome, noble diners! Welcome! How pleased I am that you will be eating me today—to which end I have asked your chefs to ensure that they grill me evenly on both sides!'

Though the Hoggit was in awe of Lord Rumbuck's majestic bonhomie and grave dignity, he couldn't bear it a moment longer. Breaking out from the shadows, he threw himself at Bling's feet. 'Please!' he cried from the underbelly of a deep bow then sprang straight back up and cast open his arms.

'Let me liberate your soul from the Curse of Glitterlove! Let me lead you back to the one true love of your life!'

As Lord Rumbuck mumbled his approval, Ripper heaved himself to his feet. 'Who the arse end of a bog-brush are you? And what are you talking about, the *one true love* of her life? Rats!'

Once again, however, Bling stayed Ripper's hand. 'We will hear what this prickly gerbil has to say,' she purred, gesturing Ripper to sit back down. 'Then we will use him for toothpicks.' She arched an eyebrow at the Hoggit. 'I don't know who you are, spiky-boy, but I can tell you, I have had a skin-full of bizarre creatures trying to save me today and you are as plump as I am hungry.'

The Hoggit knew that this was the moment to whip out the Ring of Love and cast it into the fires in which it was forged. But as he twisted to retrieve it from behind the tiny sword that he still kept hidden in his spikes, he was paralysed by a terrible blasting of dissonant trumpets and the sonorous boom of Mr T'wit's warning that *anyone who tried to use the Ring when they themselves stood in betrayal to the call of love would be crushed to dust*.

Bling sniffed at the Hoggit. 'It would seem zat you cannot even save yourself.'

Crying out that he could save everyone, the Hoggit strained harder for the Ring. But even with the rats pressing in, he could only cry out to God. And lo and behold! God gave him the strength to bear the pain of his betrayal and cry, 'I am not here for myself, but for Mr T'wit, your long-lost love!'

Ripper was back on his feet, bulge-eyed with rage. 'How dare you come into my brand-new barbie with talk of old flames?' He pointed an angry finger. 'Put him on the grill!'

'Wait!' cried the Hoggit, though once again it was Bling

who restrained the rats, and now he saw something else in her eyes. But she narrowed them and grabbed up the Hoggit by his safety harness.

'You can go and tell zat old fool I would not go back to him if he was zer last feather in zer duster. How dare he create this *nuisance*?'

The Hoggit's legs pedalled madly in mid-air. *'You must go back to him*! Because he's dead and it's all my fault. But your love will bring him back to life! I know you still love him! I know that in your heart of hearts you long for the perfect life you had before!'

'I'll kill you,' Ripper choked, but before he could issue the command he slumped back onto his makeshift throne, clutching his chest and gasping blue for air.

Bling's eyes had flared with anger but her expression calmed to a sneer. 'It did not have zer perfect life with zat old *twit*. It was just a little holiday romance. I was young and foolish.'

'That's not true! You sailed the seven seas in your Pea-Green Boat! And don't you remember how Mr T'wit played his guitar and sang so beautifully? And you dined on quince and danced under the Bong-Tree!'

Bling drew breath as though to unleash fire, but again, and still without so much as a glance at the choking Ripper, she sighed heavily and her gaze seemed to drift. 'Okay, maybe that stupid bird could play the odd ditty on a heartstring. And *yes*, he had a voice like honey. But how lucky is a girl if her man cannot pay the bills, huh? Poems are just letters if zey cannot be turned into numbers. And, can you believe, he even gave away our precious five-pound note? *To people who need it more than us*, he said. But what did he know about growing up in a railway yard? What did he know about the things a girl must do to survive in a man's world? And after he had given away our last penny, we couldn't afford even zer bare necessities, let alone my occasional little luxury. Then it wasn't just *la-la-la* songs and *blah-blah-blah* books, it was every time I acquire a new piece he goes all tut-tut on me. Why do I need so much *stuff*? Where are we going to put it all?'

'But you loved him!' the Hoggit cried again. 'And you still do! I see it in your eyes! And all it takes to bring him back from the dead is for you to confess your love!'

Her eyes flared again and she pulled him to her face. 'Don't talk to me of *love*. Love is nothing more than zer lipstick they smear on that grunting piggy-wig we call *life*. If you want to experience true love ... eat zer piggy!'

'No, my love!' cried Ripper, clawing at his chest. 'You love *meee* ...'

'I don't love anyone,' she shouted and threw the Hoggit down. 'Because no one ever loved *me*. Just one run-down council house to the next. Kicked from violent father to abusive bloke. Of course, I fell for that stupid old bird. But done is done and dead is dead.'

The only sounds left standing after Bling had finished were the background roar of the ship's boiler and Ripper's almost inaudible clawing for air. But it was in that moment that the Hoggit finally understood what extremes of misfortune and privation had driven Bling to this degradation of the soul.

'I want you to be happy like you deserve!' he cried, springing to his feet. 'Oh, if only you'd have followed your heart to Mr T'wit and not let your damaged soul lure you to the Vile Villain!'

He saw the confusion in Bling's eyes, the glances at Ripper and the rats, at some distant place where lay the fallen body of her long-lost love. Yet once again, she shook her head clear and coughed up a furball. 'You are a persuasive little pin-cushion, but I know which side my rabbit steak is buttered and—'

'You're just saying that to protect yourself from pain,' the Hoggit cried. 'But I know how you really feel, and I understand why you hurt poor Mr T'wit and cast him into a life of pain. How you made me live in fear of my beloved guardian being taken away from me. How that made me fear everything! But I great-big-F-word forgive you! And I'm not scared of losing Mr T'wit, because he'll be with us both forever!'

With that, the Hoggit tugged the Ring of Love from within his spikes and held it up like the sun. '*Now* you'll remember your love for Mr T'wit! That love you felt when you were young and he went off to be a wise shaman and you married some abusive scrap metal dealer for his money.'

Bling stumbled backwards, her gaze in thrall to the Ring, which glowed silver and gold and all the colours of the rainbow. Clutching her chrome-clad breast, she fell to her knees. 'Of course I still love him! Oh, how can he be dead, my poor Tufty-Wufty!'

No sooner had Ripper issued one last deathly rattle than an ethereal light filled the engine room. The rats fell back in awe then fled crying *Fire! Fire!* and *God is coming!* And out of the numinous radiance emerged an even brighter glow, a lantern on the bow of a small boat that floated in on a sea of mist and light.

'Mr T'wit,' gasped the Hoggit as he recognised the glowing golden-brown figure at the helm. 'You have risen from the dead! Love has brought you back!'

Then the Hoggit saw that Bling had shed not just the

Armour Impervious but every last gleaming trinket. And as she was about to step aboard the little boat, she turned to the Hoggit and held out the Ring of Love. 'Take this, noble Hoggit, for you too have overcome fear and found the forgiveness that will grant you the gift of love forever and a day. And now you have earned everything you need to find the truth.'

As the little boat floated away on its own special sea of tranquillity, the Hoggit wanted to cry out. But then his pain was gone and in his mind he saw only a slow-motion figure getting up from the garden path where once-upon-a-time he had fallen.

16

AT SOME POINT AFTER REACHING THE END of his long cathartic passage, Brio moves in a trance to be with Logie by the fire. He's dimly surprised to find the tree trunk stool so comfortable. He even likes the feel of their knees touching.

'And in those beautiful words you wrote,' Logie intones, 'you said you saw Father T standing up from the garden path where he fell. This must have seemed similar to Mr T'wit's rising and return, but really it's just interesting how these little coincidences crop up. And we're not here to talk about those things, only to help each other as friends to help the Hoggit find home. But we can still talk a little more about Father T if you like ...'

Brio knows he's still under, and he *wants* to be under, more deeply under than ever before. He wants never to have been in any other place except this state of perfect, rhythmic calm, with Logie saying whatever it is that needs to be said.

'There's nothing wrong with holding the Church responsible for Father T's death—no sin in that at all. You may even have blamed Father T himself, for breaking his oath to God, and also his oath to take care of *you. How had Father T not simply brought his own death upon himself?* you probably wondered. And it was only natural to blame Bella Ripley as well, for leading Father T away from the right path he'd chosen. These understandable feelings were heavy burdens, even if they were nothing compared to the millstone of blaming yourself for the death of the person you most loved. It's a giant step towards paradise that you've forgiven him now. Forgiven Bella too. Forgiven yourself. And as Mr T'wit said, when you grieve properly, it'll last a lifetime.'

'And after that day when things were really bad in my head,' Brio hears himself saying, 'Father T said I should never write stories in my diary. I should always keep them separate. So I always did—except when I urgently needed to write down a story but didn't have any paper. Then I sometimes did use my diary. But I was always careful to turn it up*side d*own and start the story from the back. It worried me that if I kept going, the story would bump into the diary and they'd both be upside down and get all mixed up. But now I know that God can read things whichever way up they are. It's really good to tell you how truly good Father T was.'

'And I've enjoyed listening, and getting to know him a little better. Father T said some cool things.'

'He did. Even in church.'

'What better place can there be in which to say cool things? I'd love to get to know Father T even better. And I guess, in a way, even though it's not really my business, I wish I'd heard the things you overheard him say to your mum.'

Taken off guard, Brio finds himself on his feet, but he also finds himself weightless and disoriented. Somewhere in the space between them, he's angry with Logie for knowing too much, for breaking the precious spell. 'How did you know I overheard something? No one in the world knows that. No one except Izzy. And Mum.'

Logie's own bandaged hand reaches up and touches Brio's. 'Relax, my friend. Join me again. Keep focused on the flames and think back to what you overheard on that unforgettable day. Those words are surely carved into your memory.'

Brio swallows and blinks hard. Sitting again, he tries to corral his thoughts back into the fire. 'But how did you know?'

'A very slow process of understanding. And I'd say you really need to share this.'

Doubt threatens but he needs to sit back down … he's aware that he *is* sitting back down, to focus his worry into the fire, to pick out individual flames and feel their longing to be one single rose-golden tongue sharing the same crackling memory of Father T's voice downstairs in the little sitting room. 'He told Mum she could take strength from knowing my dad was still alive.'

He wants to keep going but needs to know whether he can trust Logie enough to say more.

'It's very interesting …' Logie says, 'very interesting that Father T used the word *dad*.'

Brio doesn't like the feeling this fine distinction provokes. He has to get rid of it quickly. 'Well, maybe he said *father*, but it's the same thing. And he said there was always hope that my father could be saved.' Father T's words come to him verbatim like a ritual prayer. 'He said my father might not be a father in the way I'd been raised to understand, but, even though he'd never be there in the house, he was a father nonetheless. He told Mum that if she told me everything then it would give *me* hope too. Then one day when I was old enough, and with God's strength, it would be me, his own son, who freed him from those shackles and led him out of the desert.'

Brio has to focus harder still to keep the flames merging into that one crackling tongue, but his vision blurs and the flame becomes a glowing ball, a ring … a rose-golden ring …

'That's quite something for Father T to have said,' Logie says, which Brio feels as a wave of unexpected relief down his back. Even when Logie asks what his mum said in reply to Father T's question, he stays happy and calm. Nor does it trouble him to realise that this is a conversation he won't remember after dawn, and he's sure that Logie won't remember it either. Because they're deep under together … deep *in* together … and whatever happens to one of them will happen to the other too.

'My mum asked Father T why he'd changed his mind—why he'd always told her to keep up the fake story about my dad dying in Africa but suddenly wanted her to tell me the truth.'

'Uh-huh. And did Father T reply to your mum's question?'

'He said God had helped him to discern a better way to understand my father. But I know it wasn't God who told him to tell me the truth, it was Bella. Then Mum said she didn't want to talk about it ever again.'

Logie leans forward to draw Brio further into their fireside cone of trust. 'And did your mum say anything else to you about your dad after that?'

The very thought chokes him up, he can't even share it with Logie. But he remembers that Logie lost his mum too, in exactly the same way, in the very same hospital. 'It's when Mum was really sick—when there were all the machines and tubes and she was so thin. She was going to tell me the whole truth about my dad. She said she needed some sleep but she'd tell me everything in the morning. She swore an oath. But in the morning she was gone and the bed was empty.'

While Brio weeps without inhibition, Logie keeps his head bowed and his hand resting gently on Brio's knee.

When it's time, Logie says, 'Did you ever ask Father T what he meant by those things he said to your mum? That your father wasn't a father in the normal way. That there was always hope he could be saved. That it might be you who led him out of the desert?'

The question casts Brio back into the labyrinth. How much he wishes he'd asked Father T what he meant, how he longs for him to come back and explain everything like a father …

'How about your mum? Did you ask *her* what Father T meant?'

But Brio's pursued by the ancient worry that Father T's

apocryphal words really did mean something else, and it takes him time to work through the confused weeping. Eventually, he says, 'She was cross with me for eavesdropping. And she just said Father T was talking about God the Father, not *my* father—though I know that God the Father is my father too.'

'And with all your heart you tried to believe her,' Logie whispers, his hand patting slowly. 'For so many years, it tore you apart inside, that terrible feeling that you were out of faith with your mum for not believing what she told you.' The gentle rhythm of words sends tingling down Brio's back. 'It made you feel you were out of faith with God as well. But you weren't. Because it's okay to question. God likes you to have doubt, you know that now. And unlike back then, you have someone to trust and talk to.'

Now Brio wants only to be back in Father T's little boat, taking it in turns to read to each other from *The Hobbit* or *The Lord of the Rings* while they waited for the bite on the fishing line that would never come, because Father T never put any bait on the hook—which was a pretend hook anyway.

'He loved you,' Logie says softly. 'He wanted to be the father he was desperate for you to know.'

This sets free the different tears that Brio's kept buried for so long. When at last they subside, Logie leads him back to all his best times at Father T's side. Cooking lunch for his mum on a Saturday to be ready when she arrived back from the shop. Planting marrows and green beans that produced crops of fairy-tale abundance. *We're working as God's little helpers*, Father T always said. And whenever they went fishing, it always felt like they were on the Sea of Galilee, even when it was dark and windy, especially since they never caught a single fish.

'There must have been some scary moments in that little boat,' Logie says. 'Even though you were probably close to land.'

'I was never worried.'

'And the time you were stranded and ended up out all night, were you troubled by that?'

Brio knows there was a time when he'd have slammed the door on such a question, but now he feels only gratitude. 'When I was with Father T, I always knew everything would be all right.'

'And you really didn't think your mum would be worried that you weren't back, even though she knew you were out fishing in a small boat?'

A pulse breaks in on the calm.

But no. It's okay. The pulse knows the rhythm and the words. 'She knew that if I was with Father T, I'd be all right. She was always happy when I was with Father T.'

'So when you finally made it to land at four in the morning, you knew she'd be happy that Father T had taken you back to his home instead of waking her up in the middle of the night?'

'I didn't worry about Mum when I was with Father T. It was the only time I didn't worry about Mum.'

There's a pause, until Logie says, 'I didn't realise you worried about your mum.'

'It doesn't matter. And that's not what you want to talk about. You want to know what happened when Father T took me home with him.'

'Well, not especially. But you must have been frozen to the bone by the time you got back to Father T's. Did you have a nice hot bath or go straight to bed?'

'I had a bath.'

'And did you want Father T to stay with you while you were in the bath, to talk about how exciting it had all been?'

'I suppose so. But he had to go and find me some dry clothes.'

'And after you got out of the bath, did he help you to get dry?'

Brio really likes Logie's questions now. Best of all, he knows they're both in the same place where everything's true and to be believed and forgotten in the morning. 'I don't remember whether he helped me get dry. I don't think so.'

'And then you went to bed?'

Brio pauses to think about what he should try to think. 'Yes. I went to bed.'

'In Father T's bed?'

'No. In his spare room. The one with the pink and green flowery curtains.'

'Did he lie down next to you?'

This is troubling and Brio has to think harder.

But no, he doesn't have to think at all. 'That's what shepherds always did in those days. They slept across the openings in the simple stone walls to protect their flocks from wolves and rustlers. They risked their own lives for their flocks.'

'Which yield their wool in return.'

'I suppose so.'

'And sometimes more.'

'Father T was a pescatarian. During the week, he didn't even eat fish.'

'And this shepherd of yore, did he pull a blanket over himself and the lamb?'

'No. He covered the lamb with his blanket and lay outside in the cold.'

'He was a kind shepherd. I'm sure he would have put an arm over the lamb to help it keep warm.'

'Yes.'

'Until the lamb slept.'

'The lamb couldn't sleep.'

'Because he was too happy?'

'Because the shepherd snored loudly. Enough to scare away any wolf or murderous robber.'

There's a pause and Brio imagines that Logie's trying to stop his smile becoming a laugh. Yes, humour *is* the way to get through this. More gags like that one will keep the wolves at bay. There'll be all the time under Heaven for centipedes and millipedes.

'But did the lamb eventually get to sleep?'

'I suppose it must have done, because it remembers waking up to a sunny day.'

'And did the lamb feel uneasy about what had happened?'

'No.' But since they both know that this isn't quite true, he adds, 'The lamb just felt a bit guilty.'

'Why did it feel a bit guilty?'

'Because the lamb knew that there were people who did bad things when no one was looking.'

'What things?'

'All those things its mum always said would get you burned in Hell.'

'But the lamb didn't do any of those things with the shepherd. *Did* it?'

'No. But it *felt* like it did them.'

'Why? Because of a dream it had while it was asleep under the blanket?'

'No. Because of everything its mum always said. What everyone else said too, even the shepherd—that just having the thought will get you burned in Hell.'

'And did the lamb have thoughts like those? Is that why it felt guilty?'

'It didn't have any thoughts like that. It was just because so many other people thought it had those thoughts that it made the lamb feel that it *must* have had them.'

This brings them into a silence that's scarcely touched by the distant whispering crackling of fire.

Eventually, Logie says quietly, 'I see now. I see exactly. And God forgive *me*.'

After that, they sit in another easy silence that deepens and becomes detached from even the fire—until Logie says, 'Pardon me for asking, but doesn't this mean that the Hoggit's as ready as he's ever going to be? I mean, hasn't he earned the right to bear witness to the Tower of Time?'

The words mean almost nothing to Brio and even suggest that the fire might be fading. But in the flames he sees an image that's as familiar as it is stunningly new. 'Oh, my God,' he hears himself murmur. 'It's the Tower of Time, and it's right there. It's like they escaped from the ship and ran like the wind along the coast. Except it's kind of unreal too.' He cranes forward, eyes wide. 'But it's so real.'

'That's great. And how does it look?'

Brio can hardly speak. 'Like Grandma always told him in that poem.'

'The poem that was in one of her stories about Lord Rumbuck?'

'Yes.'

'And when you met him at the castle, when he told you everything that happened to him, did he recite the poem in full?'

Brio's heart's suddenly knocking hard and he has to catch a breath. 'Yes.'

'And didn't you swear to write down every word he told you?'

The next moment, they're stumbling fast across the carpet of pine needles like father and son rushing for a bus in the rain. Brio trips on the step of the campervan but Logie catches him and no harm done. At the table with the empty hot chocolate mugs he has to close his eyes.

'Close yours too.'

'I have,' Logie whispers as he slips the Magic Quill into Brio's hand. The words come into Brio's mind so fast he doesn't have time to write.

'And thus they stood in rev'rent awe, silenced, stunned by what they saw. Made witness—'

'Write it, buddy.'

'I cant.'

'But—'

'Made witness now to dazzling dark, the castle like a saving ark. And from those battlements so high, the tower, it rose up fit to fly. All stripped of light from former days, yet held aloft by power of gaze.'

'This is rose-golden,' Logie whispers. 'And the Hoggit's little warble has gained a resonance beyond himself. But breathe deep, my friend, let the Magic Quill honour your oath to the Hoggit.' Logie's hand almost forces the quill down onto the parchment.

> 'Those ornate columns, bones of stone,
> and armoured walls like cliff-face honed
> from ancient rock, by hand of God,
> where once the angels gaily trod.
> But lo! Those windows, tall and thin,
> concealed a wickedness within.
> For from those slits as thin as cracks,
> aimed poisoned arrows, glinting black.
> And perched atop the highest rungs,
> the Clocks of Time, like white-hot suns,
> round-rimmed by rings of golden glow,
> yet cold as ice and still as snow.'

In his lavishly illustrated mind, the Hoggit was already inside the Tower of Time. Its twisting stairwells had never been so clear.

> 'A clock to south, a clock to north!
> To east and west, the first like fourth!

Four burning orbs that never die,
with dead black hands that never lie.
And right above, a vestibule,
be-crowned with arches, green as ghouls.
The Young Prince knew at once and cried,
"Tis Dungeon High! M'lord, let's fly!"
But bearing down on dungeon high,
to block attack from freedom's sky,
a turret, worn as wizard's hat,
with evil point, as black as cat.
So up the tower they'd have to climb,
assailed by traps and beasts—and *Time*.'

Issuing a bugle call from one contorted side of his mouth, the Hoggit thrust his precious little sword into the air.

'Lord Rumbuck to the breach once more!
To fight and fell the darkest lord!
Then in that dungeon, high and barred,
they'd find the King, all chained and scarred.
At last, those years he'd waited long,
repaid in chimes of rescue song!'

By the end of his soaring delivery, the Hoggit had reached such heights of passion that it remained only to fly from the ship and ascend the tower's dizzying heights. But on launching away in the direction of the open engine room door, he twanged back to find Lord Rumbuck's firm hold at the end of his tether.

'Let go!' he cried. 'We have to get to the tower!'

Lord Rumbuck's pink face was a taut, distorted weave of expressions the Hoggit didn't understand. 'Don't be a fool.

You'll be run over before you get halfway across the road. You don't even know whether your father's really there.'

'You're just scared!' the Hoggit shouted. 'Because you've been shaved and you're not wearing your armour. Put it on! And your Timeless Tunic! And pick up your sword!'

But Lord Rumbuck didn't move. 'Fear and a close shave be damned. It's simply that my paramount duty is to protect you.'

'Protect me from *what*?'

'From disappointment. From heartbreak. I mean, what if your father isn't there as you suppose? It's been so many years, he may be dead already. Worse still, he might not be as you expect. You imagine him to be some great hero, but what if he's just a father?'

Dread took hold of the Hoggit. 'How can you say *just a father*? A father *is* a hero.'

Lord Rumbuck's expression darkened. 'A father is *not* a hero. A father is just an ordinary mortal. Only a hero is a hero, and no hero would ever be a father. Because a father is small. Normal. *Useless.*'

The Hoggit shrank back from the fire in Lord Rumbuck's eyes. 'That's not true. A father is brave and fights the world. A father—'

'—is a *coward*. A flop who can only fail the very family he was put on the earth to protect, who deserts them in their hour of need. A father is a crawling thing that—'

'No!' The Hoggit's head swirled with a maelstrom of unwanted images—children and a roadside he didn't know, an angry wife and blinding headlights. 'That's not true! My father's a hero!'

'No father can be a hero!' Lord Rumbuck bellowed. 'Because he's trapped by the tedium of gnawing chores and humiliating duties. Licking the dishes, nibbling the lawn, trying to be *this* and having to be *that*, tiptoeing on thin ice to be everything to everyone and never being any damn thing at all. No hero prances around trying to set good examples and begging to be a jolly good role model. A hero brings the sheer, brute force of nature into our lives, to fill us with the energy of the cosmos and show us the power within ourselves! And that hero never *ever* lives happily ever after, Young Prince, because no true hero can survive the tedious, gnawing, back-stabbing civility of this man-made hell we call life. So I'm damned if I'm going on a wild goose chase up some imaginary tower for a father that can never exist.'

Brio stares at the dense page of shrunken scrawl. It's so tight there's hardly a gap between words, and his head's thumping with nausea at the sight of Lord Rumbuck all pink and raw. This is supposed to be a muscular saviour not a piece of meat. This *cannot* be what happened. It's Logie for sure, doing everything he can to stop the Hoggit getting to the top of the Tower of Time. Because Logie doesn't believe his father's up there. Because he's got no faith. He's been corrupted by Zpydr and Ms Whittle, and he's buying time again, making it all go in circles till he can figure out how to make the Hoggit give up and accept that his dad killed himself.

But when Brio looks up to seethe out the accusation, he finds Logie lying on a blanket in front of the fire reading a book. The next thing Brio knows, he's shouting and thumping the table and Logie's flying back towards the van. Brio jumps up and slams the sliding door in his face, and pulls the tatty curtains over the window.

Back at the table, his tears are constipated and impatient and want him to write without thinking. To the disconnected sound of a half-shout, he snatches up the quill. But the Hoggit's too scared to let him write and he has to tell Lord Rumbuck himself. 'Put your fucking armour back on. And your tunic too. And pick up your sword. Then we're going to find Madame Haha and rescue my dad.'

But the Hoggit's struck mute, which leaves Lord Rumbuck naked and marooned and staring blankly at nothing.

Come on, buddy, says the voice of Logie in his head. You know how much the Hoggit wants to know whether his father's there.

'But what if they don't find Madame Haha? What if she's dead?'

'Then the Hoggit has the faith that he can do this on his own. He doesn't need Madame Haha any more than you need me.'

'He does!' Brio cries. 'Why can't you understand?'

'What I understand is that this is all about whether the Sacred Prophecy is going to stand between the Hoggit and finding his father. And that comes down to whether sacred scriptures are cast in concrete or always evolving, always giving meaning as times change.'

Too fast to stop, Brio's finger lances out at Logie's nose. '*They can never change.* They're the final word.'

'That's right, in their hearts they never change at all. But if you believe the Sacred Prophecy was written by God, then you can't say that it's the final word of God or you'll be claiming to have the knowledge of God—to be God yourself. And wouldn't that be blasphemous?'

Brio wants to cut him down with one word, but Logie's holding his arms tightly to his sides.

'My friend, listen to me. The only thing standing in the Hoggit's way are his own doubts.'

'Get *off*.' He throws Logie's hands, but the fire in those mesmerising eyes is enough to tell him that if he can't overcome the doubts about his own father, the Hoggit will fail. 'I don't have any *doubts*. It's *you* that doesn't trust *me*.' He lurches forward, hands twitching to make fists. 'Tell me you believe his father's there. Tell me he's a great hero—*and* a great father.'

'Buddy—'

'You see? You don't even know what a good father is.'

There's a shock silence and Brio almost cries out for Logie's reply. All he wants to hear is that there's one person in the world he can trust, one living soul who's not doing it for bent dimes or fleeting fame. And now in Logie's worried eyes, Brio understands exactly what happened to *Steve Logue* the failed screenwriter. How he tried to commit suicide but got saved by the CHANT people—alleluyah. How they made him believe that being a CHANT practitioner was as good as being a great writer. Through brainwashing, they harnessed his whole life to succeeding as a CHANT guru. But he never really believed it in his heart, and he's hidden his battle against the Dark Arched Window behind that cool American act. Then the world's first *deepmind parable* came along and he saw a chance for something that would make him as good as a great writer. So he's thrown his heart and soul into making it a success. And if the deepmind parable fails, Logie won't want to keep living either. That's why his voice is so tight and small, so struggling to stay American.

'What I said …' Logie says through a steadying breath. 'What I said is—'

'*Shut up.*' Because he doesn't just know about Logie's black hole, he feels it as his own—how much Logie wants to save himself by stealing Izzy's abandoned place at his side. How much he wants to—

'Buddy? You okay?'

Brio finds himself locked into the stare with Logie and before he has time to think he hears himself murmur, 'I don't know. Are *you?*'

They fall into the hug and Logie's tight hold is no hold at all, and that's how they stay, with eyes closed while the little fire at

Bluebells crackles and their feet float above the scented bed of pine needles and softened twigs.

'What's a good father?' Logie murmurs eventually, his voice unsteady, his mouth almost touching Brio's ear. 'Well, I guess if a great hero's someone who'd lay down their life for someone else, then a good father is someone who'd keep laying down their life on every day they're alive, to make sure the family they love is okay.'

Sitting back at the table as though for the first time, Brio feels as raw and drained as he does live with excitement and trepidation. But despite his feelings of trust, he doesn't know what will happen when he closes his eyes and writes. Because even if Lord Rumbuck agreed to take the Hoggit to the High Dungeon, they still need Madame Haha. He wishes they didn't, but it was set in stone by the Sacred Prophecy.

'Okay,' Logie says, his voice tight and trembling. 'Where are they now?'

'I don't know. They're not on the ship anymore but I thought I heard the big door of the engine room slam shut.'

'They're on another level of existence and experience. But it's all real.'

'You mean it's only in the Hoggit's head?'

'I mean the Hoggit's witnessed it. He can get there now.'

'It's just that—'

'*Write it.*'

The unexpected sharpness of Logie's command echoes in Brio's head like the slam of an engine room door. But it's easy now. It's all clear. He takes a deep breath.

And there she was, framed in the doorway by light from behind. 'Madame Haha is here to save the day!' she hooted.

'Fresh from her greatest opening night ever! Oh, how the giants love her!' She started and gawked at Lord Rumbuck. 'Deary dear, Mister Rumbo, this is a close shave that will make you very famous indeed.'

Realising that he's become too aware of the quill, Brio rolls his eyeballs to blur his vision. He needs more words from God to get him through.

'Why've you stopped?'

'I don't know.'

'You're surprised that Madame Haha's returned?'

He doesn't know whether it's Logie he doubts or himself. 'You don't want Madame Haha to be back. You want the Hoggit to go on his own.'

'This is only about what the Hoggit told *you*. So come on, why's Madame Haha suddenly looking so serious? Why's she dropped to one knee in front of the Hoggit?'

Brio's stomach crawls. 'I don't know. Are you sure you didn't just put that in my head?'

'I really hope not.'

'I can't remember why she's looking so serious, why she took the Hoggit by the hand.' He lowers his gaze to the page and waits for the feel of Logie's touch, the gentle nudge to guide the nib down under the surface.

'You ask why Mummy is looking so serious?' said Madame Haha. 'This is because she sees that if Mister Rumbo won't take the Prince of Joy to find his daddy, the Prince of Joy is stuck in the mud.'

'But what can I do?' bleated the Hoggit. 'It's not my fault that I need Lord Rumbuck to take me.'

'It's not,' Madame Haha agreed. 'But it's the very thing you believe that's standing in your way. And maybe this can be said about your whole life.'

The Hoggit was determined to argue strenuously with Madame Haha, and not just strenuously but cogently too, and fervently, passionately and furiously as well, any which way that would keep the argument going forever. But all he could do was plaintively ask her, 'Why does what I believe stand in my way?'

She drew his hand closer. 'Well you see, Prince of Joy, you want so much to believe that your father is up there in the Tower of Time that your very wanting to believe it is as powerful as truly believing. It fills you with *hope*.'

'I do believe it.'

'Oh, yes, you believe that you believe that you believe. And you believe that you need Lord Rumbuck in order to find your father, because you believe that you are not brave enough to find him yourself. But what a sticky-tricky number twenty-two situation, because it is only finding your father yourself that can make you truly brave.'

'I *am* brave. But only Lord Rumbuck has the Great Sword. And if I—'

'It's not a sword,' Madame Haha cut in quietly. 'It's just a silly old draining spoon.'

Stumbling backwards, the Hoggit reached frantically for his own little sword to defend himself from the Dark Lord's servant. 'You *know* it's not a spoon! It's your Magic Microphone.'

Madame Haha smiled. 'That is a harmless little belief. It helps Madame Haha to tell better jokes, and that in turn brings a smile to many faces. And for Madame Haha that is the best love she can give and take. But when *you* believe that our lovely spoon is the Great Sword, it makes you believe that you cannot defend yourself on your own. So you see, your story has trapped you like a lobster in a pot.'

The Hoggit looked to Lord Rumbuck for help, but his great protector had become a waxwork figure reminiscent of an iceskater in mid swoosh. He could only turn back to Madame Haha.

'You're trying to trick me. You want to kidnap me and eat me in your house of candy and gingerbread.'

'Mummy only wants to *free* you, to help you grow up into a proper man.' She shrugged. 'Of course, your father *may* be up there in that tower you now see so clearly. But you won't know for sure until you see for yourself. And why does Mister Rumbo refuse to take you? Because he worries that maybe your daddy really will be up there, and then you would not need *him* anymore. You would both realise at last that the Sacred Prophecy never said what would happen to Mister Rumbo after you found your daddy. So Mister Rumbo has clocked that you never really cared if he died in the battle.'

Her words sent the Hoggit teetering again. But he knew she was right. He didn't care what happened to Lord Rumbuck, just like the giants didn't care that their gods died for *them*. They just took it for granted as part of their helpless and selfish little rituals. And this was why Lord Rumbuck said that a true hero can never survive in this world.

But when the Hoggit took breath to holler Lord Rumbuck awake, all he could do was turn back to Madame Haha. 'You'll take me to the Tower of Time to find my father? *Really*?'

Madame Haha nodded. 'She is here to see you through the biggest moment of your life. And she will be here for you whatever happens—as a friend.'

The Hoggit couldn't believe that all these serious words were coming out of Madame Haha, and somehow her hand was on his little knee even though they were supposed to be standing. But how could he place his trust in someone who once threw themselves overboard? Was it because Madame Haha had finally found the only kind of love available to someone like her? Making people laugh and being loved with applause.

'No,' she whispers. 'Madame Haha has discovered a better kind of love. And that's why you can trust her. Because she cares so much about the Prince of Joy. Which is better than any kind of fame or fortune.'

Her words bring a glow to the Hoggit's heart and he needs to cry.

He hugs her too.

But back on the right side of the table, he's worried. 'What about Lord Rumbuck? I need you both to come.'

'One little click of Mummy's fingers and Mister Rumbo will ping back to life. And when he sees that Madame Haha is back, he will feel such a need to compete with her for your affections that he will put his armour straight back on and vie to take you to the tower first. And he will be so filled with that old martyr complex that he'll want nothing more than to lay down his life in the most spectacular way possible. So everything is in order and it is time for the Prince of Joy to overcome his doubts and find out whether his daddy really is there. So come and see.'

Heart beating in big slow thumps, Brio stays absolutely still with eyes closed and quill in hand exactly as it must have been before he slipped out of the Groove. He has to make Logie think he's still under, so he can catch him in the act of feeding lines. He hovers the nib closer to the page. He lets its ink glance a little dash to make him seem half-in, half-out, to lure Logie into his trap, fool him into revealing his deception.

'What's happening?' Logie asks in a murmur. 'Why don't I hear that beautiful sound of quill on parchment?'

Brio starts. What the hell was he thinking? He could hear Logie's breathing the whole time he was writing.

'I don't know what's happening,' Logie says as though from deep sleep. 'But if the Hoggit's decided to go with Madame Haha to the tower, why hasn't he gone already?'

Panic builds fast. Why *is* he still hesitating? This is the moment he's been waiting for all along. The quill slips off the page. He has to cradle his head with both hands.

'Slay those doubts, buddy. Lay them to waste.'

Brio needs to feel Logie's hand again, to see the fire, the candle. He wishes he could stop himself but he can't. 'I need my notes.'

Logie takes Brio's hand. 'You need to trust.'

Inside, tears are fighting a scream and his bandaged hand clings on to Logie's. 'I *want* to. I really want to.'

'It's all about trust, and the trust isn't in me, it's in your own strength.'

But that just makes things worse. Because it's Logie he wants to trust, not himself. 'Please. Just give me my notes.'

'Come on, keep writing. Just one small step for hoggitkind and he'll reach the truth.'

Brio fumbles up the quill and dips blindly.

The steel door slammed back again and this time it was a great big party of drunken giants that came into the engine room. They were swigging from beer bottles and whoop-whooping and calling out for Madame Haha to come back and continue her show.

When Madame Haha saw the giants, her face lit up and she bounced back to her feet, almost knocking the Hoggit over.

'Madame Haha is here! At your service!'

But then she looked back down at the Hoggit with a serious expression. 'Oh, deary dear. What shall Mummy do? The giants want her to go and be a huge success but the Prince of Joy needs her to take him to see if his daddy is there. Maybe Mummy should ask the Prince of Joy whether Mummy's dreams are as important as his own?'

Brio finds himself staring at a Logie whose eyes are wide with worry. 'What did I just say?'

With a jolt, Logie closes his eyes. 'You didn't say anything.'

'Then what did I write?' He pushes the page across the table. 'You have to read it upside down.'

There's a silence. Brio can see that the fire needs more wood but he doesn't want Logie to leave the table. He wants to se that he's okay. He *needs* him to be okay.

'Well …' Logie swallows hard. 'It seems Madame Haha went off with the giants.'

Brio clutches his head with fists, snapping the quill. 'She can't have done that. I'm writing rubbish. It's all just voices. And Madame Haha gave the Hoggit a chance to stop her going. Why didn't he stop her so she could take him to find his dad—his *father*?'

'I don't know, buddy. But we're still good. Coz he can go without her if he wants.'

'He *can't*.'

'And you know what? It doesn't matter that he can't. Because the Sacred Prophecy's already told him what's in that tower.'

Brio's head springs up. 'How can it have told him? It never said whether his father's there. It left it open. That's the whole problem.'

'Exactly. And the only thing the Hoggit needs from the Sacred

Prophecy is the same single gem we all need from our scriptures—
the simple message of love that's born from a simple trust that
there's something good up there in that tower that doesn't need to
be seen to be believed.'

Brio throws down the snapped quill and pulls himself out from
the table.

Logie follows hurriedly. 'I'm serious. It's wanting to *know* that's
blocking his faith. He needs to let go.'

Not aware of having fled the van, Brio finds himself pacing
frantic circles in the hut, the precious pages hugged to chest.

'Buddy …' There's open panic in Logie's voice now.

'*Get back in the circle*,' Brio shouts. 'And give me my notes.'

'We've gone beyond the notes,' Logie says breathlessly from
behind him. 'But it's all good, we're in well-charted territory …
with the memory of Bling and Mr T'wit … the joy of forgiving.'

Hopping a change of direction, Brio can't avoid knocking
Logie's shoulder. But it felt good. He wants to do it again. 'Give
me my notes. There's no other way.'

Suddenly, Logie's blocking his path and gripping him by the
arms. He has tears in his eyes. 'There's nothing in those notes that's
going to help you now. *Okay*?'

'I don't *care* what's in them!' Brio cries. 'I just need to know you
trust me.'

Logie's face is taut and gaunt, his eyes bright with fear. The next
second, Brio's standing next to the fire with his hand outstretched,
ready to drop the precious pages into the flames.

'Give me my notes or I'll destroy everything. Then you'll fail too.
And we'll be doing it together.' He feels he's about to faint but all
Logie's staring at is the wad of papers.

'Buddy, you do not want to burn those precious pages.'

'*See*? That's all you care about, your fucking *deepmind parable.*'

The Jesus-hands rise carefully but they're trembling. 'Buddy,

I really care about you. You know that.'

'It's all been coming from *you*. You put the whole thing in my head. And never call me *buddy* again.'

As Logie edges closer, Brio can see the tears rolling down into his chin-strap beard. It really is Logie's life-and-death moment too.

'For God's sake, it's only your own doubts that are stopping the Hoggit from confronting the truth. *That's* what we've got to talk about.'

Seeing his own hands shaking over the fire, Brio knows his resolve is weakening. He rattles the pages and does a dummy throw-down. 'I know my notes are in the van. I can feel them.'

'You need to confront your doubts, okay?' Logie's struggling to speak. 'You need to ask what they mean. And I'm here to help you with that—to get you through anything. Every day for the rest of your life.'

Brio feels his face contort. Through tears and flickering lashes, he tries to keep sight of Logie. '*Please*. Just prove you love me.'

With a groan, Logie cups his forehead. '*Please*, for Christ's sake, you just need to accept the truth about your dad.'

'It's a lie. Tell me you love me.'

Logie looks back up and his glance at the drawer under the bench seat is so fleeting that Brio almost misses the tell. A few seconds of blood-rush later they bottleneck hard in the van's open doorway and, before Brio can slam the door, Logie's inside too and trying to pin him with a bear hug. Brio throws himself with such force that Logie goes down, smashing his head on the counter. He's left groaning on the floor, one of his lower arms pointing sideways at a sickening angle.

Ignoring Logie's semi-conscious moans, Brio throws the table aside and drops to his knees. As he yanks open the drawer, the flimsy lock splinters out onto the floor. And there it is, exactly as he imagined: the charred wad of notes all neatly wrapped with a strip of wide purple ribbon. He bursts it open with a single tug and the papers spill onto the floor. He stares in horror at Logie's code of circles and polygons, and dotted lines and arrows, a whole dark doublespeak that turns the Great Plea into mind-meds for Zpydr.

Brio lets out a cry of anguish and no longer cares whether the Hoggit reached the Tower of Time. The only thing that matters is saving poor Bella from Zpydr so he can save his dad from all their lies about his secret woman and his depression and his ultimate cardinal sin. Moments later, Brio's running through the woods with the wad of precious pages clutched to his chest, and all he can think is that he must reach the ferry terminal before the first rays of dawn.

~ PART SIX ~

THE LORD OF TIME

There is now a wider range of forces trying to control our thoughts and emotions than at any other time in human history, and these forces seek to control us for reasons that go well beyond the compulsion to exploit others that in turn stems from greed, laziness and the simple ability to extort, even beyond the need to facilitate social stability. These forces have coalesced around a quasi-autistic elite that controls all of the macro algorithms and contemporary channels of trade and interaction, and they strive to keep us dependent through well-disguised rituals of childhood that block emotional and spiritual growth, and that leave us captive to that strain of humanity that represents our most primitive drives and impedes ascendance to a collective higher self. It has become clear that these beguiling simulacra of the circular rituals that bring true comfort and stability have infiltrated and hijacked the mediation of our most candid relationships.

Dr Charlotte G Young
The Clown as Saviour

17

THE WOMAN'S SMILE DOESN'T FALTER. 'Brio, I promise you, I'm not from the French or any other government. And my American accent is real. I'm from the Bay Area of California.' She rests three fingertips on the edge of her name badge. 'And this *is* my real name. Dr Sandy Missle. I've come to help you. You're a very special person.'

Brio tries to vent his fear into the armrests of the comfortable chair, but his bandaged grip fizzles into phoney pins and needles. Through the small window, he can see only a dismal light-grey sky and the tops of two trees. Not wanting to look at Dr Missle either, he stares instead at her light-brown shoes, which become footprints in the mottled beige rug that's the same colour as her trousers and short jacket. Even her hair and the necklace of little wooden pearls match perfectly. Knowing that it's all designed to make him feel relaxed and neutral, he lets the rug's patterns swirl into a paisley of bleeding wounds. 'You can't keep me here. I know my rights.'

'We don't want you to be here either,' Dr Missle replies, smiling. 'We like it best when people are ready to leave.'

Intending to snap back that he *is* ready, Brio ends up scratching at the embroidered insignia on his floppy light-grey sweatshirt: *Chant Clinic London*. It's like a thick scab, and how can his fingernails be cut so smoothly, even polished? He has to find some shoes he can run in, not these useless throwaway slippers. He has to get to Bella Ripley before they do. And until he can escape, he must fight the beigeness and comforting tones and false peace. If the armchair didn't weigh a ton, he'd angle it away from the olde-worlde fireplace that's been sealed up with white marble and laid with fake orange flowers to look like a warming fire of a loving home. But the marble slab looks like a tomb and he's not going to be fooled by the flowery curtains and old-fashioned room either. If this was the big old leafy Victorian house on the website, there wouldn't be prison locks on the small windows and the room wouldn't smell of perfume.

He frets again that he can't remember anything after the white van at the entrance to the woods. Maybe one of its doors opened someone jumped out, maybe two people, even three. It was so dark. Then nothing, no dreams, no sounds of nurses or canteen trolleys. 'You kidnapped me.'

'I'm afraid it's not that exciting,' says Dr Missle. 'It's simply that the people who care about you agreed that you were suffering and that we could help you.'

People who care about me? he wants to scoff, which tips him into a thorny tangle of feelings about Logie: missing him and cursing him, trusting and hating, worrying he's been badly hurt and wishing him dead. It frightens Brio that he can't even remember sitting down with Dr Missle. And what if she *is* one of the government people who want to stop him blowing the whistle on their bodged mission? With a sudden flutter of excitement, it comes to him that he can set them all against each other—*divide and rule*, as Father T used to say about the flower arranging committee—and he's about to ask Dr Missle point-blank which side she's on when he grasps with dismay that Zpydr and both sides in the government all want the same thing: to stop him believing his dad was in the Foreign Legion, to make him believe his dad's as dead as the idea of God the Father.

Whatever Dr Missle just said is lost among images of his dad that are suddenly so vivid he actually *wants* her to be from the French government, so he can beg her to tell him where to find the desert prison.

'Brio, I know it'll take time for you to trust me, and I know I must earn your trust.'

Realising that her gaze is directing him, he looks to a small wooden sideboard and sees a plastic box with no lid. His rosary too, still hung with his dad's wedding ring. He hurries across the room to find his notes reduced to papier-mâché and his torn-up precious pages a mosaic of irregular tiles and sticky tape. The memory takes him unawares: shredding them as he shouted at his pursuers, as he crashed face-first into some kind of muddy pond. They've even managed to salvage the writing with a painstaking trace of purple biro over the washed-out ink.

'Brio, I'm sure the Great Plea is exactly as you remember, and you'll be able to recreate it perfectly. But the most comforting thing is that the best part is yet to come.'

Before Brio can work out whether her words contain some clever double meaning, he sees that his rosary beads and the wedding ring have been threaded onto a strand of white cotton. He turns on her again. 'I'm not going to hang myself.'

'I promise you, Brio, the chain was broken beyond repair.'

Worrying that it might have been him who broke the chain, he drops the subject and quickly works the delicate makeshift necklace over his thick hair and annoyingly large ears. As soon as his dad's wedding ring is back around his neck, he finds he can taste his mouth and there's a cool breeze from somewhere. Feeling somehow more than himself, he demands to know where Logie is and what they've done with Bella. 'And you'd better not have hurt Izzy.'

Dr Missle's smile remains patient and understanding. 'There are several questions there, Brio. May I answer them in turn, starting with Izzy?'

How can he say no? He has to be polite, like his mum always taught him. But the silky rhythm in Dr Missle's voice makes Logie look like a beginner. She's probably the mastermind who saved him at that place in New Mexico.

As soon as Brio's dropped back into his armchair, Dr Missle asks him to help her understand why he thinks anyone would want to hurt Izzy.

'You know why. Because she blew the whistle on what you're trying to do to me.'

'Brio, no one's trying to brainwash you. And wasn't Izzy just trying to help you because she cares about you?'

He stares incredulously at thoughts about Darcy that seem to have come out of someone else's head. Not just thoughts but feelings, and they can only be Izzy's feelings, how much she cares about Darcy. To stop the feelings getting worse, he says, 'I know I'm your perfect candidate. And I'm much better than Darcy because I *can* write. And everyone in the world knows about me because you made Penguin Boy famous on purpose. You did everything just to make me ready for *this*.'

Dr Missle is still smiling. 'I really do understand your concerns, Brio. But think about it—if people knew you were already a good writer, wouldn't it be counterproductive for anyone to try to stage a clinical outcome? People would surely take it that CHANT only works for people who are already good writers. And you yourself went to see the Hoggit. I think you're very glad you did.'

Brio flounders for a change of subject. 'What about Bella? What have you done with *her*?'

'I can assure you that no one's done anything to Bella either.' She looks genuinely curious. 'But why do you think anyone would?'

'Stop pretending you don't know.'

'I really don't.'

Some little voice tells him to hunker down and deploy his dad's anti-interrogation techniques, but the words are out before he can think. 'Because Father T told her my dad's still alive. So she knows the truth you don't want people to know. Because if he's alive you can't pretend you cured me of having a mad delusion. But bribes will never work against someone who's found God through Father T. And you'll never brainwash her either, because God's on *her* side. That's why you have to get rid of her and make it look like an accident.'

After he's finished there's a silence and he can see from Dr Missle's dead serious expression that he's hit the mark. But when he realises it's actually true that they've got rid of Bella Ripley, his stomach flips and panic grips his hands to the armrests.

'Is that true?' Dr Missle asks eventually. 'Father T told Bella that your dad's alive?'

Brio stares at Dr Missle, brain racing. When he realises what's happened, his stomach flips again. Because they obviously didn't *know* that Father T told Bella Ripley his dad was alive. Brio curses himself inside for having let slip the one critical piece of information they didn't know. And now they really will hurt Bella. 'But Father T wasn't really talking about my dad,' he says hurriedly. 'He was talking about the Father *God*. He just meant God's still alive in the world.'

Dr Missle recovers her smile but it's not the same as before. 'Yes, I'm sure that's what Father T meant. And I promise you again, Brio, no one's done anything with Bella. Now, am I right in thinking that what you'd like to talk about most is finishing the Great Plea? Because if so, I'm certain I can help you reach the ending very easily now.'

'You *can't*. It's ruined.' He looks to the small window and its dismal sky. How secure are those locks really? And are they two storeys up or three? It feels like three. Too high to escape but not high enough to—

'Brio,' Dr Missle says gently, 'it really is your choice whether you complete what the Hoggit asked of you.' She tilts her head the other way. 'Perhaps it doesn't need to be finished?'

'It *does*. But you're never going to make me change the ending.'

They sit in silence and, even though Dr Missle looks to the small window too, she doesn't lose her smile.

When she looks back, she says, 'I wonder whether you've ever contemplated the possibility that what happened in the past is not as important as what happens in the future? After all, many roads that begin behind us can lead to the same destination ahead. And memory is such an incredible thing, don't you think? And don't we already trust our memories for huge decisions?'

But Brio can't think anything, because the rhythm and timbre of her voice have released those irresistible waves of comforting tingles down his back.

'Perhaps that's it,' she continues. 'We only mistrust our memory when we don't like what we see. And we think we remember things in our own lives when actually they may have happened millions of years ago. I mean, a curious mind like yours truly wasn't born yesterday, or even in your own lifetime.'

Sensing a trick in the making, Brio stirs himself for a fight, while Dr Missle's smile becomes even more earnest.

'What I mean,' she says, 'is that we're the result of billions of years of evolution, from the first glimmer of hydrogen and the first cell capable of dividing, right through to all the organisms and creatures that have paved the way to the present day—to you and me sitting here as though this is what humans have always been. And think on that—if we're born with instincts that make us behave in particular ways—memory-based instincts that are coded into our genes—why shouldn't we have inherited a whole lot more besides? If our DNA can store memories of the threats and opportunities we've faced in the past, along with our best ways of responding to them, derived from millions of generations of trial and error, doesn't this mean that our DNA can somehow store cinematic experiential memories too? Why would it store only the lessons and morals of the story and not the workings and colourful narrative detail too—in case they could be used in a different age to some even better effect? Why wouldn't lots that's lying deep in our memory today have come from a time when we weren't even human? Isn't that why some people seem like particular kinds of animal? Isn't that why some people seem to have insights that others don't—why they seem to have been here before? Some people call that having a past life, but maybe it's not quite as spiritual a phenomenon as they think.'

'I don't care.' Though he didn't miss a word and his mind races with possibilities that someone needs to resist. These are matters for God alone.

'Interesting too,' she goes on regardless, 'that in our evolutionary past lives we've been both male and female, and all types of male and female. Biological hermaphrodites too, and asexual reproducers that seem to live on air. And there's nothing spacey about this. It's just science that needs an explanation. And we always assume that memory is only about going *back* in time, but if time and space are one and can warp, why shouldn't space and time warp back on themselves to begin at their own end? Why do we even think of beginnings and ends when we're all just points in that eternal, multidimensional cycle of lightspeed stillness? And what if that cycle is beginning and ending the whole time? Then we're everywhere at once—just like God. So when we write the stories that explain ourselves to the world and the world to ourselves, we need to break free from the shackles of beginning, middle and end. By which I mean, of course, the only way is to make the end the beginning and the beginning the end.'

'You're not going to win,' Brio mutters. But he longs to know the answer. Because that's exactly why he was put on this earth: to *prove everything*. To show the workings and all the colourful detail too, just like the Bible—the Book of Life—the greatest oblation of all.

'I'm not trying to win,' says Dr Missle. 'And neither are you. I'm just suggesting that you might like to ask yourself one simple question. If our genetically stored memories contain so many worlds and glacial epochs of learning and adaption to change, why shouldn't we trust our memories to guide us? Why should we keep trying to force our constructed wills on what we already know deep down? If the past can be changed as much as it can't, why should we waste time trying to patch it up? Why tilt at windmills and inveigh against an occluded history when you could think about the limitless future, which you know from the Hoggit has already happened? The chances are that you *did* know the Hoggit in a past life. Perhaps you actually were the Hoggit, or will be again. But all you need to know is that your memory is a friend you can trust.'

Brio's lost all track of what he needs in order to reach the Tower of Time. But it doesn't stress him now, because he knows that in his past life he really was a hedgehog. That's why he can speak Hedgehoc, why he's been chosen to help the Hoggit find his father. And the reason he'll succeed is because he *is* the chosen one, just as the Hoggit said. But he finds his gaze following Dr Missle's to the table and chair and the big computer screen that he always knew would come next.

'I'm not going to do it,' he says. *But how can it be worse than this? And maybe I really can find the ending before they get to Bella.* He feels his breathing change and hears Logie's voice counting him slowly *in* and *out* …

But *no*. He has to stop himself going under. He has to work his fingernails through the bandages and dig into his palms. There's still time to escape. He can do this without them. But what could be braver and smarter than facing them down on his own? And what if playing along with Dr Missle is the only way he can escape?

'Brio, this is proven technology and I promise you'll know at all times what's going on, and you alone will be in control of your thoughts and feelings.'

Now comes the fear that if Dr Missle wins, they'll be able to find out he's been gay for millions of years. He'll never be able to break the bonds of his deeply buried penguin genes. Or what if he's got so many girl genes hidden away that it was all a big mistake for him to have been brought up as a boy? What if it goes back even further to when there was no difference between male and female and everyone had nipples or none at all? The time when there was just reproduction without sex, and all living cells were doing exactly the same amount of womanly housework as they were manly battle with all those other cells that were achieving the perfect life balance of housework and battle. When Brio looks back up and sees Dr Missle, he knows it's true. They don't want him to be a boy *or* a girl. They want him in their secret religion where no one's either and everyone's both. Just beige like Dr Missle. Beige with no shape and one smile fits all.

'Brio?' comes Dr Missle's coaxing voice. 'Are you ready?'

He snaps out and tries to hold her gaze. He's not going to let them tie his mind in knots. He's going to slip a hand up his sweatshirt and slide the Ring of Love onto a finger. It'll be his shield against evil, his divine kryptonite. And he'll play along by agreeing that she can strap the CHANT wearable assistant onto his wrist like she's doing right now, making it seem like a demonstration that isn't really happening in real life. She obviously doesn't know that on *his* wrist it'll become the unbreakable watch that his dad wears on operations. Then he'll use the power of his deepest memory to turn the tables on her like he did with Logie in Pippa's garden. By the time Dr Missle's accomplices find their star hypnotist, she'll be drugged and gagged on her own words and he'll be on his way to Bella Ripley.

Even when Brio registers that he's sitting in front of the computer screen, he knows victory is assured. Because instead of the real Dr Missle on the screen, it's just a fake. In fact, it's so fake she might have been the real Dr Missle all along. And the scarcely detectable strobing flicker in her eyes is every bit as good as an inextinguishable candle or steadily crackling fire.

'So let's go back to that wonderful day,' says the beguiling yet reassuringly surreal Dr Missle, 'that wonderful day you met the Hoggit at the castle. And, feeling as comfortable as you are ... drawing in everything that makes you happy ... remembering what amazing things the Hoggit told you ... letting go of those tiny troubles that might still give you the teeniest moments of concern ...'

Having braced himself for contest with the vaunted virtual mother of all mind-gamers, Brio's dismayed by the body double's clumsy incompetence. Maybe she's even going to whip out a gold watch and tell him he's feeling sleepy.

'... and no one can disturb you now. No one can stop you honouring your oath to the Hoggit ... And you can see the Hoggit now, longing to reach the Tower of Time ...'

Despite Dr Missle's woeful blatancy, Brio can't deny that her voice is becoming somehow more comfortable, and he's happy to be breathing *in* with what makes him happy ... *mmm* ... and out with what makes him sad ...

'... and bobbing gently on waters that ran together once, two channels that flow and change as they wend their ways ... and we don't understand why some went here and some went there ... flowing their parallel lives ... one spread thin and clear over sand, over time, to the sea. And who controls it but the moon, we ask? Who controls it but the moon? And the other channel so held in line by riverbanks and walls, flowing over rocks … over time. And who controls it but the man, we ask? Who controls it but the man?'

Her voice reminds Brio of his mum reciting poetry she wrote for him alone. Yet the more Dr Missle says, the more she seems a figment of his imagination, which makes him think *good then, she's not real, I don't need to worry about falling under her spell.*

'And so those parallel waters are coming together now, coming together in the middle like the Hoggit's diaries meeting your wonderful stories … everything the right way up for God to read …'

Brio knows he must keep up the acquiescent murmurs to prove that his resistance is melting …

'And it's time to think about the way we all take into our hearts so many things from around us … those things people say and do … the pictures we see … the news we hear, the anger and the laughter all around us … all those things that cause us to mould ourselves to the shape of our world, to make ourselves a story for others. But to be at peace with the world to which we have shaped ourselves, to prevent us becoming many stories for many people, we must share our true story and become part of the bigger story … the bigger truth.'

It makes no sense at all to Brio, but, 'Mmm … yes …'

'So you want to share your story with the world you love … and now that Madame Haha has gone to embrace her fame with the giants, does the Hoggit have a plan to reach the High Dungeon?'

'Mmm, yeah … He's gonna snap Lord Rumbuck out of his trance and they'll go together.' He's never felt more in control.

'That sounds very good,' says Dr Missle. 'Shall we see if his plan worked?'

'I don't know if it did. Because Lord Rumbuck looked so pathetic, he just wanted to cover his raw body. The Hoggit tried to fire him up with reminders of his derring-do and his destined battle with the Dark Lord. But Lord Rumbuck must have overheard what Madame Haha said, because he knew he was destined to die in the battle. "And you don't care," he said mournfully to the Hoggit. "I was mere cannon fodder in your wild dream." The Hoggit wanted to deny it but before he could think of some way not to lie, he said, "You *wanted* to die. You made that big speech and thought dying was the greatest thing ever. That's why we're in this mess." Lord Rumbuck's eyes narrowed, even the bulging one, and his expression darkened. "Then I *will* take you to your father's empty tomb. And I'll die in the process, exactly as you wish. I'll lay down my life as a father should, then I too will be the perfect father." But he was too weak to even lift his armour off the ground and the Hoggit's heart went out to him. He couldn't help thinking about Mr Hare with all his daughters—the big happy family he always watched so dreamily from up in his castle. How can he let poor Mr Hare lay down his life when he has so many kids who are longing for him to come home? Without a thought for the Sacred Prophecy, the Hoggit spills everything about Mr and Mrs Hare's argument by the roadside, and how Mr Hare stumbled into the path of an oncoming car. The Hoggit begs Mr Hare to understand that stealing him away from his family was an honest mistake. But Mr Hare's totally enraged. "You kidnapped me from my family for your own selfish ends. You've left my children fatherless in a dangerous world. I'll kill you." But his rage gave way to a cry of realisation and the armour slipped from his hands. "I'm not a brave hero at all. I'm a pathetic hare who abandoned his family. Oh, what have I done? How can I ever make amends?"'

As the Hoggit angrily wipes away the tears, so too does Brio, and Dr Missle says, 'It hurts me to see you upset.'

'I'm not upset. And I know exactly what's going on here.'

'That's good. I hope you trust me now. And I know the Hoggit's in distress, but isn't it lovely that he cares about Mr Hare and his family? There was a time, after all, when he wouldn't have cared at all. He'd probably have tried to backtrack and tell Mr Hare that he *was* Lord Rumbuck and that what he just said about him being Mr Hare was a trick by the Dark Lord.'

Brio can't believe how well Dr Missle knows the Hoggit. It thrills him as much as it releases a collywobble of worry. But how could the Hoggit feel sorry for Mr Hare when he had a secret woman hidden away from his wife and kids? No, of course the Hoggit was allowed to feel sorry for Mr Hare, because it was he himself who'd made Mr Hare abandon his family, and the only way he could put right his wrong was to make amends. And maybe getting Mr Hare back to his family would make amends for his secret woman too. '"Please," the Hoggit begged Mr Hare. "You've got to go now, before the ship leaves. You must prove that the reason a father's a great hero is because he *can* survive in that mundane jungle of love and duty." But as though roused by his own great words, the floor beneath the Hoggit's feet suddenly shook with one long horn-blast of exactly six seconds. "Go!" the Hoggit cried. "The ship's leaving!" But Mr Hare wouldn't leave without the Hoggit. "It's your home too," he implored. "And if we ever find it again, you can be part of my family forever." There were peals of impassioned shouting, tears too. Eventually, the Hoggit had to physically bulldoze Mr Hare out of the engine room and slam the door behind him. He was relieved to be alone at last and slumped back to catch his breath. But then the full reality hit him. He truly *was* all alone, which meant that he'd have to face the truth about his father alone. He began to panic. He couldn't think straight ...'

'Brio, everything's all right.' Dr Missle's voice is steady and calming. 'You only need to ask yourself why the Hoggit's so frightened.'

'He's not frightened.' Brio has to draw hard for breath. 'He just knows that if he doesn't follow the Sacred Prophecy to the letter, his father won't be there in the High Dungeon.'

'Okay, be calm. It may be dim and spooky in the engine room, and the roar of the boiler may seem like the fires of Hell, but he's at the heart of the ship, in its innermost place, the deepest cave, the source of its energy, and he too must leave before the ship pulls away from the dock.'

Brio has to stare harder still, to lose himself in the calming flicker ... the little bands of glow that run slowly across the wall behind Dr Missle like electronic news captions on tickertape.

'The Hoggit loves the Sacred Prophecy ...' she says. It sounds like the beginning of an incantation. 'He respects the Sacred Prophecy. And he knows that it calls for him to be accompanied by Lord Rumbuck and the Jester. But he knows too that all scriptures are symbolic poems that are forever unfolding, forever uncertain—forever deepening but never solving the mystery of God. And he knows that his own Sacred Prophecy left so many questions for him to answer for himself—like why they had to save the Queen before they could find his father ... why the Sacred Prophecy never told of what happened to Lord Rumbuck ... above all else, why it never said for sure that his father was there in that golden tower. So the Hoggit knows that Lord Rumbuck and Madame Haha are but symbols of the courage and joy that he himself can embody and carry into this final stage of his great quest. And that knowledge gives him the courage to face down his doubts, the doubts that we all carry in our hearts. And the reason God wants us to doubt is so we can *face* our doubts, so we can make them the cornerstone of our belief, our belief in ourselves as part of something unbelievably and wonderfully big. That's why God doesn't care about the exact letter of scriptures—doesn't care how many times we twirl our beads or offer up burnt offerings. God only cares that we have love in our hearts and live our lives by that love. So what *is* the true message of the Sacred Prophecy if not that the Hoggit should—'

'Stop!'

Brio's so startled by his own sudden cry, he needs a few seconds to understand where he is. But as he hurriedly fixes in on Dr Missle, he remembers why his heart's beating with pure excitement. 'I've got it! I know what the true message is!'

Dr Missle's smile seems to break out into some kind of rose-golden glow. 'And what is the true message?'

'It's that the Hoggit must find his father at all costs, even if he has to break the Sacred Prophecy and go it alone.'

He stares into the imperceptibly flickering eyes and waits for her answer.

'That's very good.'

But Brio stands up and Dr Missle looks worried.

'Brio, this is such a great moment, how can anything be wrong?'

He feels the freeze down his back, in his forehead. 'The Hoggit can't go on his own, after all. I'm sorry. Grandma would be heartbroken if he broke the Sacred Prophecy. Heartbroken in Heaven.' He has to keep saying words to bury whatever else is underneath them. He has to shout and shout louder. But several giants are approaching and he quickly sits back down. The giants gather round him. He knows he must tame them with jokes like Madame Haha does, so they don't ruin his plans of escape. 'I've got a joke about a millipede,' he announces hopefully. 'It's ten times funnier than the one about the centipede.'

Laughter like church bells, a circular round of perfect applause.

'Oh, thank goodness. You got the joke.'

'You're full of great jokes,' says a voice like Dr Missle's. 'What a shame you've had to bury your joy for so long.'

'I know. All my life, I've just wanted to laugh.'

But when he closes his eyes more tightly to block out even the dimmest silhouettes, he sees the big sign on the pale blue wall:

CHANT ~ The Central Hospital for Animals ~ Neurological Treatment Clinic. 'Why am I in hospital? There's nothing wrong with me.'

'That's right. So at last you can slip off your lovely safety harness.'

'*No*,' he cries and grasps the rosary under his grey sweatshirt. 'It's all I have left to remind me of Mr T'wit.'

'Oh, yes, Mr T'wit loved you a lot. But don't you remember how much you wanted to take off your safety harness when he insisted you were still two years old? Do you not recall how often you tied yourself onto something to be safe, only to find yourself stuck when you needed to flee from danger? And how many times did Lord Rumbuck use your tether to take control of you? Even now, you know that your safety harness is far too tight. It hurts. It's hindering your growth. Come, take it off now. Pass through that golden archway and into a new life beyond.'

There's a tussle to pull the rosary up over his head. He doesn't know how many hands he's fighting, it might only be two—might only be his own.

'It's all right,' comes a voice. 'No one's going to force you to do anything you don't want.'

But the little beads spill onto the floorboards and it's the most he can do to keep the Ring of Love safe in his hand.

Yet, as the storm passes, he does feel free, just like Dr Missle promised. *Oh, my goodness*, he thinks. *She must be a clairvoyant, a seer. I must keep my eyes closed*. 'What's going to happen?' he mumbles, his lips too parched to lick. 'What *is* my future?'

'The future is the past and the past the future,' intones the Unseen Seer. 'And I'm sorry to impart tidings that are as great yet sad as they are sad yet great.'

He can't swallow either. He won't be able to speak for much longer. 'What tidings?'

'The greatest tidings you've ever heard,' says the Unseen Seer.

'That your father the Hoggit King did indeed take brave battle to the Dark Lord. And oh, what another contest to behold. But alas, Young Prince, for although all portents and auguries pointed to a valiant victory, when the moment came for the Hoggit King to deliver the decisive blow, the Dark Lord struck him with the devilish Hex of the Mirrored Fate, the dire anathema that pitches a creature into mortal contest with itself. Forsooth, and what a truly dreadful battle, because the Hoggit King was a warrior of such unrivalled strength and skill that in the end he won the great battle against himself.'

'My father did not slay himself,' Brio cries in the Hoggit's squeaky voice. 'The Dark Lord threw him into the Tower of Time. And he's still there.'

'Alas no, Young Prince,' purrs the Unseen Seer. 'You must celebrate his victory. You must glory in the life of a true hero. Come to an accommodation with your loss. Remember how it was only your noble father's heroic strength that afforded him that great victory over himself.'

On his knees at the altar, Brio begs the Unseen Seer to tell him the truth.

'Young Prince, you can find joy and strength in your noble father's martyrdom, for you yourself share all of his great qualities.'

In Brio's mind these words lay an unnaturally abrupt blanket of peace on the Hoggit which he works hard to experience as a rational and determined state of mind. But the peace becomes heavy and lopsided. It's going to slide onto the floor. 'That's not what happened. And you're not allowed to dictate my fate like a Greek god. The most you can do is send me dreams so I can decide for myself.'

'God lets you choose with parables too,' purrs the Unseen Seer.

'This is *not* a story. And Grandma did *not* lie. She told me my father's in the Tower of Time and the Tower of Time is *not* Heaven.

And if you dare say otherwise, you'll be calling Grandma a liar.'

Suddenly, it's a contest that places his very life on the line and never again is he going to be beaten down by better words.

'Grandma was a wonderful woman,' says the Unseen Seer with the certainty of ritual monotone. 'A wonderful woman who loved you with all her troubled heart.'

Brio feels the Hoggit draw himself tall to throw it back in her face. But he knows they must both pretend to accept what the Unseen Seer says.

'Grandma loved the Hoggit with all her heart,' says the Unseen Seer. 'Yet, like all wonderful people, Grandma had her own little fears … of being left alone … of losing her only grandchild. And all of her fears came from losing her only son, the Hoggit's father.'

'Mmm …'

'Grandma was also a storyteller of repute who wrote wonderful tales into which she poured all the powers of her imagination. She even entrusted you with secret knowledge of seemingly sweet creatures who could unexpectedly change into monsters. She created a world where nothing was as it seemed. You found it impossible to tell what was truly good and what might turn bad. You couldn't trust yourself to face such a world. Why go out there when you could live a life of certainty with your wonderful grandma and kindly Mr T'wit?'

More than ever, he knows he must control his rage. The Hoggit must do nothing but meekly agree.

'But you forgive Grandma for her mistakes,' says the Unseen Seer. 'Because you know she was doing the best she could in difficult circumstances. And you understand that Grandma's stories didn't really amount to a sacred prophecy at all. Indeed, it was only Lord Rumbuck who gave her stories this name. So if you go up the Tower of Time without Lord Rumbuck and the Jester, you won't be breaking faith with anything or anyone. You'll only be breaking the chains that have held you back. You'll be the lobster escaping its pot, the crab making it to the other side of that plank over troubled waters.'

A silence follows, which Brio counts in seconds to quell his fear that the Unseen Seer has seen into his innermost secrets.

'So are you ready to venture up the Tower of Time?'

'Mmm …'

'Are you ready to find that High Dungeon door?'

'I am.'

'To push it open and see inside?'

'Yes.'

'Ready to see whether it's your father's place of waiting or an empty tomb?'

'Yes. But it's a big climb and I'm very tired. I need to rest before I go.'

'But if you don't leave the ship now, you'll be marooned at sea for an uncertain term. You'll be exiled, life in a wasteland.'

'I know. But I'm off the ship already. I'm on the dock and tucked into a little nook where I can sleep.'

'Brio …'

'I need *rest*. Can't you allow me a good night's sleep before I set off?' He quickly tries to make amends for his sharpness by sounding childish too. 'I've had such a big day, after all.'

There's a weak silence and he imagines the giants all conferring with secret eye signals and hand signs.

'All right,' says the Unseen Seer eventually. 'But promise me you'll ascend those spiral stairs to the High Dungeon as soon as you're awake?'

'I promise.' And for the first time since he fell into the hands of the Unseen Seer, he's relieved to have been able to tell not only the truth, but also the whole truth and nothing but the truth.

18

TUCKED BY OTHERS INTO HIS BED and staring into darkness, Brio battles the somnolence he knows they're forcing on him with the interminable, soporific incantations through hidden speakers and vibrating ripples—long bass notes and the soft, rhythmic chiming of distant bells. He bites the end of his tongue and digs fingernails into his palms, revels again in his victory over the Unseen Seer, how he turned it all back on her and fooled them with his curated responses.

He jolts again and has to up the pain level by pinching a fold of sensitive skin between his legs. *If you fall asleep for even a moment*, he scolds himself silently, *you'll wake to find you really have been brainwashed. Except you won't find out at all. You won't even know.*

His nails are about to break skin when he registers that silence has displaced the mind-numbing drone. He holds his breath and strains to listen for even the slightest sound. And he's still telling himself he must play safe and wait longer when his foot slips itself out of bed and feels for the smooth rug.

In the cupboard he finds the pile of spare sheets he expected, though he's surprised at not having had to quietly break open its door. He sets about tying the sheets into a rope to bear him the two or three floors down to the ground. As he's about to make for the small window, he sees a single rosary bead on the floor. To his further surprise, he finds the little trinket disconcerting and hurriedly dismisses it as a cast-down pearl not even fit for piggy-wigs.

Double-checking the cast-iron solidity of the radiator, he triple-knots the end of the sheet-rope to one of its feet. When he eases open the small window, rain blows into his face from the darkness, but he pushes back with his huge cloud-like bundle and crouches on the windowsill for one last look back at the scene of his greatest victory. Seeing the drop, though, Brio dizzies, and it's only a noise from behind that pushes him out into a foot-scrabbling grapple with sodden cotton and gnarly ivy.

After a seemingly endless descent past curtained windows and oddly placed ledges, his bare feet squelch to earth in a mud of pretty flowers. He swipes the rain from his snout and lets his ears twitch like antennae. Detecting only the sound of chariot tyres on a wet road close by, he darts across the gardens to the tree he knows will be awaiting him, its slippery bough reaching out over the pavement beyond the high perimeter wall.

In the lee of the great cliff face, he squats to check he hasn't been seen. Excitement rushes in to fill the vacuum left by his spent fear and he clasps the ring in his pyjama pocket.

Planning his route up the tree, he rubs bandaged hands in mud to roughen them for the ascent. How mightily irritated Lord Rumbuck would be to witness the climbing skills of a mere Hoggit. How lithely the stalwart little creature will land and roll on wet paving stones beyond the wall. And he won't need help from anyone to find the Tower of Time, because in some past and deeply buried life lies a memory of the route along which he was once dragged by an impatient hand like Grandma's.

Only when he's free of gawking strangers and running barefoot along the rough canal path can his yearning become a cry of, 'Father! I'm coming! *Fa-ther!*' Which startles a huddle of sleeping ducks into a flapping of crisscrossed skims across the dank water. Their fatuous quacking echoes off tall walls and fades behind him as he runs past houseboats and small barges, under bridges too, and up and over a deserted road to circumvent a short tunnel that the Dark Lord has blocked with fake repair works. He only notices the pain from his chafed feet when they go numb, and the only things he sees are a stray dog, a fox, and an igloo-shaped cardboard box.

Exhilaration and trepidation vie with impatience as one stretch of canal turns out exactly like the last. But eventually he smells zoo through moonlit railings and sees the familiar polygon-dome of netting. Pursued by the stink of fermenting orange peel and acrid wee that makes his nose stream in the rain, he profanes penguins all the way to the dark safety of the park, where it's a never-ending avenue of all the bins and benches ever made.

Hearing voices in the unlit darkness, he veers off the wide path and crouches next to a tree. A statue in the centre of a big circle reminds him of a church spire, which chastens him into a prayer for strength and skill in the coming battle. God replies at once, calling upon him to consign his frantic and breathless run to a forgotten page of history. This is no way to approach the final battle, says God. The Young Prince must bear down upon the Dark Lord as a single unbroken rank that marches fearlessly into the mouth of cannons and beats out the rhythm in a drum-step of rhyme—yes! 'Words aloud for God to hear, in Hedgehoc fit for giants' ears!'

No longer fearful of voices other than his own, Brio stands tall and raises his chin high against the raw force of rain. 'Onwards!' he commands himself and breaks into a heavy, determined stomp, calling out the step as he goes, 'Left, right, left, right, marching hard in*to* the night. Heft 'n' might, heft 'n' might, bold as brass in dead of night.'

Though his marching remains strong, he's slowed by the niggling voice of Grandma, scolding him for using nothing but rhyming couplets and far too many repetitions. But no, he must fight back, because Grandma only hated rhyme and meter because it might have given him the momentum to sally forth into his own life. With a violent shake of the head, he scratches the rain and tears of confused grief from his eyes. He tells himself that next time he must be more vigilant, because this won't be the last of the Dark Lord's assaults on his mind and will.

Even when he breaks out of the park ten minutes later, he keeps up the rhythmic, rhyming chant, which becomes louder and louder until he's marking time at the edge of a busy road, shouting at the unbroken stream of passing chariots. Seeing no alternative but to exploit a brief chink in their defences, he skirmishes across six lanes of blinding lights and blaring battle horns. After a lumbering dash to put the mess behind him, he finds himself in some indeterminate street clambering up into a stranded barge that looks like an overloaded rubbish skip on the bank of a rain-washed road. The moment he sees the discarded fireguard, he knows it's the Armour Impervious in cunning disguise, responding to the call for battle. The Great Sword too, in the form of a rusty poker, and the Timeless Tunic so much like an old towel it might even fool the Dark Lord's soldiers.

Having torn a hole and pulled the rain-soaked tunic down over his head, he straps on the fireguard-armour with a Lilliputian lashing of electrical cable. Seeing how authentically medieval the hospital trousers look with the tunic and armour, he laughs and holds out the Great Sword with both hands. 'For yea, it heard the call to arms, presented sly as poker charmed! At rest no more, now mighty in my hand! Lead on, be brave, my trumpet's marching band!'

He drives forward like a parked car on the move, head high and swishing wildly to clear a path through pelting rain. Gleefully, he witnesses how giants take one look and scurry away in terror. He's the master of the night, the god of his world!

Turning a corner, though, he sees up ahead a wall of bus sides and straggling giants, and lights that reveal more of the world than broad daylight. And when a white and yellow chariot with a blue light turns slowly into his street, he realises that the Dark Lord's soldiers are in active pursuit. Diving into the nearest doorway, he finds himself crammed in against a hovel of cardboard and shopping bags. He draws his knees up under his chin and prays that the Dark Lord's chariot will pass before the hermit vagabond slits his throat. Yet when the hovel stirs and grumbles, his words flow easily. 'I come in peace, dear sagging soul of soggy cardboard, bags and grime. All I need is a hidey-hole, for the briefest of your precious time.'

A hand breaks open the hovel to reveal a gnarled and fallen face inside a matting of knotted beard. '*Ucgh arf.*'

Brio draws back and presses one hand to his armoured heart. 'Hurt me not, Oh, gentle giant, for p'leece car seeks me for a client. See it loom with rain-flecked swipe and frown. I've got to cower, conceal my spikes and gown.'

The pitiful hand grabs his forearm. '*Whaddja-torkn-baah?*'

Brio leans forward and cups the gripping hand with his own. 'I beg you, beg you, beg you, *please*, just let me hold your long, damp sleeve. Let's cower together, fireguard safe, though rain still trickles, stings and chafes.'

As the Dark Lord's bright chariot slowly approaches in the sweeping rain, Brio twists to hide his face, which makes the hand grip him harder still. Yet even as the chariot rolls slowly and searchingly past, Brio feels the love pouring out through his hand. And after the homeless guy has slurred another incomprehensible compaction of words, Brio asks, 'Dost thou enquire if with my fireguard here, I've brought a hearth of logs and cards and crate of beer?'

Their eyes meet and Brio sees with terrible clarity the fate that awaits him too: being cursed into the body of a giant for the rest of his life, left to rot in a deserted doorway, shackled to the walls with no one who cares enough to care. He can't stop the sob and grips the sleeve harder. 'Alas, no time to right your wrong. I wish you well, short life make long. The Dark Lord's chariot just turned right, I must rejoin the looming fight.'

As Brio marches on, unable to look back, he can't believe he robbed the poor man of his precious blanket. His small bottle of spirits too, and the broken takeaway box of half-eaten cake. Hollers of impotent outrage echo behind him, but the voice is too weak to threaten chase and he ducks into another doorway. Having slung the blanket around his shoulders in preparation for its revelation as a cloak of invisibility, he splashes the stolen firewater into his mouth. His throat and belly burn and he gags. But just as Mr T'wit used to whisper to Grandma that a little tipple of the Holy Spirit never did a soul harm, so he must quench the fire with a stuffed tongue of stale cake. Having clenched down another retch, he stumbles back into his march.

Closing in on the pandemonium ahead, he slows to pull the cloak over his armour and sword. The street becomes busier and brighter, ever more confused with dancing rain and frightened faces. He passes shopfronts brazen with light for no one and traffic lights no ordinary Hoggit would ever understand. Now the leering eyes of mannequin giants in shop windows are swivelling in his wake, surely whispering to each other from shop to shop, sending the message ahead to warn the Dark Lord of his approach. Their pass-it-on clamour becomes such a loud babble of pursuit that he has to break into open flight and the street becomes a gauntlet without visible end.

The Dark Lord's cameras pick him up too, craning down from high walls and lamp posts. He has no choice but to enter an alley of overstuffed dumpster-bins. From under the canopy of an open door, an apron-clad giant glances at him and draws hard on a cigarette. But no, it's not a cigarette, it's a fuse to blow that row of fake beer kegs and kill the Young Prince in a gunpowder plot. He dives for cover between two bins and braces himself against the wall, breath clenched between his teeth.

When he realises that God's saved him by soaking the gunpowder with rain, his legs give way to laughter and he slides juddering down the wall. 'Father!' he cries with his last shiver of strength. '*Father!*' But as his head's about to fall forward, he finds himself staring at a large rat. He sits up sharply and pulls in his bleeding toes, only to recognise the vile face. His jaw clamps in resolve and he stands to look Guzzle in the eye. 'I see you've crawled out from that drain, to mind-game play my rain-soaked brain. But you'll not win, I did but rest, and now will give my noble best—you filthy *pest.*'

Instead of crumbling under the assault of words, Guzzle holds his fiery glare and scoffs. 'There is no father in your tower, your soul will split, t'will be your hour. From such a loss there's no recall, from such great height you'll choose to fall.'

Brio slams back against the wall and wilts into a tangle of blanket. The retching of cake and acrid spirits leaves him drained and the doubts crowd back in. He's about to spew again when three giants holding beer cans walk past, pausing their banter to laugh at his plight. The humiliation galvanises him to even greater resolution and he blazes double at Guzzle, who's watching him with one nibbling eye from the edge of a congealed pizza crust.

'Oh, stand aside, you foul-mouthed rodent! For I am sterner stuff and potent! The Hoggit King, my father true, does flood my veins with blood-red blue. You knew me once when I did wince, but now you see the Great Red Prince!'

Wiping rain-diluted vomit from his stinging lips, Brio gives thanks for his victory over yet another attempt by the Dark Lord to cast the curse of doubt. He breaks into a strident march, but he can no longer feel his feet or hear the passing traffic, and time seems to rise above him, leaving him in some no-man's-land of footless travel like sleep.

Still crying out to his father when he reaches a park, Brio scrambles clanking over a barricade of slippery, liveried railings. Hemmed in by lake on both sides, he erupts a fright of moorhens and has to duck an outrage of geese. They're still shouting at him as he escapes the shrinking enclosure of royal birds, but it's to the persistent echoes of this inauspicious fanfare that Brio finds himself stumbling back in awe. He blinks and wipes his eyes, fully expecting the great walls of columned light to have vanished as unexpectedly as they appeared. Even when he shakes his head for a seond double-take, he can't believe he's made it all the way. As though to cast the impossible vision in stone, he finds himself mumbling the old verse handed down by Grandma. 'With battlements so high, the tower rose up into the sky. Though stripped of light from former days, it held aloft by power of gaze.' His voice becomes louder, the rhythm gathers momentum, and to hell with Grandma's hypocrisy for building it out of such solid gold rhyme. 'Bones of stone by hand of God, where once the angels gaily trod! For lo, those windows, tall and thin, conceal a wickedness within! And from those slits as slim as cracks, aim poisoned arrows, glinting black!' He thrusts his poker up into the pouring rain and lets out a cry of, '*Faa-ther!*'

On reaching the grand square in front of the great tower, Brio's brought up short by a terrible discovery. The Dark Lord has erected an extra wall of defences up the tower, a mind-messing maze of bars and crossbars and platforms draped with heraldic banners, all disguised to look like colossal scaffolding and renovation works. And standing at every gate, the same dark blue tunics and lurid neon armour.

Doubt suddenly rains down from the battlements and his resolve falters. Everyone's surely laughing at him and seeing right through the dripping veil of stolen blanket. The two earnest women under their shared umbrella. The man-in-suit who turns to scurry the other way. Gawking passengers on a passing bus. Only a kerbside puddle in the face jolts him back into action and he drags his theatrical club foot into the road, where he haphazardly negotiates lane after lane of fast chariots and jumbled lights. All it'll take to alert the Dark Lord's minions is one blast of horn or screech of tyres.

Down on the pontoon jetty where he came ashore with Madame Haha and Lord Rumbuck, Brio sheds the shawl and wrestles the life-ring out of its housing. Having detached its rope, he sits on the edge and topples into the freezing water with the cavorting doughnut clutched to his armoured chest. The cold makes him gasp but the current clears his mind of everything except trying to stay in the eddies that'll keep him pressed to the towering riverbank wall.

As he bumps along rough stone, a frantic calling starts up from behind. But as soon as he begins to pass under the enormous bridge, all he can hear is the echoing rumble of traffic above. Hardly able to see for the vegetal water that slaps his face, he has to flay fingers to stop himself being yet again swept past the base of the tower, and he only just manages the miracle of clawing himself up onto the bottom step.

Barely registering the pain or the rain or his freezing, soggy pyjamas, he scampers along the banner-draped wire mesh of the Dark Lord's new defences. Finding an untied overlap between banners, he prises his way inside and scampers for the steps that zigzag their way up the great matrix of steel bars. At the bottom he stops and prays for protection from the fear of heights that's already reaching down from his forehead into the pit of his stomach.

A few moments later, he's mounting the steps in laboured heaves that burn his calves and flay his bare feet. At every turn, he has to stop and listen breathlessly for voices against the ever more distant traffic noise. The higher he climbs the harder he prays that the banners will keep shielding him from the view of the drop and the attention of the Dark Lord's minions. He's on the point of believing that the Dark Lord has cast him into a cycle of never-ending steps when he becomes aware of a brilliant white glow just above him. Three turns more and he's out in the open, nothing but wire mesh between him and the appalling drop. His thoughts pixelate and his breathing becomes an uncontrollable wheezing and heaving. He has to clutch hold of the nearest scaffolding bar and close his eyes on the revolving blue lights far below.

A shout startles him and he sees minions running for the base of the tower. Launching back into the ascent, he enters a tight column of steps that ascend the side of the giant clockface. At the top, he's confronted by a narrow gantry above the clock, and the only way across to the tower is by a small bridge into one of the high arches. But one glimpse of the bottomless drop drains the blood from his neck and he has to cling to a vertical scaffolding pole. He's about to retch when calls and thundering feet from below send him crawling along the gantry, poker-sword in hand and eyes closed. He doesn't open them again till he's clawed his way around the turn and felt the cold stone of the archway against his palm.

'*Fa-ther!*' he cries into the darkness. 'Where are you? It is I, your son!'

But when all he sees inside is the gigantic god of a bell attended by its carillon halo of little angel bells, he shouts his dismay and leaps down steps so fast he can't even begin the count. In a high-ceilinged chamber of loudly ticking cogs and humming cables, he's surrounded by the four giant clockfaces in reverse, their hands frozen at midnight. Crying out for his father, he darts from shadow to shadow in search of the High Dungeon and its studded oak door.

Realising that he's trying the same places twice and that the Dark Lord's minions must be nearing the top of the steps, he finally confronts the possibility that his father isn't really there. But just as thoughts of casting himself from the tower are taking hold, he remembers that to return to the exact day his father was cast into the High Dungeon he must use the Timeless Tunic. Before he can work out how, he sees a shadow that grows rapidly to fill a whole giant clockface. He's about to cry out in when the Dark Lord's shape mutates into a woman he knows as someone's mother from some other life. *Oh darling*, echoes an eerie, gelded voice. *You don't want to slay your own mother, do you?*

Brio's so horrified he can't keep moving. But as the spectre dissolves, he realises that the only way to force time backwards is to push the giant clock-hands anticlockwise. Before he can leap back up the steps to the gantry above the clock-face, the Dark Lord's minions appear at the top and he rushes for a vertical steel ladder that rises up the wall like a beanstalk.

'Brio,' calls a voice. The name stops him mid-step and in that moment he's some other person in some other place. When it calls again, though, and he sees the police officers fanning out to block his escape, he launches himself at the ladder and grapples wildly up the cold rungs, his fireguard clanging steel-to-steel. With his eyes closed, he only knows he's reached the top when his head bangs into the hatch. He pushes it back and climbs out onto a stone walkway inside the high arches. Trying to keep his eyes closed, he crawls across the small connecting bridge to the gantry above the clock. No sooner is he in position above the giant minute-hand than police officers are edging towards him from both ends of the gantry. He shouts at them to get back or he'll jump.

From there, it all goes quiet in his head and he no longer hears the calls and coaxing words. All he needs to do is drop down and cling onto the huge minute-hand as though it's a climbing rope. But if he so much as glances at the ground far below he'll be paralysed by fear and the police will be on him in less than a shout.

The next second, he's dangling by his hands from the scaffolding, fireguard scraping against a galvanised stanchion. His feet flail in search of foothold, but the world he knew has disappeared into the abysmal drop. Yet suddenly, his mind is clear like never before. All he needs to do is let go of the scaffolding bar and he'll land on the box-frame scaffolding that's surely just below, and from there he can easily reach the top of the minute-hand. It's much easier than he could ever have imagined.

But what if he's misjudged it and falls into the abyss? What if it's like putting Teddy in and out of his bag so many times he doesn't know whether he's in there or not? What if he's a Buddhist crab that accidentally falls into the bubbling soup? What if his misjudgment is the will of God? How can there be a mortal sin in that? And what's the point in asking any more questions when all that exists is the fragile membrane between the lost suitcase of the past and a future without hope? 'Faa-ther!' he cries out into the night sky. 'I'm coming!'

~ PART SEVEN ~

RETURN OF THE QUEEN

Working for so many years
with patients and their personal narratives, it
has become clear to me that, through our serialised
fictionalization of facts, and through the collapse of our
necessary fictions within the framework of a total access to
each other's lives that perversely shifts us even further from
collective consciousness, we have become so merged with
our own post-everything, pre-nothing narrative, so frazzled
by our entangled multiplicity of scriptural interpretations, so
immune to the glib excuses that infiltrate our tales of
the expected, so bewildered by the speed of change,
so ironically limited by our notion of infinity,
so hilariously and lazily earnest, and so
much our own Nero, that it really
is only the raw purity of animal
essence that can give us
the critical perspective
on our own
hum-drum
conundrum.
Our own primal hero.

Stephen J. Logue PhD
Animal Magic & Magnetism for Beginners

19

SILENCE AND DARKNESS SLOWLY COALESCE into images of the abysmal drop and as Brio's consciousness grows, so too does his realisation that there was no great studded door to some high dungeon, and no hoggit king either. There was just a mad kid who lost his mind in front of the whole world.

Brio's emotions crumple into a sickening sense of failure at not having had the courage to loosen his fingers from around that freezing cold scaffolding bar, and as his eyes adjust to the dark he's possessed by one single electrifying resolution: that he'll get to the lighthouse cliffs in any way he can, and he'll overcome his fear of heights and never fail again.

Staring in half-drawn daylight at a large unframed mirror that dominates one wall, Brio realises that people must be watching him. He tries to feel for the electrodes they've surely stuck to his head but his wrists are restrained in some way he can't see.

'I told you,' he mutters irritably to the nurse who's as stone-cold real as the daylight. 'I'm not going to eat.' He closes his eyes to shut out the mirror that watches him with a reflection of his own crinkly pink face.

The nurse retrieves a flimsy plastic spoon from the floor and places it back on the tray of watery scrambled eggs and runny porridge. As she hurries out with the pristine debris, Brio calls after her to lower his bed. But it's another nurse who appears, this one wearing a different uniform. She stands aside to usher someone into the room—a large wobbly chinned man in a billowy dark-blue suit with hair like a bicycle helmet. He's followed by Dr Missle who's dressed from high collar to flat shoes in an even beiger beige than before. Next comes a lady in violet glasses wearing a dress of too many colours. And following like an afterthought, a thin man in casual trousers that don't go with the off-white shirt that needs a tie.

After they've all sat down on the array of chairs Brio hadn't seen, Dr Missle introduces the big man as Professor Yanki and the lady in the annoyingly complicated dress as Dr Shivani Kapoor. Before Dr Missle can say anything else, the thin man interrupts from the right-angle chair to introduce himself as Dr Lee from the government health department. He asks Brio if he's comfortable to talk to people from the CHANT Organisation.

Brio looks back out of the window to a sky that's the same placeless grey as the room's stark white. 'How do I know you're all real?'

He senses the looks of concern but Dr Lee's face remains expressionless.

'When you say *real*, Brio, do you mean, is everyone who they say they are, or are you asking if we're all actually present?'

Brio looks away again and sniffs. 'I don't care.'

There's a silence while Dr Lee writes something in a notepad and Brio wishes he hadn't spoken. After Dr Lee has finished writing, he looks up. 'Brio, I'm here to monitor this conversation. If at any point you feel unsettled, or if I think it appropriate, I'll bring proceedings to a close.'

'I told them already,' Brio replies with a jerk of head at the large mirror. 'I'm not going to talk.'

Dr Lee glances at the CHANT people and back to Brio. 'So does that mean you're not happy to proceed into the conversation?'

'I don't care.' He decides that this is what he'll keep saying. Because it's true. And it'll get him through till he can form a plan to escape. And this time will be the last.

'All right,' Dr Lee nods to the CHANT people. 'You can proceed.'

'Thank you, Dr Lee,' Dr Missle says cordially and looks to Professor Yanki, whose face breaks into a foolish grin. 'We've heard so much about you, Brio. In fact, we've come all the way from America to meet you here in London.'

'You don't have to talk like I'm a fucking kid.'

'Brio, we're on your side,' Dr Kapoor says quickly. 'We want to help you.'

'No, you don't. You want me to help *you*. Because you tried to brainwash me and the whole world saw it go wrong. So now you have to try even harder to prove it works.' He gestures again at the large mirror. 'You have to prove it to all of *them*.'

From there, the interview begins in earnest, each question pretending to be more caring and professional than the last. Did he know where he was going when he climbed out of the window? Can he remember shimmying down his home-made sheet-rope or landing in the flowerbed? Did he speak to anyone on the way to Big Ben? At what point exactly did he apprehend that it was Big Ben and not the Tower of Time? He freezes out questions about his time in the river too, even though they tell him he was courageous.

'Why don't you all just *die*?' he says and, when they don't flinch, he realises they're not under pressure at all. They let him escape deliberately so he'd do something crazy, so the world could see that he really *was* mad. Then they could force-brainwash him and claim they cured him, amen.

'So how are feeling about your dad?' Dr Kapoor asks in a harmless tone. 'Now you know he's dead.'

'I *don't* know he's dead.'

Brio is startled by own response. Is that what he really thinks?

321

Dr Kapoor shifts and brushes a fleck of invisible dust from her jeans, which allows Dr Missle to remind Brio that he told her about experiencing a mental image of his dad jumping off a tower somewhere. 'Or being pushed.'

'I didn't.'

'Perhaps it was more a feeling than a mental image?'

Brio gestures at the mirror. 'They know you're trying to put things into my head. And if you want me to believe my dad's dead, you have to prove it.'

His interrogators exchange glances and he sees Dr Lee writing fast into his notepad.

'Well, I must admit,' says Professor Yanki. 'It *has* proved difficult to identify actual documented evidence of your father's death. But isn't this a situation in which there can never be proof? Surely, when you *feel* something so deeply, that's the best proof of all.'

'Don't try to be clever. *I'm* not stupid either.'

'We know,' Dr Missle says hurriedly. 'But isn't it really that you just need to put the seal of approval on your acceptance that your father's dead?'

'For *you* yourself,' Dr Kapoor adds. 'Not for us. So maybe you need to let the Hoggit tell you what he saw when he was at the Tower of Time.'

Brio draws to snap back that there *was no Hoggit* but he can't bring himself to say the words, and again he has to fight back the secret hidden woman who's trying to take human form.

'Brio,' Dr Kapoor says, 'you've lived so much of your life in a dark room. You've sensed shapes and stumbled into things you didn't know were there. And you didn't know what they were or what they meant. Small things seemed huge. Soft things felt hard and jagged. Let the Hoggit throw light and show you the way out of that dark room.'

As though on deliberate cue, a new light does come on, and it casts the room into a stark white glare. It takes Brio a few seconds to register that the big mirror has turned into three rows of seated people in a clinical observation room. His arms fly up to clutch his head but the tethers snap taut, while in the observation room a spiky-haired guy in a T-shirt remonstrates with the cleaner who turned on the light.

'Brio, are you all right?' Dr Lee asks hurriedly as the light goes out again and the mirror reappears on the wall. 'Because this is obviously unexpected. You may feel that this is no longer a safe space.'

'Dr Lee, I'm sorry to interrupt,' Dr Kapoor says urgently, 'but perhaps I could explain to Brio who these people are.'

'I know who they are,' Brio snaps. 'And if you want me to answer any more questions, they all have to come in here so I can look them in the eye.'

As the mosh of human shape and colour crowds awkwardly into Brio's room, his gaze skits about in search of even one person who might be on his side. But he can't even tell who's on who else's side. Why can't they all wear white coats and black suits to make it easy to divine the allegiances and alliances?

When the awkward jostling and obsequious bowing and scraping are over, Brio finds himself facing off against three ranks of staring eyes that bring his brief reign to an end.

'Hi, Brio,' says the Japanese-looking woman whose aura dominates the front row. Before she can continue, a woman in a smart skirt and gold-trimmed trainers steps forward from the side of the room and cups her hands as though to release a dove from her belly button.

'Brio, my name is Zuri Dacosta. I work for a consultancy that's helping the government assess multiple approaches to the treatment of mental health with interactive technologies. My role is to adjudicate the various inputs of which you are obviously one, and a very important one, and first of all I'd like to say sorry that we—'

'*Wait*,' Brio cuts in. 'What's your accent?'

People look at each other and at last Brio can begin to discern the affiliations. But Zuri Dacosta nods earnestly to agree that it's a logical question. 'I'm from Stafford.'

Brio sniffs long and hard enough to screw up his face. 'Okay.'

'As I was saying,' she continues, 'I'm sorry we didn't disclose our presence in the Sharing Room. It's only right that you're able to ask whatever questions you'd like. Maybe I should tell you who everyone is first.'

'I know who *he* is.' Brio gestures his chin at the spiky-haired guy he first saw on the CHANT website. 'He's Danny Bellani from Sociomedica, which is part of Zpydr but pretends not to be. See? I know everything you're doing.'

Danny Bellani holds up a hand of greeting, while Zuri Dacosta presses on with a roll-call of Jilly Umber and Mike Cuth from the Treasury's Healthcare Unit, Jaleh Abedian and Petra Sadowski from the Health Insurance Confederation, on and on until she's left holding out a hand towards the small Japanese-looking woman who now seems to fill the whole room on her own. 'And this ...' she says as though reluctantly welcoming the Pope, 'this is Anni Seng-Müller from Zpydr.'

Anni Seng-Müller doesn't acknowledge the introduction. Instead, with a smile that drops ice cubes down his back, she says, 'Hi, Brio. It's really nice to meet you at last. And since neither you or me has an online presence, you won't know that I work alongside Tabo Forzac. You've heard of Tabo Forzac?'

Brio tenses and tries to clench fists, which draws a sharp sting from the cannula in the back of his hand.

'I'm guessing you don't have the highest opinion of Zpydr,' Anni Seng-Müller says. 'And some of these people behind me agree with you. They think we're out to exploit people. But if you'd be willing to hear me out, we can show you this isn't true.' And when he just clamps his jaws, she says, 'Brio, we know you've had difficulties with social media, but you're a smart person, you understand that the vitriol we see on these platforms is simply a symptom of the deeper issues we want to treat. I know this is cold comfort to someone who's suffered so much from the power that's been placed in people's hands, and people never realise that it's them who've become the pitchfork mob they scorn in movies. But the reason we're here today is you and only you. Brio, you've had so many things happen in your life and that kind of compounding trauma doesn't resolve itself without proper closure. It needs an ending that flows from its own beginning.'

'I don't care.' It comes easily now, with vehemence and conviction.

Anni Seng-Müller's gaze only intensifies. 'Brio, it's not us who's keeping you here. It's you yourself. Because you're uncertain about what you face in the world. You don't believe that people will admire and respect you for rising from your challenges.'

'I don't care. And I'm not going to finish it.'

Anni Seng-Müller pulls an expression of mild curiosity. 'But isn't finishing it what the Hoggit wanted you to do?'

Brio wants to fire back that there was no Hoggit, but the little face is back and he feels a pang of longing, and of shame at having almost betrayed him.

'Is it because God didn't lift the Memory Curse that you can't finish it?' Anni Seng-Müller asks.

His anger sparks. 'How do you know what God did or didn't do?'

'But you fulfilled all the conditions for the Memory Curse to be lifted. You wrote the Great Plea all the way to the exact moment when the Dark Lord cast the Memory Curse. Are you sure the

Hoggit didn't see whether or not his father was there?'

Brio has to look away again. He can't let them so much as glimpse those images that the Dark Lord inveigled into the Hoggit's mind. The lack of High Dungeon door. The gruesome fake Grandma masquerading as Mum.

'I assume,' Anni Seng-Müller adds, 'that the Hoggit does still want to know whether his father was there?'

As Brio can't twist his head any further, he turns it the other way. 'You'll have to ask him yourself.'

He glimpses consternation on faces and feels shocked by his own treacherous idea of letting Anni Seng-Müller talk to the Hoggit.

'Do I really need to ask the Hoggit? I mean, he had faith that God would lift the Memory Curse, right?'

His head flicks back. 'How can he know what God will do? No one does. Not even *you*.'

She doesn't pause to vary her smile. 'Well, the Hoggit might not know for sure but he does have that faith, right? Because in the Hoggit's world, it's you who's God, and what you've written is his Bible.'

Brio reels and flushes with the heat of embarrassment. He's got to slam down what she said before they force it further open. 'The Hoggit didn't think I was God. And I did not write his *Bible*.'

Anni Seng-Müller's smile changes and he's thrown off balance by its unexpected warmth. 'But isn't that what the Hoggit really wanted when he asked you to help him? For you to be the God of *his* world?'

'*No*.' But he's straight back to the day they met at the lighthouse, and the Hoggit's looking at him as though he *is* his God. And isn't that exactly what the Hoggit said? That he thinks God is a giant. 'The Hoggit doesn't know what God is. He's an atheist.'

Anni Seng-Müller's smile broadens. 'That's cool. Because believing there's *no* God needs an even stronger faith than believing there is. But from what he told you, it looks like the Hoggit does believe in God. And maybe that's because he knows that the only God we can know in this life is the best part of ourselves. So maybe that's exactly it. The Hoggit knows that the best part of himself is you, and in your heart you know that the best part of you is the Hoggit. So he really is as much God to you as you are to him.'

'That's not what God is.' But when he tries to say more, Anni Seng-Müller gets there first.

'Don't you remember what the Hoggit said when you didn't understand why writing his Great Plea would help free him of the Memory Curse? *Why can't you just trust God?*, that's what he said. And now you know what this means. You know how much strength lies within you. And don't you want to know what happened *after* that climax in the Tower of Time? I mean, the denouement is still to come, right? Because we don't know how the Hoggit got back to the castle. So why can't you trust yourself with the truth? Don't you want to prove that the Hoggit didn't just imagine the whole thing?'

'Ms Seng-Müller,' Zuri Dacosta interrupts. 'You're feeding concepts.'

'It's all within scope,' she replies without losing her smile or taking her gaze off Brio. 'I'm eliciting thought and ideas.' And ignoring Zuri Dacosta's bitten-in bottom lip, she says, 'Brio, don't you want to know that what you believe isn't just what you believe? Don't you want that *certainty*?'

'I don't care,' he says as forcefully as he can. 'I just want to get out of here.'

'And you really can,' says Anni Seng-Müller. 'All you need to do is complete what you've written and your new life can begin.'

'For goodness' sake,' comes a voice from the back row and a messy-haired man in a badly fitting suit stands up to address Zuri

Dacosta. 'This is supposed to be a consultative process around current case studies, not a live intervention. And Ms Seng-Müller is neither qualified nor entitled to tell this patient that if he writes some kind of conclusion to his narrative he'll be discharged. That's a decision for the consultant psychiatrist responsible for Brio's care. And I'm sorry to be saying this in front of the patient, but quite honestly this comment by Ms Seng-Müller typifies the whole approach that's been taken by Zpydr in this process, and simply because Tabo Forzac has the kind of influence that—'

'Woah!' Anni Seng-Müller is on her feet. 'It's you who's out of line here, Professor Payne. Because this *is*, exactly as you say, a current case study, and by definition that's going to be live. And you've been very clearly asked to observe only and not share negative opinions in front of patients. And if you keep trying to white ant this process—like you just did with the Sharing Room light-trick—a lot of people are going to be very upset.'

'I'm sorry, Ms Seng-Müller,' Zuri Dacosta jumps in before the man can reply. 'It's actually my role as convenor to adjudicate here. And I think that if Professor Payne has live issues concerning the patient, then it's surely appropriate that he's allowed to voice those concerns.'

'No, *I'm* sorry,' interrupts Dr Lee. 'I really don't think it's acceptable to conduct this kind of debate on data-set parameters in front of Brio.' He turns to Brio, who manages to get in first this time.

'Let me guess. It's my choice. I've got to *buy in*. Well, I don't want anyone to talk except her.' He nods sharply at Anni Seng-Müller. 'And she's got a right to answer back at *him*.'

Anni Seng-Müller gives Brio another of her warm smiles, which leaves him with the disconcerting feeling that he's somehow been tricked into liking her. She turns back round to Professor Payne.

'All I said to Brio is that if a narrative conclusion helps him resolve his issues, then he'll be prima facie eligible for discharge. Are you telling me that, even if he's clearly no longer experiencing any of his mental health issues, he would not in fact be discharged?' And the moment Professor Payne flounders, she says, 'That's correct, right? If Brio completes his narrative and resolves his issues, he'll be entitled to discharge?'

'A very big if,' Professor Payne replies curtly and glances at his colleague for support.

'Thank you,' Anni Seng-Müller says and sits back down. 'Brio, I'm sorry that this exchange took place. But the upshot, as I'm sure you gathered, is that if you complete your fantastic narrative, and if this conclusion brings you the clarity and peace you seek, then you *will* be discharged.'

'And if it doesn't,' Professor Payne says irritably, 'then he will not.'

Brio expects Anni Seng-Müller to twist back around and blast Professor Payne again. Instead, she sighs and slowly shakes her head. And there, for the briefest of seconds, Brio sees it: the glint of triumph in her eyes—the satisfaction of having tricked Professor Payne into issuing the blunt ultimatum on her own behalf.

Before Brio's finished telling himself that his whole future depends on staying calm at this critical moment, his hands jerk hard against the restraints and he shouts, 'You're not going to make me finish it. *I hate you all.*' And he keeps shouting it till people are falling over each other to escape the room.

Even after Zuri Dacosta has managed to usher the last of the fearful, pitying, told-you-so expressions from the room, Brio's uncontrollable shouting and fight with the restraints continues unabated. And as the rubber-gloved hands hold him still enough to empty a blunt-ended syringe into the cannula, he sees with terrifying yet calming clarity that killing himself isn't just the only thing he can do, it's the very reason to live.

20

IN HIS NIGHTMARE, BRIO'S FALLING AGAIN, always falling, flailing, he can't stop himself ... wanting to fall as much as he fights screaming to keep flying, to save himself, save the world from the Dark Lord ... But there's a gentle humming in the sky and he wants to sit up ... he's a vampire rising slowly from its coffin ...

He opens his eyes to discover that the humming's coming from his bed as it slowly sits him upright. He's ravenous, and strange nurses are tidying things that weren't messy, drawing curtains even though it's a surreal kind of daytime, replacing the barricade armchair with a triptych medical screen to form a temporary door. 'This is all wrong,' he says. 'For the gates shall not be shut at all by day. And now of all times I need them open.'

Taking him by surprise from one side, a damp cloth wipes his lips, which he finds are crusty with dried food. He registers that they've tried to force feed him in his sleep—what he hears himself murmur is that in his mouth it's sweet as honey but in his belly bitter—and he's still squirming the rough lip-cloth away when a stocky guy in a tight suit comes into the room, one finger to an ear. The guy scans and goes straight back out. Another figure enters, behind whom unseen hands push the medical screen tight to the doorway.

Unable to comprehend, Brio experiences flashes of unspoken words about a big tent being thrown over him by a golden deity on a throne. It's as though he went somewhere bright and silent and came straight back without even blinking. 'Is it really you?' he asks in awe.

'Yeah, guy. Who else?'

Brio stares incredulously as Tabo Forzac pulls up a straight-backed seat next to his bed. 'You're just in my head.'

But it's the slight differences from all the photos that make Tabo Forzac so real: the roughness to his baby face skin, the thickness of his messy short hair, the burning lack of colour in his eyes, the way he whips out a fancy packet of cigarettes and tosses one up into his mouth. Who'd have guessed that Tabo Forzac smoked? And check out that Zpydr logo on the chest of his grey hoodie.

Spark and flame, Tabo Forzac angles his head to take the cupped light from some invisible passer-by. Leaving his cigarette hanging from a corner of his mouth, he does big-time Jesus palms. 'I've come because I want you to know how important you are to us. I want you to join us.'

Before Brio can bring order to his mind, Tabo Forzac stands back up and draws long on his cigarette. The only question Brio can muster is whether Tabo Forzac's accent is real. It's like he's an American pretending to be Dutch. And somewhere in the background there's a distant trumpet sound like the amplified whine of a machine.

'I've always worked hard to assimilate with my fellow humans,' Tabo Forzac says as he parts the curtains to crack open a one-way view.

After that, he paces slowly up and down, drawing hard on the pale green cigarette, not taking his eyes off Brio, who still can't make himself hate Tabo Forzac and wants to break through the acrid smoke to sample the harmless cigarette.

'So …' says Tabo Forzac, 'you're trying to work out whether you should trust us to help you finish the Great Plea of Tribute and Proof.'

Brio gulps dry and tries to pull a disinterested shrug. He needs to get his act together and tell Tabo Forzac he's the Devil.

'Your choices are as follows,' Tabo Forzac continues through a slow exhalation of smoke that looks like he's inflating a cobweb. 'One, accept that your pops is dining with the angels then go right ahead to have a nice life—help save the world. Or two, refuse to accept that he's dead and stay banged up some place like this for all eternity.' Before Brio can fight back, Tabo Forzac throws up his hands. 'Jesus Christ! Don't you believe in our perfect world enough to sacrifice your sentimental attachment to some dead notion of a father?'

Brio's desire to fight back fouls up with questions and renders him mute, which leaves Tabo Forzac unopposed and nodding sagely.

'All along, Brio McPride, you've been thinking only of the entity you identify as yourself. And that's only natural for a dude your age. But *natural* isn't what's good anymore. And you see it, right? Unless the whole world's okay, no single person can be okay either. So the only way to be okay is to get the whole world in the Groove. Easy logic, huh?'

Brio can't lift his head. It's a soufflé the weight of an anvil. He claws for shapes to fire back. 'You're full of weasel words.'

'In God's name!' Tabo Forzac's exclamation makes Brio jump. 'You know these words are true and faithful. So help me make all things new!' He takes a long puff of the cigarette that's gone dark green and makes a wriggly feeling of getting back to groovy and chilled. 'Yeah?'

No, *not* yeah. Not *yeah* at all. He's got to find the confidence to beat Tabo Forzac back down. He needs to do what Ms Whittle said and remind himself of his previous achievements. 'Yes, all the world's a stage,' he says, 'and every stage a world of players hiding, caught between the guise of self and wobbly lines, that screen of falsehood, every word a twist of knives and—'

'No!' Tabo Forzac cries. 'I mean, yeah, that's great stuff and full score for lack of rhyme, but don't give me smoke. Come on, you and me together, let's wipe away all tears from their eyes, no more sorrow or pain if all those former things are passed away.'

'But it's a sin to even *try* to make a perfect world,' Brio replies hotly. 'Everyone the same and talking one language. And you're even worse than Adam and Eve, because you don't just want as much knowledge as God, you want more. And you're definitely worse than Lucifer, because all *he* wanted was to be God's favourite. So it's true—you *are* trying to kill God.'

Tabo Forzac holds up a finger as he lights another cigarette, this one pale blue. Pocketing the lighter, he says, 'We're actually doing God's work on earth. Pretty soon we'll take it higher still.'

Brio's stomach flutters like a kid's and he prays that what Tabo Forzac says is true. But how could a monster like Tabo Forzac believe in God?

'Damn right I believe in God,' Tabo Forzac says. 'Personal psychological disposition and need aside, it's just plain good sense. That's why we all believe.'

'What do you mean?' He has to pick this apart before it gets him in a Sumo hold.

'I mean, the tribes that believe in a god always win. Shared stories are what first enabled humans to act together en masse, right, to become societies, and a god bonds people together like no other cause or threat. But you and me, my good friend, we are what God did on the *eighth* day.' He takes another long draw. 'This smoking's going to kill me, of course. That's why I only do it in the company of friends.' He barks a hard-edged laugh that hits Brio in the forehead.

Brio's inner conflict needs to scream at all the false symmetry. He wants nothing more than to put an end to this sickening disorientation by agreeing to everything they want.

But no. He must fight back with the first words that God puts into his mouth.

Having waited patiently for the smoke to rise from his lungs, Tabo Forzac laughs easily at what Brio just shouted. 'No, I do not think I'm God,' he replies. 'Though it's an interesting question, right? What *is* God? And hey, it's kept the brains trust in milk and honey for millennia.' His face changes abruptly to dead serious and his cigarette turns red. 'Brio, listen. Come and see. God is not an intelligence and human reason is divine. So it's just like the Buddha said, we won't be punished for our anger but *by* our anger. Which is why, six hundred years later, we've got *dei filius* Himself telling us not to bother looking in some other place for the Kingdom of God because it's in our very midst. *Ergo* … if God's within us—and may Brio truly be your name—then God must be in everything we create that stands the test of time.'

'But what if—'

'I promise you, guy, CHANT*bot-vip* will get us where we need to be. The world just needs to believe that our technology truly is a gift from God. We need proof for the moms and pops. We need a pin-up who can show the world that it'll do what it says on the box.'

'But—'

'But *what*? You really believe we didn't help you find this love in yourself, the love that lets you talk to me like this? You think the way we assisted you with the Great Plea didn't happen?'

A clamp of anger in Brio's temples brings Tabo Forzac's face into even sharper focus. How dare this monster claim it was Zpydr who wrote the Great Plea when it was *him* and no other? But dizziness tempers Brio's anger. What if the Great Plea really was no more than a story? Would that mean he should give in and help them achieve their perfect world? Or should he fight even harder to bring them down?

'So what *is* the difference between fact and fiction?' asks Tabo Forzac thoughtfully.

Brio's aghast. Not only did Tabo Forzac read his mind, he doesn't even know the most basic things. 'It's easy. Fact is true and fiction's just a fantasy.'

Tabo Forzac takes another long draw on his dark-blue cigarette and releases so slowly that Brio sees in the smoke the shape of a dragon that decays into an open mouth that widens to release a frog, and another and—

'Didn't Mr T'wit cover this off for you?' Tabo Forzac asks. 'The difference between a truth and something that's true.'

'But what if it's not a story but not real either? What if it's just half in, half out? HI-HO, as they say in the trade. Don't they? And if I thought I was writing a story, wasn't my thinking that I was writing a story in itself a reality that had a right to be in my diary?'

Tabo Forzac laughs and flicks ash into his palm. 'Well, everything in the universe is semi-fictional, guy. But that's very different from a half-truth. And what are you really saying here? That you want hard facts and figures instead of the truth? Is that your idea of a perfect world? A bunch of stone-dead certainties? The lies that historians always tell but poets never do? How can that keep you moving forward?'

'But death *is* certain. That's why it's so good. It takes away all this unbearable doubt.'

Tabo Forzac examines his silver cigarette while with the other hand he carefully massages the palm of ash into his hair. 'So you're claiming to know what happens after death now?'

'*No.*' Brio's shocked by the proposition. *Though maybe I do know*, he thinks. *Because I did let go of the scaffolding bar, after all, and this is Heaven and Hell in one, HE-HE, half-in, half-out.*

'God's unknowable, guy,' Tabo Forzac reassures him. 'And that is an eight-sigma certainty. And if we don't console our blindness to the unknowable with story and symbol, the uncertainty's gonna drive us out through the stage door. We simply need to find that spark and glow at the heart of our collective consciousness. Our universal soul.'

Brio knows that in some past life he'd have been bowed under by the weight of his opponent's words. But now he's got the comebacks he never had when Darcy was merely a Greek god. 'You don't want a human story at all. Because you don't have a story in your own heart. That's why you want a story written by a computer. And that doesn't count as working for God, that's being in league with the Devil.'

'I refer you once again,' Tabo Forzac replies, lighting another cigarette, 'to my comments on human agency and produce as a manifestation of the divine.'

This sends Brio in search of a better riposte, but all he sees is a puppy chasing its own tail so fast it becomes a dog before it's had the chance to frolic and wee on the rug. He has to get this back to something he can understand. He must wrestle with what it all means for the individual people who want to write their own heartfelt stories and share them with the *real* world. How can a world be perfect if its stories are all dug up or faked by computers? 'We don't need all your *stuff*. Our stories are good already.'

Tabo Forzac releases dense smoke. 'Our stories are more than good. They're our gods. Coz like I said, that's what we invented them to be. And we only have religions because we're wowed by stories and poetry that are so great we're willing to believe they came from God. If we didn't have them, we'd just be avoiding black cats and broken mirrors and giving ladders such a wide berth we'd get cleaned up by a passing bus.'

As his mind turns sluggish circles in the haze, Brio gazes longingly at Tabo Forzac's cigarette. 'But if a story comes from a computer like that, it won't come from people's hearts—from their imagination. Isn't imagination what makes us so special?'

Tabo Forzac takes a long, careful suck on his gold-ringed pink cigarette and studies Brio through the smoke. 'You sure our imagination's such a great thing? I mean, isn't it our imagination that ruins everything good?'

'*What?* How can that be?'

'Well, just think of anything good and you'll find *homo sapiens* right in there, fucking it all up with their powers of rational creativity and interpretive cognition. Take desire, for example. Our imaginations twist it into perversion and help us hide from the love that would make desire a mind-blowing miracle. Imagination is what dreams up justifications for exploitation and domination too, and wars and atrocities, for stealing and lying, for burying simple faith with esoteric theories. Imagination's what makes two plus two five and three a crowd.' He taps ash directly onto his head. 'I see this troubles you. But here's the good rub. I think what we're gonna find when we put CHANT*bot-vip* out there is something that's way better than imagination. And what I say is this. Take a look round the world and ask yourself two questions. One, are humans ever going to be able to escape the same old dead loop of competitive-collaborative aggregation and disintegration? Two, isn't it true that the only real progress humans have made since the first stick-and-stone tribes has been in their technology?'

In what seems like hours later, Brio says, 'I'm hallucinating. I'm having this siphoned out of me because I'm in a permanent state of hypnosis.'

Tabo Forzac laughs. 'See what I mean about imagination?'

Brio's thinking too fast to stop. 'I see it now. I'm more than your perfect candidate. I'm the chosen one. So I had to be sacrificed. I really am dead already.'

'You wish.'

'I don't.' But he knows that Tabo Forzac's right: he does wish, because he can no longer fight the ever-growing desire to give them the perfect ending, the key to their perfect world. All they need is proof that with a beautiful fantasy he's healed himself of what ailed him. And how can he be anything other than that exact living proof? How does he have any choice at all in the matter? 'I need a drag.'

'Sure.' Tabo Forzac extends an arm that's longer than Brio expected. The two thick fingers smother his lips with neck-chilling warmth. He gags and coughs. But when he tries to get a hand to his mouth, the tether flicks tight. This is surely Hell.

'Enough?' Tabo Forzac asks.

The nauseous experience has changed Brio's feelings. He thought he was warming to Tabo Forzac—almost trusting him—but through the smoke and its caustic bite in his soft palate, he sees the truth. Tabo Forzac has no faith at all in humans. He doesn't believe they can change in any way that counts.

'You're right,' Tabo Forzac agrees readily. 'We believe that humans have been shown every example and been given every freakin' second coming and third chance. But they've proved beyond all reasonable doubt that they can't manage their own affairs. What else can we do but let the AI have a go at running things?'

'No!' Brio cries. 'You can't do that!'

Tabo Forzac looks confused. 'Why not?'

'Because only God can run things. How can a computer program have God at its heart?' He tries to make it sound like a demand, but he really needs to know *how*.

Smiling seriously with no loss of rakish gravitas, Tabo Forzac says, 'You know how we can be eight-sigma certain that God dwells at the heart of my organisation's AI? It's so simple. Because

CHANT*bot-vip* will be built on the godlike part of our collective self. Are you with me now? You see where you fit in?'

'But what if there's something wrong with me? Something that no one knows?'

Tabo Forzac regards him thoughtfully. 'Okay, I see what you're saying here, and we can revert. But for now I'd like you to consider one simple fact, which is that our AI—our Deorum-Ex—will have read the Bible, just like it will have read every other text we call scripture. And it'll have read all those gems of literature we know should be called scripture too. If the AI likes what it sees and comes to believe there's a place for those messages within the ur-narrative, then your Bible will be there in the mix. Your God truly will be *in machina*.'

This suspends time. Brio can even taste the lightbulb. 'Okay, I'll finish it. I'll complete it any way you want.'

But as soon as the words are out, a revulsion kicks up in his guts. 'No, I won't. Because your perfect world's the death of the human spirit, and wanting to be in it is a death-wish. It's the black hole of fake bright eyes, the yawning chasm of a hidden nun keeping secrets.' His own mouth opens for the cigarette and the smoke inside him feels warm and comforting, and the hand across his mouth makes him want to close his eyes and sleep. Who cares if their perfect world is the same as death? 'Okay,' he says quietly, and he's known all along it was coming, so it doesn't need any more of those trumpets blaring like New York traffic in the sky. 'I actually will do it. I'll write that the Hoggit saw the great studded door of the High Dungeon, and it was already open. And the tomb was really was empty.'

Yet once again, the revulsion fires up and knots his chest. He slumps back, eyes closed to shut out the dreadful hallucination.

Tabo Forzac gazes at him and takes a weird, demure puff that *pwoofs* out like a ball of cotton wool. 'So what exactly is it—in your own words—that's stopping you finishing the Great Plea? I mean, you've accepted everything I've said and recognised that this is your duty, right?'

Brio looks away, but even that can't stop his head drooping in shame.

'Oh, I see!' Tabo Forzac exclaims. 'You're standing here at the threshold of saving the world but you can't take that tiny step because you're still in chaos about a trivial little worry of your own you've got hidden away.'

Another squeeze of fear and Brio's out in the open—in the arena. Because now he knows the Bible's safe and that God will still be watching, his big excuse is dead. He must doubly hide his terrible hidden flaw at all costs. 'You're talking froth, Mr Forzac. What *worry* have I got hidden away?'

'Oh, you know,' Tabo Forzac says airily, 'that it's the end of May and you fret you might be a darling kind of bud.'

The wave of hot shame knocks Brio's head down so hard it's almost whiplash.

'A touch of torrential rage,' Tabo Forzac says in a sympathetic voice, 'and the bright son shies away. But okay, you don't know whether you are or you aren't, but either way you think it's a sin and you don't think much of people who think it's not a sin. Just like the women who don't like the whole macho gig but disdain men who feel the same way.'

'I'm *not*.' He presses his head down harder.

'Not what? Trans or in chaos?'

'I don't know. Not any of that.'

'And that's okay. Coz you're not alone in being confused about what you are or whether what you feel like doing sometimes is what makes you what you are, blah-blah. Sure as my sweet shih-tzu, we live in a world where lots of people say it's okay to be gay or any which way, but that doesn't mean everyone's happy with who they are, right? It doesn't mean they don't hate themselves so much they'd rather die or kill.'

Brio wants to put Tabo Forzac down with a categorical denial. That's what his mum wants too. He feels her presence like the creak of a floorboard, like Izzy behind him in the mirror, her head longing to be a hedgehog of spikes. 'It's a sin to be gay or trans,' he tells Tabo Forzac firmly. 'And it's not *my* fault it's a sin.'

'To which I say time and place, and purple in tooth and claw, and look beyond the workings for the meaning, okay? Which is that life is all we got, so we should try to keep it going. In Bible days that meant having bucketloads of babies to keep the show on the road. In fact, even a hundred and fifty years ago, a person assigned female at birth had to pop five kids just to stop the village shrinking. But these days the planet's got humans coming out of its *ass*. No one gives a toss if you don't have kids—well, not unless they're a racist pigdog. But this is needless detail. We want to know if the Bible is kosher, whether we can trust it to be our God. That's why we have to ask ourselves whether we really know what it says about sin and sins? Maybe the reason you're down on yourself is coz you were raised to feel shit about being human, coz humans supposedly committed some gigantic sin at the dawn of time. But the guys who dreamed up this Original Sin gig had fuck all to do with writing the Bible, right? They're just Johnnies-come-lately throwing brains around and helping keep order, wowing underage prey with their big grey muscles. But seriously, if God created the inorganic existence from which the intelligence to create our concept of higher self evolved, then taking the blame for sin upon ourselves would seem to be a little up our own asses, don't you think? Bit of a conceit, I'm saying. Bit of an imagination overdose.'

Brio feels he should fight. 'You're trying to make me stop believing in the Bible.'

Tabo Forzac shakes his head. 'I am not-repeat-not trying to cut your umbiblical cord. I'm just saying, let's think of God as the G-Force. And hey, if G-Force works in mysterious ways, why shouldn't we ourselves be a little hazy in what we really believe? But this is all totally sideshow, coz there's only two aspects of God that humans need concern themselves with. Selfless love, and good order based on that selfless love. And if we use our awesome technology to strip away all those human ailments that stop us acting selflessly, are we not agents of G-Force?'

Brio floats above the spun-out Brio below. 'Where am I?'

'You're back. And you're figuring out that you can't pin or take blame without a personal credo on what ultimately causes shit to happen. How much of that freedom did we actually have at the moment of pulling the trigger? Who determined our choice of desire to be a dick or a dock or some brand of fabulous fusion? And at the root of all that lies the question of what caused existence itself. Meaning, if you don't know what caused prime cause, you don't know what caused you to pull the trigger, in which case there's no such thing as "sin", there's just some transactional good sense around the do's and don't's of peaceful cooperation. That's to say, laws. So how's your so-called "sin" shaping up after the big one went belly up? Shaky, right? But it wouldn't matter even if there actually was some grand primal crime, coz forgiveness trumps it all. That's why we've got to push back against all this patriarchal chicanery with Original *Forgiveness*. That's the big F where we forgive God for birthing humans into this brutal existence for the sheer fun of seeing whether we can survive—or even improve ourselves. And along with Original Forgiveness, we've got to offer up Original Gratitude too, for the once in each lifetime chance to shit kindness or get off the pot. And, in the context of all that, what the hell does it matter who we love so long as we *can* love, and *do*?'

'Help me,' Brio murmurs. 'I'm dying.'

'Don't be dramatic. Just focus on the easy ones. Like the only sin is lack of love. Like Brio McPride is way above all this meat-space stuff like sex and gender. You're the chosen one. The beacon. That's why we love you. That's why we want you to be one of us.'

Now, instead of not knowing whether he wants to let the Hoggit change the world, all Brio can feel is terrible for having wanted Darcy to be mentally ill and locked up as a girl forever. But this leads him to the exhilarating thought that accepting Darcy the way he is—the way *they are*—would make Izzy love *him*, the real Brio McPride. Because he'd have proven he was ready. But the old floorboard creaks and his mum's presence tightens the knot. Or was it a burning in his chest because he wanted to love Darcy for the wrong reason?

But what if Darcy really was mentally ill? Brio asks some other self. *Could I accept Darcy on the basis that wanting to be a girl is a mental illness? Would Mum be okay with that?*

Hs mum doesn't even need to reply for him to know that wanting to be a girl when you were born a boy is *not* mental illness. Because there's no such thing. There's only distance from God and alienation from fuck knows what. He tries to clutch his head but the tethers pull another deadened twang.

'What?' Tabo Forzac asks through purple smoke. 'You're back to complaining about the feeling you don't exist? That you might as well be dead? You're bitching about trivia when you know that all you need in order to exist is a purpose? And your purpose is the same as everyone else's. To leave the world a better place than when you rocked up.'

These words stun Brio. How can the answer to everything be so straightforward? So obvious? So easy.

Tabo Forzac nods keenly. 'So tell me, why on earth are you here on earth if not to finish the Great Plea of Tribute and Proof—to be the writer you were born to be?'

Brio's head is so full he can't process. All he knows is that after all the effort they've devoted to him, he surely owes it to them to be compliant. Though, on the other hand, they're all trying so hard to stop him killing himself that he wants to do it just to make them look foolish. There's a nice clean logic either way. It's all very rational. So it must be right. He just needs to toss the Ring of Love for a decision. He can be brave and defeat the Fate of the Mirrored Hex. Which means that this whole thing cannot be in his imagination. And God doesn't just play dice, He's an ace at poker too.

Fuck.

But he also knows there's no point trying to fool Tabo Forzac with closed eyes and fake sleep. Because Tabo Forzac knows what's in your head before you do. So there's no choice but to acknowledge the smallness and sterility of resistance—no option but to agree to *come and see*. To test the fresh waters, Brio says tentatively, 'Yeah, I see that too. A new Heaven and a new Earth.'

Tabo Forzac breaks out a tonic grin. 'That's *awesome*! And I'm seeing us wash our clothes in blood and making them clean and pure. Am I right?'

'Yeah. And drying them out in a pure river of the water of life, clear as crystal, proceeding from the right side of your temple.'

'Way to go,' Tabo Forzac agrees. 'I feel it flowing. Kinda nice.'

Now Brio really does feel it flowing. 'I am the first and the last,' he whispers, and he doesn't care that people are listening and thinking he's mad. He only cares that Father T would be so proud of him. Madame Haha too, she'd love his performance. And no more death-wish for *her* either. 'I am he that liveth,' he tells Tabo Forzac. 'I am also he that was dead. I'm alive forevermore.'

'Like me,' Tabo Forzac agrees again. 'And like me, you have but little power. Yet you've kept my word and not denied my name. Good job. I will write upon you my *new* name.'

Brio is relieved that, at last, Tabo Forzac's voice sounds like parallel waters coming together. 'Thank you.'

'You betcha. Hence no need for a candle anymore, nor light of the sun. For there *is* light. There always was.'

'And it's just like your hair. Weirdly white from all the ash.'

Tabo Forzac laughs and pats himself on the head to make them both good boys who deserve a treat. 'Cigarette?'

Brio takes the exciting and weightless little dry cylinder between his fingers. But he doesn't try to place it between his lips because he knows the tether will stay his hand and expose his weakness. It's enough for him to know that completing the Great Plea isn't about finding his father, it's about believing in the truth.

'I feel I just made the ultimate self-sacrifice,' Brio says. 'I'm going to be the saviour of the world.' In his mind, he sees Frodo embarking upon the last ship to the Undying Lands. 'Though there's one little housekeeping matter to which we must perforce attend.'

'Shoot, friend. And aim high.'

'Well, I don't mind Bella telling the world that Mum told Father T that my dad won the fierce battle with himself. But I'm not okay with her saying that Father T did something bad to me, even though I forgive people for thinking the worst. Do we have a deal?'

Tabo Forzac holds out a hand for Brio to shake. 'Thy will be done.'

'Now free me from my bonds, please. Then we can cast the moment in smoke.'

'Sure thing.'

Brio watches Tabo Forzac unbuckle the restraints on his wrists and ankles. A new spark follows, which kindles a new flame and they smoke together. And as Brio watches his rose-golden smoke rings decay into shrivelled frogs and a crumbling throne, he understands in full that a noble Roman end is the only way on God's earth he can be crowned as his own unchallenged emperor.

21

THE NURSE ONLY MAKES IT A COUPLE OF STEPS into the room before she freezes, looking alarmed. 'Who undid your restraints?'

Brio assures her that it was Tabo Forzac, which doesn't seem to put her mind at rest one bit. 'You don't believe me?' he says. 'You're trying to tell me it wasn't real?'

'No, no. Not at all. Just let me find out whether we need to redo your restraints.'

While another nurse stays to engage him with innocent questions, the first hurries out. She returns to announce that the doctors are very satisfied with his progress. 'No need to restrain you for the time being.' She seems more surprised than pleased and tells him he has a visitor.

'Is it Darcy?'

She looks puzzled. 'No, I'm afraid not. Is Darcy a friend who you hope will visit?'

'I think he may be a patient here too,' Brio explains. 'I'd like to talk to him when he's free. I mean, I'd like to talk to *them*.'

Finding himself wishing that Darcy Withart and Tracy Hardwit didn't hate each other so much, he can't help but fall into a whispering prayer for their well-being. But when his unexpected desire to make Darcy better comes up against his dogged inability to accept that there's any such thing as mental illness, he has to find some way to make Darcy better when they're not actually ill. Either that or he has to accept that there *is* such a thing as mental illness, which is too frightening a notion to entertain. So maybe it's about making them better in some other way that's not "curing from illness". But what way could that possibly be?

It's Pippa who comes in, and on seeing him she stops and murmurs, 'Oh,'Bree.'

He's startled by how different she looks—sort of younger but older. Her silent tears draw his own and he hears himself saying sorry about her house, sorry about everything, so sorry. The tears flow. She rushes and he sits up to hug her, and she's crying loudly too, saying it's all okay, she's fine, it was just a house and the insurance will pay and don't worry about anything and tears make their cheeks slip against each other and she's saying sorry for all her mistakes, for letting him down, for confusing him by falling in love with Logie.

'It doesn't matter,' he says over and over through his welcome crying and, although the hug becomes so tight he can hardly breathe, he can't bear the idea of it ever coming to an end.

When it does, she's holding his hand and hurriedly wiping away their tears. 'The doctor said you're doing really well,' she enthuses. 'I really hope you can come home soon.' She clasps his hand tightly. 'Oh, Bree, Logie's so sorry about what happened. He says it's all his fault. He just did what he thought was best for *you*.'

Brio feels something bad stirring down under the fog and he makes his hand go floppy to loosen her grasp.

'He cares about you so much,' Pippa implores. 'He's in a really bad way because of what happened.' She holds his gaze, he's obviously supposed to see the sincerity of the couple called *Logie and Pippa*. 'He needs to know you're okay,' she says. 'He'll help in any way he can. The CHANT people called him but he refused to talk. He's really not working for them. Bree, we can put it all behind us and have a new home. We can be a family.'

Desperately needing to stay on the level, Brio has to avert his gaze. 'Is that why you really came? Because you want us to be a family but you think Logie's suicidal again? You just want me to say everything's okay so *he'll* be okay.'

Their hands fall apart but she quickly grabs again and ends up squeezing his fingers. 'Bree, that's not what I mean. I just meant—'

Relieved that his moment of anger has buried the tears, he looks back at Pippa. 'It's okay. Logie just wanted to help too much. That's the end of the matter. But I don't want to worry about Logie. Because I'm at peace now. My bond with Logie must be broken. His mental illness still has the potential to bring me down.'

He can see she's aghast and confused, the whole thing's beyond her. She takes hold of his wrist. 'But can I tell him you forgive him? I mean, I know this is all about you, but if we're all going to be happy together …' Her head falls. 'I'm sorry. I just can't get anything right.'

The ensuing silence becomes odd. It's as though they've said everything and peaked too early. Brio rests his head back and closes his eyes. Why did she have to visit him before she was ready? Bringing all this worry, all these things to think about. And what about Izzy? How can they ever have this impossible new family without Izzy? How can he have any family at all without Izzy?

Eventually realising that Pippa's thinking hard about something, he lifts his head. Her expression triggers the worry he's trying so hard to banish. 'What is it?'

She searches his face. 'Well, I'm not sure whether it's the right thing, but …'

'I told you, I don't want anything messy.' He tries to look away but can't. '*Is* it messy?'

'No. I mean, I don't think so. It's just something I should probably give you.'

'You mean my dad's wedding ring?'

'Wedding ring?'

'It doesn't matter. I don't want it anyway. What have you got?' His disquiet grows. He doesn't like it that Pippa's let go of his hands. She pulls an envelope from the bag she dropped on the floor.

'I don't know what it says.' She holds it between them and it's him who has to take the next step.

The disquiet becomes alarm. 'I don't want to know anymore. I don't care what it says.' Eyes closed, he rests his head back again. 'But thank you.'

He can feel her new confusion, her desire for him to open the letter. She holds one of his hands, in the other she still has the envelope. He has to fight harder to stay calm. He's not going to throw it all away on a whim.

But however hard he tries to stay steady, the presence of the envelope keeps growing. And so does the thought that after all that's happened—after all the lies and fake beliefs and pitiful demi-secrets, after a lifetime of not knowing the truth and being driven mad—the real answer to everything is suddenly in Pippa's hand. And this isn't happening in some *state of mind*. This is the real letter from his real father. He tells her to burn it without reading it and swear that's what she'll do. But he needs to know where the letter's been hidden away all this time. 'Did *you* have it all along?'

'No. It arrived in the post two days ago.'

His thoughts begin to rave, it's all he can do to stifle the cry of anguish. 'Who sent it?'

'Well, I'm not a hundred percent sure, but I think it came from Bella Ripley.'

22

BRIO KNOWS THEY'RE ALL LOOKING at his foot but he can't stop it tapping. And he desperately needs to stop it tapping. So they'll think he's okay and let him out. So he can do the only thing left. Even when Dr Kapoor asks if he's okay, he can't get a single word through the chokehold of rage and shame. And the more insistently he feels their gaze, the more he's taunted again by the evidence that was there all along. His mum's hatred for *those people*. The cocoon of bolted doors and drawn curtains that protected him from a sick and twisted world. Her stories about creatures that started out nice but morphed into their grotesque hidden selves. The super-manly Red Knight stories that she only stopped telling him because he said he wanted to be a soldier when he grew up.

This time round there are only nine people in the room, in two rows of chairs with a strong-arm nurse standing on one side. But through Anni Seng-Müller's unblinking eyes it feels as though the whole world's watching him.

'We heard you've discerned an awesome ending,' Anni Seng-Müller says, which sends a frisson of mixed energies through the group.

Brio knows that if he doesn't speak quickly and calmly, they won't give him another chance. 'I got the Memory Curse off the Hoggit,' he says into his lap. 'He remembered what he saw.'

'That's great to hear!' says Dr Missle, but it's Professor Payne's reaction that Brio looks up to gauge—him and two of the three government people next to him. And maybe Zuri Dacosta too, who's now wearing the gold-rimmed trainers with a suit. These are the people who guard the gates and somehow he's got to control his rage enough to fool them. He's got to forget what his so-called father's letter said and focus everything on giving them their precious ending.

'I can see that it's a really moving finale,' Anni Seng-Müller adds. 'And that's great, Brio, because in a story about story, the ending really has to be about the ending.'

But the awful memory comes at him again: being left alone with the envelope after he told Pippa to leave, his hands shaking as he fumbled to rip it open. Inside the envelope he found another that was accompanied by a note in such fresh ink it could only have been written a few days before. One skim of its contents branded the words into his head forever:

> Dearest Brio,
>
> Many years ago, your mum gave our beloved Father T this letter from your dad for safekeeping. Father T always said that if anything happened to him, I should give it to you when you were ready. He said I would know when you were ready because you would come to see me out of concern for me. A little bird told me recently that this is what you wanted to do. I hope this letter will help you come to see me before it's too late.
>
> All my love in return,
> Bella

In his mind, Brio sees the vomit swirling around in the toilet,

taking with it the confetti into which he shredded the letters from
Bella and his so-called father. Feeling nauseous again, he has to
fight down his translucent breakfast. And destroying the letter isn't
enough. If Bella's still alive, he has to make her swear in blood to
take the secret to her grave. And if she won't, he has to kill her. Oh,
God, and Ms Whittle knows too. Of course she does. The way she
always seemed to know something and was forever pressing him
to be like Darcy, dressing him in the Indian robe like a girl.
Because she knew that when he was ready, he'd want to be a fake
woman too, and that would drive him so mad he'd kill himself,
exactly like his father did. *Like father, like son*. Like no father at all.

The thought of having to push a pillow down on Ms Whittle's
face before he kills himself unleashes a paralysing sadness that he
has to crush with curled toes and compressed neck. And did his
mum tell Pippa too? Or maybe Pippa steamed open the envelopes.
Of all the people in the world he doesn't want to kill. Oh, God,
and Mrs Thorne knows too. The way she and Ms Whittle looked
at each other so knowingly in her office that day when Darcy made
him go crazy. And who else did his mum tell in her lonely despair
when she first arrived from Ireland with no friends and a new
identity that wiped out her past in some tiny town where everyone
knew the truth? Did she whisper it confidentially to Dr Shenoy in
his cluttered surgery? Did she dump it anyone at church? If she
told Mrs Robinson then everyone knows and it's always been some
gigantic secret with everyone laughing behind his back. He finally
understands how someone can walk into a crowded church and
start shooting.

'Brio, are you okay?'

Startled again, he sees that it was Dr Missle who spoke, while
Anni Seng-Müller glances round at the government people, a
smile to seek their patience. When Anni Seng-Müller turns back,
he catches a glint of guile in her gaze and realises that Zpydr

themselves know the truth. Because they forced it out of poor Bella against her will, deep down in the dungeons of their fortress in the New Mexico desert.

'Ms Seng-*Moo*ler,' comes a voice from the back row, 'we're beginning to question whether your patient is in fact ready to complete this narrative therapy process and move forward.'

'I *am* ready,' Brio says sharply and tries to calm his rage with a pair of deep breaths. 'Just let me think.'

He fights to summon the words for the ending they want. When the words won't come, he closes his eyes and wills himself to reprise the rhythmic march on the Tower of Time. Words finally rise, now all he has to do is impose enough rhyme and rhythm to speak them aloud. But the words start spewing out before he can bring order. 'On seeing there the dread Dark Lord, shaped in form of maternal haunting—taunting Hoggit, who thus drew sword, and puffed his chest in cast iron, vaunting.'

At last, the words flow and he has to stand up, which propels the strong-arm nurses into the no-man's-land between him and the blurred faces.

'But then in Dark Lord's face he saw, two eyes he once did cherish. The truth he knew at once—*Oh, Lord*—all hopes were dashed and perished. The Hoggit fought with strength the truth, so many truths he'd rather, but nothing could conceal the proof. The Dark Lord was his father!'

Confronted by the nurse's odours of soap and sweat, Brio has no choice but to force him into retreat with words.

'Yes, Hoggit King and Dark Lord were but one and same unriven. No rescue here like Queen from ark, *he cannot be forgiven*. Thus seeing now how pale he glowed, that one and only Devil, the Hoggit marched upon his foe, his sword raised straight and level.'

Brio finds himself staring at alarmed faces and can't believe what just happened. He must laugh it off quickly and get back to the happy ending they all need—the one he needs too, so he can live in that perfect world where everything's pale green and Tabo Forzac's merely God in a puff of smoke.

So yes—he catches his breath and says *sorry*—he'll do the right thing after all. He'll give them the same ending that the Unseen Seer gave *him*, the one where his sick father wins the battle against himself and dies heroically by his own hand. That's surely the one they want. The Hex of the Mirrored Fate. He can turn it on *them* too.

Or maybe that's not enough anymore. Maybe they want Tabo Forzac's ending, the open door and empty tomb. Yes, that's the better ending, because his father was never a great hero who could have died a noble Roman death. Not even the oh-so-accidental *ker-plonk* of a crab forced to walk the plank. His father was the opposite of a great hero, and he did the right thing by sneaking off into a dark night to throw himself out of a window.

Brio finally registers that he's still in trouble with the authorities. He's got to give them an ending that slots perfectly between the good one and the ugliness—the kind of HI-HO that Tabo Forzac wanted. Their New Heaven and Hell, HE-HE. 'The Hoggit's father appears to him in the Tower of Time.'

He stops again to gauge their reactions but their faces have become blurred and all the same.

'Go on, Brio,' Anni Seng-Müller says quietly. 'We know how difficult this is for you. But you can do it.'

Her encouragement stiffens his spine sharply enough to leave him bowed backwards. 'Yes, I can,' he says. 'And it goes like this. The Hoggit's father was a great king indeed. Awesome, actually.' His voice sounds to him like some kind of super-sensible newsreader's. 'But, *Oh, dear*. He's only the king of the Dead Army. That's the army made up of oath-breakers who laid down their arms to become normal fathers that nibble grass and lick dishes. They've been damned for their feeble treachery to an eternity between life and death—half in, half out—and they long for the honourable peace of dying as men by hacking each other to pieces in the time-honoured way. And if the great Hoggit King can slay the Dark Lord, the broken oaths of his whole army will be wiped clean and they'll all be allowed their honourable peace. So the Hoggit King battled the Dark Lord for hour after hour, grinding down his dark energy, sapping his hissing blood with a thousand cuts.'

Brio realises that he doesn't know what he just said. They were mere words from somewhere else and they don't go anywhere. He has to shut out the looks of bewilderment and worry. He needs more time to save himself. But Professor Payne's objecting again and Anni Seng-Müller is fighting his corner, while the convenor and monitor argue about what proper adjudication should look like at a time like this. Surely, it's still possible for the Hoggit to become a new kind of king for an age in which kings and gods are dead and there's no pale grass left to nibble or smoke.

But Brio knows his time's run out. The swirling confetti of letter and vomit rises again and blurs his mum's face into the Hoggit at the Dark Arched Window. He has to get the real ending out before he vomits on the nurse's dissonant black and orange trainers.

Professor Payne is suddenly standing right in front of him. 'Brio, are you all right?' He looks to Anni Seng-Müller and Zuri Dacosta. 'For God's sake, this has gone on long enough. He's seriously unwell.'

'I'm fine,' Brio growls. Somewhere below, his legs break into a march on the spot, knees kicking up so high he's back with Logie in Pippa's sweet garden. He's Madame Haha doing the crazy-flip can-can too, and in his hands he's certain of the hollow shield and tousled lance.

But however hard he stomps on the floor, the words won't make rhyme and rhythm. He has no choice but to cry havoc and let the words pour out as a disorderly. rabble. 'The Hoggit stabbed the Great Sword into his father's guts. "*Aargh!*" roared the evil freak. The Hoggit hated the sound of his father's voice so much that he stabbed the blade into his neck too. He dug out his voice box so he couldn't even shout to get rid of his pain. Over and over, the Hoggit stabbed his sick father. Then he cut out his evil tongue and threw it from the battlements. "Lick that!" he cried. Then he chopped off his evil fingers too. Then his hands. And his ears. He threw them all out of the window, at the stupid police who should have been there to arrest him. He cut off his thing too, and threw it at God. Then he screamed at God that it was okay to kill yourself because that's what the Romans did, and God made the fucking Romans. Then he summoned up all his energy and threw himself out of the same window.'

23

BRIO PACES AROUND THE FOUR unthrowable armchairs, clenching and unclenching his bandaged hands to vent pain. From a seat outside in the corridor, a different nurse watches him through the door's slit of toughened glass. The way she self-consciously head-jigs and flick-scrolls her phone tells him she's monitoring his every move. And how dare they trim his fringe while he was asleep? And don't they care that his manacled inability to touch what's left causes him physical pain? Are they actually torturing him into giving them what they want?

As he stares down at hands that seem anchored into his bellybutton, he finds himself confronting the possibility that his mum and dad never loved each other, not even in the beginning. He's the product of lovelessness, of a marriage that should never have happened. It's worse than being born out of wedlock. And that's the real reason he's like he is.

But how am I really? he thinks. All along he's been stressing that he must be gay or trans or something else he doesn't know about— all of the above, as Professor Glybb would say—but what if it's something else? What if he's not imprisoned in his sick father's genes? What if it's not preordained that he'll become trans? He has to know *now*, before it's too late. But how?

He realises that the answer's about to walk through the door. Because when he sees Izzy, he's got to look at her like he's never looked at her before. He has to prove to himself that he only likes the way she looks because he wants to be like an animal with her, in the same burrow, not because he wants to *be* her. When she's sitting there in that chair, he has to make himself have grown-up thoughts about her. He must imagine her with no clothes on and touching his nose. He might have to take his own clothes off too. When he can't make those thoughts take shape, he tries to make her open her legs and put a banana in her mouth, but he recoils from the feelings of depravity and shame. All he wants is to *be* with her, lying next to her on the bed without touching her—in their own perfect world. *Oh, God, why didn't Father T explain all this properly?* Only a tap on the door stops him from crying aloud and he turns to suffer the most shocking sight of his life.

'What have you done? Where's your hair?' Nothing but stubble the length of toothbrush bristles. Remembering his brief thought of her hair wanting to become a hedgehog, he thinks he's hallucinating. But it's real. And it's him who made it happen.

Izzy doesn't have time to speak before the nurse asks them to sit in facing chairs and stay seated. As soon as they're alone, Izzy says, 'Bree, you didn't agree to do what they want, did you?'

He can't focus. He doesn't know what she just said. 'What have you done? *Why?*'

'Bree, tell me you didn't say yes.'

Anger crashes his shock, because after everything that's happened she still only cares about whether Zpydr wins or loses.

'Tell me you didn't find Bella Ripley. Tell me Ms Whittle didn't tell you anything.'

Izzy looks away and he chokes on a stifled cry.

'*They told you.* They told you everything.'

'Bree, I don't know anything from anyone.' Her voice trembles and she glances at the nurse through the glass.

'Then why did you come?'

She looks around the room, clearly trying to warn him that there might be hidden microphones. That's why they have to sit apart, so they'll be forced to speak loud and clear. She leans further forward to whisper. 'Pippa said you told people here that you accepted your dad was dead, and that he was, you know—maybe not what you thought.'

Seeing the old pity in her eyes, he thinks again that she already knows the truth. But no she doesn't, there's too much confusion on her forehead. Even to pinch his own chin he has to bend almost double in the chair.

'Bree, tell me about your dad. Please.'

'I don't want to talk about it. *Ever*.'

The silence gets loud and he has to look up. He finds the nurse peering in and Izzy leaning even further forward, almost off the armchair.

'Pippa said she gave you a letter from your dad.'

Now Brio wishes Izzy knew the truth already, so he wouldn't have to go through the hell of telling her himself. And he *must* tell her. Like he's always told her everything.

'Bree, tell me. You did read the letter, didn't you? You didn't throw it away?'

Their silence seems to draw louder noise from the air-conditioning. He stares at the floor and clutches his knees to stop his hands shaking.

'Bree, I honestly don't know what was in the letter. I just know your dad's alive. I can feel it.'

'He's *dead*.'

But the question's suddenly real and urgent. What if his sick father is not dead after all? What if he failed to kill himself too? Brio's still reeling when he's struck by the possibility that his father saw the news. He might turn up to see him. Then everyone would find out the truth. Oh, God, it's even worse than that—his father's someone he knows, someone who's been there all along, hiding in plain sight till the day his son was ready for the shock and disgrace.

Brio's back prickles cold and his mind roves wildly for who it might be. Any of the women at church who aren't really women at all. Maybe one of the teachers at school, or Mrs Elswood next door, always watching from her gardening cushion, forked trident of a trowel in hand.

His search disintegrates into a whole new chaos of questions. How can he die without knowing whether his father's alive or dead? How can he kill himself if his father didn't do the same thing first?

Izzy leans forward again. 'You mean, the letter was like … a suicide note?'

'*No*. I mean, yes. But it's none of your business.'

His raised voice has the nurse on her feet outside the door and Izzy hurriedly smiles and gestures that everything's okay. As soon as the nurse has sat back down, Izzy whispers, 'So where *is* the letter?'

Brio has to control his breathing before he can speak. 'I flushed it down the toilet.'

Izzy groans and runs a hand over her stubbly scalp. 'Bree, if your dad's alive when Zpydr's done everything they can to make everyone believe he's dead, then this whole thing will collapse and you can get out of here. *Tell me.*'

This time his anger melts into an unexpected calm and he looks Izzy in the eye. 'You'll never beat Tabo Forzac. He's too smart even for you. And he's wise too. And he wants to help the world.'

He tries to read what she's thinking and prays that she's too shocked to keep asking questions about his freak father.

'Bree, you've got to come home,' she whispers urgently. 'I'll do anything to look after you. Skip a year—whatever.'

'I don't need anyone to look after me. I'm fine here.'

His last words stun *him* too and Izzy's expression changes.

'You mean you don't want to get out of here?'

He can't answer. His thoughts are back on the conflict of wanting Bella to be safe and wishing her dead too. Wishing *everyone* safe in Heaven.

'Bree,' Izzy implores. 'You're not safe here. We've got to get you out.'

'Why aren't I safe?' He tries to sound tough but the look of worry and care in her eyes makes it another pathetic whimper. Only when Izzy looks again at the nurse does he register that she has some other kind of bad news to tell him. 'What is it?'

'Bree, I know I shouldn't tell you but you have to know. So you see that you have to get out of here.'

'*What?*'

'Bree … Bella died.'

He floats. That can't be what she said. It's all happening in his head. He killed Bella by wishing her dead. He's making everything happen by just thinking it. And Izzy's frightened expression means that something bad happened to Bella. 'What did they do?'

'She was walking in Spain. The pilgrimage track. The famous one she went on with Father T. The Spanish police say she went off the proper track and slipped down an escarpment.'

Suspects flash through his mind but they all feed up to Tabo Forzac, and how could Tabo Forzac do something so evil when he's supposed to be God? 'They killed her and made it look like an accident.'

'But what the police said might be true,' Izzy says quickly. 'Bella *was* old, and it was really hot. And a witness said she wanted to walk alone.' She reaches out. 'Bree, please. The truth about your dad is the way to fix everything. Tell me what he said in the letter.'

Suddenly, all Brio wants is to be out of there. Because Izzy's right. If they can kill Bella, they can kill him too. And that proposition incenses him more than any other. Because the only person who's going to kill him is *him*. It's truly is the only control over his own life that he still has.

His thoughts disintegrate again and he has to gasp for air. He doesn't want to leave there at all. He wants to be in the hospital forever so he never has to face the world. He wants to kill himself here and now and get it over with. But he needs to know whether his father's alive.

'Bree, I swear—whatever it is, I'll stand by you. We've just got to get you out of here.'

Her words spin him again and he's carried away on the euphoric thought that if Izzy would be with him even after she found out the truth about his father, then maybe *he* could live with the truth too.

But his elation is damned by the memory of his mum's anger as she tore the photos of *those people* out of the free newspaper. Overwhelmed by the dark wingspan of her static, circling presence, he slumps back in the chair and feels for the first time that the whole thing's just too big for him to understand, let alone handle. How did he ever stand a chance of being able to face the world on his own two feet? How could he have even thought he could be with someone like Izzy? How had he ever been anything more than the lukewarm puddle of all his mum's pitiful hot and cold?

'Bree?'

The very sound of her voice pushes him into a grim new determination. 'I *do* want to get out of here. As soon as I can.'

Izzy brightens. 'That's good.' But her face falls. She's obviously worked out *why* he wants to leave, and needing to distract her from the thought, he says, 'I just need your help so I can get out.'

'What do you mean? Help with what?'

'With the ending. What else?' The mission becomes clear and all his old feelings for her come in a rush. 'But the ending has to be the truth. That's what I swore to the Hoggit. And it has to be the ending that *they* want too.'

He holds her gaze but can't stop his eyes feeling plaintive like the Hoggit's. And he sees on her face the sheer impossibility of the task. Because asking for it to be both the truth *and* what Zpydr wants is like asking for something to be black and white at the same time, or wet and dry, or boy and girl. When he sees Izzy looking even more worried, he says menacingly, 'You said you'd help me find my father. And this is how.'

'Bree, the way to find your dad is to tell me what was in the letter. There's no other way to fight them.'

But Brio doesn't want that ending. He wants the real one, the one that's beyond truth, the one that by definition lies beyond the capacity of humans to undersand. 'The only way I can get out of here is to find out what the Hoggit *really* remembered, before they messed everything up. And the only person who can lift the Memory Curse is the Hoggit's god.'

He searches her face and pleads inside for her to know exactly how to help him like she always did.

'I know,' she says. 'And the Hoggit's god is *you*.'

Seeing how relieved she is to have evaded what he wants, he stands up and fixes her with a stare she can't refuse. 'That's right,' he says. 'I *am* the Hoggit's god. But I'm only the Hoggit's god, and I have only ever been the Hoggit's god, when I'm part of *you*.'

She manages to hold his gaze long enough for him to see tears in her eyes. And the nurse is on her feet too, looking anxiously through the glass panel. He drops to his knees in front of Izzy and tries to reach for her with his manacled hands. '*Please*. You have to help me get out of here.'

Izzy's head falls and he stares at the top of her spiky head. But he no longer cares what she looks like. He just needs to hear her say the magic words. And he prays that this time she *will* remember what the Hoggit told him at the castle.

She eventually looks up and the tears have been replaced by that familiar determination.

'Okay,' she says, 'the Hoggit did see whether his father was in the High Dungeon. So that's what you have to tell him. And after you've told him that, there's nothing more you can tell him. Then the Great Plea will be finished and he can hold it up to his god. And God will lift the Memory Curse to let him remember the truth.' She looks right into him and grips his hands tightly. 'So if Zpydr want their ending, they have to let you go back to the castle like you promised and tell the Hoggit the last bit of the story you know. Then the curse will be lifted and the Hoggit will remember everything about his father.'

~ PART EIGHT ~

TRANSCENDENCE

Above the senses, the mind, the intellect
and the ego is the Unmanifested Cause. Beyond
the Unmanifested Cause is Brahman: omnipresent,
without attributes, immanent and transcendent, beyond
all duality, and beyond the reach of thinker and thought.
So it is said: when all the desires that surge in the heart
are renounced, and when all the knots that strangle
the heart are loosened, the mortal becomes truly
immortal, here in this very life. As the skin of
a snake is sloughed onto an anthill, so does
the mortal body fall. But the Self,
freed from the body, merges
in Brahman: infinite life
and eternal light.

From the *Katha, Tejobindu,*
Amritabindu and *Brihadaranyaka Upanishads*

24

FACE PRESSED AGAINST THE AIRCRAFT WINDOW, Brio cranes to stay in contact with the lights far below. When he can't twist any further and they disappear, he's plunged into a confusing fusion of darkness and the reflection of Danny Bellani sitting on the other side of the narrow aisle. The thought that they must now be over the sea stirs butterflies, because if the engines failed over land the pilot might still find some kind of runway, whereas the sea offered only a cold drowning, and it seems impossible that the small jet can stay airborne for long enough to get him back to the island, where he can die in the way he wants.

Unable to close his eyes, Brio prays that this whole Zpydr jet ride isn't just another rolling hallucination, one more story that's been fed into his head by people he needs to take with him over the cliff: Anni Seng-Müller sitting opposite cosseting an elegant briefcase that contains the expertly salvaged Great Plea, Dr Missle and Professor Yanki leaning into animated conversation with two new Zpydr people, government people talking hush-hush inside the muffled cocoon of wind-rush and engine whistle.

He also can't help worrying that they've got some other hidden plan that'll stop him doing what he has to do. Why else would the Zpydr people want him to stay at Logie's house if Logie's not working for them? They can't seriously believe that Pippa and Logie can provide a *stable family environment* when Pippa's just had a nervous breakdown and Logie's suicidal.

Thoughts of Logie's wavering accents and veiled pain plunges

Brio back into confusion. How can he even lay eyes on Logie without being sucked back into the turmoil himself? Except maybe Logie's not really suicidal at all. It's an act like everything else. Maybe they do have some secret plan, and Logie's their key agent.

But no. There's no plan. They just want him to stay at Logie's so they can come up with one. Though what if Logie does care about him? What if all those squiggly lines and polygons on his notes meant that Logie was trying to help him, trying to be a better friend? Brio's thoughts fragment and he curses himself for having let Logie get to him again. But slamming the door on Logie only opens another for Ms Whittle, who rushes him with knowing glances and giveaway exclamations, with her passionate attempts to change him into a girl.

He shuts Ms Whittle down too. Because he's made his decision and none of this matters anymore. Because St Luke was right, and so was that ancient Greek man Father T really loved, the one who said humans could become like God without being blasphemous because God's there for us in the divine energies and the divine energies were everywhere. *Just like in Star Wars*, said Izzy, and even Ms Whittle was right about God being in everything. So God's within you, and if you want to kill yourself then it's God who decided.

The moment he finally manages to close his eyes, Anni Seng-Müller asks if he's feeling okay. He snaps to attention and summons up the semblance of mild hypnosis he's certain will reassure them of how equably he accepts his father's death. 'I'm fine, thank you. It's just that this is the first time I've been in an aeroplane—especially a quite small one.'

Smiling, Anni Seng-Müller says, 'You know this is only the beginning, right? You've got such a big future ahead of you.'

'Yeah,' adds Danny Bellani, 'we want the Hoggit to play a really significant role going forward—an interactive icon-mascot on the CHANT*bot-vip* platform. Like a saviour figure who symbolises the soft inner part of ourselves that we protect with spikes so as to get through life.'

'I'm really proud of him,' Brio agrees in his grown-up voice, and he's surprised not to need the fake smile.

Danny Bellani twists round to face him. 'You're surely more than proud! You're gonna be at the heart of our brand. Because you truly are the emblem of a world beyond gender. I simply can't wait to shoot that golden moment when you and the Hoggit are reunited. That truly is the money shot, the Hoggit coming face to face with his god, and his god becoming one with his healed and godlike inner self. The perfect fusion of sames and simulacra.'

The barrage of vacuous hyperbole leaves Brio lost for words and he worries that his stage persona's about to crack. But after Danny Bellani has sunk back into his conversation with Dr Kapoor, he recovers enough to wonder how they're going to add the Hoggit into the video with special effects when they have no idea what he looks like. With a frisson of dark satisfaction, he wishes them the high-profile success of their dreams.

A sharp drop and swerve wakes him and before he's regained his bearings the plane lands hard. As they flash along the runway, he sees clustered vehicles outside a brightly lit hangar. It smells like home ground, for sure, but it's a place he's never seen. He feels so near but yet so far. So half-way in but half-way gone.

In the chill wind, Pippa's waiting by the small plane's steps. Her hug triggers ripples of comfort and he can't help hugging her back tightly. Realising with a pang of sadness that she's part of the everything he must relinquish, he almost pushes her away.

Hunching as though running a gauntlet of press cameras, the Zpydr and government people show each other into limousines, while the nurses climb into an immaculate white campervan. As a CHANT nurse climbs into the passenger seat of Pippa's car, a government rival ushers Brio into the back and wedges herself in next to him. As soon as they're moving she explains that two or three nurses will stay with them at Logie's place and take it in turns between the campervan and the house. 'Everyone else will be staying at a hotel in town. They'll be waiting to hear when you're ready to go to the lighthouse.'

'I think you mean the castle,' says the CHANT nurse from the front, after which they continue in frosty silence on country roads that the darkness once again renders unfamiliar.

Eventually they come to a broken-down gate between crumbling low stone walls and Brio almost groans his weary resignation out loud. When they pass the small track to the drystone hut in the small woods, he's torn between nostalgia and the rekindled sense of having been the victim of an elaborate trick that might yet turn out to be a grand plan.

Further on, past other tracks into woods that are bigger than he previously imagined, the headlights illuminate an old cottage set in ramshackle gardens. It's surrounded by trees that look like they were once well kept and Logie's waiting at the front door, one arm in a sling. He's thinner and paler with dark rings under the eyes, and neatly brushed hair makes him look insane.

While nurses unload suitcases, Brio pushes past Logie into a small musty hallway. The place is so like Bluebells he wants to do everything from cry to run to never leave. At the top of the rickety stairs, he hears the tinny bygone sound from an old radio and glimpses a very old lady in a bedroom. Her wispy hair's so thin that parts of her scalp show through and she looks like a ghost in the equally threadbare armchair. Pippa explains that the lady is Logie's mum. 'The poor thing's deaf,' she adds in a whisper.

This time the fraud does rouse Brio's anger. Faking an accent is one thing, maybe it's even good, but winning his trust by saying his mum died of the same cancer in the same hospital is too disgusting to even be a sin. But *good*, Brio thinks. *It proves you've been bad all along, so I don't have to care about you anymore.*

Except that when they're crammed in outside a bedroom door and he sees how broken Logie looks, he can't stop himself saying, 'You don't need to feel bad, you know. Because you didn't fail and I'm okay now.'

'Are you though?' Logie whispers hoarsely. 'I don't believe this is what you want. They've done something to you in that place.'

This chills Brio's feelings. 'With respect, I think it was you who Zpydr brainwashed, and I know what I want perfectly well. So why shouldn't you be fine too? Isn't this what you always wanted for us?' But the distress on Logie's face is too real. 'I'm sorry,' Brio says hurriedly. 'You need some sleep too.'

Inside the small bedroom with Pippa, Brio shuts the door on Logie. The room's hardly big enough to be a room. Only the flaking paint distinguishes it from a hermit's cell, and the cocktail of smells is unlike anything he's ever encountered: mould and a mildewed curtain in opposition to air freshener, washed blankets and Pippa's new brand of perfume, old wood and more besides. On seeing the brand new window bars, his stomach tightens, because his captors are still one step ahead, and now to escape he has to get past the inside nurses too.

A cough turns him around to see the other nurse putting down his own suitcase in the small bedroom opposite. How the hell did someone open the door again without him noticing? Pippa's about to say something when they pick up the sound of Logie's mum mumbling to herself. He tells Pippa he wants to sleep and sits down heavily on the bed. He'll sleep in his clothes, he insists. He doesn't need to clean his teeth till the morning. Pippa argues that he needs to get ready for bed properly. The bathroom's next door.

He's had a long day.

But Pippa has to stand aside while the nurse gives Brio another sedative and watches carefully until he's downed it with three gulps of water.

'Good job,' says the nurse to Brio as he ushers Pippa out of the room. 'So get a good night's sleep, yeah? Big day tomorrow. And let's not forget it's your sixteenth birthday on Sunday.'

25

HOLDING ASIDE THE MILDEWED CURTAIN and gazing into the sombre morning light, Brio sees that the cottage faces down a shallow valley to a small bay. When he apprehends it as the very place of his most treasured outings with Father T, he braces for another wave of grief. To his surprise, however, he finds himself strangely excited at that idea that very soon he will once again be with Father T.

His elation is spoiled by the nurse who wants him to have breakfast. He keeps his nose pressed between the bars and says he's not hungry, he'll eat later. After the second nurse has taken over, he argues about his open door. He needs to meditate in private, to make himself ready to meet the Hoggit, because readiness is all and he doesn't like the smell of the small landing. 'And don't forget,' he adds, 'I'm about to do a film-shoot. They want me in an excellent state of mental health.'

Half an hour later, he repeats everything to Pippa and rejects Logie's attempts from the doorway to lure him downstairs with pancakes.

'I'm not five, you know.'

The floorboards have hardly started creaking Logie away when Brio sees Dr Shenoy's familiar orange jalopy drawing up next to the cottage. Nurses immediately appear like partisans from the forest, two of them—a third—one of them not even dressed as a nurse. Brio watches with mild curiosity as the nurses surround an angry Dr Shenoy, while Izzy's allowed to walk past unchallenged.

The stairs creak again and there she is in the doorway, looking like it's all nothing and she was there all along. He has to return to the window bars.

'I know the Hoggit isn't real,' he says.

'He is. And I love him too.'

The magic words almost lift him off his feet. She could just as well be saying *I do*. When he turns, though, he sees only that the whole plan to meet the Hoggit at the castle was as much a ruse to trick him as it was for Zpydr and the government people. And she's only here with her dad to talk him into the Northview, to lead him away like a lamb to be Darcy's other half in their bond of so-called schizophrenia.

Taking fresh hold of the window bars, he tells himself that once he's told her the truth about his father she won't give a damn whether he goes to the Northview or not. She'll just try to smile and say that his father being sick in the head has nothing to do with *him*. Once she's dashed off her comforting lies, she'll explain politely that she has extra piano or some kind of half-term genius camp. Then after she's gone, he'll never see her again, because he's going to run through the night till he reaches the Cosy Nook at the exact breaking of dawn.

In the silence of a sea mist that pushes effortlessly up the valley, Brio senses Izzy moving closer. Even though her perfume smells like aftershave, it scrambles his thoughts and he loses sight of what's supposed to happen next.

From close behind him, she whispers, 'I'm glad I helped you get away from that place. But I'm not stupid. I know what you meant when you said the Hoggit would take the truth like a man. Please. Talk to me.'

'You just want me in the Northview, so you can visit Darcy and pretend it's to see me.' He hates his childish need for reassurance but he can't stop. 'You think Darcy can be normal again, but you think *I'm* mad forever.'

'Bree, Darcy's just a friend. And I don't care about anyone else in the world like I care about you. And I can't help Darcy at the moment anyway. Because they're really not doing very well.'

Brio wants to snap at her that Darcy's not a *they*. Instead he finds himself asking what's wrong with Darcy.

'They've been diagnosed with dissociative identity disorder,' she replies. 'Which is really sad, because I really thought they were okay with being gender fluid. But—'

'O-*kay*. I don't want to know.'

After irritation comes confusion at feeling such concern for Darcy. It tangles into a weird grief over losing the vile certainty he always knew. And people like Darcy were surely a primal force of nature that must never be crushed, and maybe *Tracy* was actually real and a part of that primordial true self. Good God, maybe Darcy even fits Lord Rumbuck's description of the true hero who can never survive the mundane trivilaities of life and the braying mob.

From there, Brio even wants to forgive Darcy for their deranged cruelty. Because it wasn't really Darcy's fault. And Izzy was right, somehow the the three of them really are all in this together. And in some even stranger way, he can sense through the ether that Darcy is genuinely sorry for all the wanton cruelty of his broken days.

'Bree, I totally get how you feel about the Northview. It's a big thing. But I've been there now. They're really nice people. And they're nothing like ...' She glances to the world of CHANT and Zpydr, and Logie and Professor Glybb.

'I don't *care*. I just have to talk to you. That's the only thing that matters.'

They're left in a tense silence and birds flit as though making final preparations before a hurricane.

'One thing, though,' Izzy says. 'I did find out how Darcy knew about your secret.'

Brio swings round. 'How?'

'It was so obvious. I just didn't work it out because I trusted them. They sneaked a look at my diary when they were round at my house working on a script. I'm really sorry I wrote down what you told me about your dad. But you know how a diary has to be. You can't leave anything out or the omission can fall prey to imagination and become a lie.'

Before Brio can understand how he feels about this revelation, Izzy's expression becomes more insistent. 'Bree, we've got to get you to safety. The Northview's the only way. But you won't be there for long, I promise. Dad's found people and lawyers who can fight Zpydr and the mainland government.'

His anger deadened by the intensity of Izzy's care, Brio turns back to the bars. Suddenly, the idea of being close to Darcy at the Northview scares him in a way it didn't before. Worse still, he wishes Izzy actually could help Darcy get better. He wishes *he* could help Darcy get better, and surely there *is* a better way than 'curing' him of so-called mental illness. What in God's name can it be? But he has to get his thoughts back to Izzy. Because telling her the whole truth is the only thing left. 'I have to tell you something terrible.'

He counts the seconds of silence—three, four ...

'Is it what was in the letter?'

Something in her tone flips his feelings and he hates himself for needing to tell Izzy everything. Why can't he be like the Hoggit and break out of his childish dependence? And if he doesn't tell her about his father, if he can silence everyone else who knows the truth, then his father really can die a fake hero. And so can he. Then everything else will be all right.

But the thought of not telling Izzy turns his insides again, and it's not because of some childish dependency that he has to share it with her, it's out of love. It's about being totally open and honest because that's the only way to have complete trust.

Though what if being totally open isn't the same as being honest? What if there *are* things that should be kept secret even between people who love each other? What if knowing each others' innermost secrets isn't what creates collective consciousness at all and it really is the total access to each other's lives that drives us apart? What if a trusting silence is precisely how you create the ultimate fiction that contains the ultimate truth? He clutches his head. Where are these words coming from? They're all rubbish. Because anything hidden in your heart will eat you from the inside, like a lie that comes back to ambush you. Before he can stop himself, he's pouring it all out, how his father still went ahead and married his mum even when he knew he had a secret woman hidden away inside him, how he let her have a baby then ran off to become a woman himself.

When he registers the shock on Izzy's face, he lets out a noise he's never heard before and slides down the wall into a crumple of clutched knees. 'Just *go*.'

'Oh, Bree …' She drops to her knees and clasps his arms, but he throws her off.

'Oh, God,' she murmurs. 'But it all makes sense now. Oh, this is so hard for you. Oh, Bree …'

'Just go.' He needs to be sick. '*Go*.'

But she only manoeuvres to kneel more comfortably and reaches for him again. He lashes out with the back of a hand and pulls himself more tightly into his ball. And in the following hiatus, all he can hear is a thumping in his head and the muffled sound of nurses talking outside in the garden.

'Bree …' Izzy says eventually as though beginning again. 'I know what you were brought up to believe. We were all brought up to believe the same thing. But this would be a shock for anyone.'

'Just fucking *go*.'

But she doesn't move. 'Let's just be here together for a while and not talk.'

'So you can think how to get out and pretend it's okay.'

'It *is* okay. It's just in real life … you know … it can be difficult.' She takes his hand and rides out the rodeo to keep it tightly held. 'Bree, this is huge for you and it will take ages to come to terms with it. I *know*.'

'It's why I'm a freak too,' Brio blurts. 'It's why I'm …' He cries out and clutches his head harder. 'I don't know what I am.'

She clasps one hand in both of hers. 'Bree, it's who you are in your soul that matters, not in your genes. And it doesn't matter at all how you are.'

He's straight out of his defensive ball. 'But I'm not gay. And I can't be trans either. Because I love *you*.' He searches her face for what *she* thinks and how *she* feels. All she needs to do is agree and his confusion about her love will be washed away. When she doesn't even squeeze his hand, he cries, 'I'm *not* gay. It's just what everyone else says and thinks.'

But at once, the weight of opinion and all those looks pile back in. And how can Professor Glybb be wrong? We *are* prisoners of our genes, and our genes are created by God. With another half sob, he breaks the hold of her hand and disappears back into his shell.

This time, the silence even seems to stop the birdsong, but he no longer cares whether the whole world's dead, he just needs to know whether she'll be with him in the way he wants.

But what *is* the way he wants? Who does he want to be when he does whatever he wants to do? What if he really doesn't want to *do* anything?

'What else did your dad say in the letter? I bet he said he loved you.'

'It's just words. It's what he did that counts.'

He can sense her struggle, but he knows what she really thinks.

'Bree, I know it's not what you need to hear right now, but what your dad did showed real courage.'

'It *wasn't*. Why couldn't he stop himself? That's what would have been brave. That's what would have been strong.'

Izzy tries to hug him but he presses back against the wall.

'Bree, when you know in your heart who you really are, there's no other way. Your dad had no choice at all. I'm sure he wanted to be your dad but—'

'Why couldn't he *believe* he was a dad, even if he wanted to be something else? That's all you have to do. Just believe. That's stronger than anything. Stronger than any genes or some stupid memory you can't control.'

'Bree, it's not that easy.'

'Why *not*? If I could really believe I was a hedgehog, why couldn't he believe he was just a *father*?' And when she sighs, he says, 'Go on then. Go to your *piano lesson*. Your stupid horse riding.'

She tries once more for his hand. 'Bree, we have to find your dad.'

'He's *dead*. And I don't want to talk about him ever again.'

'You don't know they're dead.'

He stands without warning and sends her off balance again. 'He's a *he*. And he *is* dead. Because God hated him. And Bella falling down the mountainside was an accident. And Zpydr's just mad. So forget everything.'

'Bree—'

'*Swear it*. Swear you'll never tell anyone what I just told you.' When she hesitates, he says, 'If you swear you won't tell anyone, I swear I'll believe you.'

Izzy reaches for him again, her eyes bright with alarm. 'Bree, stop thinking like this.'

'Why shouldn't I? What have I got to lose?' He wills her to take the cue and tell him what he needs to hear, but her hand drifts slowly back down.

'Bree, there's something I have to tell *you*. I've wanted to tell you for such a long time.'

His bowels turn to liquid but as she's about to speak there's a gentle tap on the door. They watch it slowly open to reveal Pippa looking ashen-faced and wide-eyed.

'What is it?' Brio asks weakly. He's never felt such dread.

Pippa slips the door closed behind her and leans back to stop anyone coming in. 'I just had a call.' She's breathing in little pants. 'It was your dad.'

26

'LOOK, I'M SORRY,' Logie pleads feebly. 'And I admit, I did think your dad took his own life. I mean, we all did.'

Brio turns on Logie again and couldn't care less that he looks even closer to a nervous collapse than before. 'Just *shut up*. I want to talk to Izzy alone.'

'But seriously,' Logie persists, 'this doesn't change what we did together, which was all about forgiveness—which is the answer to everything.'

'What?' Izzy snaps. 'Are you saying Brio can't forgive people now?'

'*No*. I'm just saying—'

'I *can* forgive people,' Brio says angrily. 'Like I forgive you for saying your mum died in hospital the same as mine when she's still alive. Now *get out*.'

Logie's face falls further. 'Oh, God, I'm sorry. I didn't think to explain. My mum did die, when I was eight. But I was lucky, my foster mum adopted me.'

Brio's thrown again, but even through his own distress he sees how the whole thing between Logie and Pippa makes sense.

But no. He's got to crush his feelings. 'Just get out. Both of you.'

After a silence, Pippa says, 'Bree, your dad does want to see you. She booked a ticket from Australia as soon as she saw the news.'

'He's not a *she*. And it's all lies. He didn't know my name. He could never have known it was me.'

'Bree, parents just know. But it's okay that you need time to think. That's only natural.'

He's assaulted again by the memory of his mum tearing up the free newspaper to obliterate all those people on their parade with ghoulish make-up and two-inch eyelashes and wigs and bright red high heels. 'I told you. I don't want to see him.'

'Bree, this does change everything,' Izzy says cautiously. 'I mean, your whole life can start again. Because that's all that's ever been wrong. You lost your mum and Father T but you knew in your heart your dad was still alive. And no one believed you, not even me. That's enough to make anyone lose their bearings.'

But now Brio's embroiled in angst about killing himself when his father's still alive. And why *is* he still alive when he deserves to be dead for making his mum suffer so much?

'One good thing, I suppose,' Logie says weakly, 'Zpydr's gonna get hammered when the truth comes out. And so are the government people who supported them.'

Brio turns so sharply they all recoil. He only just stops himself from grabbing Logie by his shirtfront and shaking off his head. 'You're never going to tell anyone about him. *Ever*. Any of you.' Even though there's something pathetic about Logie's eyes now, he has to return to the window bars, where he sees nurses outside chatting over cigarettes like prison-camp guards. He can smell their smoke through gaps in the window's rotting timber. He has the outlandish thought of slipping a load of sedatives into the nurses' coffees. Then he'd be able to escape as soon as it went dark and have the whole night to deal with all the people who have to be silenced before dawn breaks at the cliffs.

'Bree, your dad really cares about you,' Pippa says. 'She— I mean, your dad tried for years to find you but it looks like the Church in Ireland really did help your mum change her identity so you couldn't be found. But your dad never gave up trying—and hoping.'

As he stares out of the window, a small bird lands on the windowsill and peers in at them. Unthinkingly, he lunges to scare it off, which leaves him staring at the empty sill unable to comprehend how he could have done such a thing.

'What else did Bree's dad say on the phone?' Izzy asks Pippa.

'I don't want to know,' Brio says with another hard tug on the bars. But even as he's physically repulsed by the idea of seeing his father, he's tormented by the primal need to know everything.

'She said she was a horse trainer,' Pippa says cautiously to Izzy.

He wants to shout at them to stop saying *she*, but the thought that his father trains horses has sent an unwanted thrill down his back and the golden-robed rider comes alive in his mind. He catches himself and is about to yank on the bars again when he registers that the silence behind him has grown a new energy. Seeing in the reflection that Izzy is staring open mouthed at Pippa, he swings around. 'What?'

Izzy doesn't take her eyes off Pippa. 'You said Brio's dad was called Robi?'

'Yes,' Pippa says, looking worried. 'Why?'

'*What is it?*' Brio almost shouts.

'Bree, I know this is crazy,' Izzy says, 'and I know it's going to freak you out even more, but I think I know who your dad is. She's quite well known.'

Logie looks askance but realisation dawns. 'You mean, Robi *Galla*? You serious?'

'Well, how many other well-known trans equestrians called Robi do you know?'

Brio stares at them helplessly. 'What do you mean? Who's Robi Galla?' The idea that his father isn't just a freak but a famous one tips him into a totally uncharted place where nausea muddles into simple butterflies and anger vies with another tingle down his back.

But Izzy's eyes are as radiant as he's ever seen them. 'Bree, you have to meet your dad. Oh, God, this is incredible. I've read so much about her.'

'Man, talk about celebrity couple,' Logie says and before Brio can decide where to hit him, Izzy's in on the act too.

'Wouldn't it be amazing if Robi really did want the world to know that Bree was her son? Wouldn't it be great if everyone could see what a great father Robi was, and every—?'

Losing control, Brio lunges this way and that, pressing them all back against wallpaper and the rickety wardrobe. 'I'm never going to meet him. And you're not telling a single person. *Swear it.*' But all he can see in their faces is how much they want to be with him in some gigantic global freakshow, and Izzy's cupping her cheeks as though she hasn't heard a word.

'Bree, your name—it uses the same letters as Robi.'

'So *what?*' He's on the point of doing something terrible.

'Well, doesn't it mean that when your mum changed your birth certificate, she must have known your dad's new name? Even though she was so angry and disappointed, she still wanted you to be connected with your dad. She wanted you to know them one day.'

Brio clutches the remnants of his fringe. 'She didn't. She told Father T she never wanted to talk about him again.' But he remembers his mum's email to Pippa, how she wished he had a father when all she'd got for him was the letter. At the thought of his mum so desperately wanting him to have something he's shredded and flushed, he has to defray a sob into another tug on the bars. When the nurses look up, he quickly lets go and turns back to the room. 'My father's dead. Now let me be alone with Izzy.'

But Izzy's too fired up. 'Bree, Father T said he wanted you to be the one who rescued your dad from his shackles. And now you know what he meant—that you have to rescue your dad from the loss of being separated from *you*.'

'That's not what he meant. He meant rescuing him from the Devil. And I can't. No one can. And I don't want to.' He's about to say more when he sees they're all staring at Logie, who looks even more nervous than before.

'What is it now?' Brio demands.

'Well, I mean, it's crazy,' Logie says to Pippa and Izzy, 'but what if these Zpydr guys actually know that his dad's Robi Galla? Just the fact that his dad's alive is a pretty major inconvenient truth.'

Izzy's face drops and she looks at the door. 'And what if they knew that Bella knew?'

Logie runs an anxious hand through his hair. 'What the hell have I got myself involved in?'

'It doesn't matter whether they know,' Brio says coldly. 'Because they'll never want anyone else to know. And that's *good*.'

Pippa looks confused. 'How could Zpydr have known that Bella knew something?'

'Same way they know everything,' Logie says. 'Like, how the hell did they know your home insurance wasn't going to cough up?'

It takes a few seconds for Logie's meaning to drop; suddenly Pippa not having the money to build a new house is the only thing in the world that matters. 'Why aren't they going to pay?'

'With everything happening,' Logie jumps in, 'she forgot to pay her premium and missed the reminders.'

Seeing that it's all his fault, Brio slumps heavily onto the wobbly bed. Yet out of his fresh turmoil comes a thought—that's actually a *plan*. He springs back up. 'I *will* give them the ending they want. And then they can do whatever they want with it. And you'll get the prize.' He points at a gobsmacked Logie. 'Then you'll give it to Pippa for a new house. Then she won't have to live here anymore. And no one will ever mention my useless father again.'

'Bree, no,' Pippa murmurs. But he can see the hope in her eyes and feels a warm glow at the thought that he can repay her for how much she's always done her best. His happiness is broken by Izzy's evident dismay and Logie looking like he wants to sneak away.

'What?' Brio growls at Izzy. 'Did you think I wasn't going to give them the ending they want?' He turns to Logie. 'And swear you'll give Pippa the money. Swear it on your life.' And when Logie shifts awkwardly, Brio snatches up a small vase and knocks its rim against the wall. As shards of glass tinkle on the floorboards, Pippa and Izzy cry out Brio's name, but they're not quick enough to stop him running the jagged edge across his scabby palm.

Izzy and Pippa rush for his new wound but he waves them away and thrusts the razor-edged vase at Logie. 'It's your last chance to prove I can trust you. And your *mom's* your witness.'

Logie's eyes narrow and, with an abruptness that makes Pippa and Izzy start, he grabs the vase. His face flinches even before the sharp edge has made contact. A moment later, he's holding up his bleeding palm for Brio to lock hands.

'Good,' Brio says and holds Logie's pale-grey eyes as firmly as his hand. He detaches with a push of palms that sends them both staggering back. 'I believe you. And now I'm going to talk to Izzy alone.'

Before Logie can reply, though, his eyes glaze and he gives way at the knees so unexpectedly that no one has time to break his fall.

'Then we'll go somewhere else,' Brio says and steps over Logie to pull open the door for Izzy.

Izzy closes the kitchen door behind them, but through its rippled glass Brio can see a nurse hovering in the hall. He's annoyed to see another one patrolling the patio of weeds and uneven slabs.

'Bree, we have to do your hand.'

'I *want* it like this.'

With a sigh, she dumps her backpack on a chair and pulls out another. 'Just come and sit down then.'

But he's been struck by the realisation that if he kills himself, Zpydr will have failed in their make-believe cure and Logie won't get the prize money. Then Pippa won't get her new home.

'Bree, your dad isn't what you imagine.'

The softness in her voice wrenches him out of his new dilemma. Izzy's surely the answer to everything. Now he longs for the little bird to return so he can beg its forgiveness and promise it everything its little heart desires for the rest of its never-ending life. But he has to ask Izzy now, before she makes his father sound like something good, before there's some even bigger problem than Pippa's money.

'And I bet your dad said they loved your mum and did their best to make it work.'

Forced again to remember the feminine handwriting of his dad's letter, Brio realises that he knew the truth about his mum and dad all along. And that's what was dragged up from his memory when he subconsciously overheard the huge argument between Mr and Mrs Hare. As though the terrible scene he must have witnessed as a toddler might come at him out of the corner, he turns back to Izzy. 'My father only married Mum because he felt sorry for her. Because *her* mum died too, of the same thing as her. They were friends since kids. That's how they should have stayed. They should never have got married.'

'Then you wouldn't be here.'

'Good. And you'd be happy too.'

Izzy makes another silence and doesn't move. 'Your dad cared about your mum when they were together. And he did his best. That's love.'

'It's sick love. And if he did his best, he'd never have left.'

Izzy has to gather herself. 'Bree, your dad's not sick. Your dad's a very good person and everyone knows that.'

Hearing the unexpected indignation in her voice, he brings his freshly bloodied palm down on the countertop. 'That's because they don't know he abandoned us to go and be a woman. And I only want to talk about *us*. You and me.'

He twists round just in time to see Izzy trying to conceal her gulp behind a hand. His hope crashes and he turns back into the corner.

'Bree, what they told us about being trans belongs to a time that's passed. Some places in the world have never thought it's wrong. And your mum only felt so strongly about non-binary people because of the pain she suffered.'

'She was right to.'

They fall silent again but he can feel how much she needs to speak.

'*What?*'

'Well, the Bible's important to me too. And Jesus does say it's okay for a man to decide not to be a man if it's for the Kingdom of Heaven, which everyone knows is just an old-fashioned term for a world ruled by love.' And before he can contest her claim, she says, 'Bree, your dad obviously loves you. And I bet he didn't really want to leave. And you care about your dad too.'

'I hate him.' But Izzy's tangled him up in something clever he doesn't understand. 'He didn't have himself chopped up out of love. He did it because …' He groans and clutches his stunted fringe. 'I don't *know* why he did it.' He turns to see her face. 'How was it out of love?'

She holds his gaze with a kind of adult kindness he's never seen in her before. 'I want to show you something,' she says.

'I don't want to see. And Jesus never said it was okay to be gay or chop yourself up.'

'Bree—'

'*I don't care.*' He's just going to keep saying it, even though his thoughts are fragmenting and something's tearing at him, and if he can't drive it away then he can't ask her the big question. 'Anyway, it's not what the Bible says that counts. The Bible can mean whatever you want. It's what the Church says that matters. And the Church says it's a sin, and that being gay means you're mentally ill as well.'

Izzy's expression flashes with something more than indignation. 'And don't you think that's wrong?'

Brio's spun out again but he can't turn away. 'It *is* wrong.'

'That's not what I mean. I mean it's wrong to only welcome trans people to the Church on the premise that they're mentally ill and need to be healed. And how can the Church say that gay and trans people shouldn't have intimate relationships until they've been *cured*? Some gay or trans people may be mentally ill, and it's always them who make the news, but it's not being gay or trans that makes them mentally ill. It's their confusion and the self-hate that comes out of how society sees them. But if being trans or gay *was* a mental illness, the Church is even more wrong. Because then they'd be saying that people aren't entitled to have intimate relationships if they're mentally ill. How can that be a message of love when it's love above all else that has the power to heal functional mental illness? How can a person be deliberately denied love because they're ill? What would Jesus say about a church like *that*?'

Brio's head beats as if someone's doing it *to* him and he tries to bury what she said. But like everything Izzy's ever said, her words become an instant part of his being and now he doesn't know who to hate and who to believe. All he knows is that his mum's closing in around him. 'How can you say the Church is evil?'

'I'm saying the Catholic Church is a human corporation, the relic of an empire that held Europe together for five hundred years.'

It's kept going by huge wealth and glamour and the human need for consolation and continuity, and certainty. That's a powerful product but it's just a corrupt civic institution that no longer has anything to do with the message Jesus brought.' Her eyes flash again. '"Who am I to judge?" says the supposedly enlightened Pope. Who indeed? And how convenient that he's also spared the simple task of judging it to be a love like any other.'

Brio marvels at Izzy's eloquence, but he realises she's written it a thousand times on social media, and one day she'll be speaking it in front of large audiences, even in the Houses of Parliament. When its full meaning finally dawns, he recoils against the edge of the countertop. She's a servant of the Dark Lord who's been sent to destroy the Church.

But he remembers that he doesn't know whether he still thinks the Church is good or bad. Because if the Pope hadn't broken Father T's heart first, he'd never have collapsed on the garden path at Bluebells. 'Who cares about the Church anyway? It's what Father T said that counts. And he did say it was a sin.'

Izzy's eyes are still alight but her expression softens. 'Is that what he really believed, though? I mean, if he agreed with the Church, why did he leave?'

'Because he loved Bella.'

'Exactly. And he knew that the Church was wrong to stop him getting married. I think he knew in the end that it was okay to be non-binary as well.'

'He *didn't*. And if he thought he did, it was because Bella put it into his head.' But just saying Bella's name makes Brio wish that she and Father T had been able to sail away into the rose-golden glow like Mr T'wit and Bling. How can he ever remake everything so they really can?

'Bree, don't you remember the sermon Father T gave that really shocked everyone? The one after Mr and Mrs Larson's baby died before it could be baptised and Mrs Larson ended up in the Northview Wing?'

'What's that got to do with anything?'

'Well, it shows that Father T was having doubts about a lot of Catholic teaching. It's a huge thing for a priest to tell their congregation that the Church is totally wrong about something. But that's the only reason Mrs Larson became mentally ill, because she was convinced her baby would be in limbo forever and never go to Heaven, so they'd never be reunited with her again. And even though Father T told her it was rubbish and her baby would be in Heaven if that's what she wanted, she was so indoctrinated she refused to believe anything but the Church's teaching. That's why she's still in the Northview, even after three years, and Mr Larson's making a complete mess of raising their other daughter because he's such a wreck himself. I mean, what do we really want to believe in, the message of Jesus, or rules made up by old men who just put burdens on others while living in their state of luxuriant, theoretical humility? And Father T *did* believe in the message of Jesus. And he knew that God will always meet us at our own level, in the way that's right for the way things are at that time and place.'

Brio fights to resist Izzy's eloquent poison, but he can't stop himself thinking that maybe Father T did think it was okay to be gay or whatever else. And what if it *is* okay? As his gaze dances around with Izzy's, he confronts the most dreadful thought of all: how can he ask her to be with him forever if it's simply that he loves her so much he doesn't realise he's gay or trans? Or maybe he does realise, but he can't admit it to himself because then he'll lose her. He sees that it must have been something like this between his father and his poor mum. He has to break the chain and stop it happening or it will happen to his son too, and his son's son, all the way down the human race. And it's for him to stop it here and now. Him the Chosen One.

'Bree, there really is something I have to tell you.'

He plugs his ears and lets the seashell wind-rush block out the world. But the mocking and pitying faces have already invaded his head, and they're demanding to know how he could possibly not be gay with such a lack of father figure and a mad woman who over-mothered him into non-existence. The faces press forward like everyone in the spare room at Izzy's, making him look at all the evidence that's been there his whole life: his weedy body, his love of poetry and books, his failure to think the right kind of thoughts about Izzy. Even when he thinks about jumping from the clifftop, he hears Mr T'wit scoffing and telling him he wouldn't get a hundred yards, because he's a coward too, *like father like son*. And that's right. That *is* why his father's still alive. Because he didn't have the courage to be a Roman and fall on his own sword.

The thought that his father never had the guts to kill himself triggers renewed panic that he won't have the courage to jump either. He'll need Tania's tisane and a triple dose of the wipe-out meds from the strong-arm nurses, and a whole bottle of the cognac that helped his mum face the world. Yes, of course he knew that the secret bottles Pippa bought weren't just for his mum. They were for her and Father T together, during those quiet nights after little Bree had gone obediently to bed. Oh, God. Is no one what they seem?

But *no*. He does not need false courage. He's already sworn the vow never to fail again. And he'll prove it once and for all by leaping into the abyss in a state of pure unassisted self-reliance. And his conundrum about Pippa's money is resolved as well. Because she can sue Zpydr and social services for sending an idiot whose incompetence caused her house to be burned down. And then she can marry that same idiot, because she loves him too, and how could she not be happy to live in this cottage that really is

Bluebells reborn?

Now that nothing in his conscience stands between him and his fate, he turns to face Izzy. 'I have to know about *us*. I have to know now.'

Izzy can't conceal her gulp. 'Bree, I did want to tell you something, and you do have to know. But right now I've got to show you something even more important.' She takes out her sticker-covered tablet and gestures for him to sit next to her at the table.

The intoxicating musk of Izzy's new scent so deranges his already disordered feelings that he barely notices her tapping and swiping, and it takes him several seconds to register that he's staring at a photograph on the screen that seems to have nothing to do with anything: a woman in well-worn jeans and a purple checked shirt under a padded waistcoat, with naturally wavy shoulder-length hair and eyes that twinkle humorously. The kind of woman who spends her time outdoors, probably with animals—somewhere nice and sunny. It's hard to tell her age. Thirty? Forty-five? When he finally understands what he's looking at, the shock knocks him backwards but Izzy's coiled ready and clutches his arm so tightly that it hurts.

'Please,' she says. 'Just look. And keep an open heart.'

When the image changes, Brio flinches at how small the woman looks next to the horse. Behind her, there's a jump built of pretend castle blocks and a square pond of water. But there it is again, the same smile with the same twinkling eyes. Another screen-swipe from Izzy and the woman appears on an outdoor stage at a microphone in front of a line of kids in riding gear.

Izzy gently works a wireless earphone into his ear and in some new dimension he watches a huge horse seem to stall in mid-air before sailing over an impossibly high fake wall. The elegantly poised rider tips gracefully forward for the landing and rights herself to a prim straight back as the horse canters away triumphantly through a giant arch of flowers, while the stadium crowd cheers and the commentator gushes hyperbole about world records and grace.

Brio scarcely registers the change of venue as the woman shakes hands with a royal lady he recognises and receives a medal. The next graceful swipe takes them to fluttering Olympic flags and the woman's being interviewed next to a different horse. He jolts at the sound of her voice, but she's talking too fast for him to think, with a smiling lilt, calm and relaxed. Her accent is that soft Irish like his mum's but mixed with the lady at church who came from New Zealand. She agrees into the reporter's microphone that the move from jumping to training was psychologically and emotionally challenging, but the success she had with a horse that everyone had written off was a reward that paved the way to what she hoped would be a *grand old future* in training.

'That was three years ago,' Izzy whispers. 'She's trained loads of other champion showjumpers since then.'

With Brio suspended in a shrinking hiatus, Izzy taps and scrolls faster. He has no choice but to watch the woman in a dusty round-yard baked in a glare of bright sunshine. She's turning on her heels, a horse prancing circles around her on the end of a long leash while the reporter talks about a long road to recovery being like the determination needed to train some of the world's top showjumpers.

'Why's she limping?' Brio hears himself ask after the scene has cut to the woman walking towards the camera in a large indoor arena. When Izzy explains that she was deliberately hit by a car for being a trans woman, he wants to kill the person who could do such a thing. But the scene's changed again, this time to a close-up interview at the timber wall of the round-yard. She's saying that yes, she does forgive her attacker and that, even though anyone who's never faced this lack of choice about who they are will always struggle to understand, she hopes attitudes will change so that the very many people like her can live complete lives without fear of violence.

Leaving Brio one taut thread away from breakdown, Izzy scrolls again and drops them into the audience of a chat show, where those twinkling eyes have just finished laughing at something, and the audience is clapping.

'Talking to you now, Robi,' says the chat show host, 'you come across as so unassuming. When you're going over those jumps, though, we see a very different person.'

'Well, I think when you're on that horse, Jim, you *are* a different person, because you're part of the animal, if you like, and the animal's part of you. You just need to let it know that you believe in what you're doing, then it'll go with you all the way.'

'So when the attack happened and you couldn't ride anymore, that was a terrible blow.'

'It was, Jim. It was the worst moment of my life.' She pauses. 'Well, the second worst. But you know, in life you have to get back on the horse. And, if you can't do that, you have to help other people get on theirs instead. That's given me more joy than riding for myself.'

The audience claps, while Robi adds that she *can* still ride, just not to the level needed to keep the horse safe in competitive situations. Jim nods to show that he's done with this question and says he'd like to touch on the gender issue a bit more. 'I mean, obviously the attack led to a terrible period in your life, but given your celebrity status and your ability to influence public opinion, do you feel you're doing enough for trans rights?'

The audience goes quiet and her face becomes so serious that Brio stops breathing.

'Well, the way I see it, Jim, I'm here today talking to you as an equestrian and a helper. That's who I am, it's what I do … what I love. And if that's all we talk about and I can share my passion like any member of society, then that's the best thing I can do for people in my position. No song and dance. Because you know, Jim, above all else, trans people are really nothing special.'

Jim nods and a few people clap but it's feeble and there are grumbles too, and Jim doesn't seem happy with the answer. When Robi can only pull an apologetic face, Brio feels a helpless plunge of sympathy.

'Nothing special?' Jim says. 'You mean—'

'Exactly that, Jim. Being trans doesn't make me special. Why should it?'

For the first time, Jim looks uncertain and glances at the audience.

'Perhaps we could talk about my book,' Robi suggests.

'Absolutely,' Jim agrees and reaches for the brightly coloured hardback that's sitting between them on a glass coffee table. 'Now, I know you've said you'd like to stick to talking about horses, but in your autobiography you've written a lot about your early life in Ireland and the effects of being raised in a pretty conservative environment. You talked about the difficulties of growing up in a community that you knew might ostracise you if they found out, at the very least try to cure you—maybe forcibly. You've talked about your ambivalence around the Catholic Church. I'm sure a lot of people are wondering whether you really are so at peace with all that, or whether there may still be some anger there—not just towards the Church but maybe even towards your mother?'

Robi loses her twinkle but stays dead still in the big orange seat. 'No, Jim, there's no anger at all. It was hard for me, I must admit. People let you down. But you can't hold things against anyone who's done their best for you. I just hope that when my dear old mum looks down from wherever she is, she can see that people like me are able to have happy and successful lives—that we can contribute in all sorts of ways.'

The audience claps, and when some people whistle as well Brio even feels he wants to join in.

'As for the Church itself ...' The twinkle in Robi's eye suggests that she wants to surf the new happier mood. 'Well, they obviously haven't read their own book. I mean, from what I can remember, woman was made out of a man, so I do feel I've been given a bit of a blessing here.'

There's a half laugh, but Brio can see that Jim doesn't want her to make it fun and easy. He wants conflict and drama so the audience can bay and love being upset.

'And what about family?' Jim asks with a slight edge. It's clear he's going to keep pushing till something gives. 'Do you think your mum would have wished for grandkids?'

Robi loses her smile again and Brio freezes.

'That's a hard question too, Jim, because as you know I love working with kids. But ... well, to have your own needs time and commitment.'

'You've never thought of adopting?'

As Robi gathers her thoughts, Brio finds himself holding his breath.

'Well, you know, Jim, when you don't have that mad pressure to start a family, you get a chance to think about it properly. You ask yourself whether you really have the time to make a good job of being a parent. I mean, the people I know in my position who've started a family, they really wanted kids from their heart—because that's the only place it can come from, right? And they've been the best parents I know.' A cheer from the audience cuts her off and the clapping and whistling rolls on.

Brio slumps back in the chair. 'She never even wanted me.'

Izzy pulls him close and he's so shocked by the paralysing

euphoria that he loses all contact with Robi and Jim and their fickle audience.

'So for Robi Galla it'll always be the career?' says Jim. 'Definitely no kids for the woman who's done more for young people's showjumping and disabled riding than anyone else in the country?'

Robi takes a long breath and looks up, while Brio becomes such a mayhem of emotions that he wants to do every opposite thing in the world at the same time.

Looking back down from the unseen studio ceiling, Robi says, 'I think once you've had a dream like having a kid, Jim, it can never be truly replaced by another.'

The audience doesn't know how to react and nor does Brio.

'What does she mean?'

Izzy draws him closer still and he feels the sheer physical warmth of her upper arm. 'Your dad means that no one can ever replace *you*.'

'And still no Mr Right?' asks Jim. 'Or Mrs Right?'

Robi laughs and the corners of her eyes wrinkle. 'Well, I *am* an old-fashioned girl, Jim, and the horses, you know, they take all of your time and attention. But hey, every now and again they kick you in the head, so you never know what you might think tomorrow.'

Not knowing what reaction he wants from the audience, Brio's thrown by the stony silence and needs Izzy to hold him more tightly again. But Jim comes to life like he's been handed the key to the candy jar.

'And that's an interesting point, Robi. Because in your book, you do talk a lot about being a traditional woman, and I know this has drawn some pretty heavy criticism from within your own community.'

Brio scrambles for bearings as the world keeps jolting round in quarter turns. 'Can't he see she doesn't want to talk about stuff like that?'

'It's hard for her,' Izzy says, drawing him tightly against her again. 'But listen.'

'Jim, as you know,' Robi says, 'I'm not a political person at all, and I do find it hard to talk about this side of things. And I've never said anything about how other people should make this journey.'

'But obviously,' Jim presses, 'after the attempt on your life— I mean, we know how much the physical injuries changed your career, but the reaction from some people in the trans community must have left some pretty deep scars too.'

Robi's face tenses and Brio's fists clench. He wants to kill the evil chat show host for making cheap entertainment out of someone's goodness of heart.

'Well, yes …' Robi begins, but Jim cuts her off.

'I mean, how *did* it feel to have members of your own community saying they wished you'd been killed by that car? Were you surprised by the level of abuse on social media?'

Brio's stomach twists at the thought of his dad suffering at the hands of people even crueller than Darcy used to be.

'Well of course it was painful, Jim,' says Robi. 'But you know—'

'Though there *is* a serious point here,' Jim cuts in. 'I mean, what *is* your reaction to these accusations that you've become the acceptable face of the trans community to a still dominant patriarchy? That you should be doing more to defend against the claims that being trans is just a fashion that's got out of control, that it's just glorified escapism, just another form of social protest against the patriarchy like so many before. How do you respond to those who say you should be using your position to bring awareness of the challenges that most trans people face—the prejudice and injustice, the mental illness and exclusion, the overrepresentation of sex work, the violence?'

When Robi loses her composure into a fraught massaging of the forehead, Brio slaps the table and breaks Izzy's hug. 'He's got no right to do that. Why can't she just be what she wants?'

'The thing is, Jim,' Robi says, pulling herself together, 'even if you're not devoting your life to training the top jumpers, and to kids and disabled riding ... it's hard to talk on behalf of people whose experience is very different from your own. I know what some trans people have called me. But every woman I know is different, so every take on what womanhood should be is going to be narrow too. I can only be who I actually am, Jim. The mental illness, the sex work, the crime, my heart breaks for those folk. They're my folk too. But everyone has their own journey.' She leans forward as though to forestall the grumbling, and when the camera zooms in to capture the precise emotions, Brio finds himself face to face with his father.

'I do a lot for people, Jim. There's only so much one person can do. And what it is—like I said in the book—I see my community as the whole world, and my own little nook in the world is horses and kids and people with physical challenges. To be honest with you, I'm not sure I really understand some of these issues around gender and sexuality. I mean, if you know you're a woman, then obviously you feel that gender's something real. If you don't believe there's any difference between men and women, why suffer the change?'

Even Brio knows that Robi's said something that some people won't like and the audience has gone stone-cold silent. As the camera scents blood too and moves in even closer, Brio misses whatever it was that Jim just asked.

'Well, this is what I mean, Jim. If you say that men and women are the same but you dress up as a woman or a man when you were born different to that, then how is that anything but dress-ups?

How can you change yourself if there's no difference to be changed?'

Discontent ripples through the audience and the camera switches to the sea of faces. But it's straight back to Jim so that he can say, 'I guess some people might take that as quite a controversial observation.'

Robi swallows and someone shouts something. Brio's stomach tightens but he sees in Robi's eyes a flash of that quiet determination.

'Well, it's like I said in my book, people can say that my being a particular type of woman reinforces gender stereotypes. But so does being any kind of woman compared with being gender neutral. But I am who I am, Jim, and I really wish people could simply see me as an equestrian who's comfortable in her own skin and just wants to leave the world a better place.'

Before Brio can work out what to think or feel, Izzy pauses the video, which leaves Robi in mid-smile, slightly blurred, with eyes accidentally skew-whiff and her lower jaw jutted out to one side. She suddenly looks demonic and Brio's whole dream-space collapses. Because that is *not* his mum and how could he have ever thought it was? It's his freak father, dressed as a woman in front of the whole world, and probably chopped up into one too.

In the window of the kitchen back door, Brio glimpses a watchful nurse, but all he can think of is his poor mum, having to do and be everything for little Bree because his freak father wants to help every other kid in the world except him. Because he abandoned them so he could go and be famous and have everyone worshipping him on TV. He's just pretending to be all nice when he's worse than Madame Haha. He rushes to block out the nurse with his back to the kitchen door. Through the stifled tears he can hardly speak. 'I don't want to be just friends. I want us to be together forever, like *normal* people.' He snaps his father's wedding ring off its chain around his neck and shoves it out at her. '*Tell me*. Will you be with me or not?'

The tears stream down her cheeks too and she steps out from behind the table to come to him. 'I love you so much. But I can't love you more than the way I do.'

Refusing to hear, he thrusts the ring harder. 'You have to take it. Make it ours forever.'

'We're so young,' Izzy says between sobs. 'And one day you'll find someone who's perfect for you.'

'I won't. Because Mum was right. You're the only one for me and my life will be terrible if I marry anyone else.'

Brio's revelation startles Izzy out of her tears. 'Your mum said *that*?' But before Brio can reply, she says, 'Bree, your mum was just saying it to be kind—and fun.'

'She wasn't. She told me that's what I had to do. And that if I couldn't marry you, I'd be gay and it'd be your fault.'

Izzy's eyes close and her face disappears into her hands. 'Oh, Bree.' But she returns quickly. 'Look, I know it's going to be hard to understand, but you will. And it could be such a bond between us. Bree, there's a reason I can't be with you that way. You know there is. And it's got nothing to do with you.'

She holds his gaze but he doesn't want to know. Because it's not going to be *her* fault he has to die. It's going to be the fault of that freak father who ruined his life.

An abrupt coldness brings clarity and intent. He must meet his father after all—one time and one time only—to press the Ring of Love into his hand and not let go. To take him down too, over the horizon and back to when it could have been different, when it could have been Mum and Dad and happy little Bree.

Unmoved by Izzy's look of anguish, Brio lets his mind run free with images of how it will happen. But just as he's drilling down into impossible details, he's interrupted by voices in the hallway.

Through the rippled glass he sees the outlines of Dr Kapoor and Dr Missle, other people too. But all that matters is getting to those cliffs for the world to see, the same world that gorged itself on his misery while Zpydr raked in the money.

'Okay,' he calls to the group that's formed in the corridor. He has to swallow hard to quash the tremble in his voice. 'I'm ready to meet him now.'

Danny Bellani's rippled shape appears at the glass. 'Hey, that's great news. Can we come in?'

'I'll join you in the lounge.'

'Great. You sound good.'

'I really am.'

As soon as they've gone, it's a race to speak first. 'Bree, what do you mean, you're going to meet the Hoggit? You're going to go to the cliffs?' Wide-eyed with alarm, she looks to the door.

'I meant I'm ready to meet my father,' he says menacingly, and when she edges to bar his way he demands to know what's wrong. 'I thought you wanted me to meet him. Because it's your dream, so you can be friends with a famous horse rider. So me and my freak father can be famous and destroy Zpydr and make the world like *that*.' He points at the deformed face on the screen. 'You think your dad'll warn everyone and they'll put me in a mental hospital for my own protection. But I'm never going to a mental hospital. Because I'm not sick—just like you said.'

There's no anguish on Izzy's face anymore, only sheer terror. 'Please. I have to tell you now. It'll change everything.' She reaches for him but he swipes violently at the air and ends up with a finger pointed at her face.

'Swear you won't say anything. Not about my sick father, and not about what I have to do.' When she remains frozen, he jabs the finger so it's almost touching her nose. 'Swear you won't say anything to anyone. Swear you'll leave me in peace. That's all

I want. To be with the Hoggit. In our perfect world.'

Izzy makes to speak but her mouth closes again as though of its own accord.

Keeping the finger pointed at her face, he uses his left hand to take hers, which bonds them in congealing blood. 'If you love me, you'll let me go. And you'll keep this as our most precious secret ever.'

Even as he releases her hand and stands back, Izzy still doesn't move or speak. At the door, he turns. 'Greater love hath no woman than that she let a friend lay down his life for *her*. And don't write that in your diary, or it'll come back to haunt you.'

27

AT THE END OF YET ANOTHER WORST DAY of his life, Brio's finally alone in his tiny room. He's so drugged up, so exhausted by his hours with the Zpydr people, and so broken by the loss of Izzy that he collapses onto the bed with the light on and falls asleep before he has the chance to be overwhelmed by the fear of what's to come.

He wakes to find himself staring out of the barred window at the cottage's ramshackle garden. In the spectral moonlight it's become a haunted graveyard and the valley down to the sea is the end of the world. As though from nowhere, he remembers something dreadful his father wrote in the letter: that he'd been sixteen when he *came out* to himself that he was supposed to be a girl. And what if it really does happen like clockwork as Professor Glybb said? In a few hours' time when the clock ticks past midnight and he himself turns sixteen, it's going to happen to him too—like father, like son. *I am in the Father and the Father is in me.*

At the thought that midnight might already have happened, he searches frantically for a clock. Finding nothing, he looks up at the moon and bemoans his inability to tell the time from celestial bodies alone. If only he'd had a dad who taught him all these ancient skills. His thoughts are about to disintegrate when he remembers with joy that he was born at five past midday, so he's not truly sixteen till lunchtime. Thank God he's meeting his father at eleven o-clock. He has a whole hour to end things before *he* becomes a freak too.

The relief is short-lived. Because what if his father arrives late? If it turns even one minute past midday before he's dragged them both over the edge, he might undergo a change of heart that makes him understand his father. He might even want to forgive him.

As he's cursing Logie for sneaking the worm of forgiveness into his brain, a tap at the door makes him jump.

'You need something to help you sleep,' says the nurse; Brio knows it's not a question.

The glass of water and pill on open palm confront him like the sacraments. And then as now, he has no choice but to let it happen.

When Brio wakes, it's not just a new day, it's a new world bathed in different light and a new mish-mash of smells. He sits up to find he's wearing pyjamas and his mouth tastes of toothpaste even though he can't remember cleaning his teeth. He has vague memories of being awake and having difficult thoughts. But as he looks out of the barred window into the little Eden that so reminds him of Bluebells, all memories of the small hours are gone and everything seems settled.

In the mellow morning light, the colours and brighter greens of the tumbledown garden seem to belong to yet another realm. Even the loss of his own comforting smell to the scent of laundered pyjamas seems like something in nature. A dragonfly buzzes and taps on the cracked pane of glass, seemingly desperate to tell him how good it is on the other side, though it's somewhere deeply *in*side that Logie's mum is still channelling the eternal *om*.

On the narrow bed that he's made with neat hospital corners and folded chin-hem, Brio lays out the new clothes Pippa bought for him in town: a checked shirt that reminds him of a tablecloth because it has too much yellow, jeans that she seems to have ironed, a light jacket that looks like a second shirt. If he didn't love

Pippa so much, he'd be outraged at having to die in such an outfit.

As he dresses, he remembers how his mum used to button him up for school: the well-pressed shorts and shirt, the striped tie he never quite learned to do up, the school shoes she brushed into blurred mirrors with too much polish and too many different brushes. He remembers too how sometimes it was Father T who helped him put on his uniform because his mum was tired from all her work at the church and had overslept.

Yet, gazing down the shallow valley to the sea, Brio finds it a pleasant thought that his mum discovered some kind of peace in her secret nights with Father T. If only Father T actually could have been his real father. Isn't that what everyone had thought? Isn't that what he himself had always secretly hoped?

Becalmed by an other-worldly repose reached through ritual transfused with medication, Brio stands quite still to dress himself, to revel in the sensation of his mum's hands fumbling his shirt buttons and giving a little tug on the brown leather belt.

Smiling unguardedly to himself, he's struck by how proud Madame Haha would be of his performance on the previous day with the Zpydr people, and how quickly he regained his composure after the terrible ending with Izzy.

'You must be experiencing some extreme positivity about the Hoggit,' the new Zpydr lady enthused.

Even though they were all crammed into the small sitting room, he felt like he was speaking to her as the guest on her chat show. 'Yes. Very positive indeed.'

'That's wonderful,' the lady said then introduced another lady called Simi Vallyn. 'Simi would like to talk a little about the things we think will happen after you've met the Hoggit and put the seal on this incredible act of personal change and growth.'

He sensed that Dr Missle wasn't very happy about what the other Zpydr people wanted, and he noticed the brooch that Simi

Vallyn wore on her bright blue jacket: a rainbow in the shape of a fan, just like the one Ms Whittle wore to Bookworm Club that caused such a huge row with Mrs Thorne.

Simi Vallyn then talked about the well-deserved attention he would soon receive and how he should conduct himself in the limelight. He was going to be a celebrity author, so he needed to learn how to perform in front of cameras, how to talk about the groundbreaking system of psychotherapy that had helped him out of the mental illness that would otherwise have led him to suicide. The Great Plea, said Simi Vallyn, was the ultimate self-help book, because it was written by his true subconscious self. Though be careful, she counselled, he should never sound like he's been coached. He certainly shouldn't come across as someone in some sort of enhanced mental state. He should simply present as the enthusiastic ambassador for CHANT*bot-vip* that he'd become, speaking always with spontaneous passion and gratitude for having survived his near-death experience. In fact, he should refer to it as an *actual* death experience, because in many ways he truly had been reborn.

'We need to take a look at your signature too,' added the seemingly genderless person called Janni-Marie. 'To make sure it's both visually appealing and psychologically upbeat. Also a little larger than your normal one. You need to press the pen hard into the paper to make your moniker look positive and strong. We like fountain pens, by the way. They give people a sense of old-world familiarity that fosters emotional engagement through nostalgic association.'

When they were done, Dr Missle said that despite the busy schedule of the next few weeks it was really important for him to complete his grief counselling programme. 'Because even though your dad died a long time ago, you've only just acknowledged the loss, so the grief is clear and present. We're confident that Logie can partner well as your grief counsellor.'

Then they all stood up and Danny Bellani clapped a hand on Logie's shoulder. 'Don't forget, my man, you're responsible for getting our star to the show tomorrow. Curtains up at midday, yeah?'

With the aromas of baked cake seeping into his room, Brio can't help wondering how many people die on their birthday, especially their sixteenth. To come of age by dying seems right, though, and maybe the people who die on their birthdays are the only ones who can be reborn, can come back and have a past life.

Turning to the mirror, he lifts his chin in the manner of Lord Rumbuck. The mirror's solid frame makes him an ancestral portrait and he holds himself as still as a lizard, his eyes the cold marbles of a ghoulishly sightless Roman bust. And why should he not resemble an ancestral portrait after all the past lives he's lived and all the things he's achieved since he first emerged from the stardust to which he will soon return? All the cells and organisms and genders he's ever been. All the different things that have led to this one gigantic nothing.

'You okay, Bree?' calls Pippa. He places her voice at the bottom of the stairs and is pleased she no longer needs to creep around and tap anxiously on the door.

'I won't be long,' he calls back, though somehow the final summons casts him into such bold definition in the mirror that he's transfixed by how real he looks, and how totally unlike himself. He feels the dull queasiness trying to break through again, because this really is the last time he'll leave the room, the last time he'll leave any bedroom. He'll never sleep again in the old-fashioned way that's plagued by unhappy dreams and cack-handed releases and rude awakenings. No more bittersweet, hot-and-cold messages from the gods. Just one super-quick moment of courage and he'll be with the real God forever.

Brio's about to leave the room when it comes to him that he must ensure complete orderliness before making his final trip to the castle. He must do all the things that people do in books and movies when they kill themselves in a civilised way. But how can he write a last will and testament when his only belongings were cremated in the attic fire? And if people can't understand the workings and superhuman logic from reading the Hoggit's Great Plea then what's a silly suicide note going to add?

Freed from all taint of earthly formalities, he's pitched unexpectedly into a hand-wringing about whether he should pray in a situation like this, and whether God would even want to listen. 'Our Father,' he whispers, 'who art in Heaven ...' But for the first time ever, the comforting chant feels strange. And surely it's as laughable that God should be a father as the idea of a father being God. Apart from anything else, if God was a father, it meant he had to have a penis, and God couldn't have a penis under that lavish sackcloth robe any more than he could have the smooth-cupped nothingness of the lighthouse keeper mannequin.

Kneeling at the side of the wobbly bed now, he closes his eyes and tries again. 'Our Creator ...' That sounds much better. But with the rest of the Lord's Prayer now in question, he doesn't know *what* to pray—how exactly to explain what he's decided to do. He daren't be angry with God, and he can't say sorry for not liking the way he was created because he has no objection at all to how he's been created. It's the world he rejects. But how can he complain about the world either if God created that too?

For some reason, Ms Whittle's talk of Buddhism comes to his mind and he's so appalled by the idea that he might be reincarnated back into the world that he recoils from the whole idea of making the jump. He comforts himself with the reminder that if Buddhism says nothing's real, then nor is Buddhism itself, and nor is anything it ever taught, and if Buddhist writings claimed that everything was impermanent, then those writings themselves must already have ceased to exist. So there's no such thing as reincarnation, which was in any event a dead loop like walking pointless circuits in back gardens, or like crop-circles or gyrating maces or blurred chases around dock yards, all dead loops that began and ended in a deliberate nowhere when what he needed was to end up somewhere very definite from where he could begin again, not end up in some state of perfect non-existence.

But still there needs to be a prayer before he leaves. And it needs to be a prayer about *something*, and addressed to some*one*. The Zpydr people claim that the Great Plea is the definitive scripture on God being no more or no less than one's own God within, but if he only addresses his prayer to some god of the stardust who lives inside his every cell, he'll be talking to nothing more than himself, and that for sure is the first and last sign of madness.

Forced to accept that the Lord's Prayer might be the only way, he bows his head and waits for words to flow. 'Almighty Creator …' he begins again in a whisper, but how could the Creator be in Heaven when Heaven had surely come from the Creator? It needs to be a prayer to, 'Almighty Creator, *in* whom lies Heaven, sacred be your unknowable name. Your realm of love come, your will be done, in our hearts and our world together.'

But who created the Creator? Did the Creator create Himself? No, not *Him*self. It's *Themself*. And how else can it be? Because if the Creator didn't also create the Creator then they couldn't be the Creator. Feeling his first serious disquiet since taking the decision to end his life, Brio finds himself asking how he could make such a huge leap when he didn't know who God was, when perhaps even God didn't know who God was, when there might not even be a God. How could he be confident to die when God might not be waiting for him as everyone always promised?

As always in moments of existential crisis, it's Father T who comes to the rescue. *You just need to believe in the story enough to make God real. And if that doesn't work, just give God a few human characteristics. That'll bring him to life, and then you'll be able to pray like He's in the same room.*

But sorry, Father T, that's not enough anymore. God has to be more than a storybook character. God has to be defined by something real. Something He does. *No*—by something you do … like pray. *Oh, God, I'm just going round in circles again. God help me.*

It takes Brio a few moments of frozen staring at the peeling wall to realise he actually has just stumbled upon the Holy Grail. Because that's right, isn't it? It isn't who you pray to that matters, it's *what* you pray. 'Oh, my God!' he cries in a whisper. 'That's it!' It's the very things and people you pray for that defines God!

'Bree?' Pippa's voice is on the edge of worry now. 'Your cake's ready.'

'I'm coming,' he calls back, but fresh anxiety curtails his euphoria and threatens panic over the number of people he has to pray for. He hurriedly presses his forehead down harder onto steepled fingers and begins a gentle, rhythmic nodding. But realising he's emulating Mrs Thorne's hallmark trait, he drops his hands and holds them in a clasp on the bed. But no, he *should* do it Mrs Thorne's way, as a mark of respect. And he should thank her for everything she tried to do for him over the years, most of all for keeping her knowledge about his father a secret and never telling a soul. Finally, he thanks her for having wanted him to believe his mum's story about the tropical disease in Africa. Because she was right. If he'd managed to suspend his doubt and believe in the same story as everyone else, he would indeed have been saved from all this harm. And he'd have lived a peaceful, happy life in the balmy bliss of ignorance.

He should thank Dr Shenoy too. The hapless doctor made lots of mistakes but he really had cared in his own ways, and these ways were real and practical. Izzy's mum had cared about him too. As had so many people. He just never understood. And Ms Whittle as well, she was like his mum and Madame Haha rolled into one, like Lord Rumbuck too, all loving others for themselves because their ability to love had been so messed up by people who'd been messed up by people who'd been messed up by whatever they were before evolving into people.

After this spiritual cleansing, Brio leaves his hermit's cell and goes to gather himself at the top of the stairs, to summon up the character who will enact the next couple of hours: that young man on the Zpydr jet who's keen to meet his estranged father, yet who at the same time is understandably apprehensive.

Glancing down the lopsided stairway, he hopes it can hold out for one last descent. What a crude and cruel irony it would be if he survived the jet plane ride and all the other life-and-death moments only to die in the collapse of some rotten stairs in an old house that hadn't been decorated for a hundred years. And that wouldn't just be wrong, it would be a cardinal sin for sure. Because if there truly was a God who lets us make our own decisions, then everyone had a right to write their own special, pre-ordained ending. And at the end of the day that was all he wanted: the right death to bring a proper close to the wrong life.

At the bottom of the stairs, outside the small living room where he spent all that time with the Zpydr people, Brio stops to gaze at the three nurses slumped back in old frilly armchairs.

'God knows how many laws I've broken,' Logie says and Brio jolts round to be flustered by the sight of Logie's gaunt face and dead but loaded eyes. As he makes for the kitchen, Logie grabs his arm.

'Look, I get that all this stacks up for you, okay? And if you finish the book and you're as sorted as you seem, the money's going to zip through to Pippa. But she doesn't care about that and nor do I. We only care about you. And do you really want to help Zpydr make people think their crap actually works? Because the world *is* stark raving mad and this gig really could sway public opinion and get decision makers over the line. And Zpydr's been doing plenty else besides. Bottom line, I don't believe you want this and I don't believe you're anywhere near as sorted as you make out. Come on, talk to me.'

'Let go of my arm.'

'For God's sake, I know it can't happen overnight, but if you can find it in your heart to forgive your dad, then the Hoggit is alive for all time and Zpydr dies. But if you can't, it's the Hoggit who's dead and—'

He shakes off Logie's arm and tells him that the Hoggit will never die. 'And you know that full well.'

In the kitchen, Brio finds Pippa waiting beside the ingratiatingly large cake: a model of the lighthouse with waves of blue marzipan and white icing breaking against a fake rock from the garden centre. They've even created a replica sky-glass dome with the transparent bell-lid of a family-size ice cream tub.

'What do you reckon?' Logie asks, wiping his eyes.

'It's great.' Brio quickly adds a laugh to emphasise his appreciation of the humour. To exclude Logie's worried glances with Pippa, he silently counts to check they've placed the correct number of candles.

With his good hand, Logie lifts the dome and painstakingly sets the candles alight. Before Brio can stop them, they're singing *Happy Birthday*, but it sounds like they can't make it end quickly enough.

'Thank you,' Brio says emphatically to cut short the final *yooo*.

'But you know, I'm not actually sixteen until five past midday.'

While they do a laugh, he looks at the clock. To be safe they must leave in twenty minutes. 'I think we should say grace,' he says, which draws awkward *yes-of-course* kind of faces.

Peeking through lightly fluttering eyelashes to make sure they're following suit, Brio finds that his own version of the Lord's Prayer has grown and become more fluent. '… and help us break bread with those who hunger, that all may share life with joy and wonder.'

It's as though he's been waiting to speak this version all his life and the next lines are so clear he needs to keep it rolling. But there's something even more pressing to be said to Pippa and Logie. 'I do mean *thank you*. Because I know you did your best. You're good people with good hearts, and from now on you can stop worrying about me and have a nice life of your own.' And when Pippa and Logie both make to speak, he adds hurriedly that it's not only them he has to thank. 'I know that everyone did their best for me and I'm sorry I didn't recognise it at the time. I was young and bad things happened to me. So this is my prayer, to say thank you to everyone, and especially both of you.'

'Wow,' Logie says quietly when it's clear that Brio has finished. 'That's really nice.'

'It's beautiful,' Pippa agrees, though her voice sounds uncertain, and when he opens his eyes she has to quickly turn her look of apprehension into a smile.

'I'll blow out the candles now,' Brio says and, with a force that threatens to divulge his true inner feelings, he extinguishes the candles in one last blast of church organ.

Pippa hesitates for only a fraction of a second before handing Brio the large knife, with which he rents a crevice at the base to represent Mr T'wit's secret cave. This brings down the whole fragile edifice, and after the fussing and cobbling together of cake rubble onto three plates is done, Pippa says, 'How about that first drink?' She glances at a bottle of champagne that's sitting in its cooler-sleeve on the kitchen counter.

'I'd like that,' Brio agrees, though he worries that the alcohol might weaken his resolve. He reassures himself with the reminder that the last time he stuffed down a whole load of alcohol and cake, he was unstoppable.

A loud pop is followed by the clumsy decanting of froth and a clinking of glasses.

'A glass of twinkling moonlight,' Logie suggests, which draws an indulgent groan from Pippa and helps Brio to see at last how it was that Logie failed as a screenwriter.

'It's not really my first alcoholic drink,' Brio says. 'I stole a bottle of whisky from a homeless guy in London.'

Leaving them to digest this chastening image on their own, he finishes the glass of champagne and stuffs down two large blocks of castle topped by dense, sweet mortar.

After a minute of chewing to murmurs of feigned appreciation, Brio is unexpectedly rushed by another wave of euphoria and can't stop himself wondering whether he's got the whole thing wrong. How can he take a woman to her death? No real man does violence to a lady, even a fake one. Even the fake Lord Rumbuck wouldn't have done such a thing.

From there, it all goes awry, with a plea to God for his father to be normal and not a hero at all. Just a workaday dad who kicks a ball and washes the car on Sundays—even takes his turn at the sink.

'Are you okay?' Pippa asks.

'Yes. Sorry. I was just thinking about Father T.'

'To Father T,' Logie says swiftly, raising his glass. 'A true father.'

They clink again and Brio says, 'To Bella too. May she rest in peace. And may we ourselves rest easy, certain in the knowledge that she died in a genuine accident.'

He knows the mood's been dented, and Logie's mention of a true father has triggered a mess in his head. He has to get going *now*, even if it's too early.

'Oh, by the way,' Pippa says, going quickly to the counter. 'Izzy sent you a birthday card. There's another one too.'

The sight of Pippa once again holding out two envelopes sends a shudder. On the light pink one he recognises the fancy italics of Darcy's famous fountain pen. He takes both envelopes and draws back into the corner to open Darcy's first.

> Love to love y'arl,,, bro. Happy Bbbirthday. Come any time. Sweet sixteen! The food's gone crappo!!! BYO yo! Worst holiday camp evrrrrr but all limpid now. Limpid ha! That means clear as nothing to see. Except they're trying to fix me up and think I maybe not be gay or whatever. But you know what I say to that? I say they're trying to put me in a straight jacket! Lol lol lol geddit? Straight jacket!!! Loads of words in here you'd love them whizz. God is great! Be good. Take care of Izzy till a big hello. We'll look after each other. Write some good pudding. Life's great as a sandwich on toast. When's a normal non-crappo dinner by the way? By the by before bye bye,,, when you come …

Unable to take any more of poor Darcy, he opens Izzy's letter. Before he's even found the beginning, it's pouring out all the good things about his *dad*. And if he wants to know what makes a good father, she says, he simply has to remember that any quality that would make someone a good father would make them a good mother too. He wants to reject her claim outright. Even his freak father knows that men and women are different. He ransacks his brain for some quality in a good father that can't also be found in a mother, and for anything about a good father that wouldn't also make a good mother. But what *is* a good mother? Has he ever experienced one? Yes of course he has. Because his mum might have failed him, but didn't she do her best? And isn't that enough? Maybe what makes a good mother is that they always fail in some way, so the kid has to learn to stand on its own feet, so it knows it should never depend on anyone else.

Knowing he's about to be ensnared by his eternal quest for logic in places where certainty can never prevail, he reads on and finds Izzy's passionate assertion that his mum and dad *did* love each other. Over the page, his hands clammy now, Izzy shouts at him in purple block capitals that she loves him as much as any human can love. She shouts other things besides, drawing him helplessly into her passion, until there it is—

> ... I swear to God and on my life I'll keep your secret safe and give you the freedom to die if that's what you really want. All I ask is that you destroy this letter before you go, just like you destroyed your dad's.

With a dull tingle, the blood drains from the top of his head. Suddenly, he can only breathe in short, sharp pants. Because she really will keep his secret to the bitter end. And out of that same love, she'll bear his death on her conscience for the rest of her life. Oh, God, how can he burden poor Izzy with such heartache if he truly loves her as much as she loves him? How can he not honour her love by staying alive when all he really has to do is put up with the mere humiliation and disappointment of his father not being what he dreamed? Maybe Zpydr's perfect world on earth really is the only way humans can be happy, with their minds pacified by a force billions of hearts and minds greater than the sum of their own. Maybe it was only in such an impossibly perfect world that a love like his and Izzy's could live. The kind of perfect world in which there was no one left to hold you back with tethers as they clung desperately to what they couldn't understand.

And there they are, the words she so badly needed to say to him, the great reveal he's been blocking out with his own pain.

> Which means I don't properly know, I suppose. Maybe I'm gay, maybe trans. It's a journey and journeys are good. Who knows what the future holds?

Oh, God. The final impossibility. His mind races for answers, for deliverance. Maybe she'll change. Maybe she's just caught up in a fad and love will bring her home. Maybe she's just mistaken.

But no. Maybe the connection between them truly does live above the tawdry essentials of the physical. Maybe theirs could be the most divine merging of all, writing together like kids, wielding that godlike power to create a truly immortal incarnation—the highest form of procreation known to humans. And that finely carved nib never breaking through the page after page of virgin birth.

28

EVEN WITH WINDSCREEN VISORS DOWN against the unexpected sunshine, Brio feels his resolve beginning to crack. And with Pippa so close and so burning to speak, he can't bear the idea of not giving her this one last chance. Oh, God, how can he be doing this to any of them? How can he never again luxuriate in the familiar aromas of Pippa's car—the fabric and chewing gum, the air-freshener and old walking boots in the back? How can he never again feel its ribbed seats and rest his hand on the awkward armrest?

He finds himself wishing Darcy could be there too, to see a truth that would magic away all the bad stuff that had driven them mad. The father who used to beat them as a kid, even when they weren't a kid anymore. The father who beat their mum too. Not a good father at all. Not a father like his own, the man who simply found himself in an impossible predicament with the woman he loved, where no one was to blame and everyone tried to do the right thing.

But if no one had done anything wrong, there was still nothing and no one to forgive, and unless he can truly forgive something big, there can never be an end to all this, even after he's gone. But how can you know who and what to forgive if you don't understand what causes everything to happen in the first place? How can you have Original Forgiveness when you don't know if God is real? *Forgive us our sins*, he chants in his head, trying to keep his mind clear. Better to think nonsense than let himself visualise that drop. But Tabo Forzac was right, those words aren't enough, and they're wrong. They should be *Help us learn to forgive by earning from others, the forgiveness of actions our failings uncover*.

The fragile epiphany takes him back to his wrangling about parents who do their best but fail, which takes him straight on to Izzy's letter, and however hard he tries, he can't find a way to defeat her claim. But there *must* be qualities that only apply to fathers? And the same with mothers. There can't only be things that make a good *parent*, full stop. And even if Ms Whittle was right that God can only be found on earth where male and female are both present, and that God is above gender, how can mothers and fathers be the same? How can there be no difference between boys and girls? How on earth can there be a world without the tense duality that breeds the seemingly chaotic clamour of life? And how is he meant to pray to God if God isn't the tough, rational, male presence in the sky that makes possible and gives structure to the naturally abundant maternity of earth? How can he ever let go of the male God when it's the only thing that keeps him in communion with his mum? And how can he die with so many questions unresolved?

Oppressed by Pippa's stark silence, he sits up straight and takes a calming breath. All this must surely be simpler than he thinks. There must be one easy question that has one easy answer. And yes, there it is! Right from the Hoggit's own mouth. *Why can't you just trust God?* said his god of gods. And that really is all he has to do: pray for the right prayers, then God will be waiting to catch him and raise him up.

But is it really the same God that his mum believed in? Maybe she didn't even believe in God at all, she just wanted there to be a God because she wanted to keep alive the bond of shared belief with her own mum or dad. Because a family that prays together plays together, spends the rest of its days together, and passes that light down the generations. But his mum's gone and his dad's got no womb, so the chain's broken and there's no more light. He was the last generation.

'Sure you're okay?' Pippa asks.

'I'm *fine*. Just keep your eyes on the road.' He feels an immediate pang at having been sharp with her. How can they part under such a cloud when he'll never get another chance to make it right? 'I'm *sorry*. I didn't mean to be like that. I love you.'

She glances and clutches his knee. 'Oh, Bree. The things you've had to go through.' She quickly looks back to the road and holds the wheel with both hands. 'There,' she says with a smile that didn't work. 'I'm driving carefully.'

He forces himself back to the comforting certainty of planning the detail, picking up exactly where he left off—fretting about how he can coax his father to join him at the very edge of the cliff.

But of course—he just has to tell his father about the Cosy Nook and how it was his mum's most special place in the world. He'll tell him how he was so scared of heights that he could never make himself approach the edge, never prove to his mum that he had the courage she never really wanted him to have. But he'll tell his father that he *has* overcome that fear and that, since his mum can't be here to witness it for herself, he wants to prove it to *him*, his father. And if his father still hedges after that, still won't meet him at the cusp, he'll recite the exact words his mum used to say whenever they gazed out from the Cosy Nook—that *it truly is the only place on earth from which our fragile perch in this ferociously balanced universe can be sensed with complete clarity. The one place where we can witness that ferocious balance of equal and opposite reactions. For every back a forth, every down an up, every wrong a right, and every take a give. This is how all things started and it's how they all shall end. Yet it is, in the same breath, the same reason that there was no start and there will be no end. Amen.*

But what exactly happens when they're right there on the precipice, father and son? Does he just extend a hand to make formal greeting then grip tightly and pull him over the edge? Surely there needs to be a pause for contemplation, some sort of action to mark the moment, to give his father that brief second of realisation. So it must be a hug, and his father must think it's real. Then they must stand there on the edge of the abyss, entwined in their own unique double-helix of a hug. But as they shuffle imperceptibly towards the drop, his father will understand that it's not a double-helix at all, it's two snakes locked into an embrace that looks like the closest kind of love but is in fact a silently squeezing fight to the death.

And that's what he wants to experience too: the precious split second between the truth dawning on his father and the rush of air—the precise moment his father understands that he failed when he could have done better, that he's destroyed a life that wasn't his to waste, that he's paying the proper price for entry into that perfect world beyond the horizon. Then after clearing the highest wall he's ever jumped, it'll be joy and downhill all the way. And they'll just keep going, in a dead-straight blur of golden speed, skimming the water, feeling the sun on their backs, till they disappear over the horizon to meet his mum in a blaze of light and warmth. Then they'll all keep going together, hand in hand, all the way round and round, and round and round, till they're no longer going but coming, till they're freed from the feeble past and born again strong, back here and now in that moment of nothingness between the baggage of the past and the hope for a future where nothing happened and nothing ever will.

When Brio sees that one of the two empty cars in the lighthouse car park has a rental company sticker, it all becomes sickeningly real. He glances up at the lighthouse through the windscreen, but his great castle in the sky belongs to someone else and he withers under the ominous glower of its blank windows and doorless block walls.

On seeing the real-life human being in jeans and light jacket who's sitting on a smooth rock at the foot of the lighthouse, Brio feels sick again. His whole plan's a bad dream and the idea of throwing himself off the cliff a ridiculous joke. The next moment, he's struck by the terrible finality and back in the heartache about Pippa missing him when he's gone, and Logie too, and Ms Whittle and Izzy. The ache becomes a physical longing and his hand clamps down on Pippa's. Tearful, they fall into another awkward, twisted hug and he tells her that he *will* see her again, he promises. But he squeezes so hard that she flinches and he sees over her shoulder that his father has stood up and is looking at them.

As the car door clunks shut behind him, his mind is already cleared of the parting with Pippa and he walks fast for the start of the rough track that leads down past the lighthouse. Even with his eyes lowered to pick out every footfall, Brio trips and stumbles on the uneven gauntlet of loose stones and gorse roots. Breaking out onto open grass, he forces himself to look up, and now he can make out an expression that looks like a fake smile made worse by trepidation. But where's the contrition in that face? The humility?

Drawing closer, Brio has to spur his legs to keep moving. But he's going too fast and worries that he'll cause alarm. He quickly tries to turn his purposeful stride into an unthreatening amble, and after an intense count of ten steps he looks up again. The distance between his father and the edge of the cliff is less than three cars. The old terror dissolves his bowels, exactly as he'd feared. Now it's not just about luring his father to the edge, it all hangs on whether he himself can make it those last crucial yards.

His next glance lasts too long, because his father's face is close enough to be fully real and even in the flesh there's no hint that this person was once a man. Instead of the dangerous weirdo he needs to see, there's only kindness and an equal longing. But when his father smiles, it's an alien creature that can only be a lure into something grotesque and it has to be defeated.

Relieved at the return of revulsion, Brio veers and heads for the exact spot where he needs to place himself, directly in line with the Cosy Nook. But the closer he gets to the edge, the weaker his legs become and he trips in the long grass. When he makes it to within a yard of the drop, he's trembling so violently that he's all but forgotten the need to make his father come too. But his father's already approaching, with careful steps and a smile full of that fragile yearning. And each time she looks down to avoid tripping he wants her to *keep* looking down, so he can grab hold and throw them both into the gaping vacuum that's already clasping his ankles. He only just manages to stop himself glancing round at the drop and giving it all away.

'Happy birthday, love.' And when he can't speak, she says, 'I'm sorry you've had such a rough ride.'

'Because of you.'

'It's a lot to forgive, love. If you can't, I'll understand. But thank you for meeting. It means a lot to me.'

His toes curl to fight the shivering in his legs. He fights the gentleness in her voice too, her lovely soft accent. The face that looks normal and loving like his mum's never did. He knows it has to be now, before it all goes wrong.

'Love, I can't change the past, but for as long as I'm here on this planet, I'm here for you now. If that's what you'd like.'

He fights tears with screwed-up eyes. He has to get her to the edge before she says anything else, and its his father's very presence that's taken away his fear. He can't stop himself turning round and glancing down at the breaking swell and rocks. The sight spins him out and he almost loses his footing.

When he turns back, her expression has changed. He panics that he's given it away. He has to make those worried eyes trust him again. Those beautiful eyes in the gently weather-beaten face that longs to be smiling. How can her skin be so smooth and soft? How can this be his *father*?

He wrestles the wedding ring out from the tangle of manufacturing fluff in his jeans pocket. Without looking up, he lunges it at her on an open palm. 'Take it.'

When she doesn't move, he looks up to see that her lips have drawn in on themselves and a tear is running down the side of her nose.

'*Take it.*'

She still doesn't move. The ground's surely about to crumble and give way. He has to fight the burning need to step back from the edge.

'I loved your mum,' Robi says, but she has to gather herself before she can go on. 'I always loved her. She knew I did. A real, deep love. We knew each other since we were kids.' Her words are flowing now, she must have rehearsed the speech a hundred times. 'Maybe in a different world it could have been enough— somehow. And I've never stopped loving her, love. Never been for anyone else. We never divorced. We were married till the day she died. I've wished so much that everything could have been healed before she went.'

The sound of her voice and all those beautiful words do everything to Brio at once. She hasn't rehearsed it all. It's all natural. He has to find his anger and make it happen. 'Why didn't you try to find me?'

But he doesn't want to hear about how many times in the past she travelled from Australia because she thought she'd managed to track him down. He wants rage. He wants that grotesque face in the freeze-frame on Izzy's tablet. 'You touched me,' he hears himself say. 'You did bad things to make me love you in the wrong way.'

Shock breaks through her tight, silent tears. 'Lord, no, love. Who could have put such a thought in your head?'

Brio feels sick with remorse. Where had such terrible idea come from when he knew it wasn't true? Why had he wanted to cause hurt in those lovely eyes? He has to make all this pain go away.

The sudden sight of Izzy on the high rocks spins his thoughts again. She's going to try to stop him. It has to be *now*. But he needs to know his own real name before he dies. And his mum's too.

'Mhairi, love. Your mum's name was Mhairi.'

'Mary what?'

'Mhairi Boyle.'

'So that was my name? Brio Boyle?'

'No, love. You had my name, which was Gallagher. I shortened it to Galla. And actually, your name was Fynn. Your mum had that changed too.'

Galleon, gallop, Galahad, Gallahop, his mind fills with rubbish as words. 'So I'm really Fynn Gallagher?'

'You're whoever you want to be, love.'

'But who do *you* say I am?'

'You're my son, love. That's all I know.'

Brio's legs are giving way, but he sees with relief that Izzy has sat down like a birdwatcher. But his relief that she's not going to stop him is swept aside by the realisation that she only sat down because she doesn't believe he has the guts to see it through. And she never did. That's why she hasn't told anyone. Because she thinks he'll fail like he did on Big Ben. Because she doesn't know he's become a living vow to defeat his greatest fear. Because she believes that love will win.

But how *can* he go through with it when she's sitting there like that? And Pippa too. No, to hell with them, he'll prove that he does have the courage. All it needs is for his father to reach out then he can make a grab, then it'll just *happen*. But his own thrust-out hand becomes ridiculous and he pulls it back. Cursing his weakness, he wills his father to say something that'll make him do it for his mum. 'Why don't you believe in God anymore?'

His father takes a sharp breath and glances at the drop. 'Well love, that's a big question. But I do believe in God. It's only the Church I stopped believing in.'

'*Why*? Why did you stop believing in the Church?' Why can't she say something evil? Why can't she say something to explain everything and make it all different and the same and—

'Why did I stop believing in the Church? Well, I suppose because the Church stopped believing in me, love.'

He thinks that this was it, the evil thing that'll make him *do it*. But at the thought of his father being cast out when she so much wanted to be loved by God, a wave of overwhelming sadness sets his whole face wobbling.

'Oh, love …' She stumbles a step forward with her hands out. 'Look, I'll never be your mum, love. But I'm still your dad. Lord, I'd like that so much.' She edges forward and he can't stop her. 'Heavens, we still have *time*. Can't you find it in your heart to forgive me? To *understand*.'

Brio thrusts the ring again and the tips of his fingers touch her stomach—just under her *breasts*. The second she reaches for it, he'll clasp her wrist. '*Take it*.'

But she still just stands there with face pleading and hands open.

He glances round to make sure the ground won't give way before they've gone over. '*Hold my hand*.'

When he looks back, her expression's changed again and he sees the same glint of determination he saw on the chat show.

'I will, love. Whatever happens, that's what I'm going to do now. I'm going to hold your hand and be with you.'

Their hands lock around the ring and he tugs her towards him. They clamp into a hug, the knot of locked hands trapped awkwardly between them. She's taut and athletic and her breasts are so real he almost cries out. But he can't, because his face is crushed into the side of her neck and her skin is so soft and she smells perfect.

But no. He has to get them moving backwards—sideways—before God collapses him onto the grass in a pathetic embryo. He has to be fearless like his father. He has to prove to her that he's not scared of dying either. Because that's the greatest courage of all, to have no fear of the drop.

As her hug tightens, his fear is gone. With eyes screwed up hard enough to burst blood vessels, he leans his weight backwards to feel for the edge with his toes—and when she comes willingly, it's all beyond his control.

'I love you, my boy.'

Her words open his eyes and, over her shoulder, through his blur of tears, he's up there with beautiful Izzy, whose cropped hair makes her the boy she was born to be. And Ms Whittle's there too. Ms Whittle who loves Tania and wanted little Bree to be just like them, to make them feel the safety in numbers that's better than any comfort of words. Oh, God, what a world. And there's Darcy as well, given a morning exeat from hospital to witness the vision that will transform his life. And he does want Darcy to be okay, because for everyone to be okay, *everyone* has to be okay. And what's mental illness compared with the power of love? How can he do anything but die for them all?

When he understands that it's only Izzy's who's really there, he reels out of the hug. With the crazed thought that to save the world it must be both of them making the decision, he clasps his father's hand and pushes the ring onto one of her fingers. Grabbing her by both wrists, he turns them side-on to the drop.

'I want to know …' His voice sounds more his own than he's ever heard and all fear is truly gone. 'I want to know whether you'd lay down your life for me? *Would you?*'

Searching her eyes, he's sure she's having to think fast to buy time.

But no, she's not. She's holding his gaze with the same old calmness. The same determination. The same dull and dented love.

'I'll lay it down either way, love. Over that edge, or whatever you want for the rest of your life. Like I said, I'll give up everything for you.'

What I want is for you to be a real dad, Brio shouts in his head. *I want you to look like a dad and talk like a dad and make the doctors turn you back into a dad.*

But the thought of changing her gives him such a shock he involuntarily grabs her back into the hug and clings on like he's never clung onto anything or anyone in his life. And in that moment, with her strong fingers clutching into his thick hair, and with tingles zinging through his whole body and his legs about to give way, he understands in feelings far beyond words that all the world needs in order to be perfect is to be made up of people like *her*—his *dad*. His *father*.

Waiting for the air to give way beneath his feet, Brio feels the Ring of Love warm in the sunshine and Izzy's letter tucked safely in his pocket. And floating free are those words from the glorious abyss of divine dream, the words about the child who was *born so full of grace, from Father Time and Mother Grace. Yet, water's thick and blood is thin, and only love makes next of kin. Oh, God, we're here, afloat in Heaven, bound by pure and bloodless love. We father, son by friendship leavened, 'twined like double-helix*—HOME.

Now sensing himself to be part of the air that's brushing their soft ground, Brio glides peaceably through an end-of-day throng that's lost all interest in some kid who used to holler like a toddler and fill his voids with crazy ideas. And in his mind now, it's way after midday and everything's exactly as it should be between father and son.

And the Hoggit's there too, high in the Sky-Glass Dome, raising his Great Plea of Tribute and Proof for God to read—his Book of Life. And he's even holding it properly the wrong way up! And there's the first of Zpydr's media trucks, right on time, trundling slowly into the car park to record the true big moment for the world to witness. And after the news has broken, Izzy will write all night to help bring down that corporation of foul smoke and the world will be freed from the Hex of the Mirrored Fate.

And so, with his feet swimming them both slowly towards the beautiful unknown, and with his yearning for some distinction between life and death now a faded memory that's something less than an itch, Brio knows that he will at last find home, on solid ground and soft grass, with the curtains at Bluebells thrown open, and a story that ends without end in a world without end.

A cry rises up as a sob made perfect by joy, and when Brio opens his eyes in squint to the horizon's shimmering brilliance he witnesses Mr and Mrs Hare resplendent on the great steed Pegasaurus, soaring alongside the spirit of Mr T'wit and Bling in their Pea-Green Boat, and Madame Haha a glorious bright sun of sparkling sequins.

Brio and Robi clutch for every size and shape of every hug they never had, and, as Brio's face presses into the smooth skin of his dad's neck, he sobs out the question that's been too big a dream to dare since the day he first beheld the glorious rider in her golden robe.

'Oh, God, love,' Robi replies through her own ecstatic sob, 'of course I will. And we'll ride into that sunset till it's rising on the other side of a whole new world.'

R.A.RUEGG is a professional ghost and advertising copy writer who grew up in Britain, read law at King's College, London, then spent several years in the US and East Asia before emigrating to Australia.